COURAGE *to* SURRENDER

A Journey to Meaning and Hope

George S. Steffey

Inspiring Voices®

Inspiring Voices books may be ordered through booksellers or by contacting:

Inspiring Voices
1663 Liberty Drive
Bloomington, IN 47403
www.inspiringvoices.com
1 (866) 697-5313

ISBN: 978-1-4624-1175-7 (sc)
ISBN: 978-1-4624-1176-4 (e)

Library of Congress Control Number: 2016901857

Print information available on the last page.

Inspiring Voices rev. date: 2/15/2016

Preface

Courage to Surrender is a story of how nine American teenagers from Pittsburgh, Pennsylvania come to discover how to be the church; not the church of the 20th Century in America, but a hopeful future resurrected church for the 21st Century. It is a church fellowship where people love one another with the extravagant love and grace of God. One in which a love for those in need flows out of their relationship with one another. The story begins in 1984 and plays out in the second half of 2007.

In 1984 those teens are:

Stan Beckley, a typical suburban white 16 year old who lives in a wealthy suburban community, loves computer games, plays soccer, and dabbles with alcohol and marijuana. His father is an executive at an investment company and his mother suffers from depression and alcoholism, but she and the family are in denial about her addiction. He has one older brother who was at the top of his high school graduation class and is on a soccer scholarship at a division one university. He also has a younger sister. In 2007 he has become the owner and CEO of a billion dollar internet marketing company.

Brandon Bryce, a middle class white 16 year old who attends a racially mixed suburban high school and is an outstanding student and quarterback on the football team and runs track. His father is a teacher at his high school, mother is a teacher in an elementary school in the same community. He is an only child. In 2007 he is a Christian missionary in the Sudan.

Mel Carr, a 15 years old, white, upper middle class young man who goes to private high school, is a good student and is on the debate team. His father is a computer company executive and an elder in a suburban evangelical church. His mother stays at home. He has two younger sisters and a younger brother. In 2007 he is the senior pastor of a popular mega church.

Jorge Cruz, a Hispanic/African American who is 16 years old and lives in a poor urban neighborhood. He attends a city high school, is an average student, plays football but is not very good, occasionally uses drugs, and attends a predominantly African American church. His father is from Cuba but he has never met him. His mother is African American and a single parent. He has one older sister who has a child, three younger brothers, and a younger sister. The older sister has a different father than he does. And his three younger brothers and younger sister are fathered by a third man who is in and out of the house. The family is on welfare. His mother works part-time under the table. Jorge often sleeps at friend's homes. In 2007 he is a youth pastor at an urban African American church.

Misha Jenkins, a 16 year old African American who was a poor student when she was younger but in 1984 is an outstanding student attending a church run private alternative school. She used to dabble with drugs and was sexually active in her early teens. She is artistic. Her father is a minister. Her mother is a nurse and she has one younger sister. In 2007 she is married to Jorge Cruz and they are team youth pastors at her father's church. The have twin boys.

Odell Ogden, a 16 year old African American who lives in the same community as Brandon. He is a poor student and is a wide receiver on the football team. He has drunk and used marijuana from the age of 12 and became an addicted at age 14. He used to sell drugs. In 1984 he has been in recovery for about a year. He does not know who his father is and has an older brother who is in jail. He lives with his mother, grandmother, younger brother, and younger sister. They are on welfare. They infrequently attend an evangelical Black church. In 2007 he is the Director of Addiction and AIDS Services for Henley Health Care Center. The story in this novel is told in the first person from his perspective.

James Smith, a 16 year old African American, lives in the academic and professional community of Oakland. He is a good student who loves acting and he plays basketball. He has a younger brother. His father is a professor at a university and his mother is a nurse. In 2007 none of the others know where he is.

Kara Stevens, a 15 year old white girl who lives in the suburbs and attends the same private school as Mel. She is an average student and a cheerleader. Her parents are both physicians. She has a younger brother. The family attends a one-fits-all downtown church. In 2007 none of the others know where she is.

Emily Stewire, an upper class, white 16 year old, who lives in a different wealthy suburban community than Stan. Academically she is at the top of her class and the class Vice President. She sings and acts and is an outstanding soccer player. In her childhood she suffered depression. Her parents are divorced and she lives with her mother who is an alcoholic. She has two younger sisters who live with them too. Her father is a millionaire bank president and lives nearby. In 2007 she is married to Brandon and with him serves as a missionary in the Sudan. They have two boys and a girl.

These teens, when they are juniors and seniors in high school, bond together on a trip to Kenya, Africa in 1985. After high school they go their separate ways and then when six of them are brought together twenty two years later, in 2007, their lives are turned up-side-down and a new journey begins.

Jesus is misunderstood today because Christianity gets mix in with so much other stuff. As a result the Church becomes a self-centered institution.

If you long to experience authentic biblical Christian discipleship or you are someone looking for meaning and purpose that you can get passionate about and that address problems in the world, then, this story may challenge you. My desire is that it will enjoy reading it, be encouraged as you read, and be left with a lot of hope.

One

My alarm clock unlocked a deep sleep interrupting a wonderful dream. I was surrounded by family, close friends that I had made throughout my life, and by many others who I felt knew me and whom were known by me. We were at a beach party, the sun was warm, the ocean breeze was cool, the food was good. It was in such a deep, peaceful, sleep. It was a dream that made me fight my return to reality. I didn't want to wake up.

As I hit the off button, clock numbers glowed 4:30 a.m. I threw the covers off, swung my feet to the floor, and walked groggily into the bath room. Turning the light switch on was like the flash bulb from a studio photographers' camera.

After putting on my running clothes I went out into the dark morning for my daily run. The air was fresh and the stars still sparkled.

Running for about ten minutes and going through my stretching routine finally woke up my body. I began to run again; settling into a nice pace that felt smooth and energizing. Reflecting on the new day made me feel fully alive. The birds also welcomed the new day with their singing. Then, strangely, I began thinking about my life journey.

I thought, I am thirty-eight years old and have been trying to follow Jesus for twenty years, yet I still feel I haven't found a church where I feel safe and at home. Where are the people who love me like they love Jesus, who care more about those who suffer than they do about themselves? I reviewed the five or six churches where I'd been a member or a regular participant. There were even a couple of churches where I'd spent more time at meetings and programs than I did with my wife and kids. I'd never found a church that felt to me the way I thought it must have felt at the beginning of the church after Pentecost, or even two hundred years after Pentecost. I wondered again where to find the church I'd read about in the gospels and the rest of the New Testament. Every church I'd been involved with seemed hung up with traditions and the values of their culture. Most were self-absorbed. I was getting tired of trying one more church in the hope of discovering where I belong.

I considered suggesting to my wife Deb that we attend a new emerging church that was starting up in an old reclaimed church building in our neighborhood. And then, just as I was deciding that maybe I should try again, a kid passed me jogging about twice as fast I was and he wasn't even breathing hard. My mind shifted to my running and the thought that I was never going to get my youth back, either.

One of the reasons I ran almost every morning and often lifted weights was because I always hoped to restore and maintain the body I had when I was eighteen, or at least twenty five. This kid running past me had the body that I'd had and was in the condition I was once in. The devastating realization came upon me that I was approaching middle age and would never be twenty years old again. It felt naive to think that I could actually imagine myself with a body restored to its youthful prime. And, oh yes, I also planned on being able to run a six-minute mile with no pain because I could remember running a five minute mile in high school with energy to spare, and with out pain. But the blur that ran past me at that moment popped my bubble. Reality hurts. I was never going to get back my twenty year old body. Maybe I also had to face the reality that the church was never going to look like it did when it was in its youth either. I realized that maybe I should stop hoping for a biblical community of Jesus' disciple, let go of fantasizing about some extended family of surrendered sinners and just meld in with what was available.

Rather than being challenged to run faster, my pace slowed down and I felt a wave of sadness like I hadn't felt since my brother was killed. The rest of my run was a labor of discipline. It was 6:00 a.m. by the time I finished my post run stretches. I walked for another five minutes to cool down and then went into the house for a shower.

After a shave and shower and some fresh clothes I made myself a cup of coffee and got the Sunday paper off the front porch. The rising sun peeked through the glistening Japanese Red Maple that grew outside my kitchen window. In the quiet of this fresh morning, only the birds were singing. The memory of my dream came back to me. It reminded me that I had not lost my ability to dream. I guessed I wasn't too depressed after all; just despondent about the church.

I sat down with my coffee to read the Sunday Morning Post-Gazette. I always read "*Prince Valiant*" in the comics first. Then I began to scan through the front page. *Same old-same-same-old*, I thought. But on page three in the bottom left hand corner, the heading read,

> "Dr. Brandon C. Bryce Assassinated.
> Malakal, Sudan
> Sunday, June 10, 2007
> International Associated Press
>
> In broad daylight, the Children's Army of the Kalif Resistance Forces (KRF) interrupted worship services at the Day of Hope orphanage today and

opened fire, killing the worship leader, his wife, two of their three children, and ten orphan children. The worship leader was Dr. Brandon C. Bryce from Park Hills, Pennsylvania. He, along with his wife, Emily, their fifteen year old son, William, their ten year old son, Odie, and their eight year old daughter, Faith, had been serving as New Hope missionaries in Uganda and the Sudan since 1997.

Known as "Papa" to hundreds of children who had fled the military inscription of KRF, Dr. Bryce had been instrumental in negotiating the recent peace talks between KRF and the Sudanese government. Since the Plano meetings in October of 2003 Dr. Bryce has been a part of the Church Alliance for a New Sudan (CANS). Those who took part in the attack are a small brutal band of 12 to 16 year olds who the Islamist government in Khartoum and the KRF has disavowed.

The Day of Hope orphanage is located in northern Sudan near the ancient Christian Kingdom of Nubia where the local tribe had experienced an attempted genocide prior to the peace agreement in 2005. Out of compassion for the future of the orphans in Sudan, Dr. Bryce had been instrumental in helping the Khartoum government to secure U.S. support for the Khartoum government to moving forward with the damming of the Nile to flood the Nubia Ravine and was now with the President of Sudan working of new peace talks for long term peace. But now with Dr. Bryce's death, President of Sudan, Omar al-Bashir, has reportedly said the new peace talks scheduled in the coming months will not continue as planned.

Mbumbla Gengeci, the Director of Sudan New Hope (SNH), in reporting the assassinations, confirmed it was very unlikely that Mr. Bashir will entertain any Christian considerations of peace now that Dr. Bryce

> will no longer be involved. A spokesman for President al-Bashir said Dr. Bryce had spent ten years building his relationship with Mr. Bashir and it was only out of his respect for Dr. Bryce that the peace talks were even being considered. Five other children, including the Bryce's son William, were injured. Twenty boys under the age of 14 were abducted. William and the other injured children were taken to the hospital in Malakal and were being treated for gunshot wounds. All the children are in stable condition.

It was as though a bolt of blinding lighting thundered out of a brilliant clear blue sky and struck my heart. I sat stunned in disbelief. Brandon and Emily were due to come home on furlough in just a couple of weeks. Finally after ten years they were beginning to see an answer to their prayers. *Hope*, was not only the word that punctuated their mission but the expectation that had been oozing from their spirits.

There had been no one, except perhaps my wife, Deb, to whom I was closer than this brother and sister. We had been through a lot together, high school football, our African mission trip, our romantic rivalry over Emily, serving as his best man at their wedding, the many nights Brandon vented his frustrations with his doctorate program, naming their second son after me; and helping them pray through their call to the mission field. And now their lives were all at a sudden end.

As much as I tried to put my total trust in God, I couldn't help my first thoughts. Why, God, why Brandon and Emily and Odie and Faith? And what must Billy be experiencing? Why did this happen? Why did this happen now?

I felt catatonic. I tried to take a sip of my coffee but instead watched my hand shake as I realized I couldn't competently pick up the cup. Tears slowly began running down my cheeks until I could feel my whole body shaking as I silently sobbed. I must have cried for fifteen minutes. “No God!” I yelled. “No!” “Oh, God, this just can’t be! How could you have let this happen?”

It was good that Deb and the kids had spent the previous night with her parents; I don’t know how I could have held it together if I were not alone with this catastrophic interruption.

I slowly lifted my 6’3”, 210 lb. frame, got up, went into the den and fell into my easy chair. There I sat limp and silent for maybe an hour. Sobbing, numb, why, why, why, letting go, letting go again, trying to put it all in God’s hands. I had given the care of my life and my dear friend’s lives over to the care of God every morning, and now I was struggling to turn them and myself over to God again. So much came flooding through my mind as the cloud of emotions burst and poured down over me. My mind drifted back almost twenty years to when Brandon and I meet in high school.

Two

An African American from the East End of Pittsburgh, I was being raised, along with my two brothers and two sisters, by my mother and grandmother. We were a third generation welfare family. The men in our family, even my uncles and cousins, going back to my great-grandfather, had either died in prison or just disappeared into the streets.

I had met Brandon at football practice the summer before we started ninth grade. Brandon was a tall lanky quarterback. The coach was putting his hopes on Brandon to be the quarterback of the decade. I had my hopes of being a stand-out wide receiver.

In 1984 when I met Brandon, my older brother, Jocko, was serving five years in Blueville State Prison for armed robbery. Jocko was only three years older than me, but he had already done jail time twice, first for possession and then for intent to sell. He had been addicted to drugs since the age of fourteen.

My name, by the way, is Odell Ogden. I too, had started to drink and use marijuana at the age of twelve. Without a father at home I found my sense of belonging with Jocko and the Franklin Street gang. I would make deliveries for him and be rewarded with a dime bag of grass. In the beginning I would sell it, but as I hung out with the other drug runners we would smoke it along with the wine one of us would contribute. By fifteen I was depending upon my daily joint to help me relax before having to go home after football practice.

I loved football and I was good at it. I didn't have time to study, what with helping Jocko sell drugs, the gang, and football, so my grades were always borderline but passing. I was smart enough to do the minimum and get by.

The beginning of the summer before my sophomore year in High School, just as things were getting out of control and I was about to graduate to filling Jocko's leadership role because he was being sent to the County jail. The Youth Minister from North Avenue AME Church asked me if I wanted to spend a week in Colorado – for free. That sounded good to me, especially since Jocko wasn't around and my good friend Brandon was also going. And it sounded intriguing to get out of Pittsburgh and see the Rocky Mountains.

The week in Colorado was going to be at Frontier Ranch, not exactly a church camp but a camp run by Young Life Campaign, a Christian youth organization.

My grandmother had always taken me to church with her, and I never really protested. It made me look good and less likely to be a drug dealer or part of a gang. I had gotten to know North Avenue's Youth Minister and thought he was OK, just a little out of touch with reality sometimes. He was part of a fellowship of youth ministers in the East End of Pittsburgh that was coordinated by the Young Life staff representative. This trip was designed by Young Life to attract "at risk" kids to an evangelical week of high adventure through the relationships that the youth ministers had developed with kids throughout the year.

On this Frontier Ranch trip, thirty kids were going, ten of them were guys, the rest girls. I liked that idea. I knew them all and a couple of the girls were hot and available. I also noticed that several of the kids who were going were my regular customers. So, that was another good reason to go. I decided to take a good supply of grass with me.

The bus trip from Pittsburgh to Colorado took only two days. We left at night and drove straight through the second night. By the time we got there my stash was almost gone. I arrived tired and high but was blown away by the overwhelming greeting at camp. About thirty "work-crew" and camp staff charged the bus on horses, shouting and welcoming us. As we got off the bus a marching band led us to the Meeting Hall where a rock band was preforming. A great steak dinner was provided and we danced until it was time to go to bed. I was into it. This was like a dream. The mountains were so huge with snow on them. The huge pine trees and the forest were like out of a Robin Hood movie. Everyone was so accepting and happy to see us. They paid so much attention to me that they made me feel like I was the only kid in camp and that this was all for me. No one seemed suspicious or paranoid that a black kid might have drugs with him or even a gun. I thought to myself, *"Are these people really this naive? Do they live in a fantasy world? And if they do, how can I get some of it."* By midnight I was exhausted and went to bed without a thought of what the next day might bring. I think that must have been the first relaxed sleep I had had since my mother nursed me as a new born.

The next morning breakfast was really brunch at 10:00 AM and then the day was packed: as was every day the rest of the week. I smoked and sold what marijuana I had left during the first two days at camp. I experienced more 'first time' stuff in such a short time that my emotions whirled. I rode a bucking mule. I climbed a snow capped mountain. I jumped thirty feet at a time down a mountain gravel slide. I swam in hot springs. I panned for gold. I learned to clog. I talked with girls without thinking about sex. I rode a horse and even raced with 25 others on horses. I went on a breakfast trail ride on horseback.

Every day there were two "club" talks about the love of God in Jesus. At first I pretended to listen, just like I had been doing at church all my life. But by the fourth day at camp, without my drugs, I was feeling way out of my comfort zone. I couldn't pretend any longer. With the extreme activities and everyone being so nice, I was confused and felt lost inside. I was craving to get high so I acted out by picking a fight with Brandon. It was not an easy fight to break up because we were both big kids, well built, and had been in fights before. But a couple of the staff were men from the city streets who had been just like me and they got us separated before either of us were really hurt. Brandon and I both knew though that our friendship was too tight for us to really try to hurt the other. We both also knew I started the fight just to release my tension and I think we both liked the contact and enjoyed putting on a show.

What took me off guard next was that instead of the camp staff and counselors getting on my case, the man who was the speaker at the late night meetings took me aside and asked if we could go for a walk. He wanted to show me something.

It was about an hour before the "club talk" and I knew the speaker had to be back for club. And besides he was an old man in his thirties and I was sure I could take him if he wanted to rough me up. So I went for a walk with him in the dark to a remote opening in the forest. We must have walked in silence for about ten minutes. I began to get a little nervous. Maybe he had others out there someplace waiting for me.

It was a clear night, there wasn't a moon, and it was very dark under the trees. As we came into the clearing away from the camp lights, he looked up and so, I did too, and what I saw took my breath away. The sky was totally filled with stars. I was awestruck. Rather than a few bright and flickering specks in the dark sky like back home, this sky was shining white with stars. They made the whole huge sky glow. I was blown away by the beauty. Some sections of the sky even had shades of color; red, green, blue, yellow. The whole sky was lit up. I had never before experienced creation without the intrusion of the city lights. It was as though the whole universe was really one bright spectacle of light interrupted by the dark contrast. We stared up at this amazing spectacle and then the speaker, by the light of the stars, smiled at me and simply said, "The *Creator* of *this* universe *knows* you --- *and* --- He *loves* you. He loves you so much that He became a person and died on a cross to forgive you." And then he just turned around and went back to give his talk at club and left me standing there. I was stunned by the calm trust of this man and at the same time in awe, not just by the sky, but by his words about God's love for me. It was like a revelation, something that had never really dawned on me. I felt like this man not only wasn't mad at me but he accepted me. I now stood there all alone, but I felt save and at peace. I looked around and realized I was in the same place where the day before the camp had a picnic and we has been surrounded by hillsides of amazing multicolored wild flowers. I thought, what an awesome creator. As I stood there looking at this spectacle I even thought I could also hear the stars singing.

That night I prayed, "Jesus, they say that you are God and that you created all this because you love me. That's crazy, I'm not worth loving. But, if that is true, then you know the mess my life is in and I want you to create a new life for me. So, right now I give my life to you. Forgive me for all the hurt I have caused and for only caring about myself. I really want to be who you created me to be, just like you created each of these stars." It was the first time I turned my will and the care of my life over to Jesus.

When I got back home I left the drug scene and become a fixture at an NA home group. And with Brandon we went on to win the Quad A State football championship our senior year.

Three

My thoughts returned to the present. There was a restored sense of peace starting to return to me. I went back out to the kitchen, got the paper, and turned to the obituary page, but there were no mention of any of the deceased.

I decided to call Brandon's parents. Bill, Brandon's dad answered and I could tell that he too had been crying. I shared his shock and sympathy. He shared with me that the director to New Hope in the Sudan had called them about 7:00 a.m. and told them of the tragedy. The family's bodies would be flown home in about four days. Billy, had been shot in the chest and through his left side just above his hip. The bullet in his chest had entered at an angle from the side and had exited under his arm not striking any internal organs or bones. He would be in the hospital for about two weeks. Brandon's parents and Emily's father were trying to work out the logistics of going to go be with Billy and at the same time planning a funeral service. Bill told me he would let me know what was worked out.

We prayed for each other over the phone.

Brandon was the Bryce's only child. Both his parents had been teachers in the Park Hills Schools for over 40 years and had both retired in 2005. They had taken their first trip to the Sudan just six months ago and enjoyed Christmas at the orphanage with Brandon, Emily, and the grandchildren.

I told Bill I would be over in the afternoon and we hung up promising to continue to pray for each other and for Billy.

The bodies arrived in Pittsburgh a full week later. Just as the bodies of the Bryce family left Africa, the believers at the Day of Hope orphanage had an African Church memorial service of celebration, rejoicing in the joy of their brothers and sisters being welcomed into the glory of Jesus open arms. Billy was permitted to attend the celebration but was then taken back to the hospital.

The U. S. memorial service at the Park Hills Presbyterian Church was scheduled for Saturday, June 23, 2007 at 2:00 a.m. There were over twenty five hundred people at the service. The church, which seated eighteen hundred, had extra chairs in all the isles, in the narthex and up front. The overflow was seated in the fellowship hall where closed circuit TV broadcast the service. It began with an opening prayer, welcome and April Pease singing, "It Is Well With My Soul." I read Psalm 150 and the congregation sang "Amazing God" and "How Great Thou Art." This was followed by the pastor of Park Hills reading Romans 8:18-29. Then Brandon's aunt, Barbara Bryce, the U. S. National Director of New Hope Ministries, shared from her experiences with the family. When she was finished it would be my turn to share.

As I sat listening to Barbara my mind recalled a time when Emily and I where kids and were falling in love. It was like I had to remember in order to finally let her go. I thought I had let her go many time, and I knew I had, but the memory was still there. Shame and guilt mingled with my grief and I drifted back.

I was in Africa in 1985, the night Emily introduced the banquet speaker for the Impact Wrap-up Dinner. If it were recorded in a love story it would read like this.

Emily drew Odell's eyes and held them with her magnetic radiance as she stood at the podium. She had kept her hair pulled back during this mission immersion, but now it hung long, auburn, and wavy over one shoulder, and her big brown eyes seemed to focus only on him. He also had not noticed before how smooth her ivory skin was nor how cute her button nose. What caught his attention the most was her perfect lips and well dimensioned figure. During their time together she had always wore jeans and a sweat shirt but now he noticed every curve.

The bonded community that the Pittsburgh group felt could have been expected but the connection that he and Emily had found during those past six weeks had taken them both by surprise. He knew that at home she would have not even noticed him, even though he was an outstanding athlete with a cut and well developed physique; and was a very attractive young stud. Emily was a soccer star, his fame was football. Emily graduated Valedictorian. He barely graduated. Emily was white from the wealthy bedroom village of Shaffer. He was black from the streets of a "changing neighborhood." They lived just 15 miles from each other but the cultural extremes were at different ends of the world. Emily's father was a millionaire Fortune 500 company CEO. His father could have been one of several men who visited his mother.

But on the mission trip, where the playing fields were leveled by dying children and the smell of abject poverty, they were just two people overcome with the needs of the world and a love for Jesus.

What had caused them to first connect happened one night after the group debriefing when she had sought him out to offer her support. He had shared in the meeting some of his struggles with addiction and his involvement with Narcotics Anonymous, and she wanted to tell him that she had been involved with Alateen. She told him that her mother was an active alcoholic and that if it hadn't been for the 12 Step program of Alateen she herself, might have become an alcoholic. From that evening on they had had something special and had begun to share with each other at levels deeper than either of them had ever shared with anyone. And the fact that they were in this liminal experience together added to their freedom to be vulnerable. And honestly, neither one had paid much attention to how the other one looked.

But now seeing her at that podium in a dress and looking so radiant his feeling for her scared him. After she introduced the speaker, he studied her for what seemed like an hour as she walked to her seat and sat down.

My thoughts were brought back to the memorial as I heard the pastor say, "Emily's sister, Betsy would like to say a word now." As Betsy stood up I saw her dad sitting in the front row with a woman I didn't recognize. I then remembered that their mother had died from liver disease complications about five years ago and that her dad had remarried to a woman from France. I had met Emily's two sisters and her father at their mother's funeral but I never did get to know them. In the second row I could see Emily's other younger sister, Joanne, sitting with what looked like her children.

Betsy share about her love for her sister and her sister's love of Jesus. When she was finished speaking the pastor said, "Odell Ogden would like to share next." When I was finished the service was opened up to the congregation to share if they liked. Ten people or more got up and spoke, including Stan Beckley and Misha Cruz. Both had been on the Kenya mission trip in 1985 with Brandon, Emily, and me. As people came forward and spoke about the amazing witness of each of the martyred family members, it moved everyone in the congregation to not only get in touch with their grief but to also reflect on the meaning of their own lives. You could hear the sobs throughout the church. The music leader sensitively began to play quiet music and a large baritone Sudanese man sang "Give Me Jesus." The pastor then gave a short homily that focused on Bryce family's part in furthering God's mandate to make the whole earth a place that worships God: Father, Son, and Holy Spirit.

The service concluded with everyone praying the Lord's Prayer.

The Interment was in the church cemetery and was followed by a reception that was spread throughout the church campus.

Four

Stan Beckley and his wife, Karen, Jorge and Misha Cruz, and my wife, Deb, and I all found ourselves gathered together at the same table in the Fellowship Hall. Except for Karen and Deb, when we had all been teenagers we had been with Brandon and Emily on what we had come to call the "Liminal Plunge" to Kenya, African. That was twenty years ago. We were now in our late thirties. No one planned for us all to sit at the same table but we did seek out each other and intentionally wanted to be together. Over the years, we had all gone on with our individual lives. But the loss of Brandon and Emily brought back the bound we felt with each other from our month together in Africa.

After college Jorge and Misha had gotten married and had been youth workers in Pittsburgh ever since. Stan had met Karen in college and he was now an extremely successful venture capitalist who had been the major contributor for Brandon and Emily's ministry. The LP members that were missing were Mel Carr, James Smith, and Kara Stevens. Mel had become the founding pastor of a growing mega church in a suburb of Pittsburgh. For the past five years everyone had lost track of James and Kara. In fact no one had heard from Kara for about ten years. On the day of the funeral Mel was on a speaking tour in Texas, but his wife Elizabeth had come to the funeral. As the group gathered she was talking to Stan and Karen, whom she knew because Stan and Karen attended Mel's church, and they ask her to join us at our table.

I began the conversation. "Now what? I blurted. "When I first read about Brandon and Emily and Billy, Odie and Hope I was in disbelief, questioning God. I still can't belief it and I am still overwhelmingly angry at Satan, but I am finally letting God be God again."

Jorge and Stan smiled. Jorge was what, if I were British, I would have called a 'portly' looking man, about 5'10" with a receding hair line and a mustache. Stan looked like the stereo type of the Corporate CEO that he was. He was clean shaven, had freshly cut hair, and wore a dark silk suit over his trim 6'1' body.

"All this is making me really evaluate my call like I haven't done since the plunge", I continued. "I have been trying to stay clean, give back, and seek God's Kingdom in all I do, but I feel like I haven't even begun. I have been seeking to follow Jesus for 24 years but I am questioning if am I really a disciple of His. Brandon and Emily just gave their lives and the lives of nearly all their children so that the Kingdom of God would come on earth as it is in heaven. And, on top of questioning my faithfulness, Brandon's dad reminded me just this week that Deb and I are named in the Will as the guardian of Brandon and Emily's children in the event of such a tragedy as this. When Billy is released from the hospital, he will be added to our family. This is going to be a very hard thing for him and for us to accept. I wonder if we will ever adjust. I have never felt such a need to depend on God. I feel so inadequate. I am surely not nearly the model of a disciple that Brandon was providing."

There was silence for about thirty seconds but it seemed like five minutes. Maybe I had said too much. I started to feel like I wanted to disappear. A couple people walked by whom Stan and Karen acknowledged.

Then Karen, whom I hardly knew, said, "I think God is calling us to pick up where Brandon and Emily left off." She didn't say it with any hint of self-righteousness or "thus saith the Lord" attitude. It was simply an assumed, matter of fact, comment. Stan didn't blink an eye. I had seen Karen at couple of other gathering and she had always struck me as a very cut to the chase blunt person. If you wouldn't have known that Stan and Karen were married and you just saw them in a room full of people you would still have picked them out as two people who went together. Karen looked like the wife of a millionaire. She was about 5'8" and had the appearance of an athlete. She was dressed in a dark dress with white trim that accentuated her very well developed body. Her beautiful dark hair and tasteful make-up and jewelry made her look like a model or a movie star at the Oscars.

Defensively, Deb asked, "Do you mean that you think our family should move to the Sudan with Billy instead of him coming to live with us?

"No, I wasn't implying that you should go. I'm not sure what I mean. But I for one, cannot let this tragedy be the end of their ministry and the hope for those kids' lives in the orphanage. If someone doesn't pick up where they left off those kids and other kids like them could be forced to become part of the Children's Army of the KRF." Replied Karen. "They will either become killers or be murdered."

Then Jorge said something which I didn't quite hear because someone was laughing loudly at the table next to us. Misha, began to share a story, almost as an attempt to change the subject. In my desire to become invisible my mind again slipped away as she began. I again remembered my experience in Africa. This time not about Emily or Brandon, but about the babies that I watched die. It was what Karen said about children that prompted my distraction.

Five

It was August 1985 again. I sat on the hard dung polished floor cradling Yakenya, a two year old in the last stages of AIDS. Her four pound body felt boney and cold, her skin stretched against her skull and cheek bones. Her sunken big black eyes were wide open with a glassy gaze into nowhere. Her tiny torso rose and fell with laboring breaths and I knew that with each breath it may be her last.

Yakenya was the fifth orphaned AIDS baby that I had comforted while she died in the past two weeks. With each one I had felt blessed with the privilege of caring for these little one. The repulsion that I felt at seeing so much suffering when I first walked into Olenjoy Christian Orphanage three weeks earlier had been transformed by the powerlessness of these helpless children. God seemed to have said to me, come enter into my suffering so that you may know my joy. I didn't understand but I felt so blessed.

For almost a month I had been at this orphanage but before that I had spent two weeks in a Maasai village where I had been included as one of an extended family. The village was a part of the Christian revival that had started nearly two generations ago and was now moving throughout this part of East Africa. I had been welcomed into the clan, lived with a family and even given the Maasai name, *Oinono-ayioni* (Powerful Son). I had learned to live without electricity; the nearest water from a stream was about two miles away, and the large outhouse, a quarter of a mile walk. Sometimes in the middle of the night, the wild animal sounds felt like they were only a few feet away.

Two weeks had not been enough to get used to walking to the toilet at night.

But strange as it seemed, I had felt like I had come home when I first walked into the village. My budding lanky muscular frame and ebony skin made it possible for me to blend in among the Maasai young men. But although I was as old as these young men, I felt like a child among them. They had gone through their rite of passage some years ago and were now responsible members of the tribe and had their own families. It did not matter that I was not from their culture; they included me anyway. They took me with them as they herded their goats and cattle and they taught me how to identify the signs of lions or hyenas nearby. They even took me on an antelope hunt with them but they were unable to make a kill because I had made too much noise. I had not learned well enough how to walk in silence through the thick underbrush. They still let me come with them the next time. They told me they were one; all succeed or fail together. The experience of being a member of a tribe was such a contrast to trying to survive on the streets. Even gang membership did not come close.

The Mara was so different from the asphalt jungle in Pittsburgh. The 'noise' was different than streets noise. At first I thought it so quiet but after a couple of days I realized it really wasn't quiet, for during the day the birds music filled the air and at night the animals seems to be having their own parties.

The contrasts sights, sounds, and combine smells of garbage, animal urine and feces, and human body odor. Eronitok, was one of the poorest villages in the world and yet they were the most generous and hospitable people imaginable. Life was extremely hard and yet the adults had smiles on their faces and the children laughed and played without a care. Starvation, disease and death were assumed as part of life and yet instead of despair, generosity and joy seemed to fill their lives. Violence from both the corrupt government and the Islamic militia occurred almost weekly yet their Christian worship was a celebration without fear. They were a people of faith and peace and they prayed at all times. It was as though they had let go of their fears. Life was held with an open hand. I noticed how they prayed when they left the hut and when they returned. Before and after almost every activity they prayed. When they introduced themselves to someone new they shared their testimony of Jesus' love for them. Sharing the love of Jesus seemed to come so naturally. In the midst of their miserable circumstances, their joyful, grateful, gracious attitudes was so distinctive I could almost taste it. Because of their joy and grace to others it was no wonder that people had been turning to Jesus, and this revival did not have an end in sight. I had learned that the elders from my tribe alone had sent out ninety "barefoot evangelists" in the past year to further remote areas of the Maasai Mara.

I remembered thinking how those six weeks in Africa had shown me such a contrast to my privileged life growing up back in Park Hills, Pennsylvania. The squalor of the slums of Nairobi, the rutted roads just outside the city, the dirt floors and dung walls of the homes where we had received such sacrificial hospitality, and the dying children made the "ghetto" of Pittsburgh's Gatetown and my apartment in Georgeburg seem like the affluence of royalty. Yet, I remembered that I had wanted to stay and spend the rest of my life with this tribe. But my Maasai brothers said I was an American and that I should be part of the Christian tribe in America; to be their brother in America sharing the love of Jesus in America.

Even back then I knew that if I walked the streets of Nairobi, dressed appropriately, and kept my mouth shut I could look like I belonged, but that would be a mask.

Six

Deb poked me and I returned to the present. Stan and Karen were getting up to leave.

"Where have you been?" Deb quietly said to me. "You haven't said a word. Are you alright?"

"Yeah, I'm finc, I was just thinking about the past."

"Well we just decided to get together as a group and be open to what God might be saying to us through all this."

"Yeah, I heard what everyone said. Didn't we also say we were going to wait until Mel could join us and ask for his wisdom, and also something was said about James and Kara too? Right"? I asked.

"Yes, that's right," assured Deb.

We got up and said good-by to Stan and Karen, and then as we began to leave to go home everyone gave each other a hug and promised to pray for one other. It felt good, but it also felt a little forced.

On the way home Deb and I mostly talked about how we were going to relate to Billy. He was due to get released from the hospital in a week. During his time in the hospital he was surrounded by so many loving and caring friends which for him was a time of both physical and emotional healing.

The families of Bill and Emily had decided to go ahead with the funeral before Billy got back to the States, feeling that one more emotional traumatic event for him would be more debilitating than healing. The plan was for his grandfather, Bill, and me to fly to Nairobi in a couple of days and bring Billy back to the States with us immediately after his discharge. To ease his adjustment to American culture we felt if at first he lived with his grandparents he might feel more secure. So for the first month after coming home he would live with them and then after the Will was read he would move in with the Deb and me and our 14 year old twins, Jenn and Jimmy. Now we would be adding a 15 year old to our family, and one who had spent the last 10 years living in a village in the Sudan.

On our ride home Deb and I talked a little about the changes that we might anticipate for our family. Then I vented my apprehensions about Mel and was glad Deb is such a good listener. I had a lot of distrust in the much anticipated, so called, wisdom Mel would bring to our need to hear what God might be saying to our little group.

"Deb" I said. "I didn't want to say anything at the table."

Deb interrupted and said, "Well, yeah, you weren't exactly your usual wizard of wit."

I continued, "I have a hard time believing that Mel is going to help us all find our way forward. You know how much I think the church is more of the problem than the solution. I've been down all the roads that the church has to offer and they are all dead ends. Remember, we even gave Mel's church a two year try."

When Jenn and Jimmy were born in 1993, Deb and I felt it would be a good idea in a couple of years to get involved in a church on a regular bases, if for no other reason than so the twins would have some friends who would support them in the faith of their parents. I had visited my friend James' church whenever he came home from college, but after that I had lost touch with him. I felt some ties to the North Avenue AME Church from my Young Life days. It was a flourishing urban congregation. But Deb wanted the twins to develop a diversity of friends, economically, as well as racially, and almost all of the kids at North Avenue AME came from the low income predominantly African American community of Henley. Because our friends Jorge and Misha were co-youth directors at Misha's fathers Church we had attended their Church at times. But it too was not culturally or economically diverse and did not expose our kids to the wider Christian fellowship. We shopped around a little and attended a couple of churches that were attempting to be mixed but "mixed" seemed to define their theology as well and we wanted our kids to hear the same thing at church that they heard at home. Then in the spring of 1995, we read in the Post-Gazette that my old "Plunge" friend Mel Carr had returned to Pittsburgh and was starting a church about 30 minutes away in Apple Orchard, so I gave him a call to see what was up. Mel said he would love to come visit me at work in Henley to see the Health Care Center and what I was doing. He'd also share what was happening in Apple Orchard.

Mel met me at the Henley Health Care Center one Monday morning. I gave him a quick tour of the Health Care Center and its Recovery Center and then we went to lunch at Luigie's, a local Pizza hang out. I shared how my life had been transformed over the past ten years and Mel told me about his. We sat there for better part of three hours. Mel finished his story by telling me that it was through another Plunge pilgrim, Stan Beckley, that he got the financial seed money to move back to Pittsburgh to start a church. I had touched base with Stan over the years, but we had not had much time together. We were both so wrapped up with busy lives and our lives were on such different paths.

After my time together with Mel, I filled Deb in and we decided to try Mel's new church. The only drawback was that it was thirty minutes out in the suburbs. So, Deb, the twins and I were among about twelve hundred people who showed up for

Mel Carr's church's their first worship service the week-end of July 4th 1995.

The turnout for that service was phenomenal. It was shocking to everyone, especially Mel. We attended for about two years as the church steadily grew. We would see Stan but I never really shared my life with him because he seemed to be so wrapped up with his own important world of making money. It was great for the twins but Deb and I felt we were in a desert dying of thirst. Everyone seemed so out of touch with the realities of the pain and suffering of the poor. Deb felt that everyone in the church had to be hurting in some way but no one ever said so. The music was great, Mel was a good preacher and the programs were educational, entertaining and well done. There was even a focus on foreign missions. But it all seemed so removed from our daily lives. Though I had the same sense of suffocation as Deb, I was finding my sense of acceptance and belonging and experience of new life and hope at the Narcotic Anonymous meetings and with my co-workers at the Health Care Center. Deb was a nurse and also worked at the Health Care Center and she too said felt that the Health Care Center was more like church than church, primarily because of the staff would openly share their personal needs and pray together,. We kept going to Apple Orchard for the sake of the twins but the church got bigger and bigger, and buildings started to go up. It started to feel more like attending a convention than a community of the beloved. So we decided to look for someplace else. And besides, we weren't so sure that the values that our kids were learning there where the values we were teaching them at home. At the time we weren't ready to say that Apple Orchard Community Church wasn't preaching the Gospel but it didn't seem to us that it was making disciples of Jesus either. We shared our feelings with Mel and Liz but we came away from our dinner time with them feeling like we were patronized more than really heard. I thought at the time that maybe there were just too many cultural differences between us and between Henley and Apple Orchard.

Now ten years later, Mel had moved on to fame and fortune and I wondered if it would be possible for Mel to hear, above the noise of his success, what anyone, anywhere had to say. My feeling was that Mel was living in denial about Western Christendom's addiction to individualism, wealth and power. And I was now convinced that the prosperity gospel, clothed in benevolent paternalism, was nothing but a ploy of Satan to distract would be disciples of Jesus from the cross.

I continued to express my skepticism and anger to Deb. "The church that Mel represents is nothing more than a baptizer of self-centered greed and power made up of arrogant leadership, self-interest programs, and consuming buildings. Mel is the world's quintessential churchman. He missed Brandon and Emily's funeral because he is off teaching the church how to do church. I wonder if he has a clue about what it means to be the church. And besides he hasn't experienced firsthand any more than the rest of us about the needs in the Sudan or East Africa?"

"I know you are angry "O" but don't you think you are being a little hard on Mel? He would have been to the funeral if he could have," replied Deb.

"He could have been here if being self-centered wasn't so important to him. If we have asked him to give us guidance about how to be disciples of Jesus we are just feed his already puffed up self-image. If it weren't for Stan and Karen's money, I imagine he would consider meeting with the rest of us as a waste of his precious time. I'm not really interested in hearing what he has to say. Sure he understands corporate growth strategies and so called leadership principles but what do they have to do with following Jesus? And to tell the truth, I really wonder why Stan and Karen Beckley care about getting together anyway. What do we have in common with them except for our grief and an experience we had together as kids?" I was so angry I was almost in tears.

"I know, honey, but you have shared with me how much that trip to Africa meant to all of you. The least we can do is be gracious. I think maybe you are taking your anger at God out on Mel." admonished Deb.

"Mel has changed a lot since then. And maybe I have too. But like I said, I know Mel's story."

I paused, tears were rolling down my face. "Why did Brandan and Emily and Odie and Faith have to die?"

Seven

As a teen, Mel Carr attended Shady Academy, an exclusive private high school. He was a soccer player and in the top of his class academically. He had two younger brothers and a younger sister. His father was a computer company executive. His mom wasn't employed but worked at home taking care of the kids.

Mel grew up in the church growth movement of the late 1970's. His family was part of the Monroe Community Church, a homogeneous non-denominational white middle class suburban congregation. In high school Mel was active in a large youth program at the church and in 1985, when a junior in high school, he was part of The Liminal Plunge mission trip to Africa. It was the same trip that Odell and the others were on. It was organized by Pittsburgh Youth Impact and supported by the Monroe Community Church and several other churches.

During the Plunge he and Kara Stevens had become an item. Kara, like Mel, was also a year younger than the rest of the group. She also attended Shady Academy and the two found that they had much in common.

When Melvin Carr and Kara Stevens started their senior year of high school after their plunge together in Africa that summer they were both floating on cloud nine. They were inseparable and very much in love they thought until one night when Mel had a family commitment Kara went to a club with some of her girlfriends. She drank too much and smoked too much marijuana; which led to her telling everyone about Jesus and bragging about her and Mel's intimate relationship. The following day Kara's "night on the town" was all over school. Mel heard about it before Kara could explain and wouldn't talk to her for over a week. Then Mel told her that He had realized that he really was in love with Jesus more than her. It broke her heart. She pleaded with him to forgive her. He just gave her the silent treatment even until he was in college. Mel went to Wheaton College in Illinois and majored in English Literature and Religion and Kara went off to Boston College to be a sociology major. The beginning of his freshman year in college Mel finally wrote her a letter that was more a sermon temptation than an acknowledgement of his self-righteousness.

At Wheaton Mel dated around but nothing serious. He joined and help lead the Christian college movement called Student Ventures. During the summers he was on the staff of Student Ventures Youth Camp on Lake Michigan. The middle of his junior year he met and developed a serious relationship with Elizabeth Felter, who to his delight was from State College not far from Pittsburgh. Everyone called her Liz. Liz's father was a Physics Professor at Penn State. Their relationship grew and they were married the summer before their senior year. Mel graduated at the top of his class and, as the Class President, gave the class graduation speech. Liz, however was not able to be present for their graduation as that same day she gave birth to their son; the first of what would be two children, a boy and a girl.

After graduation, Mel went to Gordon-Conwell Theological Seminary to prepare to be a pastor. His freshmen year at GCTS he secured a job as a Youth Pastor on the staff of a new mega church in the suburbs of Boston. In his middler year, he and Liz with their son Elijah attached themselves to an experiment in 20th Century New Testament Christian living. They moved into Boston to live in a Christian community called Kerygma

Fellowship Church (KFC). Mel commuted about an hour to Gordon-Conwell for classes.

KFC was started about five years before in the inner city of Boston by 30 adults who were dismayed by the lukewarm discipleship and politically correct fellowships of the churches that they had been a part of over the years. They had gotten together to study the Sermon on the Mount, and decided to put into practice what they understood the Bible meant by church. They said church was a verb not a noun. It had more to do with what it was, it's Being, than with what it did, it's ministries. What Mel and Liz saw made their hearts sing. This radical fellowship of believers lived together in the South End of Boston, a multi-ethnic neighborhood where many of the poor lived. Mel learned that, because Harvard, BU, Boston College and about 10 other colleges were nearby. Because of the 41 different ethnic groups, all located in these 20 dense blocks in this eastern end of Roxbury it was the most studied neighborhood in the world. KFC was an intentional residential church community.

It had three large households, each with three or more families and a couple of single people. There were about 15 in each household. Each household shared all their meals together. They shared cars and expenses and coordinated their schedules.

KFC had begun out of the hope and dream of a small group desiring to live out the teachings of Jesus. They envisioned a live where they could share their lives with other each other like the new Christians seemed to right after Pentecost. After a period of Bible study and prayer, they decided to begin by making decision by consensus. They chose leaders and selected their name, Kerygma, which in Greek means "to proclaim". With their love for one another that wanted to proclaim to their neighborhood that they were followers of Jesus.

They also set-up a financial system that incorporated the establishment of a common purse. Everyone contributed all their assets and monthly pay checks. They chose to locate in the South End and to live their daily lives on the standards of the welfare system. Everyone who owned a home sold it. They bought four multi-family houses which they renovated to accommodate common meals and living space for several families and singles and children. They incorporated as a 501 (D) not-for-profit status, which meant from the governments perspective they were considered a monastic order.

They slowly shared their honest needs and joys with each other. They began to have a shared life together. They began to feel accepted even when they shared their weaknesses. They challenged each other to live Christ-like lives. They trusted each other with their fears and their dreams, their money and their family. They gave permission and felt free to involve one another in the personal decisions each one had to make. In their free time, when not at a job or caring for children they intentionally built trusting relationships with their neighbors. The kids played with the neighborhood kids while their parents visited to each other on their front stoops. They became part of the neighborhood and felt the pain and struggles of their neighbors.

Mel and Liz learned about them in 1991. What they saw looked like the church in Acts. Mel said to Liz one night "These people are Theopollis, the 'Friends of God'. This is the book of Acts in the flesh." So, they became "intentional members" and moved into a household with their son, Elijah and lived there for the next three years.

Mel and Liz, discovered that because of close living quarter their struggles between each other were exposed. The members helped to support them in the care of their son and later with the addition of their daughter. They learned that this vulnerable life-style led to deeper levels of acceptance and supported. Though the members would from time to time hurt each other, they also brought healing to each other. Because of the acceptance that Mel and Liz felt free to share their needs. They felt that their perspective on things was respected as a gift to the others and they were not judged. The people in their household became their closest friends.

Those experiences in this church-community shaped Mel's understanding of church far beyond his studies. The life-style of the community put flesh of the bones of his academics.

The remainder of his middler and senior year at GCTS, Mel focused on learning about leadership in the Church. His internship was with KFC, where the elders let him sit-in on all their meetings. His Greek exegesis paper was on Romans 12. His Hebrew exegesis paper was on Nehemiah. With the encouragement and support of his professors and one of their publishers, Mel put his experiences at KFC and his studies on leadership together and submitted a book for publications. It came out the day Mel and Liz's daughter, Andi was born, on July 21, 1993, just two months after he graduated.

They stayed at KFC for another year but never committed themselves to full membership because they felt called to become part of the institution of the church that had been passed down through history so they could bring biblical life to it. One of the things they were learning at KFC was that this 'new monasticism' was great for a few. However, because of such a focus on loving one another, it did not have the time to express a call to outreach that engaged the culture. It seemed to remove discipleship from ministering to the needs around them. It seemed to imply that to follow Jesus meant that one had to separate oneself from being in the world. And to Mel that did not match up with what it meant that Jesus was God in the world. He and Liz did not believe the Bible taught that Jesus' disciples were to withdraw from the world. They believed that disciples of Jesus must be in the world, though not of it. In the life of KFG they saw how those who were members spent most of their time 'fixing' each other. From their perspective not enough time was spent on servicing the poor. They believed it should be just the opposite.

They also noticed that the life-style of KFC limited the callings, dreams, and aspiration of those member focused on raising a family and needing the support of others. They noticed that an unusual number of single adults and couples without children seemed to leave after just a few years of membership.

So, Mel and Liz left KGC and with the financial support of their old friend Stan Beckley, in the spring of 1994, they moved back to the greater Pittsburgh area to the new developing suburban community of Apple Orchard. They joined a local Presbyterian church and Liz got a job as a Librarian. Mel was very open with people he met at church. He was not a bit shy about sharing his call to start a church focused on outreach to those in need. Liz met almost every new young family that moved into Apple Orchard when they visited the town library. After about a year they invited Bob and Barb Franks, a couple whom they had meet at church, to their apartment for dinner so they could share their vision more fully. The Franks had taken an early retirement and moved to Apple Orchard. The two couples seemed to hit it off from the first time they met. This led to making a list of all the people they had met, whether or not they thought they were Christians, and inviting them to a cook-out at Western County Park. Liz made a list of over 200 names of people to whom she had introduced herself at the Library. Against Library rules she got their addresses off the

Library computer. Mel had been gathering names at church and in their neighborhood. The Franks put together a list from the people they had meet in their first year at church and in their housing plan. On the invitation they suggested people bring their family members and friends. The Franks said they would provide the hot dogs and hamburgers and buns and asked each family to bring a side dish or dessert that they could share with 4 or 5 people. The invitation made it sound like a big block party to meet new friends.

Amazingly about three hundred and fifty adults and maybe two hundred children showed up for the outing. They had planned for a hundred and fifty at the most. Miraculously there was more than enough food. Most of the people who came brought food for ten or twelve and one man who owned a local grocery store chain brought enough hot dogs, buns, and mustard, relish, and ketchup for three hundred. The three softball fields filled up quickly. A group of young adults organized an Ultimate Frisbee game. Some young families got together and organized races for the kids. Families introduced themselves to each other and went for walks in the nearby woods.

Near the end of the day, with a great deal of anxiety, Mel went to his car, got a bull-horn, and asked everyone to gather in one of the softball fields and have a seat. Nearly everyone came to see what was up. He thanked everyone for coming and then asked if he could say a prayer of gratitude. He prayed in a casual, conversational, yet respectful, way. For many it was perhaps the first time that they had experienced anyone who seemed to be sincere and casual speaking to God. Then for about 20 minutes Mel shared his pilgrimage with Jesus. He began with his growing up years in a traditional middle class church and then went through the African plunge, Youth

Ventures, meeting Liz, Gordon-Conwell, writing his book, *Peak Leadership*, the birth of Elijah and Andi, and their experience in KFC. There was something in what he said with which everyone could identify. Everyone seemed to be captivated. At some points the whole crowd was laughing hysterically, even the children. At other points there were tears coming down many peoples' cheeks. He wrapped up his talk with a straight forward explanation of God's love in Jesus and His death and resurrection. He was not so much preaching as simply sharing Jesus' acceptance, grace, and love. Later Mel told Liz that when he was talking, it just flowed and he didn't even feel like he had to think about what he was saying.

At the end he asked anyone who had at some time in their life asked Jesus to come into their heart to raise their hand. Bob Franks said he estimated that about 10% of the people raised their hands.

Mel then asked if anyone who would like to explore how God intended for them to live to please stand. After a few second, a couple of teenagers in the front stood up and then some men off to the side stood up, and then, like a wave, nearly everyone was standing. Mel, Bob, Liz, and Barb were stunned. Mel hadn't even planned to ask the question, let along know what to do next. So, in a very spontaneous outburst, he shouted "Great, let's all get together next month and do just that!!! This week, I'll send you all a letter letting you know when and where. Thanks, for a great day! See you then."

Most people stayed and helped clean up and talked about Mel's talk and the day together.

The Carrs and the Franks went back to the Carr's apartment and talked about what to do now. They decided to find a place to meet, and to not only send out a letter to their original list but to also put a full-page ad in the Pittsburgh Post-Gazette, that is, if Mel could get Stan to pay for it.

1,200 people showed up for their first worship service the week-end of July 4th 1995.

Within two years the new Apple Orchard Community Church had a weekly attendance of five thousand and by 2006 more than twenty thousand people attended one of the four Sunday morning worship services. In 1998, Mel wrote his second book entitled, *Driven by Intimacy: Growing the Church through Home Groups.* It was on the best sellers list for two year. In 2000 his publishers reissues an updated version of *Peak Leadership*, his first book, under the title, *Servants Modeled After Their Master.* And then in 2005 he wrote, *Choose Mission or Die.* His books were popular all over the Christian world. If you wanted to have him come speak at any kind of an evangelical or mission event you had to schedule him at least a year in advance. He limited his speaking engagements to 100 days a year and scheduled himself to preach at Apple Orchard once a month, except on rare occasions such as the one that had him out of town for the Bryce family funeral. At the urging of President Bush he was on ten day preaching and teaching tour in Texas. He was perhaps the most sought after preacher in the country.

He believed the Apple Orchard Church was the result of the miracles of God. The first outing, the first worship service, the phenomenal growth of the church, the popularity of his books, his fame as a teacher and speaker convinced him that only the power of God could have done it all. He knew it sure wasn't him, he was only a spectator.

Mel's resume' was the dream resume of the preaching profession.

I knew Mel's story and that is why I did not trust his walk with Jesus.

Eight

On Monday morning, June 25, 2007, Bill Bryce and I boarded the plane at the Pittsburgh International Airport bound for Malakal, Sudan, Africa. The trip was going to take two day, most of them in the air. First, we would fly to Amsterdam, have a six hour layover, then to Nairobi, with a ten hour wait and change of planes, and finally arrive in Malakal in the morning of Wednesday, June 27. We were to stay in Malakal at the home of Director of New Hope in the Sudan for four days. Fifteen year old Billy Bryce was to be released from the hospital on June 29th. We were to return with Billy to the U. S. on Monday, July 2nd and arrive in Pittsburgh on July 4th.

When I first realized I would be going to Africa, I was thankful again that Deb and I had visited missionary friends in the Bahamas just a year ago and I had a current Passport. I was anxious, however, about Bill and I both not having time to get a Visa. However, Bill told me that Mbumbla Gengeci, the Director of Sudan New Hope (SNH) had made arrangements with the Sudanese government for us to have Visas issued to us at Customs when we arrived in Malakal. From what I had heard about how things can work in these unstable countries, I had my doubts. But I thought I don't know what I am doing anyways, so just go with the flow and trust the Lord.

To my surprise as we were going up the escalator towards the rotunda that led to the concourses, coming down the other escalator was Mel returning from Texas. Our eyes met, we both smiles slightly, and waved. At first I couldn't identify my emotions but I was sure I wasn't looking forward to the Plunge reunion meeting at Stan's when we got back. I thought, I don't think Mel has a clue what the will of God is, yet I'll bet he will try and get us all on his band wagon and want us to propagate the blessings of American prosperity in the name of Jesus. Well, he is not going to sell me that idol. It made me aware that my anger was stronger than I had realized. I consciously put Mel out of my mind and walked toward the concourse that led to international flights. I felt safe with Bill and was relieved that he was not a part of the group that would be meeting and so we won't be talking about it.

The last week had been emotionally and physically draining. I knew it was going to be a long exhausting trip, so as soon as the plane took off I told Bill that I was going to try and get some sleep.

But I couldn't sleep. My mind began to flash back again to the last time I had been in Africa, twenty two years ago. I thought, since the murders I have been reminiscing and living in the past most of the time.

I started thinking about the end of the Plunge. I remembered thinking back then: what was I to do with all that I had experienced? Why had God introduced me to His awesome love? How was I now going to live? I remembered feeling like my youth was over and I had lost my innocence. I no longer cared about high school popularity. The experience had made me feel like I had been transported light years into the future. The trip was coming to an end. In two days the group would be returning home. How could I just leave? I felt like no one at home would understand anything about how I was feeling. I thought then that I would feel like an alien from a different world.

The last evening before our final day in Africa the group gathered to eat and then as we had done each night during our experience talked about our day. I remembered that it seemed as we shared that everyone was feeling the same things. The experience had brought us all to the limits of our faith and understanding, it had created among us a bond that we thought would never leave us. At the group gathering that night I shared that Ya died in my arms that day. Brandon shared that Kaluki died in his arms as well and others shared that three other babies died that day. Everyone shared their sense of deep connectedness with those dying children, our unexplainable peace and joy, and our fear of returning home. We were all feeling that we were returning to a cocoon that would insulate us from Jesus. Larry, the leader for the trip from Pittsburgh Youth Impact closed our time in prayer and shared that tomorrow we would be traveling back in the van across the rut tracked road to Nairobi and join the other groups that had been throughout East Africa for a dinner. We would attend a wrap-up presentation by Rick Marker. Rick was the Director of World Impact Foundation.

We spent that night at a Sheridan Inn. There, literally surrounded by suffering, we were in the comfort of a five star motel, which could have been in any American city.

The next day before boarding the plane for the United States we spent the evening relaxing around the pool. It took two full days, with a lay-over in Amsterdam, before we flew into Pittsburgh International Airport.

And now twenty two years later I was making the return trip back to Africa. It felt very strange.

I remembered our final banquet.

Emily had introduced the speaker. Dr. Marker had talked about the needs of the poor, the great disparities all over the world, that following Jesus meant serving the least, that the poorest of the poor were really the spiritually poor who were believing the counterfeit gospel of Western Christendom.

I couldn't believe that I remembered what Dr. Maker talked about. That was 22 years ago. I also remembered that his talk was split in half with the meal in-between. I remembered that after the first part of his talk we had argued at our table during the meal about whether or not what Dr. Marker had said was true.

The second part of the talk was about if you were to be a for-real disciple of Jesus you must have a preference for the poor, and that Jesus' power came from being powerless. Dr. Marker's punch line had something to do with total surrender to Jesus in your life. I remembered thinking about what that would mean for me.

The mandatory time alone after the banquet was like yesterday for me as I took myself back to that evening.

Emily and I had walked out together but neither made a whisper. When we got to the entrance to the hall I turned right and went down the hall towards my room. Emily turned left. I was hoping that my three roommates would not think of going back to our room and that it would be a good place to be alone.

When I got there the room was empty. I turned on the TV to make some noise so my roommates if they came to the room would realize it was occupied. I waited for about five minutes to be satisfied that no one else was returning. And when finally I felt like I was going to be alone, I turned off the TV and knelled beside the bed.

"Lord, Jesus, what do you want me to do with my life?" I prayed.

These thoughts and memories of the past where now in the twilight of sleep for me and with that memory I fell asleep.

I was awakened by the Flight Attendant serving a tray of "flight food." The layover and plane changes were uneventful. They were long periods of hurry up and wait, eating airport mall food, and people watching. Both the Amsterdam and Nairobi airports were crowded with a sea of world travelers.

When we finally arrived at Customs in Malakal we were greeted by Mbumbla Gengeci, the Director of SNH and his wife, Mary. The Customs official was all prepared to give us our Visa. Mbumbla told us later that a little green always helps to make a more efficient bureaucracy.

We drove to Mbumbla and Mary's home where Billy was waiting for us. Billy had his arm in a sling. He smiled when he saw his grandfather and me. He gave each of us a hug as best he could. We both hugged him and he winced from the pain in his shoulder. He didn't say anything and neither did we. Mbumbla told us later that, except for the "home coming" celebration when Billy laughed and cried and sang in worship, that he had said hardly a word. When Mbumbla told him that he was to go back to the States he only asked with whom he was going to live. Mbumbla had explained to him that he would at first be living with his grandparents for a while and then be adopted by Deb and me. Billy simply responded with some nods and a slight smile.

That night during dinner and the next morning at breakfast Bill and I tried to not to impose too many questions on Billy, but when we did ask him something he answered us with a short honest answer. For example, after dinner, just before we were about to go to our rooms, I asked him if he was worried about what it would be like to live in Pittsburgh. Billy's reply was, "There are people in Pittsburgh and I like people so I think I will feel at home. No, I'm not worried." I was a little surprised at his simple direct response.

Over the next two days, Mbumbla took Bill and me to visit the orphanage, school, health clinic, and other outreach efforts of SNH. Billy went with us but rarely said a word, except when at the orphanage.

When we pulled into Day of Hope and Billy got out of the car, someone yelled in Sudanese and the whole orphanage went wild. Kids of all ages came running from everywhere. Billy ran, arm in sling, to join them. The sight looked so strange to me. Billy, about 6' tall, all the little children, and the kids his age about 6" shorter than him. It came home to me that the children that murdered Billy's family probably were about the age and size of these friends of Billy's. It seemed to me that the greeting Billy got was way beyond what he had expected. I asked Mbumbla why Billy was greeted with such joy, didn't the kids understand that he had recently lost his family.

The Director explained. First, these children and Billy as well, truly believe that "Papa" and family are rejoicing in the fullness of God's presence. And second, the whole lives of these children had been filled with the fear that they would be captured someday, taught to kill, and forced to become part of Children's Army that massacred the Bryce family and so many of the families of these children. Even the raid on the church was part of the desensitizing and training of the children. But they had not been successful in killing Billy, who was a particular target, because he was the eldest son of the "Papa." He had been spared; he not been killed and he was not captured. He was a sign of God's favor and of hope. A sign of victory over the KRF. A sign that their reign of terror was coming to an end.

I asked, "How did he survive, if he were such a target." Mbumbla said that Billy had been shot twice, once in the chest and once in the side. The first just broke the skin on the side of his belly. The second shot was at an angle that went through the flesh on his chest and out under his arm. It didn't hit a bone or any vital organs but it knocked him down where he hit his head on the hard floor and passed out. The shooters saw him get shot and when they examined him they saw a lot of blood coming from his chest and side, so they believed he was dead or at least would die and was not worth taking as a captive. Their mission had been accomplished. But God had more for Billy to do.

I thought to myself how hard it was going to be for Billy to leave his orphan family and find a new life in Pittsburgh.

As we boarded the plane on the fourth day of our visit, I noticed large tears running down Billy's cheeks. Billy hadn't said anything since his goodbyes back at the orphanage.

When the plane took off he just sat at his window seat staring out at the rapidly fading earth. His grandfather was next to him in the middle seat and I was on the isle. As the plane climbed high above the city and began to move north, the dwellings began to fade into the distance and the landscape began to grow, revealing the lush vegetation, mountains, rivers, and lakes, and the distant horizon against a clear dark blue sky. Billy spoke, as if to himself, or maybe it was a prayer. In a quiet soft voice, but one that I could hear, I heard him say, "Yes, I see, you are doing a whole new thing, all of your creation is groaning with the birth pangs of the coming of your reign. I think I can hear the earth humming your praises." It reminded me of my experience in Colorado when I was about his age and I felt I could hear the stars singing.

When we got back to Pittsburgh at 4:30 a.m., Deb, the Twins, and Grandma Bryce were there to meet us. It was a warm but quiet greeting with everyone feeling a little awkward, not really knowing how Billy was feeling and not sure what to say. Billy went to stay with Grandma and Grandpa Bryce.

I felt such a relief. It was good to get back to the familiar. Yet at the same time I felt the anxiety of a new season in all our lives.

It was about 6:00 a.m. when we finally were home and the sun was planning a hot summer day for everyone in Pittsburgh. However, I was exhausted in every way. Thanks to a gift from Deb's parents a couple of years ago the house was air-conditioned. So I made my apologies for being so tired but said I just had to get some real sleep. I laid down in my own bed, thanked God that I had one, and oh it felt so good. In less than two minutes I was fast asleep.

Nine

I didn't wake up until the following morning at 6:30 a.m. Deb was still sleeping and so were the kids. I wondered what new challenges and how many email awaited me at work, but before I went in to the Health Care Center I just had to clear my head and get some kind of handle on what to do next.

I decided to go to what I called my "office" and be alone. First I took a long shower in my own bath room, wrote a note to Deb to let her know where I went, stopped by Mickey D's for a cup of coffee, and went to my private space for a time with the Lord.

My "office" as I referred to it when talking to Deb or the twins, was an abandoned church that had become my personal sanctuary for the past five years. It had been abandoned and boarded up for as long as I could remember. When I first explored the building, maybe twelve years earlier, I did so out of curiosity. The back door had fallen off. I went in looking for anyone who may be homeless so I could offer them a blanket or a bed in the shelter if they wanted to have a place to sleep. I had learned, however, that some of the homeless preferred to be alone, so I was always prepared to do what I could if they didn't want to the shelter at the big church in the center of Henley. I explored the building but did not find anyone. The idea came to me that this might make a good place for me to get some space alone. When you are on the streets and in an outreach ministry for years and you have kids at home, it gets to be that there is no place that you can go to just get away and be alone. This abandoned church seemed like it could be a place for me to hide, not from God but from the constant pressing of unmet needs. The idea that I was trespassing did not cross my mind.

Now, after five years it almost felt like the building belonged to me. At one time, maybe during the 50's it must have been a magnificent place. None of the hardwood trim had ever been painted. The stained glass windows that weren't broken were extremely detailed. The Sanctuary, was a huge gothic auditorium, cold and dark. It was designed to seat perhaps 1,000 people including the choir. The high roof in the Sanctuary had several holes in it through which I could actually see some of the stars on a clear night. The rain had destroyed most of the interior. There were 18 rooms that I thought must have been used for Sunday School, possibly one for each grade plus a few for adults, as well as a couple of offices. Under the Sanctuary was a large room with what must have had a kitchen attached to it, but all the appliances had been removed and most of the walls had deteriorated.

I went to the room on the second floor that I had slowly cleaned up over the years. I had made it my personal space and had even put a lock on the door to keep curiosity seekers, like me, out. Only once in five years had I found someone sleeping in the church. It happened to be someone I knew well. When I shared that I had set this space aside to be alone with God and wanted it to be special, private, and protected, my friend said he would make sure no one from the street invaded it.

I sat down in my prayer chair and began to review my life since Brandon and I had returned from the Liminal Plunge in Africa twenty year ago. I had been the director of an addiction recovery program for the Henley Health Care Center for the past twelve years.

As I reviewed the past I remembered that I expected to go to Penn State on a football scholarship. But when we returned from the Plunge my mother was diagnosed with HIV and went back on the street using drugs and prostituting. And at the end of the summer we learned that Tesa, my fifteen year old sister was pregnant, and at the same time my grandmother who was sixty years old and trying to keep my two younger sisters from dropping out of school, was diagnosed with breast cancer. It could have been on an undoing time for me but I was surrendered to Jesus and at peace.

My granny had been the one solid person in my life. Not only did she drag me to church with her but she was always there when I was headed in the wrong direction. I could count on her to block the way. One time when I was about ten years old some of my friends and I were having an apple flinging contest. We lived in an urban neighborhood where there were lots of trees. Our hood must have at one time been an apple orchard. Lots of apple trees anyway. All sprinkled in among the houses and apartment buildings. Not all urban areas have always been crowded, some started out as really exclusive communities, but after the 50's a lot of those communities changed and home owner occupants were replaced with renters and large homes replaced with projects and high-rises. My friends and I would cut some thick twigs about 2 feet long, trim off the little branches, make a point on the end, and presto, we had an apple flinger. We would stick an apple on the end and then fling it to see how far or how accurate we could fling the apple. On the end of a stick you can fling an apple a lot further and faster than you can throw it. But can you flinging it with as much accuracy? To practice our accuracy we would fling them at a tree or at a telephone pole.

As it often did, our targets turned to moving targets and we would start to fling our apples at each other. Well, we were fling away and one of our friends became the primary target. Out flung he began to retreat and eventually ran towards his house for refuge. We followed and to make a long story short, I flung an apple right through his living room plate glass window. It was a great fling. I missed my mark but the crash was great. We all took off, but later when I had got home my grandmother was waiting for me with less than a sweet Christian smile on her face. In the hood, even in those days, grandmothers looked out for each other's childin'. Granny didn't't yell or scream or even take my prized apple flinger to use as a switch on me. She just stood in my way. She seemed to know the little rush I had gotten from the sense of power in breaking that window. I don't know how but I was sure she could see inside my feelings. She saw that I enjoyed the damage that I had done and the sense of released anger that I felt. She told me that tomorrow, I was going to go to the hardware store with the money I had been saving for a bike, buy the window pane and hire the handyman on our street. Then she, the handyman, and I were going to go over to my friend's house and I was going to apologize and then help the handyman fix the window.

It was maybe the hardest thing I had ever done in my first ten years of living. And it was maybe the best thing I had ever done in those ten years. Granny knew how to point me in the right direction.

Her cancer was just one of a hundred reasons I decided to I put my football and college plans on hold and get two jobs, one washing dishes for the University of Pittsburgh dining hall and the other as a waiter working for a caterer. After a year with the caterer I became a banquet waiter and then eventually started to do fine dining waiting. And because I worked for the University, I was eligible for free tuition, so I began to take a class in the General Studies program one night a week. I was able to make enough money to pay the rent, buy food and clothes, and pay for transportation, but I couldn't get my mom clean and sober, heal my granny's cancer, or prevent my sister from dropping out of school, sleeping around, and becoming an addict like my mother and Jocko. Because of lack of information and access to good health care, my grandmother had been diagnosed very late in her cancer and she died the year after Tesa's son Derick was born. My youngest sister, April, stayed in school. By myself, I essentially made a home for her and Derick. Jocko who was released on parole in 1986, just after Derick was born. Jocko went right back to the streets and pushing drugs. To keep from using drugs myself, I attended as many NA meetings as I could and was determined that no matter what I would not pick up a drug or take a drink. I refused to let Jocko or my mother live with me as long as they kept getting high. I was overwhelmed enough trying to take care of Granny, April, and Derick.

Jocko, was shot to death on December 20, 1988. I was only twenty one at the time.

As I reflected there in my sanctuary I remembered how through those years, I continued to go to church, sometimes to the church on the Northside where James and his parents went. But mostly I worshipped at the House of Praise where Misha's dad was the pastor and Jorge was on the staff as the youth pastor. However, my primary support came from the fellowship in the rooms of Narcotic Anonymous.

In the process of trying to get my granny help for her cancer I took her to the Henley Christian Health Care Center where Misha's mom was a nurse. That was in 1990. The Health Care Center had been in existence for eight years and had a staff of twelve. They now, seventeen years later, had a staff of seventy five. When I discovered the Health Care Center and learned what it was all about, I felt it was the best kept secret in the neighborhood. The doctors and nurses at the Center prayed with the patients and spend an unusual amount of time with each visit, listening to the patients concerns, not just making a quick medical diagnosis and prescribing medication. Eventually, everyone in my little household selected the Center as their Primary Care Physician. The Center made the last year of Granny's life one in which she felt surrounded by more love than she had experienced nearly all of her life. And in the process they made me, April, Derick, and even Tesa feel like we had an extended family at the Health Care Center.

As I got to know everyone at the Center and as they got to know me, one day Dr. Fred Billard, the founder and Medical Director of the Center, suggested that I consider joining their staff and developing an outreach to the homeless and addicted. He said I would be a great fit because of my love of Jesus, my understanding and compassion for those who lived on the streets, my experience with addiction recovery, and my obvious intelligence and gifted ability to establish rapport with almost anyone. I was blown away by his affirmation and confidence in me. I had never felt such a validation of my life. The only requirement, he said, was that I continued to take classes toward my college degree. He even said they would help me with the tuition since I would have to quit my job at Pitt. So, in August of 1990, I began to get paid for befriending the homeless and helping to connect them with medical care. I quickly learned that I needed a network of support from others in the neighborhood who were also homeless providers and it was not long before we had a support fellowship of homeless outreach staff from several different providers. We became a networking team. And maybe by coincidence or by a higher powers design – I knew it was the Spirit – we were all seeking to follow Jesus.

While taking classes at Pitt I met Debra Welsh. Debra wasn't from a perfect family but she also wasn't from a severely broken one, like mine, either. She was on a scholarship in Pitt's School of Nursing. She was three years younger than my 24 years when we met. We both graduated from Pitt in 1992 and were married that summer. That fall Deb started working at Children's Hospital.

Tesa, then twenty two, had found sobriety in 1990, gotten a job as a waitress, been reunited with Derick, who was six, and had her own apartment with a roommate whom she had met at NA.

April, was twenty years old and going to college in Ohio, at Findlay University. Then when Deb and I got married, April lived with us for the summer but then the following spring graduated and got a job and an apartment in Toledo.

In August of 1993, Deb gave birth to our twins Jenn and Jim. She quit her job at Children's, and the Health Care Center hired her part-time.

As I reflected on those early years, I just marveled at God's faithfulness. All I had done was simply try to do the next right thing for my family, for any who crossed my path, and for myself. It was always just one step at a time, one day at a time; and now I had been in recovery for 23 years, had a family, a home, a college degree, and directed a ministry that offered healing and hope to hundreds of people with the chronic, fatal diseases of drug addiction and HIV. Many of those I served were friends with whom I had grown up and who otherwise would been headed for never ending suffering, hospitals, prisons, and death. I supervised a recovery peer support staff team of five and was responsible for a storefront center for recovery. And it was all a part of the integrated care of a large whole person health care facility that was a family of faith centered in Jesus.

It dawned on me, what with all that had happened in the past month, that maybe through all these years God was still preparing me for something more, a new season, a new calling. That revelation gave me a sense of peculiar peace and curious anticipation. And although I did not know what my future held and was feeling like I was starting out on an uncharted path, I felt confident that I could trust the One I knew held the future. I thought that the biggest change that I was now facing was the addition of Billy to my family. It also occurred to me that my family has just grown not only by the addition of Billy. It also now extended to the Brandon family and to Emily's family.

On Saturday, August 11, 2007, just one day more than two months since the New Hope murders, Billy Bryce moved in to live with our family at 4113 Sheridan Ave. in the Highland Park neighborhood of Pittsburgh, PA. In two weeks he would start attending the 10th Grade at Arlington High School. The day he moved in Deb, Jen, Jimmy, and I were ready. He had gotten to know us all over the past month and a half and he was also ready. That afternoon, Grandma and Grandpa Bryce and Grandpa Stewire came over for a picnic. The whole day went rather smoothly. Billy seemed to have adjusted to American life rather easily. The Bryce's only concern which they told Deb and me, was that he seemed to have adjusted too easily. They hadn't seen any anger or even signs of depression. They said he was usually rather quiet and easy going, acted appropriately around everyone, was well mannered, and always helpful. He usually got up around 6:00 AM. I thought this was really weird for a teenager in the summer. *"Could he be suppressing a lot of anger and feelings of abandonment? Did we need to look for signs of depression or the potential actions of anger?"* In many ways he functioned like a secure, stable 40 year old, not a displaced, angry fifteen year old that had just lost his whole family. The oddest thing, Bill reported, was that he never watched TV nor got on the computer; although he said he knew how to use them well. He would read, loved to swim, and often would go for a long run. He said one time when they were at a park, some teens were playing soccer. He asked if he could join them and Bill said he was amazing. At the move-in picnic, he, Jen, Jimmy, and I kicked a soccer ball around in the back yard and during meal time he shared a story about an African festival. I was cautiously amazed at this mature young man.

Ten

The follow-up meeting of the "Plunge" group was the following day at Stan and Karen's place. I was not looking forward to it, simply because I felt real uncomfortable anticipating what Mel and Liz might have to say. Deb was anxious about leaving Billy, but Jimmy and Jenn assured her that they would all be fine and not to worry about Billy. I said I would stay home but Jimmy told us that he thought Billy was more secure and mature that both he and Jenn put together. That had a ring of truth to us and I lost my excuse not to go to the group.

The Beckley's lived in a spacious 'farm house' situated on top of a beautiful hill surrounded by a forest of huge oak trees. On the property there was also a barn that stabled three horses and another building that looked like a mountain lodge.

Jorge and Misha and Deb and I drove out together. As we approached the address on Winding Hill Road in Apple Orchard Heights I was not the only one feeling a little, no, a lot, out of place. I had known Stan for twenty two years but this was the first time I had been to his home. The address was on stone pillars at the opening of a long driveway that started back through a thick oak forest. As it wound back through the trees it was almost like entering a tunnel about fifty feet in the air with the ceiling made of branches and leaves. The late afternoon sun light flickered through the branches. Along the curbs lining each side of the drive, were large flowering red Impatiens. After about a quarter of a mile the tunnel opened up into a clearing with large well- groomed pastures on either side, enclosed with white post and rail fences. There were three horses grazing in one of the pastures, one all black, one white and one an Appaloosa.

With uneasy fear, I wondered if any neighbors saw us pull in the driveway and if so what they thought about three black folks and a Hispanic, driving in here together. After we drove around the circular driveway at the front of the house and I noticed a new white Mercedes was parked there. I figured Mel and Liz had already arrived. And sure enough, standing there in the entrance to this palatial estate were these two white couples dressed in their brand named clothes looking like nothing could touch them. Stan and Karen, representing the wealth and power with Mel and Liz, representing the religious establishment. The brokers plotting behind the scenes how to influence the political decision makers secure to protect their insulation from the pain of the poor. Mel was not as fit looking as Stan and had a slight paunch but his hair was thick and wavy and he wore clothes that must have cost as much as a week in a drug rehab hospital. Liz was also a little heavier than I had expected, but never the less very attractive and well dressed. I thought she was almost over dressed for the occasion.

Everyone shared greetings and awkward hugs all around. Mel seemed to act especially warm towards me. This I found rather odd, but then I remembered that he was a hugger by profession. It was his politically correct evangelical greeting. I wondered if the grapevine had somehow let Mel in on how distrustful I was of him.

The exterior of the house was covered with white clap board siding. It was a rectangular building, three stories high, with a covered porch adorned with pillars that went across the full front of the house. But when you entered, the interior was designed like a modern home with vaulting ceilings. Stan offered to take us on a tour. The entry way was about the size of the first floor of my house. Beyond the entry way to the right was a wide, exposed staircase that went up to a bridge-like balcony. To the left of the entry way was a formal dining room. Beyond it was a huge kitchen with a breakfast nook. Between the dining area and kitchen was a hallway. There was a half bath off a hallway and it looked like the hallway went back to a couple of other rooms which I thought could be bedrooms. That area was not part of the tour. On the right off the entry way, as you passed under the bridge-like-balcony, was a Great Room. At the far end of the Great Room was a stone wall with a large fireplace that went to the top of the cathedral ceiling. There were double French doors on the right of the fireplace that went into huge recreation room. In it was a sixty inch screen TV, a number of couches and easy chairs, a pool table, a kitchenette with a long countertop and stools, and another fireplace. On the left of this room were sliding glass doors that went out to a patio. To the left of the patio was a large swimming pool.

In the recreation room to the right of the sliding glass doors was a door that went led to a hall way. Off this hallway was bath room with a large stall shower and on the other side of the hall from the bath room there was an office that looked more like a corporate board room.

Stan then took us back to the entry way where he directed us to the back of the house. At the back of the entry way as a room that looked more like an extension of the entry way than a separate room. In it were several small tables and chairs. On the left was a door that led to the kitchen. And at the back of this room were another set of large sliding glass doors that went directly out to the patio and pool. The patio was partially covered and went the full length of the back of the house. There were doors to it from the breakfast nook, the back of the entry way, and the recreation room.

That concluded our tour. The tour did not include the bedrooms upstairs or the basement or garages or what I though may be another bedroom or suite on the first floor behind the dining room. Stan said the third floor also had a full bath and four bedrooms which they used on occasion when he had extended business meetings with people from other parts of the country or world.

We all gathered in the dining room where we were served soup and salad. While we ate Deb shared with the group about the new addition to our family and I said a couple of things about my visit to New Hope Orphanage. Nobody seemed to ask too many questions and Mel was quiet for the most part. This was very unlike the Mel I had known in the past who had dominated most of the conversation.

Eleven

After dinner, we went to the Great room. Karen served some pie and Stan initiated a meeting.

First, he asked Jorge to pray.

Next he asked everyone to share a little about themselves and what God had been up to in their lives for the past twenty years. I thought to myself, and almost sarcastically blurted out loud, *"Boy this is going to be good. I just can't wait to hear Mel tell us about his life."*, but my ego also was anxious to talk about how God had blessed me. Yet I determined to stay above a 'can you top this, storytelling, game playing.'

It was quiet for a minute and then Jorge said he would start.

Jorge wasn't sure where to begin or how much to say, but like everyone there he was used to speaking to a group and even putting together last minute messages. He thought for a minute and then said, "I think you all knew me pretty well twenty years ago but a lot has happened to all of us since then. However, rather than tell you about the present, I want to start with something that happened with me back on what we experienced as our Liminal Plunge. For Liz, Karen, and Deb who weren't on the mission trip with the rest of us took in our teens, Liminal Plunge is how the leaders of that trip referred to it because it was an experience that took us to our limits. But I am sure your husbands have told you all about it, especially since it is what has brought us all together again tonight. This is something that I have never shared with anyone before, ever. If it is OK with you, Misha, and I'll need your help."

Misha smiled and nodded her head like she knew exactly what he was going to talk about. Misha had a beautiful smile as she looked at Jorge. You could tell how much she loved him. And as I watched her nod to him it reminded me of what a cute teen she had been and I thought you could still see that petite attractive kid in her. She had gained a little weight but still looked young.

"Well, remember the banquet night at the end of the liminal plunge trip. We were all supposed to go off by ourselves to listen to God. I didn't get much time by myself. I sat at the table until almost everyone had left the banquet hall. I planned to go back to our hotel room and when I got there I saw Odell in the room."

Looking at me, he said, "You were kneeling beside the far bed with your back to me. I tried not to make any noise and I don't think you heard me."

I shook my head. He was right I didn't remember hearing him.

Jorge continued, "So I slowly backed out of the room and gingerly shut the door, holding the handle down to control the click of the latch as I quietly released it into place. Then I didn't know where to go for my quiet time and I just wandered around the hotel thinking about what the speaker had said about emptying myself like Jesus did. I still think about that. Then I saw Misha. She was sitting in a corner of the lounge with her back to me. I noticed she was quietly crying so hard she was shaking."

Jorge nudged Misha, who was sitting to him, and said now you pick up the story.

Misha started, "You all know that Jorge and I practically grow up together. We met when we were four years old in the Head Start program at my dad's church where we have been the Youth Pastors for the past seventeen years. Most of you all also know that I am an only child. And as a pastor's kid I always felt rejected by the other kids. What you don't know, and what my parents didn't know then, is that when I was in Junior High, to gain acceptance, I messed around with alcohol and became sexually active. I felt ashamed and didn't like myself. To cover up my life of shame I became a leader in the Brace Ring club, a group that openly declared abstinence in sex and drugs. My dad and mom and the whole church were so proud of me and thought that I was such a good Christian. That's why they encouraged me to go on the trip to Africa.

Jorge was one of the few people who knew both sides of my life and still accepted me. We didn't have any kind of intimate or romantic relationship then. We were just friends."

Jorge cut in, "When I saw Misha crying I stopped and thought to myself, should I try and help her or go have my own quiet time. I know now that God had me stop. I walked up behind her and softly touched her shaking shoulder."

Misha interrupted, "I felt so relieved to see him that I stopped crying."

Jorge continued, "We just sat in silence for a while. Finally, Misha said, 'I don't know what to do.' I replied, 'Me either, this trip and that talk have me questioning my whole future.' And Misha replied, 'Oh, I don't mean that.' And I said, 'What do you mean?' And she said, 'I mean I don't know what to do about me."

Jorge then looked again to Misha.

Misha picked up the story, "I can remember it like it was yesterday, I felt such a relief. I said, 'Nobody knows and I have never acted on it but I am sexually attracted to girls.' I told Jorge that I knew it may be hard for him to believe, knowing what he knew about me. The trip had shaken me enough that I wanted to take off all my masks and I had to recognize my feelings and I didn't know what to do or how to feel or who I was."

Jorge chimed in again. "It was hard for me to believe but something in me said not to react. I knew she had always suffered from the fear of being rejected. And I heard Jesus within me say, 'Ask her if she thinks I have a problem with her having those feelings?' So, I did."

Again Misha picked up the story, "I thought what a strange thing to ask, I hadn't given a thought about what Jesus thought. I was only worried about how upset my parents would be, at least how upset I assumed they would be. They never ever said anything about homosexuality. So, I said to Jorge, 'What are you talking about? What would Jesus think?' And he said, 'I mean, do you think Jesus accepts you no matter what?' And I thought, yeah, I did, in fact I realized that He is the one who really does accept me. And also then on that trip, you all accepted me. Remember when I fell in the gutter where the sewage water went on the side of the street, you all were grossed out but we all laughed and you helped clean myself off; that was acceptance. But I also thought, acceptance does not make something right. God created humankind in his likeness, both male and female, not all male or all female. His likeness is male and female as one. So, I told Jorge, even though Jesus accepts me, which felt so good, I still had a problem with being sexually attracted to another girl. Jorge then told me that he too had a problem with lust, and greed, and envy and gluttony and all the other deadly sins. I remember he said if people were honest that they never stop struggling with sin, and also if they say lust or anxiety about money or eating too much are not issues for them then they are just plain lying. He said that when we stop struggling with that stuff, that is when we really have a problem, because that is when we stop needing God's forgiveness. He said the fact that I am honestly struggling with lust, regardless of sexual orientation, was a good thing. It meant that the Holy Spirit was working on changing me. I also thought at the time that Jorge was the wisest person I ever met. I remember all that because it began to change my whole life and it was when I began to fall in love with him."

Jorge then said, "It did change our relationship. That was the beginning. We have been together ever since. We went to college, got married, had twin boys, Juan and Michael, now 16 years old, and we have been co-youth pastors at Misha's dad's church since 1990. Life is full and we love it. That is what God has been up to in our lives."

I thought to myself. Now that was real. I like these two, always have.

Deb was sitting on the other side of Misha so she was next. She decided to play it safe and let me be free to share my stuff without her revealing the negative judgments we were holding about the church. I would be next and then I could say as much or as little as I wanted. So she shared some about the Health Care Center where we work and her job as a nurse and what God had been slowly showing her, first through getting to know and love me and then through the patients at the Health Care Center, the struggles of people with addiction and diseases and poverty and racism. She then talked about how our twins had also been God's teachers. Deb wrapped up her time by expressing the sad, yet awesome privilege and new challenge it was to have Billy now part of their family. She finished by saying, "Thanks for listening." And then she was quiet.

Everyone waited for me to take my turn. There was silence for a minute. I prayed silently. Then I said, "I am not sure what to say. Deb has told you about the kids and the great place where we work. All I can say is that God has truly done more in my life than I could have ever imagined or dreamed. Twenty five years ago I truly believed that I would have been long dead my now. I am a totally different person from the person I was before I surrendered my life to Jesus. I have to say that my transformation has been brought about first by the life of Jesus in me and then by the presence of God through those who suffer in the recovery fellowship. For real, the Twelve Step fellowship is where I have discovered the Kingdom of God. I don't want to be critical of the church but, as they tell us in the Twelve Step literature, when you are ask to be the speaker all you should do is share your personal experience and where you get your strength and hope. Deb knows I have tried to find Jesus in the church and it has just never happened for me. I don't see, or hear, or feel Him there. Like I said, that's just for me. Over the years I have tried your churches and others and it just isn't real for me. I am at home with Jesus when I am with the honesty, openness, humility, gratitude and fellowship of those who suffer in the rooms of Narcotics Anonymous and also to some extent at the Health Care Center. I am in love with Jesus and I have a passion in my heart to share what I know of Jesus' love for me, not because of who I am but because I know He loves them just as much as He loves me. What I have experienced of Jesus and what I have experienced of the church are almost at opposite ends of reality for me. That is what God has been doing in me for the past twenty years. The life of Jesus in me has been changing my life from the inside-out through the program and fellowship of NA. Isn't that what you are asking us to share Stan, what God had been up to in our lives for the past twenty years? He has been changing me and giving me such a full and blessed life that I am in awe about it all the time. And I rarely do I have a clue what He will do next, He has always surprised me. For now I think it has something to do with Billy, and maybe us. I also know, whatever it is, it will be good. God is always good."

"Thanks", replied Stan.

Karen was next to share. She seemed to sort of been taken aback by what she thought of as my 'confession' because of what I had said about churches and she wasn't sure where to begin. She thought, well, she would just tell her story and not react to me at all.

She began, "I was raised Karen Cranston. I grew up in a small town in the center of the state and graduated valedictorian from my high school. I met Stan at Stanford University. I first saw Stan when we both tried out for the University Choir our sophomore year. We discovered that we both were born again Christians and we fell in love with each other. It was really just like that. We got married. He got a job with an investment firm selling stock back here in Pittsburgh, and I got a job as the assistant manager for the William Penn Hotel. After a couple of years we had our daughter Brenda, Stan went into partnership with Kirk Henry and they started a telemarketing company that Stan eventually owned by himself until he went public in 2004. It is called Cyber Market. It has been, much to our surprise, an unbelievable successful. I am so proud of him.

Also, we just got back from a wonderful trip to New Zealand. It is an awesome place. No wonder they filmed "Lord of the Rings" there. We saw it all and we could just feel the battle between good and evil. Good wins you know.

Along the journey that Stan and I have been on, we have been involved with helping a number of missions such as, helping Brandon and Emily's ministry in Africa, helping Mel start our church, and a lot of other outreach. God has blessed us with so much and we've wanted to give some of it back. It is so nice to have you all here in our home tonight. Liz it's your turn.

I thought it curious that she talked mostly in the plural, about her and Stan, hardly anything just about her. So, before Liz could start I said, "Karen I think I remember at the funeral you saying something about God calling us to pick up where Brandon and Emily left off and not letting their ministry end. You haven't shared what you think God is calling us to. Have you thought about that anymore? Has God been speaking to you? What do you think now?"

Karen started to say something when Stan broke in and said, "Let's leave that till after we have all had a chance to share about ourselves. I think it could lead us getting ahead of ourselves and not giving Liz, Mel, and me a chance to tell our mini stories."

I thought, *'Just like a corporate executive wanting to control everyone.'* But I said, "OK, I understand, but I do want to know what Karen is all about."

Karen smiled. Deb thought, Odell is not going to be intimidated by Mel or Stan, I can see that.

Liz began to talk. "After what Mel and I have been through in the past month, I think he will understand if I am honest. Our life together started out like a wonderful adventure of seeking to follow Jesus but the last five or more years it has been hell. She started to get choked up and paused to collect herself. We have a seventeen year old son who is quickly becoming a drug addict and a fourteen year old daughter who thinks she is nineteen and that the world is one big party. We don't have any real friends. Except, I guess you could say Stan and Karen try to be our friends. I am very tired, not clinically depressed yet, but tired and sad and very anxious because now is when I need more energy than ever before in my life. Until the past two weeks, I didn't know how in the world I would ever be able to be what Mel and Elijah, that's our son, and Andi, our daughter, need me to be. I have no idea what God has been up to in my life over the past twenty years, especially the past ten or so. I used to see him so clearly at work in my life, but know I don't know. I think it has just been since the funeral or since Mel got back from Texas that I have begun to see some new hope. With that I pass to Stan."

This was not at all what I had expected Liz to share and I was both stunned and relieved at the same time. It seemed to me to really put Mel in an awkward position. How was he now supposed to lead us forward with his wife falling apart in front of us? And what did she mean 'new hope' since the funeral?

After a short pause Stan began, "I realize I started this, but now I'm not sure what to say. Nobody wants to hear me talk about me. Karen has already said to much about me and not enough about herself. My experience with Cyber Market has been unbelievable, but really I have just been making some crazy risky decisions at the right time in history. The really amazing part is that when the internet business started to level off Cyber Market had already diversified and begun branching out into venture capitalism in the IT industry and green energy sectors, so we grew instead of collapsing like so many of our competitors. But, like I said, I can see that nobody really wants to hear me talk about that stuff, and to tell the truth, all the stuff about business and making money is not the real me, as hard as that may be for most of you to accept. What has God been doing in my life in the past twenty years? He's been showing his great love for me with a very resilient, preserving, and loving wife and a daughter who is an angel in spite of me and He has been patiently waiting for me to surrender to him and stop serving money. As I look at my life, the most amazing and awesome thing about it has been the grace that God, who knows my heart, has shown me.

Mel, it is now your turn. I know we asked you to come to give us some direction in moving forward in the wake of losing Emily, Brandon and the kids but would you first just share with us what God has been doing in your life?"

Oh boy! I thought. *Now it is Mel's turn. I am not sure how I am going to keep my cool. Maybe I should find an excuse to have to leave.* Deb gave me a look that said, "Just chill!!" I wondered was my non-verbal cues already showing my skepticism about Mel's perspective. And how was Mel going to follow what his wife had just said about how horrible her life has been. *Regardless of what he says about himself or what he thinks about our futures, I am not going to get sucked into any of his schemes.*

Twelve

Mel began. "As Liz shared, life for us has not been what it has appeared. You may think that I am about to share with you the awesome work of God in my life over the past twenty years. How God has used me to raise up a twenty thousand member church and led me to witness for Him all over the world through bestselling books, packed stadiums, and personally to world leaders in both government and finance.

Months ago, that is probably what I would have said. But, today, I think that is all a lie, especially the past twelve years. The truth is that on this great ride of fame I have been hollow and empty. It has been as Jesus said it would be, 'I have had my reward.' and it hasn't been in heaven. It hasn't even been the Kingdom of God on earth. My children have sped through their childhood without me. I have not been available to them physically and emotionally. My self-importance has caused me to miss my son's birthdays, as well as his birth or the challenges he had to face in life. And today he is a full blown cocaine addict. I know thousands of people and I have always gone through the motions of being a part of an accountability group, but I really don't think anybody really knows me because I haven't really known me. I am alone. I don't even think Liz knows who I am."

I was stunned. I could feel his sincerity. It was like God was confronting my judgmental attitude towards him and I could feel a lump forming in my throat.

Mel went on, "For sure I am not a disciple of Jesus. And I am not leading the people at AOC to seek to follow Jesus either. Jesus didn't even get paid for preaching or teaching or healing. I have a six figure salary, book royalties, and so much conference speaking income that I need an accountant to keep track of it. Jesus had no place to lay His head and I have a large home in a very comfortable upper-income community in the wealthiest country of the world. Jesus spent most of his time alone with His Father listening. God is lucky if I have morning devotions for a few minutes. Jesus took time to care for people, go to their homes with them for a leisurely meal or a party, play with children, and sit by a well and talk with those who came to get water. I have a schedule that it takes two secretaries to manage. Jesus never wrote a letter, let alone three books. Do I follow Jesus? The truth is I don't even recognize him anymore. I have been following a big me.

I retrospect I look back today and what I used to consider the miracles of God, like the initial picnic that started our church and our first worship service, which were the beginnings of Apple Orchard Church, I now see as a diversion that Satan used to draw me away from seeking the Kingdom of God. I think I have gotten so caught up in the amazing success of my preaching, teaching, and the growth of the church that I have lost sight of the Kingdom of God. I seem to have been calling people to my Kingdom rather than God's Kingdom. I am so confused and probably depressed. For sure I am burned out. Maybe I am ready for a heart attack or some other major illness.

I thought, "Like we say in the NA fellowship, the end result of addiction to drugs is jails, institutions, and death. Could the end result of addiction to fame, fortune, and power also be jails, institutions, and death." The lump in my throat was growing larger.

Mel continued. "I met a man on the plane on my way back from Texas who is the current head of Rotary International.

We were sitting in first class, of course. And when he was finished describing Rotary I felt like he had been talking about AOC without the religious language: except Rotary requires a greater commitment. I am no different than any big business mogul. Rotary sounded like a fellowship where the business and service leaders in a community seek to use each another to further their own ends and to provide for the needs of others. It is a good humanitarian organization but it is not the resurrected life of Jesus or the reign of the Kingdom of God on earth. Our conversation made me question just whose Kingdom have I been seeking and who is King of my life. I felt like AOC looks more like Rotary than it does the Kingdom of God.

So, that is what God has not been doing in my life. I am not sure what He has been doing. And now this group has asked me to give you some direction for what you should do with your life in the aftermath of seeing the Christ-like witness of our brother, sister, and their children. I really don't know what to tell you. I am the one who needs direction."

Nothing in what Mel shared sounded like preaching or lecturing. It didn't even come out smoothly. Some of it didn't quite fit together. In some places he had a hard time staying with his thoughts because his emotions broke up his words. I thought to myself, *I think he is a genuinely broken man and he realizes that he doesn't have it together.* Tears of my guilt for judging him were coming out the corners of my eyes.

I looked around and notices that we all were averted each other's eyes, some were looked down and others leaned back and simply closed their eyes, others had tears like mine. Mel began to pray. I recognized the prayer from Psalm 51, but Mel prayed it in the first person, slowly, with obvious raw emotion.

"Have mercy on me, Lord, have mercy, please. Your love never fails, don't fail me now. Thank you that you care for me from the bottom of your heart. There is nothing in me that deserves your mercy. Please take away all the stuff that I have done to divert people from your love and grace. Wash away my arrogance and pride, forgive me for trying to control what is only yours to control. I am so aware of what a mess I have been making of your resurrected body. My whole life is a distraction from your will. Almost every place I look I see distortions of your Kingdom. I have been creating my own Kingdom. I have lead thousands of your children away from you. My self-centeredness has built a false god. Against you alone have I sinned. I am so sorry."

Mel's words sounded a little over done, yet as he prayed, I could feel the honest remorse of his heart. I looked up, Mel had paused and tears where coming down his cheeks.

Mel continued through his tears, "God, you know my self-centered heart. I feel like even before I was born I was trying to take over for you and all you have ever wanted from me is to be real about my sin and to be surrendered to you. Please, Jesus, do what it takes to change me and make me whomever or whatever you want me to be and please, please forgive me. I want to bring you joy not sadness. Break all my pride and my need to be important. I really only want to live a life that pleases you. Dear God, please only see Jesus when you look at me. Create in me a pure heart Oh God, and renew a right spirit within me. Give me the healing that comes in your presence and fill me with your Holy Spirit again. Restore the joy I knew when I first surrendered my live to you, and grant me a willingness to be satisfied with that joy.

In your name I pray, I want to follow you Jesus. Amen."

I didn't realize it but I was softly crying too. My lump was making it hard for me to breathe. As I looked through my blurred vision I could see that almost everyone else was also crying. Everyone felt the honesty of Mel's prayer and I sensed it touched the core of our sin as well.

There was several minutes of silence and then everyone, almost in turn began blowing their noses.

What had just happened was not what Mel had planned nor what any of us had expected. The group was lost as to what to do next. I think we were all emotionally drained. It was like we were without any direction for how to move forward. We just sat there stunned. But there was also a sense that God was present and that our future would be ok; more that ok.

Finally Deb softly broke the silence. "I think it is obvious that God has just spoken through Mel and he is trying to tell us something, but I am not sure what."

"I think it is obvious that he wants some things to change." Karen said.

"I agree." added Liz.

"What is obvious to me is that I need to spend more time with God and sort out what about my life is of him and what is about me." added Jorge.

"As much as my experience tells me we should now start to make some decisions about our future direction, my experience may not be the best thing to go by. I am honestly at a loss for how to proceed." said Stan.

I could only whisper what popped in to my head, "As we say in the recovery, 'if you do what you did, you will get what you got'."

It was silent again.

Then Mel said, "I don't know about all of you and I hope I have not thrown to much at us all following the Bryce's martyrdom, but I have more peace right now than I have had since I first asked Jesus into my life 21 years ago. I don't know what the future holds but I know God is giving me another chance."

Everyone nodded and seemed to agree. Again there was silence.

Finally gained my composure said, "Can we continue this next week? I think we need, like Jorge just said, to spend this week listening to God and then come back and share what we hear. And let's pray for each other too. Can everyone, does everyone, want to meet again next week?"

Everyone agreed. Stan and Karen said they would be happy to host again. Same time, same place next week.

As Mel and Liz were leaving, Stan asked Mel if they could get together for lunch the next day.

The extreme radical change that I felt taking place within me in those four short hours was by far the biggest surprise in my life of seeking to follow Jesus. It was hard for me to comprehend. I had been set in my way about the church for so many years and now I had been shaken out of that mindset by Mel's open and honest confession. I really didn't know what to expect next for my own life.

The atmosphere in the car as Jorge, Misha, Deb, and I drove back to the city was like we were all in silent shock over what had happened. For me, I had gone prepared to take Mel apart for what I thought would be Mel's sales job for the corporate institution of the church that espouses a wealth and health gospel. Instead I had found myself confronted with my own arrogance and self-righteousness. I felt ashamed and embarrassed.

Jorge voiced my thoughts for me. "God showed up tonight. What Mel shared and prayed is making me question if I have been living in denial about my surrender to Jesus. I am really confused now and cannot see what's up with my future. I feel like someone who has just experienced his first recovery meeting and everything ahead of me is uncharted territory."

"Yeah, me too and I am scarred. Yet I feel some strange peace. Can you be scared and peaceful at the same time?" Deb mussed.

I put some praise music on the car's CD and everyone except for me, as the driver, closed their eyes for the duration of the drive.

When Deb and I got home it was almost 11:00 p.m. Jen and Jimmy were in bed asleep. Billy was in bed with his light on, reading. When we looked in on him, to our surprise, he asked. "How did your reunion meeting go?" I thought it interesting that Billy identified our time together as a reunion.

I answered more honestly than I would normally have, and said, "Well, not really as I expected. I went ready to really lay out all the problems I have had with the church and I have come back feeling like I am the last person in the world who can judge anything, let alone the church. Maybe I can share more about the meeting tomorrow. Right now I need to get some sleep."

Deb and I both wished our new son God's blessing and a peaceful and healing night's sleep.

Billy said simply, "My dad always told me that the Church is all about relationships. Good night, and God bless you too."

Thirteen

I was up at 5:30 a.m. the next morning. As I went on my morning run, the birds were just getting up as well. Their morning songs felt like God's welcome to a new day. I went through my morning routine and as I was sitting down for my devotions and a cup of coffee the phone rang. Who in the world could be calling at this time in the morning? It was 6:45 a.m. I thought perhaps something had happened to one of my staff at the Health Care Center.

I answered the phone and greeted the caller, "Good morning."

"Hello, is this Odell Ogden?" the caller asked.

"Yes, this is Odell, who's calling?"

"This is James Smith. Last night I was at the movies and I am not sure why, perhaps it was something that was happening in the movie, but I started thinking about you and that trip we took together to Africa maybe 20 years ago. So I decided to give you a call this morning. I hope it is not too early. All night I couldn't get you and Jorge and Misha and everyone out of my mind. Do you ever see any of that old "plunge" group?"

I was stunned. James was the other Black guy on the Liminal Plunge in 85'. In 1990 he had gotten married and moved to Boston. He told me he was in Pittsburgh for six months to raise funds for an orphanage in Haiti and to take a class at Pitt in Public Health and World Disparities. I was in awe that his call was so timely.

We exchanged cell phone numbers and decided to get together later that day for lunch.

James and I meet at "The Diner" for lunch at 12:15 p.m. Hard as it was to believe, even though we had not seen each other for fourteen years, it seemed just like we had been together yesterday. There was a bond of trust that had been cemented on the African trip twenty three years ago. I would have recognized him anywhere. His appearance had hardly changed from high school. However, I was surprised a little that he was much heavier than I remembered him, especially around the middle.

After greeting each other, acknowledging our friendship, and both apologizing for not keeping in touch. We ordered lunch and began to share what had been going on in each others' lives for the past fourteen years.

I filled James in on the assassination of the Bryce family and told him about Billy coming to live with us. At first I didn't tell him about the funeral and the night before at Stan's. I didn't want us to get caught up in who the murders and Mel's epiphany were confronting my judgmental past; at least not before I heard his story. Besides, I wasn't really sure how to explain last night.

James told me that his wife, Sally, had died in a car accident in 1996. They never had any children. They had moved to Atlanta from Roxbury, Massachusetts to be near his parents. He said his younger brother was also in Atlanta but had gotten strung-out on drugs and was still actively using. In Atlanta, Sally had been the Director of the Social Work department at a hospital and he had a job teaching at a high school. His mom died of cancer in 1994 and his Dad died of a heart attack in 1995. He stayed in Atlanta, after Sally's death, hoping to help his brother. He said he became active in Central Presbyterian Church, a downtown church, and found some comfort and fellowship in his loneliness. He also became involved in their soup kitchen and outreach ministry to those suffering from addiction. But he told me he still got depressed and had a couple of rough years of feeling lost. Eventually, his depression resulted in quitting his teaching job. He said that what gave him new life was that some people at Central Presbyterian talked him into going on a mission trip to Haiti. There he was able to get outside of himself and again find some meaning to his life.

After returning to Atlanta he looked for a job but nothing seemed to fit. He had kept in touch with the missionary family who had hosted him in Haiti. With no reason to stay around Atlanta except for a brother who didn't want to have anything to do with him, he decided to see what it would be like to actually live in Haiti and be a part of a ministry. Most of 2001 was spent raising support and learning Haitian Creole. In February of 2002 he sold his house in Atlanta and moved to Haiti where he continues to live. He returns to the States every six months to keep in touch with friends and to raise support. When he first went to Haiti he went to do evangelism and to use his background as a teacher to teach the Bible to Haitian pastors and help them set up outreach teams. In 2003 he met Dr. Pete Palmer who introduced him to Fr. Jacque Lamont. Fr. Lamont had started an elementary school in 1962 for orphans in the area of Cange. Dr. Palmer had been supporting Fr. Lamont work since 1983. In 1985 with the financial support of a wealthy Bostonian, Dr. Palmer establish a medical clinic in Cange. When James met Father Jacque, the Father asked James if he would help with developing curriculum for the school.

He said he fell in love with the children and the school. This led to feeling called to helping to address the approximate two hundred thousand vulnerable children in Haiti who are orphans. He told me that only ten percent of the children needing care in Haiti are in orphanages. Fifty percent of the children in Haiti die by the age of five. Children live on the streets and clustered with each other and extended families who are starving. He said that the number of orphans worldwide is estimated by UNICEF at approximately two hundred and ten million. Most are homeless.

So, in Haiti, building on the relationships that he had begun to establish with the older orphans, in 2005 he began to put together a leadership team to establish an orphanage run by former orphans. The orphanage would be close to Dr. Palmer's clinic and Fr. Lamont's school.

They secured some land, built some rude shelters and began to round up abandoned children who had no one to care for them. Most of the kids came from those who were brought to the clinic for care. They were the victims of deceased parents who had died from AIDS.

James' plan for this current trip to the States was to make his base in Pittsburgh while going to school but to also make frequent trips to reconnect with contacts in Boston and Atlanta and then return to Cange the end of the year. His goal was to raise one million five hundred thousand dollars to build a campus for the orphanage and school. He also wanted to organize and mobilize volunteer groups to assist the people of Cange in building the campus.

When James was finished, I said, "James, I think God is up to something that involves you. For me, and I think the rest of the LP group, things are happening so fast and I think you being prompted to call me last night is somehow a part of what He is up to with us. While you were at the movies, the LP group, less you and Kara, were at Stan's to process how the death of Bill and his family was effecting us. We had gotten together at the Bryce's funeral and decided to meet to talk about what, if anything, we should do in response to their deaths. Their deaths had shaken all of us. What happened last night at our meeting was so unexpected. I can't really put it into words but Mel blow us away with his broken spirit. Don't you think it's just amazing that after twenty three years, last night we are together and you are in Pittsburgh at the movies, and God brings us to your mind? Then you call me this morning, and now here we are having lunch together?"

"Well, yea. I guess." He responded with a question mark in his facial expression.

I was a little taken back by his cavalier reaction, but then I thought, for James, perhaps miracles were not new to him anymore, and that God's unexpected grace had almost begun to be expected. Then he said, "I don't quite understand what you are getting at so, don't ask me to tell you why or what God has in mind. I know you can't hope to have the same perspective as God. I think it is just best to be faithful to what god puts in front of you and trust him for the outcomes whether you can identify them or not."

"Well, I don't think we need to know why right now either. Probably if we did, it won't make any sense to us anyway. Maybe God has something to tell us through you; maybe He doesn't. Maybe he wants us to be partners with you in some way. Maybe it is not about you or the rest of us at all, and then maybe it is about all of us. Honestly, after who I feel from last night, I don't need to know. It is God's Kingdom that I want to seek, not mine, anymore. Like I often hear at NA meetings, 'More will be revealed, keep coming back'". I replied.

"I know that's right." He affirmed.

Then we just sat there in silence. He sipped his tea. I finished my coffee. We each mussed with our own thoughts.

The waitress brought us the check.

As we were leaving, I asked James where he was staying and he said that for the semester he had an apartment in Oakland.

I invited him to come to our group meeting in a week and he was excited to have a chance to see everyone. Then, almost as an afterthought, he said, I wonder what has happened to Kara. I replied, that no one seems to have heard from her for quite a while. James said he had lost track of her in 1991 after she left Boston College but that he had heard from a mutual acquaintance that she had married an Episcopal priest and was living in California.

We hugged and parted. I left feeling like I was now on an unmarked path, the destination of which I did not know. As I walked to my car I heard myself say out loud, "I wonder what will happened next.

What James didn't tell me, and what I and everyone else did not find out until almost five months later, was that he had a new lady friend and she was planning to move in with him as soon as the Fall Semester started. Her name was Rita Cruz. She was in her late twenties, had a Barbie Doll body, and was a senior accounting major at Carnegie Mellon University.

For the past two school years Rita had been a suite mate of Marcie Jenkins, now also a senior marketing major at CMU. They had become good friends during their time in college. Both were looking forward to graduating. Though they were from different backgrounds they both shared a common religious upbringing in the Roman Catholic Church. Rita, grew up in New York City and was Hispanic, Marcie was from Fox Chapel, an upper income suburb of Pittsburgh. Marcie was the daughter of Barb and Dave Jenkins, two successful attorneys in Pittsburgh and Rita was the daughter of a single mom who had worked for an office cleaning company all her adult life.

Rita met James in May not long after he had arrived from Haiti to raise funds for the orphanage. They met in the stacks of the CMU Library. James was researching "grant givers" who focused on children and Rita was researching "grant givers" financial accountability policies in preparation for a course she was signed up for in the fall. Rita was taken by James' warmth and concern for the poor and James was taken by Rita's beauty. This encounter let to an intimate physical relationship between James and Rita. They decided she would move in with him when the fall semester began.

The living arrangement served both of their desires well. James didn't charge Rita any rent and was very excited about their intimate relationship. Rita was happy to save the housing expense.

What James and Rita were unaware of at the time was that just the day before they met Marcie had an encounter that would change both Rita and James life as well as her own.

Rita and Marcie both liked to jog and in May they both ran in the Race for the Cure in Pittsburgh. During the race, Rita, who was faster than Marcie, moved ahead of Marcie. As Rita lengthened her distance from Marcie, Marcie saw a runner who had just passed her and on the back of his shirt was printed, "I can do all things through Christ who strengthens me." She caught up with this runner and asked her what that meant. They got into a short conversation about God's love as experienced in Jesus and how Jesus' presence within a person gives that person's life strength and hope. Marcie slowed down her pace again but continued to think about this thought of Jesus' presence. It was new to her being within someone. When she woke up the next morning she was still thinking about it. So that morning she went to see a girl by the name of Patty Hanson whom she had gotten to know at school. Marcie approached her because she seemed to be religious. And she was smart and also very well-liked by everyone. Their friendship and discussions during the summer led Marcie to ask Jesus to bring his presence into her life on a daily basis. But Marcie's new life in Jesus would not have bearing on James' and Rita's plans until after school started in the fall and James and Rita had moved in together.

During that same time that James and I were having lunch, Mel Carr and Stan Beckley were meeting over lunch at the Duquesne Club in downtown Pittsburgh. Mel, the model of a successful church leader and Stan the phenomenal internet search engine software producer and venture capitalist.

They greeted one another with an enthusiastic hug that was most unfitting for their professional status and opulent surroundings. Immediately, they were both greeted by name and seated at their table. Over the years, Mel and Stan met regularly for lunch and sat at the same table. Stan had always been one of Mel's trustees at the church. The server brought them their water, they ordered, and within two minutes their salads were served.

And then, again, as was their custom and out of character for their surroundings, they both bowed in prayer. Each prayed sincere prayers of gratitude for not only what they were about to eat but for the deep appreciation of the warmth that they were experiencing from the meeting the night before.

As Mel started to mix his salad, he said, "Stan, I really have appreciated how over the years you have been so generous in supporting me and AOC, but now I don't know how to continue as the pastor. I no longer believe I am to be the head of AOC or any other church. I don't know what I will do but ----."

Stan interrupted, "Hold it right there. You do not need to explain yourself to me. After what happened last night, if you weren't questioning your call, I would really be surprised."

Tears began to form in Mel's eyes. What was happening was real. At this point, if the Spirit had not touched Stan as well Stan would be giving Mel a song and dance about why he should not leave the church.

Stan continued, "I need to share something with you, before you go on. Please listen to me. I need to say this and I need for you to hear it. I know we have shared almost everything together right here at this table but I need to confess to you that I have never really shared the whole picture of what goes on in my heart. The past fifteen years or so have not been what I have projected in my success stories. Most of my life has been full of internal stress brought on by feeling of guilt. Not guilt, because I have felt like I have been evil, but guilt because some place back when I was searching for meaning in life I told Jesus I wanted to be his disciple. And most of the time since then I have been a disciple of myself or of making money. Always in the back of my mind and under my heart has been this gnawing guilt that I have left Jesus in a closet. I know, I have gone to church and been a model of churchmanship and so called spiritual leader, but I have not been a disciple of Jesus. I can talk the God talk and witness with the best Christian businessmen in the country but down deep I have known that it is all mostly a mask. Karen knows how sometimes at night I have been so restless. I have always told her that it had to do with some business deal but really it had more to do with my hidden guilt. More than anything, I want to try to begin to change all that.

"So, after you share your surrender to God last night, I told Karen I wanted to sell our shares of Cyber Market, resign as CEO and go off Cyber Market's Board. I know that may sound like an irrational reactive response, but my service to both Jesus and money has been a conflict in the back of my spirit for a long time. Jesus said that whatever I don't do for the least I don't do for him. That, for me, has been a big problem. It is not what I do, it is what I don't do for him. Even John the Baptist said if you have two coat and you see someone who has none, give one of your coats to that person."

Stan eyes began to tear.

"I get an income of probably over seven thousand time as much as fifty percent of the people in the world, I know it is over 300 times as much as the average person in this country. I probably make 25 times as much money as I need. I am finished with trying to serve Jesus and serve money at the same time. I'm surrendering to Jesus and who knows what He will do with me."

"You mean, who knows what He will do with us." Mel said.

Now, both men were looking at each other through blurred vision.

There was a pause and Stan continued. "Mel, as God seems to be showing us, we have both been seduced by money, prestige, power, and pride. Being the researcher that I am, this morning I googled the financial priorities of people like me, nice Christians who make up the Church in America."

Mel listened patiently.

"Did you know that in the year 2000 Christians collected about five point two trillion dollars in income and gave about fourteen point five percent, that's seventy five point four billion dollars to the Church in the United States? But there are three billion people in the world that are suffering, dying of malaria, AIDS, TB, starvation, war, greed, egotism, religious oppression, you name it; refugees and orphans; and about half of them have never heard the name of Jesus. It is like the four horses of the Apocalypse are on earth today. The Church spent one percent of that seventy five billion dollars on sharing the Gospel with people who have already heard it and only a little more than one hundredth of a percent, on sharing the love of Jesus with the one point five billion people of the world who have never even heard about God's forgiveness and the resurrection of Jesus. Christians in the U. S. keep more than eighty five percent of their income and the U. S. Church spends ninety nine point nine percent of its mission giving on itself.

"The church in America spends nearly all its resources on itself while half the world's population is literally suffering to death. We are so over-saturated with self-centered religion that the call to surrender to Jesus gets drowned in the greed. And here I sit with you in the Duquesne Club talking about my accumulation of the major shares of an eight hundred million dollar business. What did Jesus say, something about 'If you seek to save your live you will lose it.'?"

Mel was humbled with how Stan shared what could have been extremely confrontational information. It was not as though Stan was ridden with guilt or judgmental of any church leader. He said it like it was objective reality that needed to be faced and dealt with. It made Mel feel so much better about his own revelations about the false gods he was feeling that he had been serving.

Mel responded, "Stan you don't know how refreshing what you are saying is for me. I too am rich and I have known, though not acted on, the demographics that you have shared. My self-centeredness and AOC's is a major concern. But ---"

Stan softly broke in again, "No buts."

"There is a 'but' for me Stan, because I have been seduced by what for me is an even more absurd distortion. Let me share a little about what I teach at conferences about how to be a leader. My seminars on church leadership have these Ten Command Points. I have consolidated and summarized them together from many books on leadership.

One, a leader is a person who exercises authority and has the ability to get others to do what the leaders want them to do. And also get those who follow to take ownership for it for what the leader wants done and get them to like doing it;

Two, leadership is mostly about technique;

Three, leaders above all else set a high ethical tone;

Four, leaders have a vision, know their mission, and can clearly explain it;

Five, leaders see the big picture and understand the context;

Six, leaders give good feedback and keep communications open;

Seven, leaders engender trust, are positive and encourage with realistic optimism and they are good motivators;

Eight, leaders are patient and keep cool under pressure;

Nine, leaders surround themselves with good sub-leaders, are team builders, and delegate well;

And ten, leaders adapt quickly to new situations, can multi-task, and have the skills that they expect from those they lead; and for a bonus, leaders are risk takers who make tough, timely decisions."

The ten points were so familiar to Mel that they flowed out of him as though someone has turned on a spigot.

"Mel, you could run a successful Fortune 500 company." Stan said enthusiastically.

Mel continued, "That's my point. I've been teaching pastors to become disciples of capitalism. What I have been teaching is all about how to grow and run a corporation, a corporation like the one for which you just gave financial audit report as you described the world's need and the church's use of it resources. It doesn't further the Kingdom of God or even seek the Kingdom of God. I have been teaching others to become, the 'King' of these church corporations. My egotistical aspirations in the church hierarchy is my deadly sin."

Here sat two prominent and wealthy Western World Christian men acknowledging their misdirected discipleship. Preaching to each other and themselves. Both were about to embark on uncharted futures. Both wanted to totally follow Jesus. Should they give all their money away and take jobs washing people's infected feet in a third world country?

Stan finally spoke up after they both took a deep breath. "You know, God must have some reason for shaking us up like this. It sure wasn't part of either of our long term plans. I think the wise thing to do, and probably the only thing we can do now, is simply wait on the Lord, trust him to guide us, and rest in His forgiveness and grace. Anything else would be like returning to trying to be in control again."

Mel thought for a minute and then said, "Well, I know one thing God wants me to do, and that is to celebrate my daughter Andi's birthday. She is going to be fifteen on Saturday, the 21st, and tonight I am going to take her out for dinner and try to begin a relationship with her."

After James left his breakfast at the diner he went back to his Oakland apartment. Rita was at the apartment and James shared with her what was going on with his old friends and that there might be some money to be had by reuniting with them. James also shared that, because some in the group may be very wealthy, that he would like to keep his relationship with Rita a secret. He told her their religious convictions would certainly not approve of him living with a woman. He said it could damage the trust he wanted to build with them. Rita understood. She also like the sense of intrigue it gave to their relationship.

Fourteen

It was approaching noon on that same day in another part of Apple Orchard when Curt Wheeler stopped his car, reached under the back seat, lifted it up and pulled out a sealed plastic sandwich bag full of brown shredded weed and a package of roll-your-own cigarette wrappers. He put the seat back, turned around, pulled out some marijuana and rolled it tight into a cigarette. He did it with such ease, almost grace. He lit it with the car cigarette lighter and took a deep drag. He then passed it to Andi Carr and she also took a drag, but not as confidently as Curt.

Curt had read someplace and he had now learned from experience that marijuana not only makes you relaxed but that it also heightens a woman's sex drive.

They were parked at the end of a road that went across a field and then went down into the woods where the road ended and a trail began. They could not be seen from the main road about a half mile away and Curt was sure no one would venture down that old dirt road on a Monday. The only worry he had was whether someone might drive by and see his car tracks. But then the traffic on the highway was moving too fast for anyone to really notice unless they were searching for a car parked in the woods. Besides he and Andi would only be there for a short time.

Curt was a drug dealer friend of Andi's older brother, Eli. He had met Andi one day after school when he and Eli had picked her up to take her home. Andi was excited when Curt first asked her out. He was nineteen years old, great looking with cut muscles, and lots of money. When she first met him he made her feel like she was no longer a little girl in her big brother's shadow. Curt, was a practiced smooth talker, and showed an interest in Andi for two reasons. First, her brother was a good customer of his and he saw another prospective customer in Andi, one that her brother would not reveal because of his own addiction. And second, because, though she was inexperienced, she had the body and looks of a super model. She was oh so vulnerable. He was pretty sure he could have his way with her once he loosened her up.

In the Spring there first "date", as she thought of it, was going for a ride on her way home from a swimming meet at the beginning of the summer. They stopped near this same dirt road, he introduced her to marijuana, and he kissed her. It was new and exciting for her. She was scared but it was so wonderful. Curt knew better than to take too great an advantage of her just then because he knew that later, with her father being a minister and all, that she would feel an amazing amount of guilt. Little did he know that she was looking for a way to act out her anger toward her dad. She could sense that he was holding back and softly told him. "Don't worry about my dad, he doesn't even know I am alive." She wanted more but Curt played like the respectful gentleman and said they needed to get her home.

He was right, when she thought back on that "date" she felt like she had betrayed not only God and her family but herself. She was afraid that she could have damaged her whole future just because some guy, though a good looking hunk of a man, had made her feel special. She vowed never to see him again.

He called and texted her several times over the summer but she never returned his call. She knew about his calls but was inwardly glad that she was not getting sucked into his play.

But this day he was at the swimming pool in the morning just as she was getting there with a couple of her friends and he looked soooo good. He could not help notice her in her bright yellow bikini. She smiled at him and that was all the invitation that Curt needed. Now was the time for him to make his move. They swam a little together and then he suggested that they go get an ice cream down at Busters. They left the swimming pool, intent, as Curt said, on coming right back. And now, here they were in these isolated woods, in his car.

After a few drags, Curt leaned over and kissed her. What happened next created in Andi the hardest internal struggle she had yet faced in her life. She experienced temptations and emotions that battled within her. She felt out of control. And as she realized she was about to lose a war over her self-respect and future desires, she heard her inner self crying out. *"Oh Jesus help me."*

Just then, as Curt was about to have his way with this young innocent beauty he glanced out the back window and there coming across the field towards them were four people on horseback. *This is not good!* he thought. *One of them must be the property owner. If he catches me again making out with a girl back here, he will surely call the cops. The car stinks like marijuana and I have my cocaine under the seat. This chick is a minor and the daughter of a famous minister. I am going to really be in trouble.*

Curt sat up, put on his shirt, told Andi to duck down, started the car, and took off backwards spraying dirt and gravel from his tires into the woods. He did a 180 in the field like they do in the movies and took off as fast as he could, fish-tailing and creating a cloud of dust behind him as he flew down the dirt road. He hoped the horseback riders were not close enough to get his license plate number or foolish enough to chase after him. He got to the road and looked back. They were just standing there in the field. He pulled out on the highway and headed away from returning to the pool. He wanted to give them the impression that he was from any place other than the pool. When he got on the highway he slowed down to the prevailing speed of the traffic, put the windows down to air the car out, told Andi to sit up. After about a mile he turned into a side street, driving slowly through a residential area for a couple of minutes, hoping that if the horse riders had a cell phone and called the police that they would not spot his car. Finally he stopped the car at a vacant lot, got out, went in the back seat, pulled out all his drugs. He removed a large rock and with his tire iron he dug a hole under where it had been. He buried the drugs in the hole and replaced the rock. Then he went back to the car, got a piece of paper and wrote down the address of the house next to the lot. With that taken care of he decided to take Andi back to the pool and act like nothing happened. He felt secure that even if he did get stopped there was nothing he could get in real trouble about now.

Andi had crouched down on the seat and started to cry. When Curt told her to sit up she felt like her head had cleared, either from the fear or the tears or the wind. She knew to say anything would not get a positive response from Curt so she just sat there in silence, whimpering. When they started heading back toward the pool, Curt put the windows back up and turned on the air. Neither one of them said anything. Andi stopped crying and wiped off her face. When they got to the pool, Andi got out and Curt drove away.

Back in the field the horse riders just stopped and watched as Curt sped away. Then one of the riders let out a spontaneous laugh and said, "I think that was the same kid I caught in the spring parking with a girl back here. I'll bet he was scared to death. I would have loved to have seen his face when he saw us. I hope they don't get in an accident." And then they just went on riding toward the trail in the woods.

Eli picked Andi up at the pool about 4:00 p.m. as he was getting off his landscaping job on the golf course. Their family had belong to the Northbridge Country Club for the past five years. When they got home Andi went upstairs to get cleaned up for her "date" with dad. This is going to be the worst night of my life, she thought.

At their pre-arranged time, Mel went out the back door and then went to the front door and rang the bell. Liz answered the door and called to Andi, "Andi, your date is here." Andi thought, *"How corny can you get and what a phony set up for a lecture on chastity."* Mel waited in the entrance, Andi came to the door. Mel gave her some flowers and then opened the door for her, escorted her to the car, opened the car door for her, and then went around to his side. *"So this is what going on a date feels like,"* Andi thought.

As they drove Mel made light conversation asking how her summer was going and telling her the funny story about an interchange he had had with the Rotary guy on the plane coming back from Texas. Andi politely answered his questions with one or two word answers and just smiled at his story, not really listening to it. When they got to the restaurant Andi began to open the car door and Mel asked her to wait while he went around and opened it for her. He then let her lead the way to the entrance to the restaurant. He got to the door before her and open it to let her walk through. Mel had called ahead for reservation and they were seated immediately. When they got to the table Mel pulled the chair out for his daughter and then went around to his seat opposite her. He told her to order what she liked it was in honor of her birthday. They ordered and then as the salad was presented Mel asked if they could give thanks. This would have been very embarrassing for Andi except none of her friends were around. In fact the whole date would have been embarrassing if her friends could see her. But most of the people in the restaurant couldn't see them and those who did see them saw it for what it really was, a lovely time of a father and daughter having a dinner date together. After grace Mel said, "Andi, you are going to be 15 and I did want to take you out for a birthday dinner; but that is not really why I wanted to be alone with you. I need to talk to you about something."

"Oh, no here it comes, even before we have eaten. I knew he knew. He is really upset to go to this length to ream me out. I don't think he has ever set the stage for a lecture." Andi thought.

"Andi," Mel began, "I need your forgiveness. Since before you were born I have been just too blatant self-centered. I have neglected you your whole life and I am so sorry. One of the things a father longs to hear from his children is that he was always there for them, but I have never been there for you. I am so sorry, please forgive me. I have been such a terrible father. My life has been wrapped up with saving the world and I have not even begun to show you God's love. I have been so arrogant, egotistical, and acted like life was all about me. I am SO sorry. I love you, please forgive me?" Tears began to drip out of the corners of his eyes.

Andi was stunned. She couldn't say a word. Her heart was in her throat and she was about to burst into tears. When she saw the tears from her dad's eyes she couldn't control herself anymore and started to sob. It was not a loud cry that drew attention in the restaurant but a quiet quiver. Her dad stopped talking and simply reached out and took her hand. They sat quietly, tears running down both their cheeks. After about a minute they were interrupted by the server bringing their soup.

Their hands separated and he thanked the server. Mel said, "Let's eat." Daughter and father both wiped their eyes and they began to work on their soups and salads.

After a few bites, Andi said, "Dad, I forgive you." And then she began to cry again.

Her dad replied, "Thank you Andi, I want to be a new person. I think maybe I am a new person and I will be different from now on. I won't crowd you but I will be there for you."

Through her tears Andi began her confession. "Dad you aren't the one who needs forgiveness, I am. I have been holding a lot of anger towards you for a long time. I didn't realize it though until this spring. I have so much to tell you and am so scared that you will be angry with me. And today was the worst. I have done some terrible stuff."

"Andi, you can tell me anything and I won't be surprised or angry. I am not in a place to pass judgment on you or anyone," responded Mel.

"I almost…. ." Andi began. But she couldn't finish, as she tried to hold back her tears.

"It's ok, honey. No matter what it is it is ok. I'll wait, you take your time. It is really ok." said Mel.

So, eventually, when she collected herself, Andi told her dad the whole story about Curt and smoking weed, her lust and weakness. She told him all that happened, except she left out any reference to Eli.

Mel ate his salad and soup while his daughter poured out her guilt. He then said, "Andi, before I could talk to you and ask for your forgiveness I had to first talk to God and ask his forgiveness. I had a lot that needed to be forgiven. It is not like it was the first time for me to have to ask for forgiveness, and I am sure it will not be the last time. I am thankful that Jesus' forgiveness has the power to not only restore our relationship with God but gives us the freedom to work on fixing our broken relationships with each other. When I realized my need to be forgiven, it made me recognize that I have no room to judge others. Given how I have been such a pious pomp of a preacher it was easy for me to get seduced by self-importance and forget how much I need to be forgiven. Andi, I am not upset with you or at all angry. When I was just a little older than you, I too messed around with drugs and sex. And now that I am supposed to be fully grown I still mess up. Just like God has forgiven me, and you have forgiven me, I forgive you. Now we both have a chance to start over. I know this is an awkward setting, but that is why when I made the reservation, I asked for a table that had some privacy. Would you mind if we prayed right now?"

Andi was crying again and just nodded. They bowed their heads and she quietly simply said, "Jesus, forgive me. I am so confused about so much. Please show me how to live."

And then Mel followed with, "Lord, Jesus, I want to be your disciple, not some important Christian leader, I too am so sorry and confused. Please show me how to be a father and husband and how to live. Amen."

And as they had finished praying and lifted their heads, the server was standing there with their main course. Andi had not started to eat. Mel was finished with his soup and salad. The server took his empty plates. Andi moved her salad and soup aside. The server presented their dinners and filled Mel's water glass. He asked if they were in need of anything and then politely bowed and left. Mel and Andi looked at each other, smiled and began to eat.

During dinner they shared back and forth, a mile a minute about what their lives were like. Andi talked about her friends and clothes and some of her dreams about her future. Mel told his daughter about the meeting the night before and the liminal plunge when he was 17, and a bunch of other stuff when he was in high school. Andi couldn't believe the stuff she was telling her father, and Mel wondered if most of the stuff he was sharing with her was really boring. And at a couple of points, as he listened to himself, it was boring. He thought he must sound like the adults in a Charlie Brown Special; "Wha, Wha, Wha, Wah, Wha, Wah." But they really listened to each other and it was the best time either of them could have imagined. At the end of dessert Andi asked her dad if they could maybe do this once a month. She felt it was very risky for her to ask because of how busy and wrapped up her dad's life, had always been. She was not sure if his change would really last. But she asked anyway. Mel was delighted and readily agreed. They set a date for the second Monday of each month, to mark the anniversary of this new beginning together.

Fifteen

I got back to the Health Care Center from my lunch with James about 3:00 p.m. I checked my email and phone messages, responded to the ones that needed to be returned and worked on a report to a Foundation that was helping to fund the recovery center. Deb and I left for home.

On the way home she shared that she, Karen, Liz, and Misha had been emailing back and forth during the day and were planning to get together during her lunch break on Thursday. Karen and Liz were going to drive into the city and meet her and Misha at Panera in Arlington.

I shared my time with James with her.

When we got home, the twins were watching TV. Billy had just gotten back from a run. As I was washing my hands in preparation for dinner Billy asked me if he could come to work with me the next day and see what I do. It made me happy to think that he wanted to get a window into my life in Henley. We planned to have him ride to work with Deb and me the next morning.

When we got to the Health Care Center on Tuesday, Billy went with us to devotions and then I shared with him a short history of the community and the Center and showed him around. I explained each piece of the ministry, how each related to the other, and how we tried to meet the needs of the community. We went for a walk in the neighborhood and I showed him some of the sister agencies that ministered to the homeless and hungry, foster care needs, elderly, and youth. We ended up at the Recovery Center just as the 10:00 a.m. NA meeting called "Morning Madness" was about to begin. Before we went in I tried to give him a brief description of what to expect and what a Twelve Step meeting was all about. I was most impressed at how interested and attentive he was with everything I showed him and tried to explain.

As we went into the meeting room several people greeted us with hugs and I introduced Billy to the many people I knew. We then sat down together in about the third row from the back. People kept coming in until the room was almost filled with maybe eighty or ninety people. As they came in several came up to me, gave me a hug, and I introduced my new son.

At about five minutes to 10:00 a.m. someone went to a podium at the front of the room and announced. "The meeting will begin in five minutes. This is a non-smoking meeting. If you need to smoke please go across the street. The church does not want us smoking on the property. Also, we ask that you please leave all drugs, drug paraphernalia, and weapons outside the building. And if you need to discuss something with someone else please take your discussion out of the meeting so everyone's needs are respected. Remember to keep an atmosphere of recovery."

Billy glanced at me with a look of surprise and raised his eyebrows.

Then at 10 o'clock the same person went to the podium and said, "Welcome to 'Morning Madness.' My name is Mark and I am a grateful recovering addict. Miracles happen here. Please join me with the we version of the Serenity Prayer. In unison everyone in said,

"God grant us the serenity to accept the things we cannot change, the courage to change the things we can, and the wisdom to know the difference. Amen."

Mark then said, "May we have Why We Are Here?"

A middle aged Black woman got up with a sheet of paper in her hand, went to the podium, and said, "Good morning family, my name is Barb and I am still a recovering addict." And then she began to read.

"Before coming to the Fellowship of Narcotics Anonymous, we could not manage our own lives. We could not live and enjoy life as other people do. We had to have something different and we thought we had found it in drugs. We placed their use ahead of the welfare of our families, our wives, husbands, and our children. We had to have drugs at all cost. We did many people great harm, but most of all we harmed ourselves. Through our inability to accept personal responsibilities we were actually creating our own problems. We seemed to be incapable of facing life on its own terms."

She read another paragraph and concluded with "…we sought help from each other in Narcotics Anonymous. After coming to N.A., we realized we were sick people. We suffered from a disease from which there is no known cure. It can, however, be arrested at some point, and recovery is then possible."

She then sat down and Mark got up and said, "May we have 'Who is an Addict'."

An old white, skinny, bald man, maybe in his 70's, went to the podium and said, "My name is Harry and I am a grateful to be in recovery from the chronic, progressive, fatal disease of drug addiction." He then began to read.

"Who is an addict? Most of us do not have to think twice about this question. We know! Our whole life and thinking was centered in drugs in one form of another – getting and using and finding ways and means to get more. We lived to use and used to live. Very simply, an addict is a man or woman whose life is controlled by drugs. We are people in the grip of a continuing and progressive illness whose ends are always the same: jails, institutions and death."

He sat down, Mark got up and said, "May we have 'What is Narcotics Anonymous'?"

A young well-dressed Black man went to the podium. "I'm Abdul. I am an addict and an alcoholic, in recovery just for today." And then he began to read. His reading basically said that Narcotics Anonymous is a fellowship that meet regularly to help each other stay abstinence drugs and that the only one requirement for membership, the desire to stop using.

Abdul then went back and sat down. Mark went to the podium again and said, "May we have How It Works."

Another person got up and read a short introduction and the Twelve Step. He ended with, "The Twelve Steps are a group of spiritual principles, if practiced as a way of life, can arrest the obsession to use drugs and provide a happy and usefully life free of drugs."

Next came How It Works Part II that was a longer reading and had things like:

"There is one thing more than anything else that will defeat us in our recovery: this is an attitude of indifference or intolerance toward spiritual principles. Three of these that are indispensable are honesty, open-mindedness, and willingness. With these we are well on our way." And, "...the therapeutic value of one addict helping another is without parallel..."

After this reading came the Twelve Traditions. The Twelve Traditions apply to the life of the Fellowship itself. They outline how N.A. maintains its unity and how the Fellowship relates itself to the world about it. They are the way the Fellowship lives and grows.

Then Mark ask for the Secretary report.

An older Black woman, dressed in jeans and a sweat shirt went forward, introduced herself of Maria, a recovering addict. She informed everyone the locations of the bathrooms and some guidelines for care of the church. She then said, "The most important person at Morning Madness is the one who is here for the first time. If this is your first time at this meeting we would like to ask you to please stand and introduce yourself, this is not to embarrass you but simply so we can get to know you."

Two people stood up and gave their first name and declared that they were recovering addicts. Before the meeting I had told Billy that when it came to this part in the meeting that he should just sat still.

Then Mark asked for the GSR report. GSR stands for General Service Representative. This person is the representative from this meeting that is responsible for communicating what is happening in other meetings in the area. Someone read a lot of flyers about events and anniversary meetings throughout the city. After this person sat down another person jumped up, literally ran to the front of the room and shouted, "clean time!"

And then he said with great enthusiasm, "Here at Morning Madness we like to celebrate clean time with key tags, lots of noise, applause, and lots of hugs." Then about ten people who are the home group members got up and formed a line on one side of the room. The home group is those recovering addicts who have accepted the responsibility of facilitating the meeting.

The person who had called for clean time said, "Is there anyone who wants to come get a twenty four hour key tag? If you are just starting out on this journey either for the first time or for the hundredth time, now is the time to begin. We all had to do this, come on up and get that tag!"

Three people got up and the crowd of about eighty stood up and gave thunderous applause. They then sat down still clapping and each of the three went forward to get a key tag, gave their name and stated they were a recovering addict. A key tag is key rings with a plastic tag attached to it that has written on it the length of time a person has not used drugs or alcohol. They symbolize achievement of sobriety. After being handed the key tag each one proceeded down the receiving line with each home group member giving them a hug with congratulation. And as they went back to their seats, several near them stood up and also congratulated and hugged them.

"Is anyone celebrating thirty day?" asked the person at the podium. No one stood up.

"How about sixty day?" No one stood up.

"Ninety day, three month?" One person stood up and every one applauded. A couple of people yelled out, "Keep com'in back!" "You go girl!" She went up, accepted a key tag, said her name and expressed her gratitude for her recovery. She then got hugs from the home group line. As she went back to her seat others who got up and gave her hugs.

"Is anyone celebrating six months?" No one.

"What about nine months? Three people stood up, there was applause and a couple of encouraging shout outs. They each followed the ritual of giving their name and stating that they were recovering addicts, and then went through the line of hugs, and several other hugs and congratulation from their friends.

"Is anyone glowing? Is anyone celebrating one year, glow in the dark?" One person stood up, there was the applause, with several people standing as they clapped, and some people yelling encouragement. As he walked to up to get his key tag and couple people yelled, "How you do tat?" "How you do that!?"

The man looked like he was about forty years old. After accepting the key tag he went to the podium and everyone got quiet.

"My name is Clark, my clean date is August 14, 2006. I have stayed clean one day at a time for 365 days by the grace of God and with your help. I am truly grateful! For real, this is the first year in 24 years that I have not had a drink or used a drug. That is a miracle! Every morning I get up and thank God for waking me up in my right mind. In the last couple of months I have been getting out of bed and kneeling down and asking God to deliver me from evil for that day. Every night I go to bed and thank God that I did not use a drug or drink alcohol that day. I go to meetings, I have a home group, I have a sponsor that helps me work the Twelve Steps, I make phone calls to some of you for support and I share my emotions and struggles. I try to give back at meetings by helping to prepare the coffee and clean-up. And I tell the truth today. This year has been miracle! I am so grateful for this program and all of you. Thank you! My name is Clark and I a truly a grateful recovering addict."

Everyone applauded again and he went over to the line and got his hugs, and more hugs as he went back to his seat.

The clean time facilitator then went to the podium and ask, "Is anyone celebrating multiples?" No one went forward.

He then said, "To show that this program works, anyone with a home group and a sponsor please raise your hand." About half of the people at the meeting raised their hands. "And everyone with a year or more please stand." Maybe thirty people stood up.

He then said, "The most important question is, 'Did anyone feel like using today, and wants to talk about it." There was a pause.

As things settled down, Mark looked over the crowd, it got relatively quiet and he said, "Last chance, has anyone felt like using today and wants to talk about it." It was quiet and then a young man stood up and started to cry.

After a minute he stopped and then shared how he had gotten out of the detoxification unit at the hospital just three day ago. He said he had only been clean for ten days and that during the night he had had a dream about getting high. When he woke up he wanted to go out and use cocaine so bad. But he said, thank God he called a friend in recovery instead of the dope man. His friend came over to the rooming house where he was staying. He was still in bed when his friend got there. He said he had stayed in bed desperately praying not to go out and use. His friend took him to this meeting. He said it now felt safe but he was afraid to leave when the meeting was over. He went on then to share what he was like 10 days ago and how he wanted to kill himself, that he was homeless and hungry and totally wasted on a whole bunch of different drugs. He said that he ended up curled up in a ball in the corner of an ally with urine all over him from a so called friend who discovered that he had hidden some crack cocaine and was keeping it from him. So this friend, beat him to a pulp, stole his crack, and urinated on him. He said he didn't want that to happen to him again, and that he knew it would if went back to doing what he had been doing. He didn't want to live that way anymore. He ended by saying, "Thanks for letting me share, my name is Gerome and I am a barely recovering addict." Several in the crowd responded by saying, "Thanks Gerome, keep coming back!"

Gerome sat down and Mark thank him again and then told everyone that the group would break up into a discussion group that would meet in another room and that a lead would be given for those that remained in the large meeting room. I whispered to Billy that a lead was like a testimony.

Mark said that the topic for the discussion group would be "honesty, openness, and willingness." About fifteen people got up to go to the discussion group. The remaining stayed for the lead.

Billy and I stayed. Mark introduced, "Sunny" from the "No Addicted Turned Away" home group.

I had known "Sunny," whose real name was Carl McFarlyne, for the past fifteen years.

Even before he spoke two things stood out about him. First, he was a huge powerfully built barrel chested man, about 6'4" and about 290 lb. Second, he had very dark black skin with beautiful white teeth – which I knew were dentures – and he could scare you with a smile but at the same time his presence, complete with smile, made you feel safe and warm. You could see where he got his nickname.

He began by saying, "Hi, my name is Carl, I am a grateful recovering addict and a sinner in the process of transformation. Would you all please join me as I ask the God who has been my hope, to help me say what He wants me to say." He then prayed, paused and began to share the experience, strength, and hope that he had in his life.

"I was born in 1961 in Ann Arbor, Michigan. I am the second of eight children. I grew up in a good home where my father was always an inspiration to me. My dad has always been there for me, through everything. And he always said 'get an education.' And he walked his talk. When I was a little kid, my dad went to school at night while carrying a full-time day job, got his GED and then his college degree. While I was in elementary school my dad worked his way from being a janitor in a high school to being the math teacher in the same high school. On the side he also did hauling with his truck. Even when I was young I was a big kid and some of my best memories were the times my dad let me help with hauling. We would stop for a break and he would get me milk and toast. At 47, milk and toast are still my favorite."

Sunny's big smile filled the room.

"I was caught up in my addiction from the time I was thirteen for nineteen years. One of the things I am most grateful for is that my dad saw me clean for 5 years before he died in 1998. My clean date is January 15, 1993."

Several people gave some applause.

"In elementary school my favorite subjects were science and math and when my father became a math teacher, I would help him by grading and making corrections on his student's math tests. I was what they called a 'gifted' kid. So, 'gifted', (smile) that I started listening to everyone say how smart I was. I didn't like being so smart because I didn't "fit-in" with the other kids. So when I was about eleven years old, in an effort to be cool and fit, I process my hair. And I began to smoke and wear a leather jacket. I knew my dad couldn't afford to buy me the jacket so I stole from another kid two years older than me by just taking it off his back; that is after I beat him up.

"I didn't want my dad to know about the jacket, so I created my own little room in an abandoned apartment building and after school I would go change and hang-out with the older kids on the street.

By thirteen years old, I was living in two different worlds, being smart for the adults, and hanging out with my posse, wanting to be accepted. Even though people have always told me that I am extremely likable, I never felt like anyone liked me. On the street I started drinking wine and smoking grass. And when I drank I would not just drink but get sloppy fall down drunk. That resulted in me fighting with everyone, especially my dad and anyone who thought they could tell me what to do. By the age of fifteen, I had dropped out of school. I was picked up by the cops and escorted home almost every week-end. I then became infatuated with everything related to the Black Panther movement, but never really joined. At sixteen I used my first mix of crack/cocaine and heroin. It was then that I first got started in a life of crime; like breaking into peoples' houses, assaulting them and stealing stuff. It wasn't long before I was in "real" trouble with the police. I served almost a year in juvenile detention and at eighteen I was sent to the Penitentiary. It wasn't very long before I became well known as Ann Arbor's first Black bank robber. And because of my "Sunny" personality I was very popular with the girls and on the streets. Strange though, as I think about it, back then I never felt like anyone really liked me. But for real, for real the police didn't like me. Almost every time I got picked up they would cuff and beat me. I remember thinking how I had whopped half the cops in Ann Arbor when we were in elementary school and that maybe now they saw their chance to get me back. I spent the next eleven out of seventeen years in and out of prison. But check this out. I think the reason the judges just didn't lock me up and throw away the key was because of my likable personality. I used to put on this show of pleading my case with all the judges. I knew they saw all this potential in me. I would get out of jail and rob banks until I got caught, all the time selling and using every kinds of drug. Someplace in there I also walked-on and played a little semi-pro football. When in prison I was always the strongest inmate. If someone could lift more than me they were in the record books. From 1983 to 1986, I joined the Black Muslim faith and abstained from all drugs. The first half of that time, I was in prison. I had always used when in jail but my introduction to Islam got me clean. While I was in the clink during that time I also took advantage of the trade educational program they had and learned to be a brick layer. It never really did me any good though because I never was straight long enough to want to get a job. When I got out in 85' at twenty four years old I met my wife. She has stuck with me ever since even though for the first eight years of our marriage I was having an affair with cocaine. Those three years while I belonged to the Nation of Islam was the only time I was clean since the age of thirteen, until I finally in 1993 turned my will and the care of my life over to my higher power who today I call Jesus Christ. From 1986 to 1989 I was moving around the country on the run from the police. I fled to Pittsburgh in 1989. That year, while dealing heroin, I was shot twice. I was set up. While taking a shower, my doorbell rang. I went to the door, the first time in thirteen years, without my gun. I opened the door and I got shot in the head and stomach. When the paramedics came to my apartment, they found all my drugs. I was in ICU for a month. I spent from 1989 to 1991 in prison for possessing drugs with intent to sell, but not until I was arrested again in 1992 did I seek help. I just knew that I couldn't do any more jail time. I served three months and when I got out went to detox. I was clean for three weeks and got high again. So I called Odell at 1:15 a.m., Friday morning, January 15, 1993, and he took me to the Salvation Army on the Southside. From there I came here and Odell took me to the Ligonier Valley Treatment Center. After getting out of Ligonier I came back here to the Recovery Center and started going to meetings every day. I kept coming back because there were lots of people I knew and they were clean. I remember after coming to meetings for about three months, I thought to myself this place is for real. I got a sponsor, started working the Twelve Steps and became a "trusted servant." I have been here every day since for the last fourteen years. I don't chair as much as I used to but I need these meetings. This is the best thing that has ever happened to me and I give all the credit to my higher power, my Lord Jesus. He is my strength and hope. I thank Him every day. I have learned you stay clean and out of trouble by staying honest, humble and grateful. I have a wife that loves me and kids that respect me. I am big but I try not to be a big me. And I finally believe that I am liked, first by God, who is who matters most, then my family, and for sure by a lot of you. Thank you. I am discovering a new way of life and that keeps me in recovery. I don't ever want to go back. I have a peace and serenity that is awesome! I am grateful for the blessings, so many blessings. I am overjoyed! I've been up and down and I'm on my way up!" I pray and thank God every day. For twenty years I was lonely, confused, and angry. Now I have peace, a lot of peace. I get out of the way. I'm alive. My smile is for real today – that is why I got the dentures. I write in a journal every day, I have a place to go, I can help others, it is alright today.

"In my past life I was hospitalized four times and each time I was told I should have died, but each time God saved me. I've got a contract with the Big Guy and He is living up to His part. I am being restored to sanity. My mother told me she like me today. My God is good all the time! If you don't have a God, get one. If you can't find one, you can use mine, He is just that bad! And it is just one day at a time, too. I didn't know it was so simple. I have a choice today.

"My name is Sunny and I am truly a grateful recovering addict. Thanks for letting me share."

After Sunny was finished speaking a few people share how what he had said was helpful to them.

Then Mark came to the podium and said "According to Tradition 12, anonymity is the spiritual foundation of all our tradition, what you hear here, who you see hear, let it stay here. Let's all form our circle."

The group gathered in a large circle around the outside of the room with our arms stretched out around each other's shoulders. Mark interrupted the chatter with, "Please join me in a minutes of silence for the still suffering addict." Then he said, "Whose Father?" And everyone responded with, "Our Father, who art in heaven, hallowed by thy Name, thy Kingdom come, thy will be done, on earth as it is in Heaven." And so on with the rest of the Lord's Prayer. After we said, "Amen" everyone said in unison, "Keep coming back, it works if you work it, so work it, you're worth it." We broke the circle and everyone began to disperse.

I noticed, and as I was watching Billy, I think he noticed too, that several people went up to talk to Gerome and it looked like some were exchanging phone numbers with him.

Billy and I hung around for a few minutes and I introduce Billy to Sunny. All Billy said was, "God is good and you reminded me of Him."

Sunny, gave him one of his signature smiles and a big bear hug.

On the way back to the Health Care Center I ask Billy what he thought of the meeting and his usual to the point response was, "I liked the honesty and the way people accepted each other, that meeting was a God thing."

I said, "NA is a God given program." And I thought to myself, *"If people in church around here were ever as honest and accepting as we are in NA meetings maybe what happened at our group meeting this week-end would happen in church and then who knows what might happen."*

Sixteen

The next morning, Wednesday, August 15, 2007 Billy was scheduled to go to the high school for placement tests. He had been home schooled in Africa since he was five years old and never experienced an American class room. He was scheduled, beginning at 8:00 a.m., to take an IQ test and standardized Math and English test in the morning and then a standardized History and Science tests in the afternoon. Deb had called off work for the day and was taking him to the school.

In preparation, Deb and I had tried to orient him a little to test taking. Most of it wasn't new to him. Jen and Jimmy, were going into 9th grade and had shown him some of the work they had done in the 8th. He had also gone on-line and looked at some home schooling curriculum for 9th and 10th grade. He also took a couple on-line standardized placement test. He didn't show us what his on-line scores were but he said he had done alright and that all the material was all familiar to him. But we wondered. If he was anxious about doing well or even qualifying for the 10th grade, he didn't show it.

I knew that Brandon and Emily had been very intelligent with extremely high IQ's and realized that Billy had their gene pool. He was most likely also very bright. I wondered, however, if in Africa they had the resources, even though they were both also very well educated, to provide Billy with the information he needed. But then I remembered that Billy knew his way around a computer better than I did.

When Billy and Deb arrived at the school they were met by a school counselor and taken to her office. With Deb present, the counselor asked Billy a few questions about his previous schooling and his past course of study. One of the questions she asked, which Deb found amusing, was whether or not he had taken any foreign languages. Billy's answer was "only English" and that he spoke Dinka and Arabic. The counselor responded with an open pause and a dropped jaw, which Deb was sure was involuntary. She replied, "Then we will not need to see how you place in a foreign language. If you qualify for the academic track you can choose from Spanish, French, or German." She explained what the test process was like and then took Billy to a small conference room where she administered the tests. She told Deb they wouldn't have the results of the tests for a couple of days as they had to be scanned into a computer and processed into their system.

The next day, Thursday, Deb met Karen, Liz, and Misha for lunch at Panera. It was an unusually cool day for the middle of August, in the high sixties. Deb got there first and Misha arrived shortly after her. Misha was dressed in a burgundy blazer with navy blue pants and a white open collar blouse. Deb wondered if she was dressed like that because she wanted to raise money from Karen and Liz, or maybe was feeling a little intimidated by behaving lunch with wealthy white women. Deb wore jeans, with a white cotton shirt and yellow sweater. Liz and Karen were about five minutes late, both were dressed in casual slacks. Liz had on a light weight brown leather jacket on and Karen wore a short waisted denim jacket.

They greeted one another warmly but with some reserve. After ordering and picking up their food they found a booth by the window.

Misha offered to say grace. Then Karen initiated a conversation by asking, "Yesterday, Obama said he can bring the country together better than Hillary. Where are you guys coming from?"

Deb's first thought was Oh boy, this is going to be some lunch. I don't really know where Misha's coming from but I am so excited that a Black man has even a long shot at running for President that I can't stand it. If he is a nominee it will change the way all future Black children in America see themselves. But I think I am going to have to watch what I say, I am sure Karen and Liz must be hard core Evangelical Conservative Republicans who are probably rooting for Huckabee and think Obama is the antichrist. But on second thought, Karen's tone of voice was from an attitude of genuine interest and respect for what we might think, not like someone who wanted to convince the rest of us that what she thinks is what we all should think. But, I really don't want to spend our time talking about politics. And then again, I don't want to just blow her off. Maybe I can switch the focus and hopefully shorten the political discussion.

So, Deb said, "Do you think Huckabee can raise enough money to keep his campaign going? I heard he has a hard time asking for money."

Liz spoke up and said, "This could be an interesting and perhaps tense conversation but I need to get something off my chest. You know how I shared a little of my unhappiness on Sunday before Mel owned up to his misguided live. Well, I need to share with you all that I have been a big reason for Mel's arrogance. My truth is that I have been resentful of all the attention that Mel has been getting and how he has neglected the kids and me. Not that he doesn't try and express his love but he has been blind to neglecting to show it. Since he came home from Texas we have some really good talks and I have forgiven him but I have been his accomplice. I have watch him slowly being seduced by fame and fortune and have known what was happening but I have lacked the courage to confront him. Not only have I been resenting Mel but I have had resentment towards God for the church consuming him. That resentment towards God has produced a fear in me that God would not protect Eli and Andi from drugs and sex. In the last year or two I have fought my desire to just run away from life. I have had a lot of tears this week."

As she finished she softly began to cry but was able to control her tears for fear of embarrassing her friends.

It was quiet for a minute and then tears began to seep from Misha eyes.

"I have been afraid too." Said Misha. "Filled with fear for so long I don't know what to do."

She paused to gather herself together.

"I think all of my life I have kept silent about so much stuff, mostly afraid of disappointing my parents, and sometimes Jorge and my kids, and almost everyone. I am scared to death right now that just me saying this will keep you three from liking me. I am a mess. I feel ashamed for not confronting Jorge about what I think are his misplaced priorities of administration activities and meetings instead of being with kids on the street who need his presence. And I am angry at God because He never seems to take away my anxieties and fears. What am I supposed to do?"

After a few seconds, Liz answered. "I think you just did what you are supposed to do. You shared. God hears you and we hear you and we accept you and God accepts you. We, at least I know for me, are just like you."

"Thank you." Misha replied.

"Oh boy, now I have to make a confession." Karen chimed in. "I don't care a computer chip about Obama or Hilary. You know, I am such a phony. I have been very much living in fear too. I too am afraid of rejection, but instead of being silent I have been wearing a mask of respectability. I think I am supposed to talk about politics or charities or church if I am with woman who are Christians but in reality I have been so angry at feeling like I had to perform in order to look like I am a good Christian. Stan and I also talk about what Mel was experiencing and the sacrifice of the Bryces and to my relieve Stan shared that he is sick of trying to serve to Gods, his business and Jesus. And I told him that I was sick of being such a phony Christian. We have prayed that God would forgive us. He wants to follow his heart for God and I want to just find out who I am. My prayer is that God would forgive me for not trusting in him more that I trust in Stan and money. I am avaricious and I patronize everyone but in truth I am scared that nobody like me and that I am not worth liking."

Karen paused to catch her breath; and her emotions.

"What I really want is to live with honest values that I believe are Jesus values. I want to follow Jesus and so does Stan. This week we have been like newlyweds again day dreaming about the future and all the exciting things we want to do. We don't care what anyone thinks, we are just going to be honest and be ourselves. That is once we discover who we are. That's my story and I sticking to it. I hope."

Deb smiled and almost laughed out of nervousness. The other three all looked at her at once. She responded to their stares by saying. "What?" You want me to take off my mask too? I really like Obama. There I said it. Is that what you wanted me to say? Just kidding. Seriously, thank you all for sharing and Liz thank you for getting us to get real with each other.

Yes, like you all, I have been shaken out of my comfort zone too. I haven't shared this with Odell yet but in my pray time this week I have gotten in touch with a number of feelings. First, I have told God that I have always resented and judged my parents for never accepting Odell as my equal. Second, I asked God's forgiveness for my anger at Him about the Bryce family killings and for being angry about the fact that Billy's presence was disrupting my predictable life. And I told him how inadequate in felt to raise Billy. I also asked God to forgive me for my anger at Odell for never being content with a church home. My week has been a week of tears too. Thank you all for sharing. I needed to hear that I am not the only one getting my life turned up-side down."

"Can we pray right now?" Liz asked.

They each nodded in affirmation. There was silence for about a minute and then Liz said a short prayer of thanks, resignation, and surrender.

Following her "Amen" she said, Deb just mentioned being discontent with the church. I, for one am at a loss to know what we are going to do about our life in the church. Mel has talked about resigning as pastor but then what?

Deb echoed, "Yea, now I am more frustrated than Odell is."

"That's what is on my question too, but before we start that conversation, I want to hear about Billy and all your kids." Misha, inserted. "As you know Jorge and I have twin boys, Juan and Michael. They are going to be Juniors this year at the Pittsburgh School for the Performing Arts. Both love music and Michael loves photography. Juan has two left feet but boy can he play the piano. Michael has Asperger's but he is doing well learning how to cope."

So the women talked about their kids for a while. Liz told them about Mel's lunch with Andi and asked for prayer for

Elijah. Deb shared that Billy and her twins had hit it off great and that neither of the twins seemed to be jealous of the new addition. She also told them about their trip to the school and Billy's answer to the question about foreign languages. Karen, said that Brenda had had a good summer, went to Young Life Camp and was looking forward to school starting.

"Young Life Camp! That is where "O" met Jesus. Did Brenda go out West to camp?" asked Deb.

"No she went to a camp in North Carolina. Apple Orchard has been sending kids to that camp for maybe eight years. It is awesome. But who is "O"? Replied Karen.

"A lot of people, including me, refer to Odell as 'O' most of the time. I think that Young Live experience is what started Odell expecting more out of church than what church can deliver." said Deb.

"What is the church supposed to deliver?" asked Misha. "It looks like Mel has been doing his best to provide a church that, as you say, 'delivers', and he has come to the conclusion that what his church is delivering is not the church at all. And, since I have started to be honest, my dad's church, the one where Jorge and I have been the youth pastors, has never really been what I read about in the Bible or what my heart longs for. But until now I've never had the courage to say so. I have always been afraid of disappointing my parents or us losing our job."

"I once heard a speaker say that there is something seductive and insidious about what we all have known as the church. I'm wasn't sure what he meant at the time, but I have always felt like the more I have gotten drawn into the programs of our church, the more questions I have had about what the church is supposed to be." said Liz.

"I think I know what you are talking about but I can't put my head around it. All I know is that I personally don't want to be a phony any more. I want to find out who I am and be me!" Karen shared.

"You are sounding like a 70's woman's liber." responded Liz.

"Feminist Liberators here I come!" exclaimed Karen.

Everyone laughed at such an uncharacteristic exclamation from this well-known social lite.

"So what do we expect the church to be?" asked Misha.

"I want a church where I have some honest friends; people who will get to know me and who I can get to know. And who after they know me will accept me, respect me, and challenge me. I want believing friends who will be my friends even if I disagree with them about politics or the end-times, or the State of Israel. I want to be a part of a fellowship with people I can be open with and I can trust to hold my confidence." Deb asserted.

Karen added, "Yeah, people with whom I can dream with, and confess to, and who will hold me accountable, people I can share my stuff with, both the bad and the good."

"Hey, didn't we just do some of that?" exclaimed Misha.

"Yea, we did!" Deb responded with surprise.

"But isn't the Kingdom of God more than having some real friends with whom you share life. If that is all it is then it is in real danger of becoming an exclusive click of people who get caught up in their self-absorbed lives. And that is something I know about." said Liz.

Misha continued, "What we all just did in being honest about our fears and failings with each other is exactly what I have needed all my life. I feel, because Liz was honest that I would be accepted if I shared my fears with you also. I feel like I have truly found some real friends."

Karen then spoke again, "I know I need you guys to be my friends, and I think that is one of the things that it means to seek the Kingdom of God. I also believe that for me to seek the Kingdom of God I need to have a focus for my life that is much bigger that me."

"Honestly, you guys already feel like the best friends I have ever had. It has been a long time since I have been so honest with anyone, accept Mel. I do have thousands of acquaintances but no real friends. Sorry Liz."

"Oh, I understand" Liz interjected. "Being a pastor's wife, there has been no one that I have been able to be real with either."

Karen, nodded and continued. "I have always dabbled in charity work but deep inside I have not really been surrendered to feeding the hungry, clothing the naked, healing the sick, and releasing the captive; let alone telling my wealthy social click that we are forgiven, Jesus has risen from the dead, and the Kingdom of God is here. Understand? I want to stop playing church and be the church. Friendship is a big part of that, but for me giving my life for those that suffer is even bigger."

"And I thought Mel was the preacher all these years." Liz joked.

"I'm serious, Liz. I am sick and tired of being so comfortable and lukewarm." Karen was almost in tears again.

The group was quiet for a minute. Everyone had finished eating lunch and was sipping on their Diet Caffeine Free Pepsis.

Deb broke the silence. "I don't want to speak for you all, but for me, this lunch has been church. Here we are breaking bread together, two Black women and two white women, really from different social classes too, sharing our hearts and minds together, because we all love Jesus and we want to really follow Him. It is almost like we have been praying as we have been talking, like Jesus has been here sharing with us too. Thank you. Does anyone want to lead us in a praise chorus?"

They all looked at one another, smiled at each other, and each shock their head. Deb said, "Me neither."

Karen asked, "Can we do this again, maybe like once a week?"

"Sounds good to me."

"I'm in."

"Same time, same place next week?"

They all gave a thumbs up and got up to leave. In the parking lot they gave each other another hug and said they looked forward to seeing each other on Sunday night. Each was feeling a joy tempered with wonder about what was yet to be discovered. They each also felt a subtle lack of total trust with questions like, 'Would this last?' "What would happen next?' 'Do these other women really like me?'

It was just 2:00 p.m. so Deb stopped by the Health Care Center to help out the other nurses and then went home at her normal time of about 5:00 p.m.

I had a meeting at Western Psych that lasted until 4:00 p.m. and went home from there. To my surprise, when I got home, all three kids were in the process of for a pizza dinner. They told me we were all making our own pizza for dinner. Billy was making pizza dough portions for each of us. Jen was cutting up onions, peppers, tomatoes, and mushroom. Jimmy was cooking ground beef in one skillet and ground sausage in another and while it was cooking, grading cheese. I offered to pitch in and set the table, but Jen said for me to just chill, she would take care of setting the table. I thought to myself, *where am I, have I time warped back to the days of Leave it to Beaver?*

By the time Deb got home the bar in the kitchen looked like a display buffet with the pizza shells and all the ingredients lined up. Before we dug in Billy had us all sit down at the table and he said a blessing, first an African song in Dinka and then a beautiful prayer of gratitude, especially for our family. I think Jen and Jimmy were the most blown away. I had a hard time keeping from crying.

It was a memorable meal together. We hadn't all been together for an extended sit down time since Sunday lunch. I told the kids about our confessions on Sunday night at the Beckley's. Billy share about the NA meeting and filled us in on his placement test experience. I told the kids about my lunch with James and who he was and what he had been doing. And Deb, told us about the lunch she had with Misha, Liz, and Karen. Jimmy's interest seemed to wane as Deb talked about her lunch but Jen seemed interested, especially when she talked about the need for friends. Jimmy talked a little about looking forward to football practice starting the coming week and Jen told us that she was thinking about going on a mission trip that she had read about on a web site. Deb and I looked at each other with a smile in our eyes, but didn't say anything to either discourage or encourage her. It was good to have time of sharing the stuff that was affecting each of our lives.

Seventeen

The school guidance counselor called and spoke to Deb on Friday. She said Billy did very well, that he would be placed in the 10th grade with peers his age, and that he was even eligible for the gifted academic track. His test scores had been mailed to us and that they should arrive in a day or two. Also included in the mailing would be a course list from which Billy could choose his classes, along with a list of sport and extra-curricular activities. The Counselor told Deb that, though it was not their usual practice, they had included in the mailing a poem that Billy had written as part of the English test. She said those who graded the test thought it showed unusual talent.

Deb told Billy. His reaction was only a slight smile.

Saturday morning I went for a run. It was a glorious morning, in the mid-sixties, clear, unusually low humidity, and an extremely blue sky for the morning. The birds, as usual were serenading the new day. I could even hear the trees singing God's praises at the coming of His Kingdom.

After my run I went to my "office" to spend some time alone. As I reflected on the past week, I was awestruck with all that had happened; James call and our lunch; Billy's visit to the Health Care Center and NA meeting and his placement testing; the woman's lunch and the miracle that Deb had shared about Andi and Mel's lunch together; and especially the change in my own attitude towards Mel. I wondered too, what kind of a difference was it really going to make in Stan and Karen's lives? Was Mel really going to resign as pastor of his church? Would Jorge and Misha change anything? And would my live really be any different in a year from now? If James just showed up out of nowhere, was Kara going to do the same thing? What had happened to her? Was Billy, a white teenager, adjustment so smoothly to our family a mask, and how was he going to adjust to an American school after living nearly all of his life in an African village? Everything seemed to be happening so fast and the future seemed so unclear.

I hadn't shared any of this with what I had considered my support system at work or in the NA fellowship. I wondered if any of them would understand it, or even grasp what was happening. Or maybe I hadn't shared with anyone because I hadn't yet accepted that it was all really happening, myself.

I spent time asking God all these questions and praying for everyone in the group and their families and the future. I also ask God for guidance for our group meeting the following night and that He would give us direction.

I remembered hearing a talk almost a year ago by Michael Hirsh about how we all need common liminal experiences in order to become the Body of Christ and I thought how the people in this group had already had, what for me, had been two liminal experiences together. Together we had been experienced our limits during the African plunge twenty years ago and, from what I could tell, what we were going through now was part of another common experience of reaching a different kind of limit. I also remember reading somewhere that asking questions was more important than knowing answers when it came to following Jesus and seeking the Kingdom of God. Right now all I have is questions.

Eighteen

When Sunday night came, Deb and I first picked up James and Jorge and Misha to head out to Stan and Karen's. I had emailed everyone about James surfacing and inviting him to the group, so everyone was expecting him. In the car on the way out we each shared with James the events of the last week. Jorge told him about the Bryce funeral. I shared what had happened at our last group and how surprised I was. And Deb and Misha shared the refreshing vulnerability experienced at the woman's luncheon. James gave us a quick summary of what had happened in his life since his wife Sally died.

We arrived at Stan and Karen's about 6:10 p.m. During the trip a drizzling rain cooled off what had been a very hot sunny day.

Mel was the most enthusiastic about seeing James. Everyone hugged and seemed exceptionally excited about being with each other. I wasn't sure of all that was going on inside of me. But it really felt good to be with these people. I had learned at NA meetings that honesty is a key to wellness. And if it became appropriate I was feeling free to be honest with these new slash old friends. The vulnerability of last week's meeting had come as a surprise to each of us. For me it was a revelation of secrets that only God knew about me. It confronted denial of truths that I had not yet faced in myself. I was feeling a new sense of freedom and I honestly wanted to tell everyone.

My deepest feeling this night was that I really didn't want to get into any kind of confusing discussion about anything political, theological, or intellectual. I just wanted to enjoy feeling safe.

When we were all seated and had joined hands for grace, Stan began by saying, "Remember, Jesus said that whenever we are eating and drinking together, to remember that He is our food and drink." Then Stan thanked the Lord for this daily bread. As he prayed I thought about how the Israelites in the dessert only were given Manna that lasted for a day at a time. It gave me fresh meaning to the line in the Lord's Prayer, "Give us this day our daily bread."

Karen had prepared soup and salad like she had promised. And man the soup was good. During dinner James shared about his life in Haiti. Everyone was fascinated. Karen especially asked a lot of questions.

After dinner we went into the Great Room like we had done at our first gathering. Stan got our attention by asking me to pray. He then asked if there was anything that anyone would like to share about where they had seen the Kingdom of God since last week. I said I was stunned by the phone call from James. Mel shared about his birthday date with Andi. Then Liz spoke up and said that she wasn't sure it was seeing the Kingdom of God, but that the women had had lunch together and wanted to keep having lunches together. She also said that their lunch produced a lot of questions about the church.

James looked puzzled and asked her what she meant.

Liz was sensitive to James, so rather than saying something sarcastic, like "We all know what *the* question is, 'What and where is the church?'"; instead she said, "James, after the last couple of weeks, for most all of us our experiences with the church have become a mirage, our boat has capsized and we are treading water in an ocean of confusion."

James responded, "Maybe that is what I have heard about as the 'Emerging Church' movement. People like you all who are searching for something to replace the institutions that have lost the resurrected life of Jesus."

"You could be right," said Mel, "but I think more than that is going on with me and maybe all of us. I don't want to judge. But, I think it was Nietzsche who said something like, 'Don't create a dragon to slay a dragon.' Maybe this new Emerging Church movement is creating a dragon even worse than the one created by Luther and Calvin. Because I have been upset about how I've gotten dubbed by what I thought was the Body of Christ, I have been doing some research this week.

"To my relief I am seeing what may have happened to me. You see, about eight hundred years ago, in 1271 AD to be exact, a guy by the name of Thomas Aquinas wrote what is referred to as the Summa. That document has had a distorting influence on Christianity ever since. Aquinas said that all of mankind had fallen into sin except reason. I don't believe the Emerging Church movement is at all touching one of the church's root problems. A major reason the church is distorted, and why I had bought into that distortion, is that the Western world and maybe the whole world believes that reason is supreme and if we cannot rationally understand something it is not the truth. But our reasoning is fallen too.

"Thanks, Mel, I think understand?" Misha said with a grin. "What I am confused about is what the church is for us now, and where is it? At lunch we decided it was our friendship in Christ. But isn't it more than that? Even if it isn't more than just friendship, how do we not lose our relationships with each other again, now that we are just beginning to discover what we have lost? I feel like the widow who lost the coin. Now that

I have found it how do I keep from losing it again or how do I invest it or spend it?"

"May I say something? James inserted. "You may kick me to the curb for this, but, you do know, don't you, the church is not about you, it's about widows and orphans. From what I have heard that is what Brandon and Emily gave their lives for, not so you could rearrange the furniture of your country clubs."

Stan spoke next. "I appreciate your sensitivity James, but what is happening to me is more than redecorating. And I can sure understand, how you might be feeling, sitting here in this Great Room, after living in Haiti for the past five years. But, trust me, I really believe God is about the transformation of our lives. And for Karen and me that means making some decisions about how to use the gifts he has given us."

I couldn't keep quiet any longer and I raised my voice over Stan's.

"Time out for a second everyone! I am a broken and new man and I have had a new sense of freedom this past week. I have to get some stuff off my chest before we talk anymore about the church. Jesus loves me and he has been showed me His love for me again at our last meeting.

"As some of you know, I have been extremely negative about the church for almost all of my life in Christ. I think God is angry that the institutions that call themselves churches have little or no Christ-like integrity. Last week I came prepared to tear Mel's vision for what God had for the future apart. I had seen him as the pinnacle of everything that God hates about the church and I intended to express God's wrath."

I smiled a simulated smile.

"Then he, or should I say God, blind-sided me with Mel's confession. I felt like Habakkuk may have felt at hearing God's judgement. My heart was in my throat, I was filled with conviction and speechless. My knees felt weak, and my legs began to buckle. I was brought low and saw for the first time my self-centered arrogance and small minded thinking. I have been such a judgmental, self-righteous idiot. Mel please forgive me. Jesus please forgive me. Everyone please forgive me. I am anxious to hear what God is up to."

Thanks for letting me interrupt. I'll be quiet know and listen."

Everyone looked a little stunned. I think they were stunned mostly because I was being so out of character but also because the way I spoke was with gentle humiliation.

Mel looked at me and softly said, "You are forgiven you know. But your judgement was correct."

Stan, cleared his throat, said, "Thank you Odell, you're the best." He then continued.

"Listen everybody, Karen and I want to ask you all to do something that may be way out of your experience and ours. I think, we wealthy Americans have substituted control, money, and self-centeredness as our trinity. Karen and I don't want to do that anymore. We are becoming aware that we have been seduced by the American values of the kingdom of independence and accumulation of wealth. We want to do be disciples of Jesus and seek the Kingdom of God. This may sound crazy, coming from where our lives have been, but if we are serious about surrendering to Jesus then we can't worry about whether anyone understands or not. You may or may not realize it but I am the majority owner of a billion dollar company. We think we have some major changes to make."

He paused again, looked at Karen, looked down for a second, looked up, and then said softly but with strength. "Karen and I want to turn over to this group a decision about what to do with our wealth. I mean we want this group to share with us the responsibility of being God's stewards for His Kingdom with over $500,000,000."

All of our mouths fell open with the exception of Karen's and Mel's, because of the lunch meeting that Stan had with Mel earlier in the week. We were in shock!

As much as I thought I had been purged of my arrogance, I felt a cynical disbelief popping up in my mind, saying *'I don't trust this, something is not right, I'm getting manipulated, there is a catch.'* From my experience, it was hard for me to comprehend being responsible for that much money. So I felt myself wanting to speak up and I started to say something like, *'Stan, you're not sucking me into a new scheme and using your money to side tracking me from what God might be doing with me.'* But instead, I found tears coming to my eyes and I said, "Guys, forgive me but I just found myself, falling back into old judgmental thinking, I'm sorry Stan but I started to think you are playing a game with us. Forgive me. Old habits of distrust can be deeply imbedded and are hard to break. That is shocking and awesome, I believe you, as hard as that is for me to do. What does that mean for us?"

"Yeah, what do you mean?" said Jorge as he began to ponder what this could mean for his fund raising goal.

Stan replied. "My first thought was that if I am going to follow Jesus, then like he said to the rich young ruler, I need to give all my money away. Then I realized if I gave it to someone else that would be like abdicating the gifts that God had given me, like forfeiting my ability to respond to God's love for me. Maybe someone else could do a better job of using God's money than me yet He has given it to me and with it he has called me to be a steward, to be caretaker of what he has entrusted to me. So, I can't just give it all away. So, then I thought, one of the biggest things that works against following Jesus is our self-centered value of individualism. In fact, maybe individualism is the original sin, like we are all so concerned about looking out for number one that we are kept from living in a community fellowship like Jesus had with the disciples. Our biggest fear is that we will lose the power to control our own lives. That fear is based on an illusion; nobody really controls his or her own life. What is most important to someone is what controls what they do. If drugs, money, ego, fear, whatever is what is most important to someone, that is their god and it is what controls their life. We get confused in our Christian discipleship because we keep trying to do it alone, wanting to stay in control. I think we are called to be a part of a body. A body like our human bodies, where all the members are dependent upon one another, not separate individual parts who are independent. Isn't that what Paul tells us? We are to let Jesus, who is the head of the body, be in control of our life together. That means that my gifts and my stewardship responsibilities, must be shared with the rest of the body. This group is becoming my body. So, my dilemma is our dilemma. Karen and I are turning over to this group, as a group, the decision of what to do about the wealth that God has given us. We are not giving it away to you. We are still part of the decision. We are inviting all of you to be part of that decision. We are the Body of Christ together. I guess I am asking, can we share our life with you? Are we surrendered to each other as Jesus' resurrected body? Do you think, like we think, that to be fully surrendered to Jesus also means being fully surrendered to each other?

Liz blurted out, "Whoa, you just said a mouth full, I'm blown away."

My first thought was, "This feels a lot like a principle of recovery from drug addiction. The only requirement for membership is a desire to stop using. Stan is saying, the only requirement for membership in this group is the desire to stop living as independent individuals. The first Tradition of the Twelve Traditions of Narcotic Anonymous says, 'Our common welfare must come first, individual recovery depends upon group unity.' So, after the silence following Liz's outburst, I spoke up and said,

"I think I can hear what you are saying Stan, but I don't think I am all of a sudden ready to surrender my life to the decisions of this group. However, I do desire to stop my independent individualism, in fact, I think that is a key thing I have learned in recovery from my addiction to drugs and alcohol. If you are satisfied with my desire to surrender to the group then I will join you and I hope Deb will too."

Before Deb or anyone else could respond, James spoke up and said, "I am more than a little blown away by all this. I don't know what happening to you all but I am having a hard time believing all this. Maybe, I am the one to whom you should give all your money. Just kidding. But, seriously, I do have a lot of questions. My first one is Mel, how can you blame Thomas Aquinas for the mess the church is in? Aquinas was the brains behind saving the Church out of the Dark Ages."

Then his demeanor took on a more intense posture.

"Second, and this is going to sound like someone who has been living with the poorest of the poor and always a little in culture shock by affluence after every time I come back to the States. I am maybe a little, no, I am a lot, angry about the disparity between the rich and poor in the world. I just heard you say Stan that you have more money than the total wealth of well over one and a quarter million Haitians. Do you realize that over half of the people in the world live on less than $2 a day and if you have a roof over your head, you are richer than 75% of the world? Just look at this roof.

"Now, just a few minutes ago you heard me say that I am in the States to trying to raise money for the orphans of the starving and diseased people of Haiti. So," and this he said with a lot of sarcasm. "How about seriously giving that orphanage just 1% of your 'gifts' from God! I don't want your money but they sure could use it."

I had been watching Stan and Karen as James vented his anger and the body language of both of them had remained relaxed and showed no signs of defensiveness. Their expressions were ones of concern and empathy. They gave me the impression that that had already come to accept both their complicity with the disparities in the world and the opportunity they had to respond in faithfulness to sharing the love of Jesus.

James went on, "I think it was the founder of World Vision that prayed to have his heart broken with the things that break the heart of God. There are two things that break God's heart, the physical suffering of His children in poverty and the spiritual darkness of those who hoard His abundance."

We all sort of sat their speechless. Then Karen said with a soft quiet gentleness while looking at Stan, "We would like to go with you to see the orphanage in Haiti."

Stan nodded and responded in kind, "Yeah, would you take us to see what God is up to down there?"

Stan paused and then look around at all of us and said, "I need to tell you James, and everyone. For nearly twenty years I have been caught up with being the good church goer and it has been maybe fifteen years since I have thought of Jogi, the last baby that died in my arms of AIDS in Africa in 1985. But this last week he has been on my mind constantly. He has invaded almost every thought I have had. I am a little scared, but I do think that God is turning my life around. I would like to see what you are doing in Haiti."

"Great!" answered James. It was hard to tell if he said it with honest appreciation or more sarcasm. But he then simply went on and asked, "Now, Mel, what about Aquinas?"

James' passion for the poor and then his sudden shift to Mel about Aquinas, raise a twinge of suspicion within me. I tried to blow it off but there was something in my gut that was not right about James going on about the need in Haiti and then suddenly shifting to an obscure theological historical question. But I let it pass and simply listened.

I think maybe James and possibly Stan were the only people among us that had any knowledge of Aquinas.

Mel responded to James. "Simple, Aquinas's theology proposed an understanding of man that endowed humans with the ability to discover the truth about God through man's reasoning. He taught that reason is a pathway to God and at the heart of the Christianity. Aquinas was a brilliant rational thinker and what he wrote has influenced the understanding of man's abilities in the whole Western world for hundreds of years. He was an intellectual and the excellence of reason was at the center of his theology. To hold reason up like he did was the needed correction to lead the world in his day out of a very long dark period but razing reason to such a high level has over the years since then led the church to feel that it can be the creator of the Kingdom of God on earth. So, I think, I have, like most of the Western world been seduced by this theology into believing that I have the reasoning ability to be able to perfect and manage the Body of Christ.

I now have a new way of thinking and I think I now have a new understanding. I believe that I can know God only through surrendering my reasoning powers as well as everything else in my life to the person of Jesus. The mind of God is beyond our powers of reasoning. Truth is known to man only through revelation from the Holy Spirit, not through reason. I think that may be what Jesus meant when he said in John 14:6 that he is the way, the truth, and the life.

I could talk to you later about that some more but it seems to me that how the Church, and specifically I, myself, got so messed up is not as important as what we do now about the mess we have inherited."

"OK, I am not sure I get it, totally, but I agree, if I am going to be obedient to following Jesus, I need to surrender my thinking as well as everything else. Thanks." responded James. "Stan and Karen, let's talk after the meeting also about dates for your trip." And this he said with a sincere, almost humble tone.

It still made me feel like there was something slick about James that I had seen in many crack cocaine dealer that I had known. They give you the first high for free knowing that you are going to want to get that high again and then when you come looking for more drugs you have to buy it. But this was not about drugs and what James' was selling was the needs of the poor in Haiti. Maybe it was just like we both said when we left Ritter's, more will be revealed. My life with addicts on the street must be making me paranoid. I decided to let it go, forget it, and give it to God.

Misha was next to enter the conversation. Perhaps she did so to try and lessen the tension in the room and maybe also to avoid not knowing how to talk about so much money.

"I think it is awesome how James has showed up this week and, I for one, think is it so exciting to have him with us." There were a number of nodes of heads around the room. Then changing the subject she said, "I have been wondering, what ever happened to Kara?

"Good question, has anyone heard from her?" Ask Mel.

I remembered that Mel and Kara were an item after our return from the Plunge.

"The last I knew she had married an Episcopal priest and was living in San Francisco. That was eight years ago." said James. "I think his name was Father Terry Witherspoon."

No one else had any more recent news, but James said he would try to research her where she had been since the last address he had and on the internet.

It was now around 9:00 p.m. For those of us who had about a forty-five minute drive back to the city it felt like it was starting to get late. I glanced over at Deb and I could tell she was about ready to leave. We did not want to be too late with the kids home alone.

She smiled at me and then said, "I was thinking that school is about to start soon and it looks like we are at the start of a new adventure for all of us. Why don't we have an end of the summer picnic with all our families? I think we need to have our kids get to meet us and each other.

"Great idea!" responded Karen.

"I like it!" said Misha

"Can we have it here?" I said.

"Definitely we can have it here." said Karen.

"I didn't mean to be presumptuous. We could have it at a park in the city. Like at Schenley or Highland Park." I said. "However, I know from past experiences when I've reserved a pavilion for the Health Care Center that the pavilions can get reserved pretty far ahead."

"To tell the truth, I would be a little hurt if we didn't have it here. What is a mansion for if you can't have your family over for a picnic? We have a pool, and the yard, and we will kill the fatted calf, for I was lost and now, I believe I am finally found." said Stan. "What is a good date?"

"Well, school starts on the 27th, so if we are going to have it before school, we need to have it next Sunday, the 26th." Jorge said. "We are all planning to be here then, in the evening anyway, so couldn't we just come in the afternoon and bring our kids."

"That would work, unless the kids have other plans the last day before school starts, which could be likely. But maybe we can sell it to them." Said Karen.

"We can try." Liz agreed.

"Great that's settled." I said, hoping to move us towards leaving. "Now all we have to settle is: What is the church? Where is the church? Who are we? What are we going to do with our lives from now on? How do we find Kara? Where is the Kingdom of God? Do we all have to move to the Sudan or Haiti? What does it really mean to be friends? How are we going to spend all of Stan's money?

Everyone laughed. And then Jorge added, "And if Stan's company has Steeler tickets, can I go to at least one game this fall?"

We laughed again. Stan blurted out "I do and sure!"

I noticed that Jorge and Misha started to stand up. Though fearful of prolonging the meeting but feeling we had not come to any consensus about Stan and Karen's proposal, I quickly said, "I think we need to seriously respond to Stan and Karen's invitation. Are we all open and willing to surrender our independence to this group? Could we all at least seek the Lord this week about that?"

Everyone seemed to nod with thoughtful expressions of agreement.

Mel said, "Could we have a little time of prayer together right now, before you urban folks need to get back to your kids."

I thought, *"Please God, I don't think I can take being broken anymore right now. Please Lord, make this time of prayer, a time of praise and not more breaking of my self-centeredness?"*

Jorge said sure and he and Misha sat back down.

Then Mel added. "We do have a lot to pray about and in addition to the stuff Odell just listed, I would like you all to pray about what I am going to do about no longer feeling called to be a pastor."

Liz bowed her head and began to pray a prayer of thanksgiving for new found friends. Each of us then prayed, almost like we were using my list of questions like our prayer list. We each thanked God for bringing us to this point in our lives and to a new life together. Everyone also asked God for guidance. By the end there was a tangible presence of feeling united. I was the last one to pray. I had just said Amen and James began a sing John Michael Talbot song:

> You shall cross the barren desert, but you shall not die of thirst.
> You shall wander far in safety though you do not know the way.
> You shall speak your words in foreign lands and all will understand.
> You shall see the face of God and live.
>
> Be not afraid.
> I go before you always.
> Come follow me, and
> I will give you rest.
>
> If you pass through raging waters in the sea, you shall not drown.
> If you walk amid the burning flames, you shall not be harmed.
> If you stand before the pow'r of hell and death is at your side, know that
> I am with you through it all.

> Blessed are your poor, for the kingdom shall be theirs.
> Blest are you that weep and mourn, for one day you shall laugh.
> And if wicked men insult and hate you all because of me, blessed, blessed are you!

His voice was a beautiful baritone. We all kept our heads bowed and listened. Then Mel, began to sing, *The Steadfast Love of the Lord.* This was a song that we all knew, so we joined in, and I think everyone, like me, was amazed at how good we sounded together. After that Karen started us in singing *Seek Ye First the Kingdom of God.* I think it had been twenty years since I sang that song. And then James started us with, *Amazing God.* And the part most of use couldn't remember he sang solo.

This went on for about another three or four songs and Mel closed us with a kind of benediction prayer.

We all got up at the same time, gave each other hugs and started to say our farewells. The girls said they would put the details of the picnic together at their lunch gathering during the week.

I saw James talking to Stan and overheard them making arrangements to get together for lunch on Tuesday.

As I was reaching the door Mel approached me and ask if he could have lunch with me. We decided to have lunch on Tuesday in East Liberty.

Nineteen

When Deb got the mail on Monday about 10:00 a.m., Billy was out for a long run and I was at work. In the mail was a package from the school superintendent's office addressed to us, but Deb knew it was the report about Billy's tests results. So she decided not to open it until supper time when the whole family would be together.

That night as we were finishing our dinner, Deb asked us to stay seated for a minute and then she gave the package to Billy to open. He opened it and took out a packet of material, read it to himself and then gave it to me. I too read it to myself while the twins and Deb said impatiently waiting for Billy or me to say something. The report showed that he had an IQ of over one hundred and sixty five and that he placed in the 98th percentile in all test for children entering the 10th grade. I didn't mention any of the content of the letter and only read, with Billy's permission, the poem that the counselor had mentioned on the phone was also included. It was entitled "Sunny."

Sonny

This rotting wood holds an empty tomb;
A sculptured servant hidden in its core.
Camouflaged by generations of endurance;
An icon bound by bonds of oppressions.

A broken branch of mahogany that has drifted in the water;
Assaulted by ceaseless waves, caught and freed from crevasses, washed by rapids;

A soft, dull, forgotten, and half-drowned piece of driftwood.
Yet, deep within, hope; waiting to be released.

The years have grayed its richness.
The cold water stripped its bark.
To the eye of man there is but fire wood
To the eye of God, a beam of His light.

This monument within waits to be set free.
To have his prison carved away, to have his core exposed:
Beauty to be released, wisdom to be restored.
Rays of Sonny dawning the light of the Father's Son.

When I first read the poem it took my breath away. He had expressed my own feelings about the potential I had always seen in my African-American recovery community; but it had been too hard for me to acknowledge because it was my potential as well. It made me not only feel accepted by Billy but it let me see him as someone gifted by God to see His Kingdom coming on earth.

I couldn't speak and if I could have, I don't think I could have expressed the true reasons behind my emotions. Everyone could see that I was choked up. I managed to simple say, "Billy, tell them what your report says."

"It says, I am accepted into the 10th grade at the high school." Billy responded, referring to the accompanying letter and trying to ignore that he knew I was referring to the poem. And then he added, "Can I try out for the soccer team?"

My emotions gave way a little, and with a smile and chuckle I said, "Yes, you may try out for the soccer team."

I then handed the packet to Deb.

Jenn and Jim almost in unison said, "Great!" and began to get up to leave. Jimmy had told me that morning that he wanted to be called Jim from now on because Jimmy sounded too much like a little kid's name. But he didn't want to be called James, which sounded too much like an uppity rich kid's name. Their response made me feel like the poem must have gone over their heads.

"Wait!" I blurted out to the family. "I want to tell you about something else. You all know that since Billy's family's funeral" --- I paused hoping that mentioning his family Billy would not make Billy feel too bad.

"Sorry Billy." He nodded and smiled as if to say "it's ok."

"Since then your mom and I have met a couple of times with some old friends of mine from high school. Well, something is happening to us that I think is really changing all of us.

We think it is time for our families to at least meet each other. Jim and Jenn, you probably know most of them of the people, but only from when you were little kids. They are the Beckleys, the Carrs, the Cruzes, and a friend by the name of James Smith. The Beckley's have a daughter your age, Jim and Jenn, the Carr's have a fifteen year old daughter and a seventeen year old son, and the Cruz's have sixteen year old twin boys. Well, anyway we decided last night that we are going to have an end of the summer picnic and we want all our kids to come too. It is going to be next Sunday afternoon out at the Beckley's place where we have been meeting the past two weeks. They have a really, I mean, a really nice house, with a pool and yard big enough for any sports we want to do. Your mom and I would like you three to join us for a great time next Sunday. I know it is the day before school starts, so I hope you don't have any other plans."

Jenn, Jim, and Billy looked at each other and all started to answer at the same time with, "Yea." "Sounds cool." "Sure, why not." "I think I would like that."

Deb gave out an almost audible sigh of relief and I smiled with a big "Thanks, guys!" and got up from the table. It signaled the 'meeting' was over and everyone started to clear their dishes from the table.

That evening, I called Mel and we decided to meet at the Health Care Center around 9:30 a.m. I had asked him if he would like to go to the 10 o'clock NA meeting with me before we had lunch and he had agreed.

Deb and I went to bed early with hearts full of praise. We could hear all three teens, talking quietly together.

The next day, Stan and James met for lunch at Max and Erma's. After apologizing to one another for being insensitive to each other's feelings at the meeting they caught each other up on their lives in more detail. That led into James talking about his experiences in Haiti, which in turn led to talking about Stan's offer to go for a visit. James said he would not be available until the end of the semester the first week in December. Stan said that would fit well for him too because it was going to take a few months to sort out his departure from Cyber Market. At the end of lunch Stan made out a check for fifty thousand dollars to the "Bois Joli Children's Home", the name of the orphanage in Cange, Haiti. He told James it was just "hand money" as a show of good faith and hope for the future. He then led the two men in prayer for direction in seeking the Kingdom of God. James had a glimmer in his eyes and a huge smile as he thanked Stan and gave him a hug.

Mel met me that same day at the Health Care Center at 9:00 a.m. I took him around and introduced him to some of the staff. Deb was really warm towards him. She introduced him as the author, speaker, and well known pastor that he was. He seemed a little at a loss for words. I guessed he was not sure how much to say about the changes that were happening to him without getting into a huge theological discussion. As a result he was rather quiet but ask questions about the Center.

After the tour of the Center we went to Anton's, a coffee shop near the Center. I shared with him some of the public health realities of the neighborhood including my perspective on the homeless. I told him about the food pantry, soup kitchen, the men's shelter, bridge housing, the graduated work experience program, the homeless drop-in center, addiction recovery services, and HIV/AIDS the programs. I explained how each ministry exposed the need to expand to the next additions service. I then suggested that we attend the 10 o'clock NA meeting at the Recovery Center.

We got there just as the readings were starting. Then there was clean time followed by the Chair introducing Maggie who would share her experience, strength, and hope.

There was a thunderous applause as Maggie went to the podium.

"Hello family, my name is Maggie Maloy, I am recovering from addiction to drugs. My clean date is July 28, 1992."

There was more applause.

"I am a grateful recovering addict who is continually amazed at the grace of my God. I am a child of the King and that makes me a Princess.

Maggie then share her story of a radically changed life. I could tell, as I watch Mel that he was deeply touched.

After the meeting I took Mel over to Lew's Place, a local pizza and hoagie hang-out for lunch.

Mel told me that he was even more convinced than ever that he must leave the church; not just step down from being the pastor. He shared that he also felt that he should move out of town, find a new life where Jesus' could be King of his life and where he was not thought of as the head of Jesus' body.

He told me that if he didn't move the people of Apple Orchard would still look to him as the king of the hill.

I said that I thought he was right, that there should not be hierarchy in the church. I shared that just like it states in the AA Traditions that leaders are trusted servants and do not govern, so in the Body of Christ the members are governed by the head, which is Christ.

But I also said that I thought that leaving town would be a big mistake. God was only beginning to reveal His Kingdom to us and that we needed to stay where we were planted. And if He called us someplace else He would confirm it through His fellowship of believers. I said that I thought even if everyone did have him on a pedestal, that if he was faithful, God would level the playing field.

I am not sure what came over me. I was direct and bold but uncharacteristically gentle. What I then heard coming out of my mouth was that the institutional church was our spiritual mother: that she may have adopted the values of the culture but that she was still our mother and we could not run away from that problem. I said that, like Stan was proposing, we should not make Lone Ranger decisions. Our family of believers must be involved with our personal decisions, and like it or not I was part of his family and it just didn't feel right to me for him to walk out on a church that he had grown even if it was a distorted enculturated misrepresentation of what Jesus had in mind. I also said that part of loving the Church was staying close enough to respond in love without being co-dependent with her anti-Kingdom of God choices. I asked him to stay and speak the truth in love. I said we must be who God calls us to be. And for this we needed each other's support. We needed to trust the process and just be faithful to Jesus; but no more serving the idol of the church institution. I told him that I thought in God's Kingdom there were no institutions just relationships of love.

As I heard myself talking I was being convicted that I too needed to be return to my mother, the church, and love her. Perhaps God had me say all that more for me to hear that as a sermon to Mel.

To my surprise, Mel didn't argue. First, he said that what I had just said about the church being a prostitute was also said once by St. Augustine. Instead of disagreeing with me he started to talk about the parallels he saw in the Twelve Step program and the biblical vision of the church; stuff that it had taken me years to see. Inside my heart was singing. Maybe he got it. When we were done talking, about two hours later, he said he would ask the group what he should do. He said as much as he had wanted to and was committed to do it, he had not yet resigned as pastor. Nor had he told anyone at Apple Orchard about the group and the transforming events in the past month.

That Thursday, the women met again at Panera and mostly planned the picnic for Sunday. They all reported that their kids were planning on coming, except for Elijah, Mel and Liz's seventeen year old, whom they hadn't seen long enough to talk to. Liz said he usually came home to sleep about 1:00 a.m., woke up about 11:00 a.m. and was out the door by 12. She didn't think he had had a meal at home for the last month. He put his dirty clothes in the basement with the laundry and other than a "Hey" and "Later" they didn't hear from him. She told them that Mel thought he was over at the swim club most afternoons and that he was going to go over to talk to him during the week but that as of then he still hadn't tracked him down.

Twenty

Sunday morning, as I was having my coffee and reading the paper, Jimmy interrupted me. He said that some of the guys wanted him to go to Kennywood Amusement Park with them that afternoon. It was there last blast before school the next day. I told him that I thought the family picnic was more important than one more day with the guys. His reaction was unusually strong. He started telling me that I only cared about what was important to me, and that I didn't understand. I tried to listen and gave him examples of how I did understand, but I could see his mind was set on being with his friends. So, I agreed and even asked if he wanted to ask Billy to go alone so he could get to know Jimmy's friends and experience Kennywood. He said no, that Jenn and Billy were looking forward to coming with us to the LP family gathering. LP for Liminal Plunge, was what seemed to be the name that were all starting to use when referring to the group. Then he added, "And Dad, I would appreciated it if you called me Jim. I am no longer a little kid. "Jimmy" sounds like you think I am still a little kid."

"Sorry", I responded with a hint of exasperation. "I forgot."

The addict in me felt very uneasy about his attitude but I had to let it go. When the kids were younger I learned that it is important to be picky about picking my fights. When I told Deb, she too was apprehensive.

So, one of Jim's older friends picked him up about noon and they headed off to Kennywood to meet some others. He said he would be back by 9:00 PM, in time to get some sleep so he could get up in time to go to school.

The rest of our family left for Stan and Karen's place about 1:00 p.m. It turned out to be a beautiful sunny day, not a cloud in the sky. By noon the temperature was about eighty five degrees. When we arrived, everyone was there except Jorge and Misha and their 16 year old twins, Juan and Michael. I figured they would get there later because their worship usually wasn't over until about 1:00 p.m.

When we arrived, Stan's daughter, Brenda, and Andi Carr were in the heated pool. The pool was just off a large patio in the back of the house. From the lawn on the other side of the pool you could see tennis courts through a row of Apple trees. The trees were heavy with apples.

Jenn and Billy had previously met Brenda and Andi but didn't feel like they knew them. I took them out to the pool to help them feel comfortable. Then they went in to put on their swimming suits. After they had been in the water for about 10 minutes, Karen brought all the kids out a Pepsi and some chips.

We adults sat around on the deck, talked sports, movies, family, and weather as we watched the kids swim.

The Cruz family arrived about 2:30 p.m. Their twins got in the pool with the rest of the kids and Stan and I started to get the grill ready for the chicken and steaks. Then Karen, who had been an All-American soccer player in college, came out of the house in shorts and a soccer ball in her hand and said, "Over behind the barn is a regulation soccer field, anyone up for a soccer game?"

Billy responded immediately with "Count me in." And Brenda, who was a budding star, said, "Me too!" Andi said, "Sure." Then Stan and Mel who both had played soccer in high school and college said sure they would play. And everyone else, accept Misha, Deb, and Michael, joined in too. So, that made 6 on a team.

We all went into the house to change.

As James and I were walking back to the soccer field, he got a call on his cell phone. He excused himself, and stopped while I went on. I heard him answer, with a “Hi Rita.” It made me wonder who Rita was. He hadn’t mentioned her. I thought it must be someone in his class. Oh well, it is none of my business. I don’t need to pry.

James wasn’t on the phone but a few minutes and caught up to me before we got to the field. He said the call was from a girl in the class with him at Pitt who had forgotten what the assignment was.

The soccer field was past what looked like a mountain lodge. Stan said the “lodge” was guest quarters that he had built to host out of town business associates for meetings and conferences. He said it could accommodate sixteen and had a conference room for thirty.

I was very impressed with the field. It was just not a field but it was graded, well groomed, had lines for soccer and soccer goals at each end. I remarked about it and Karen said she used it for kids’ soccer camps that she ran in the spring and that they let the local club soccer teams play there in the summer.

Karen knew that Stan, Mel, Liz, and Brenda were experienced soccer players. Stan had told her that James had player basketball in high school and Jorge and I had played football, so she figured we had some athletic ability. She divided us up so that she, Juan, Mel, Andi, James, and Billy were on one team and Stan, Jorge, Jenn, Liz, Brenda, and I were on the other team. Karen also said she thought that we should only play on half the field, a suggestion that for which I for one, was grateful.

When we started playing, we looked like a bunch of want-a-bees trying to impress each other. But slowly, Karen and Brenda got us positioned and organized and we even started passing the ball to one another and stealing the ball from the other team. Stan and Mel had not lost too much of their skills though neither moved very fast. Two things quickly became apparent. The adults, expect for Karen and perhaps I, were out of shape, and that Billy was an unusually talented soccer player.

We had a great time, mostly laughing at ourselves, and watching Karen and Billy perform, with an occasional impressive move by Stan or Mel. I was also impressed with how well Juan, Jenn, and Andi did. I complimented them on their play and learned that Andi was also on a club soccer team; and though Juan did not play any sports that he was a dancer and very athletic. Jorge, who was noticeably overweight, mostly walked back and forth with an occasional surprising sprint and impressive steal.

After about 45 minutes, Jorge, Liz, Stan, Mel could not keep going so we called it quits. The adults thanked Karen for initiating the game and said they hoped they had enough energy to make it back to the pool to cool off.

On the way back I overheard Karen asking Billy how he learned to play soccer so well. He told her that it was the only sport they played at the orphanage in Africa and that he had been playing since he was five. This was the first time he had ever played on a field that was smooth with grass and that it made it so easy to control the ball. He said that he was hoping that he would be good enough to play on the high school team. She told him not to worry, that he would be fine. It just might take a little time for the coaches and other kids to make him feel part of the team because most of them had probably been playing together for a while. Practice had already started and that there would be a lot to learn. As I listen to them, I was afraid that Billy might feel discouraged but he response was sort of matter of fact. He just said, "I will do my best and will have fun doing it."

When we got back to the pool, the guys dove in and the girls quickly changed and followed. Man, did it feel good. And boy was I hungry.

After a swim we all pigged out on the patio by the pool. The kids all seemed to be getting along well, which we adults were very happy to see. It seemed the soccer game had done the trick in helping them to find some bonding. Michael was the only one who seems to still be alone, though everyone welcomed him to be a part of whatever they were doing. He mostly spent his time behind his camera taking pictures of everything.

As we were wrapping up the meal with strawberry shortcake, Stan asked us all, kids included, to come into the Great Room. When we all gathered, James was at the piano and began to play and sing a blues song. We were all captivated. As he was finishing Stan said, "I think we have a lot to talk about."

The kids looked at each other like what does that mean.

Stan continued, "First, if we haven't already, I think we need to fill the kids in on what we have been going through. It is going to affect their lives as much as ours."

The kids turned to look at each other with confusion and apprehension on their faces. "Second, James and I what to share with you our plans for going to Haiti. And then I need to find out from you how we are going to proceed about my business."

I saw Jenn lean over to Andi and whisper, "What is going on?" Andi just smiled a little and raised her eyebrows.

After a short pause, Mel then said, "And I need to ask you all about what you think I should do about the church."

Then I said, first looking around at the kids. "We know kids this may be a lot to take in so please just be patient with your crazy parents."

And then I added, "I too have something to add. I think we also need to talk about the group this group, like how often we are going to meet, and should the kids participate, and where do we go from here, and what do we do if anyone else wants to join us, and maybe a whole lot of other stuff."

"Sounds like we have a long evening before us but don't forget the kids have school tomorrow." Said Misha.

The kids, except for Andi, were all just sitting around with blank stares on their faces.

Juan then said with a rather quiet and hesitant voice, "Excuse me, I don't want to interrupt, but what are you all talking about? This is an awesome place and this has been a wonderful picnic, but it sound like a lot else is going on besides a reunion of my parents high school friends?"

"I think I know a little bit." said Andi. "Dad would you mind if I shared a little about us?"

Mel nodded with a smile.

Andi, took a hard swallow and a deep breath, and then shared with the group what had happened with her and Curt. Everyone could tell it was hard for her but she made it through. Then Andi got a smile on her face and went on to share about her dinner with her dad and the big change she was experiencing in both her dad and mom. Everyone listened with a sense of wonder. I looked over at Mel and his eyes were filled with tears.

Jenn responded first and said, "Thanks for being so honest Andi, I am so glad to be getting to know you. I want to share something too." Deb and I looked at each with curious questions in our eyes.

"Mom and Dad, and everyone, I think my brother need your prayers. Jimmy said he was going to Kennywood with some of his friends. They aren't really friends from my perspective and he will kill me for telling you all this, but they are a drugee gang in our neighborhood. They have been working on getting him to join them. I don't know where they went, probably they did go to Kennywood, but not to ride the rides. I am really worried about him."

My insides started to get hot. I had PTSD flash backs of getting caught up with Jocko and his gang. I wanted to leave the picnic and head off to Kennywood to find him and drag him home. I was sick, angry, and full of fear, confused, and hurt. Deb's eyes were glassy. My mind was filled with tumbling thoughts. I had been there, I have helped hundreds of addicts since before Jenn and Jimmy were born, my family had been alcoholics and addicts, why didn't I see this coming, how could I be the last one to recognize the struggle my own son was facing. Shame and guilt again filled my heart.

The room was silent for a minute, everyone trying to be sensitive to Deb and me. Jenn could sense my dilemma and saw the tears in her mother's eyes and said, "Dad and Mom, it is not your fault. You know we are powerless over Jim. Like you've taught me, Dad, we need to trust God to work in others' lives. Isn't it when we surrender our need to control that the power of God can work in us and in others? I know Jim is going to be alright."

I was blown away and humbled by Jenn's wisdom. She was right, I knew it, and she called me back to Jesus. I was also stunned by how openly these two young girls were sharing in front of a group of adults. I think everyone in the room could sense the presence of God and the safety he brings.

Mel then said, "Let's pray."

Almost everyone in the room said a short prayer for Jim. Deb and I were blown away. When we were done praying for Jim, Stan said, "Does anyone else want to share or have a pray request?"

It was silent. I think we were all in a little shock at the level of vulnerability that we had just experienced. After the silent pause Stan continued, "Maybe later. We will make sure we have another opportunity before we leave. It is this kind of vulnerability that is opening us all to experience something new. Let me now give a quick summary of the last couple of months so the kids have a little understanding of what we believe God is doing.

Stan then talked about the group reunion at the funeral, our first meeting at their house when the Spirit moved us to repentance, and then James appearance. He also told everyone about his lunch with James and their plans to go to Haiti the week before Christmas.

When he was finished Billy asked if he could say something.

"This is going to sound a little bold for a fifteen year old who no one knows very well to be saying to a group that is his parent age, but I feel led to say it anyway. It is what is in my heart. I'm sorry if I will sound a little emotional and maybe judgmental. Please forgive me if I am out of place. It wouldn't be especially out of place in Africa because their most kids my age are considered adults.

"The soldiers that killed my family were children several years younger than me. They were orphaned children that were enslaved and then trained to kill. In the country where I grew up, and the countries around the Sudan, there are literally millions of orphaned children and many of them have be forced into rebel armies. In just one of those armies, the Lord's Resistance Army, there are today at least 66,000 children that are trained killers. You see, I knew the kids that killed my family. I had played with the kid that looked right at me and shot me. We had been very good friends. He was like my little brother. My parents had been like parents to those kids. And they killed them. They had been stolen, made slaves, and taught to be killers.

"I realize this is may seem far from what you have been talking about. I don't mean to distract from the struggles you are having. In fact, I think my experience is very much related to your experience. I am saying this because I believe the answer to what is happening in the Sudan will come when people like this group meet the needs of those orphans. I think, that the change you are going through may be the key to the change that in needed in the world.

"Because of what I have lived I see the need. It is part of me. In Africa forty five hundred people have die of AIDS, just today. Eight hundred and forty million people in the world will go to sleep tonight not having had anything to eat today. Every seven seconds, somewhere in the world a child under five dies of hunger. More than half the world lives on less than two dollars a day. A sixth of the world does not have clean water. Almost half of the world, maybe 4 billion people, do not have sanitation. Eighty percent of the world's population is poor, not poor, like on welfare, I mean poor, like sick and starving.

"I also see how you all are changing. I think not only should Stan and James go to Haiti at Christmas, I think that all of us have to go. The internal changes that you are experiencing must translate into meeting the needs in the world. You have got to see how people live! God is bring His Kingdom on earth. But it won't come to America unless America goes to the poor of the world. It is the orphans, widows, and refugees who will usher in the Kingdom of God."

Again, like so many times in the past month, I was so caught off guard and blown away by a young man that I was beginning to know as a quiet boy of few words. What Billy said was not only was amazing but it had the ring of truth in me.

What he had just said sounded like Jesus saying, "Blessed are the poor for theirs is the Kingdom of God." I got goose bumps just thinking of the reality that eighty percent of the people of the world were poor.

We all looked around at each other, the kids as well. Stan finally spoke and asked, "Does anyone have a problem with us all going to Haiti at Christmas?"

No one said a word.

Then I said, "What about Jim and Elijah? They aren't here. They are 14 and 17. They just can't be left home alone that long, and I don't really think either one is in a place where they will be content to stay with grandparents. I guess I have to trust God to make a way that Jim will go."

Andi interjected, "There is no way Elijah will go. Mom and Dad, I am sure you must realize that Elijah is not in a good place. In fact, he is one of the up and coming drug dealers in our end of town. Curt and he are sort of like partners."

Mel and Liz looked at each other knowingly.

"We don't know all the details but we do know things have gotten pretty bad, honey." replied Liz.

"I don't know what to say about him going, or what life will be like for him in five months but maybe God will intervene someway." added Mel.

"Does that mean, because I didn't say anything just now that I have agreed to go too?" Asked Brenda, who had come in late during James blues rendition and was sitting near the door. "I heard what Billy was saying but it is really hard for me to comprehend. I am not ready to spend Christmas in Haiti. Do I have to go? Has Billy, as much as a nice guy that he is, decide my life for me?"

"You can go honey, only if you want to." replied her mom.

"Can I stay with Carrie if I don't go?"

"We will see. Let's talk about it later."

"I realize it hasn't been said, but I assume I will pay for the trip." interjected Stan.

"Not so fast. Our family can handle it." Mel replied.

I felt weird with Mel speaking up, but also about Stan paying for it. There was no way we could afford such a trip and I knew the Cruz family didn't have the money.

Then Jorge said, "We could see if our church could help us."

So I said, "I guess Deb and I could get some support from the staff at the Health Care Center."

"No, I don't think you all understand what I am saying. What is mine is yours. I hope you have been thinking about how to be stewards of God's abundance. Remember, I need you all to decide with Karen and me what we are to do with the gifts that God has provided. So, if we are agreed to all go to Haiti together, and what used to be my money is our money, it should be used for that trip. I am sorry if I sound like I am being a sugar daddy handing out money. I don't want to be disrespectful to anyone. It is no longer my money. It really never was. If I am going to truly follow Jesus then I have to learn to get used to living with values that I had not even considered before." Stan said.

"I remember at Kerygma Fellowship Church they had a common treasury. Everything the members owned they gave to the church and then everyone made decisions together on how to spend it. Everyone's needs were being considered and addressed and shared. It was really good to be connected with that kind of trust and sharing, but it also felt kind of ridged. Like everyone had to live with everyone else watching them. I don't think church should feel like that. I think we need to grow in loving one another so that it just feels like we can trust each other. The church shouldn't be a place where we hide our needs or hoard our abundance. We should naturally feel what is mine is yours and what is yours is mine, without having to have a system of checks and balances. Stan if you are sharing your millions with us not out of a sense of obligation but because you love us then out of our love for you we are to do the same. It should be something we all feel because of our love for each other not because it is legislated. And if any of us has a need then our love for one another should free us to share are need as well. For me what that means is if Liz and I can afford to pay, we should pay. And if Jorge and Misha can't pay then we should pay for them and the same with Odell and Deb and James. Right?" Mel said with a smile. "Mutual sharing of wealth and needs should be only natural in the church."

"Yeah, that's what I said, right?" answered Stan. "So then, has anyone thought about what to do with the money I get from selling my company?"

I could see the kids looking at each other with their mouths open, just as the rest of us did when Stan surprised us last week at our group meeting.

"Wait a minute." said Liz. "We haven't really determined if we are all agreed to going to take a trip to Haiti."

"OK, all in favor of going to Haiti raise your hand." Said Stan.

All the adults raised their hands. The kids looked at each other and slowly put up their hand. All that is except, Brenda.

Stan then said. "Good, then we are going. Now what about the money?"

Liz then share that one of the thoughts she had been thinking was about was investing the money so that the interest from the investments could be given to meet the needs of orphans in the world.

This precipitated a lot of discussion in which even the children participated.

Next James filled us in on his research about the where-a-bouts of Kara Stevens. He had learned that Kara had struggled with alcoholism on and off for a number of years, but eventually had gotten sober after being arrested in Boston and finally ending up homeless. She was then befriended by an Episcopal priest who supported her through multiple detoxes, treatment programs, and half-way houses. She became active in the church, went back to school, and got a job as a website developer. Then after about 3 years, through her involvement with her church, she met another Episcopal priest by the name of Father Terry Witherspoon. They were married in 1997. In 1999 they moved to San Francisco where he became the Senior Rector of a church. That was as far as James had gotten in his research. Next, he said he was going to track down Father Witherspoon and get the rest of the story.

Then Mel brought up his dilemma about resigning from the church. He shared our lunch conversation. There were some questions which led to further discussion, but in the middle of the discussion as Karen was sharing her perspective, Mel's cell phone rang.

"I'm sorry," Mel said to the group, "I thought I turned it off. Hello. Yes, this is Reverend Carr."

Mel got up and slowly walked towards the door so he could talk without interrupting the group.

After a couple of minutes we heard Mel say, "I'll be right there."

"I've got to go." Mel said. "Stan can you take Liz home?"

"What's up?" asked Stan.

"That was Tom Barber. They have Elijah in custody. He was arrested for possession of narcotics with intent to sell. He asked them to call me to come bail him out. I have to go. Please pray for us."

Twenty One

Liz started to cry softly. Andi hugged her mom. Everyone else was silent; a little bit at a loss as to what to say. Mel went over to his wife and daughter all three of the family hugged.

James asked Stan in a whisper that we all could hear, "Who is Tom Barber?"

Stan answered, "He is our Chief of Police." And all was quiet for what seem like eternity.

Mel started towards the door.

I decided to risk saying what I was thinking.

"Mel I want to go with you and I don't want you to bail him out?"

Mel stopped. "I can't let him stay in jail!" he retorted.

Looking around at the group and then straight at Mel and in as gentle a voice as I knew how, I said, "Yes, you can. In fact that is the most loving thing you can do for him right now. Believe me Mel, my feelings are identifying with yours right now more than you know. I have a son I want to rescue too. And I have seen many close friends die from drugs and its life style. I was in that life style once myself. I know how much is at stake. But I have also seen what helps and what just feeds the disease. And just like Jenn said to me earlier, "We are powerless, but when we surrender that is when the power of God can work."

"But you don't understand, I have never been there for him and now he needs me, I have to be there for him now. God is giving me a second chance."

"Yes, he needs you to be there for him. What I am saying is that being there for him is not enough. You need to be there with him. Bailing him out is not being there for him, it is being there for you and Liz. It will make you feel better but it will tell him that he can continue doing what he has been doing and you will help him get away with it. Your emotions, right now, are clouding your thinking. And what I am telling you is very hard to hear. That is all part of the disease. Addiction is a family disease and you have got it too. Mel, this is what I know, it is what I do. I have been around it and in it all my life. I am telling you this because we are in this together. We need to go down to the police station and you need to look Eli straight in the face and tell him he has to get help and that you can't help him. He will not understand and will be extremely angry with you and maybe even more so with me. But the best way you can help your son is to show him you care more about him than you do about making life easy for you or him."

As I was saying this, I wondered a little to myself if my strong confrontational lecture was in part an expression of my need releasing some anger that I was still holding on to towards the leadership of the church. But the expression on Mel's face and his growing impatience everyone could tell that Mel was having a hard time keeping from yelling at me. I also thought, in Mel's emotional state I don't think that he heard hardly anything I had said. He interrupted me and said. "He will get be put in with some real bad people, he could get hurt. He will think I not only have been a terrible dad but that I am mean and I don't care about him at all. He will get a record. He'll never what to see us again. I can't let that happen to us."

I didn't' let up. "He already has been in with some really bad people. He already has gotten hurt. He has an addiction that brings suffering that is worse than you can imagine. And he is in the process of getting a record as we speak. Let me tell you about a similar situation."

"I've got to go!" Mel started to raise his voice and we could all feel his anguish.

I softly and firmly said, "Listen to me Mel. .... A close friend of mine, a doc, at the Health Care Center, has a son who started using drugs when he was 15. His son would get in trouble at school and he would go up to the high school and advocate for him. He went to bat for him over and over again. My friend refused be accept that his son was using drugs and just kept thinking his son was having normal growing up struggles. The boy, eventually, with a lot of manipulation of the school system by his dad, graduated from high school. He applied to college and was accepted, again with some manipulation from his dad. When he came home at Thanksgiving he told his parents that he wasn't going back to school because he was homesick. The real reason was that his drug contacts were at home and he needed his drugs. When he got home his parents did their best to help him adjust. He tried some jobs but would quit for one reason or another. He made excuses like his boss was just plain mean and stuff like that."

Mel again started to move towards the door.

"Bear with me Mel. The boy would stay away overnight. He told his parents he was staying at friends' homes, and eventually he would be away for a week at a time. When he was at home he just kept to himself and stopped relating to his parents. My friend did everything thing he could to try and communicate with his son, got him job after job, bought him cars, I mean several cars after each one would get wrecked. And he would always bail him out when his son said he owed a friend some money. He was away from the house for three months and then for six months. His dad and mom finally realized and acknowledged that he had a problem with using drugs but he would not listen to their pleas to get help. They had many arguments, and I mean really bad fights. His mother became scared to death of him, he stole money from her purse, and took stuff from the house. But his dad kept bailing him out, paying to get his car serviced, even taking him out for dinner hoping to love him into wanting to change. His son just got worse, mean, demanding, abusive, and scary."

Impatiently Mel interrupted, "Yeah, Yeah, so what is your point. I need to go get Elijah out of jail!"

"I'll get there." I said. "Then after several months of not seeing him, early one morning before my friend went to work there was a knock at the front door. There was his son. His son didn't have a key because his parents had changed the locks for fear he may harm his mother or bring druggy friends home to rob the place. When my friend first saw his son he just couldn't believe how bad he looked. He had lost about 60 lbs. since the last time he had seen him and he looked emaciated. He had a beard and long matted hair, old torn, dirty, clothes. He looked about twice his real age. His father just stood there in disbelief. His mom then got to the door, saw him and screamed. Then my friend told me that it was almost as though God spoke to him and a deep peace came over him. He went out on the front porch where his son was standing and with a strength that he knew was not his own he told his son that he could not come in the house and that if he wanted help he couldn't' give it to him but that he know where he could get it. His son pathetically pleaded with him, to at least let him take a shower and get something to eat. His dad simply kept saying no but gave him the phone and a phone number to call for help. The son eventually realized his dad was not going to let him in the house and he called the number, which was my number. I went out to my friend's house, picked up his son, took him to the men's homeless shelter were he could stay for 24 hours and then the next day, took him to detox. And then a few days later I got him into a nine month treatment facility. He was clean for about a year, then relapsed, but went back into treatment and a half-way house for two years. He hasn't used a drug or alcohol for ten years. He has a family and a job where he helps the home bound elderly. When he shares his testimony he starts with 'The best thing that ever happened to me was the day my dad would not let me in the house."

Mel responded gruffly, "OK, come on, let's go."

As we left Stan said, "We will be praying and don't worry about Liz and Andi."

On our way to the police station I didn't say any more and neither did Mel. Mel had agreed for me to come along and to take me home afterward, so I knew he was considering what I had said. It only took us about ten minutes to get to the station. As we were about to get out of the car Mel asked if I would pray for us and Eli.

I prayed the Serenity Prayer and left it like that. "God grant us the serenity to accept the things we cannot change, the courage to change the things we can, and the wisdom to know the difference. Amen."

When we entered the station, Mel introduced us to the officer at the desk. We were ushered through a side door, down a hall, and into a small room where Eli, two other young men, and a young lady were sitting with a male officer and a female officer. I had not seen Eli since he was a small child, but I vaguely recognized him. When Eli saw us he began to stand up. The officer seated next to him reached out, pushed him back down, and stood up himself. Neither Eli nor Mel looked at each other. The officer seemed to know Mel and motioned to us to follow him as he left the room. We went into an office across the hall where Chief Barber was seated behind a desk. We sat down and the officer returned to the holding room.

Twenty Two

The Chief greeted Mel as an old friend and Mel introduced me as a renewed old friend. Then the Chief described the charges that were against Elijah. He said that if Eli was convicted as an adult that there were enough charges against him for him could get three to five years in prison. But, he said, since he was a minor he might only have to serve six to twelve months at Walcott Juvenile Detention Center (WJDC). Mel said this was Eli's senior year in high school and he asked if going to Walcott would prevent him from graduating. The Chief told him no, that in fact it would confine him to the Center where he would have to go to school. He said that Eli would probably have a better chance of graduating at Walcott than if he had not gotten caught and continued to run with the other drug dealers and users. He also told us that if convicted he could get put in drug court and be required to spend at least 3 months of his sentence in a drug treatment program. Mel asked how long before the trial or whatever would determine his son's fate, and what was to happen to him until then. The Chief said there would be a juvenile hearing in about a week and then about a month after that a judgment and sentencing, if convicted. Mel said school starts tomorrow and so he wanted to know what was to happen to him between now and when he would be sentenced if found guilty. The Chief said that if Mel agreed to provide an unsecured bail of $5,000 that Elijah could go home with him. He said that unsecured meant that he didn't have to give them the money. He would be responsible for giving them the money if Elijah didn't appear for the hearing. He also said that Mel would be responsible to make sure that Elijah would not get in trouble with the law.

Then, Mel looked at me and said, "What if I don't put up the bail?" The Chief looked surprised and said that then Elijah would be remanded to Walcott until judgment where made.

Mel replied, with moist glassy eyes, "Then that is what is going to happen and I want to tell him so."

The Chief's face, to my surprise, lit up, and he said, "Mel, you are the first father who I have seen in this community who has not bailed out his son on his first offense. You are doing exactly the right thing. You're a good man. You care about your son."

Tears began to roll down Mel's face.

Then, again to my surprise, the Chief continued. "Mel, I want to say something to you. You know I am not much of a religions person. I have watched you for a number of years now and I know your popularity as a speaker and writer and pastor but I have to confess that I have viewed you as not much more than a successful business man selling people a lot of religious smoke and mirrors. I expected you come in here with cash in your hand and excuses for your son. Yell at him for embarrassing you and walk out with him in a huff. But instead, you have come in with humility and tough love. You are not the man I thought you were, you are a thousand times better. What you are about to do, I know is not easy, and you may not like what I expect you are about to experience, but believe me you are doing the right thing. Let's go see Elijah."

Mel wiped his cheeks and eyes and the three of us walked across the hall. As we walked in Eli stood up with his coat on and started to move toward the door. The Chief stopped him and told him to sit down. The other kids and the officers looked surprised and curious. Then Mel walked over to Eli, sat down in the chair next to him, looked into his eyes, and said with remarkable composure, "Elijah, I have been an appalling father, a total failure; off running around the world telling everyone about the love of Jesus, but not showing it to you. I am sorry. I can't change the past and I can't change you or the fact that we are sitting here in this police station, but I can change me. You need help that I can't give you now. I am too late. But there is help, and it is right here. So, I am not bailing you out and you will have to deal with the consequences of what you have gotten yourself into. I love you, so you are going to Walcott."

Eli sprang to his feet, almost like he was going to hit his dad. The officer closest to him restrained him from behind and Eli started to cuss his father out, telling him that he never did care about him and that this proved it, that he was a big phony &#@*!*#"!! who should have never been born. He told him he hated him and wished that he wasn't his son and that when he got out Mel would never see him again. He was shaking and crying as the officer removed him from the room. His parting shot was, "What did you bring that &#@! along for anyway, what is he, your drug connection?"

Mel turned to the others in the room and said, "Sorry you had to be a part of this, I love him more than he realizes, and we both need a lot of help." The Chief, Mel, and I turned to leave.

The Chief accompanied us to the entrance of the station, he gave Mel a hug and strong hand shake, shook my hand and thanked me for coming and supporting Mel. As we parted and were moving towards the car he yelled to Mel that he would be praying for him and Liz and Elijah.

As we walked to the car Mel apologized to me for Elijah's behavior and his language. I told him to forget it and let it go, it was the disease talking.

As soon as we got in the car Mel started to sob. I just listened. He finally wore himself out and we started back. It was only about 11:30 PM, not nearly as late as I expected it to be.

I took Mel home and when I got home Deb was waiting up for me. But since the first day of school the next day, the kids were all in bed. It was such a relief to know that Jim was home. I would wait to learn what his day and night turned out to be, for real.

I filled Deb in on how God was with Mel at the police station and we prayed for Eli, Mel, Liz, and Andi. Before joining Deb in bed I emailed the rest of the group, filled them in, and asked them to be praying for Elijah.

When I slid into bed, Deb was already asleep. I laid there for some time before I too joined the rest of our family for some much needed rest. My mind reviewed all that had happened over the past couple of months, especially the changes that had taken place in my attitude and perspective on myself, the future, and the church.

I thought to myself that most of my self-righteous feelings about the church were gone. Not my criticisms but my judgmental feelings. I still thought the church was seriously distorted and far from how the Bible taught it was to be, but I no longer saw myself as any better than those whom I had been judging all my life. I had new hope for the church. I also realized I was feeling like my life in following Jesus was just starting, almost as fresh as it was that night at the Young Life Camp in Colorado. And yet, I didn't feel at all like the past twenty five years were not that significant. I felt even more grateful than ever for God's grace and validation in my life. I was overwhelmed with his blessing in my life. Yet, I also felt like a new chapter my life was just about to begin again and that the future would not be like nothing like anything I had ever dreamed or imagined.

I laid there in awe at what I had seen in Mel and Liz, and Stan and Karen. Both couples' lives were really taking radical new directions. It boggled my mind to think that for both couples the changes they were about to make were such a sudden major about face.

And James appearance. And Andi's rescue. And Billy's maturity and wisdom. And were we really all going to Haiti?

It made me wonder too what God might be up to in Jorge and Misha's lives. Or Elijah's. Or the rest of all our kids. I prayed a special prayer for Jimmy because I was scared for him. I could see signs of him repeating my dual life when I was his age.

As I rolled over to fall asleep I looked at the clock. It was 1:00 a.m. My alarm was set for five.

Twenty Three

Monday, August 27, 2007

When the alarm went off, in what seemed like ten seconds, I woke up feeling rested but with a thousand thought swirling in my mind. They were about the Biblical principles of the 12 Step Program: powerlessness, acceptance, fellowship, service, gratitude, and much more. It was stuff I had survived on and that had taught me how to live with some sanity but it seemed to have new significance. As I came to, out of my sound sleep, the thoughts seemed to fade into one big jumble but they made me want to take another look at the whole recovery program with a fresh and open mind for the thousandth time. Maybe I had been dreaming about them because of the event with Mel and Elijah, or my anxiety about Jimmy, or both. I thought I should find some time soon to give the whole program a new open look and maybe this time more closely at its roots in the Bible.

When I came out of the bathroom, Billy was waiting for me. I put on my running clothes, we warmed up with a jog around the block, stretched, and set out on our run. For the past week, Billy and I had been getting up at 5:00 a.m. each morning to run together. We had had some great conversations. He continued to amaze me with his insights.

Today was to be his first day in an American school, outside of being home schooled, or at any school, for that matter. I started a conversation about what he might expect. We talked about education and peer pressure and different cultural expectations. He was most interested in why I thought kids his age, not only in America, but from what he had seen in Africa as well, seemed to care so much about what other kids thought of them. After I tried to give him a lot of talk about discovering your identity he wrapped it up by saying. "In other words they want to be loved the way God loves us."

So, we ran in silence for a while.

I started to think about what had pre-occupied me, on and off, for almost my whole life in Christ. It was the same issue that The Group was going to have to come to some resolve about soon; 'What is the Church in America about today?' So finally, just to see what he might say, I said, "Billy what do think about the Church?"

He said, "Do you mean in the scheme of creation, in history, in the world, in Africa, in America?"

"In Pittsburgh, America."

"I think Western Christendom, the Church in Pittsburgh, PA, has replaced the Kingdom of God on earth with an institution it mistakenly calls the Church."

Silence, a few rhythmic sounds of our feet hitting the pavement, and then he said, "We only have a half an hour before we need to jog back home and I need to pick up the pace." And he began to take off at a pace that made me feel like I am more than twice his age. Which I am. I couldn't help think, *"Thanks Billy, that really makes sense."*

When I arrived back at the house Billy was taking his shower and both Jim and Jen were ready for school and eating breakfast. I was impressed with how my teenagers were being so responsible. I didn't even sense any signs of rebellion in Jim. He was even dressed in a way that would have made him acceptable anywhere. And no signs of a change of clothes once he got out of our watchful eyes. Maybe I was just being paranoid about him starting to hook-up with the gang-bangers.

Billy showered quickly, ate and the three of them were off to meet the bus.

I sat down at the table with Deb for our coffee and we bowed in prayer for our three kids.

After our time of prayer that went beyond our kids to also included Eli and James and the rest of the group, as well as some stuff that was happening at the Health Care Center, I suggested to Deb that we start going to a Naranon meeting, the 12 Step Fellowship group for family members of drug addicts. I also said I thought that we should also asked Mel and Liz to go with us. I told her I felt we needed to do it for our kids and that it was something that I thought could also help Mel and Liz a lot as they tried to do what was best for Eli. What I really thought was that we need to do it for us. She agreed.

Before we went to work Deb called Liz and asked her about going to Naranon. Liz said that she had hardly slept all-night, and that if we thought Naranon would help her she would talk to Mel about it and get back to us.

At work that day I got a Naranon meeting list and found a Thursday night meeting about half way between Apple Orchard and our home. I thought it might be a good meeting for us since neither couple would probably know anyone there so we could all be anonymous.

That night Liz called Deb and said they would like to go. Thursday nights were good for them and they made plans for that Thursday.

On Wednesday, Stan met with his Board and top management.

On Thursday, the Panera Woman's Foursome meet again.

That Thursday night the topic of our first night at Naranon, was "Detachment." I thought that couldn't have been better, like God had planned it just for us. One person in the group shared how detachment for her did not mean abandonment but letting go of taking responsibility for another person's feelings, attitudes, and actions. After the meeting we two couples want out for some desert. Liz said what was share about not having to abandon her son but detaching was like a freeing revelation from God for her. Mel told us that he appreciated our support and that our just being with them made him feel like he was in the right place. I didn't say so but I thought, '*All my life I have been surrounded by addicts, myself, my brother and sisters, my mother, and hundreds of others with this disease. I have considered that I could have a child of mine become addicted but the reality of it actually happening is a totally new world for me.*' I also had the thought that Mel and Liz really did seem comfortable being with us, even with the racial difference. I didn't feel any kind of racial judgments from Mel and Liz, but my own racism in suspecting them to be racist surprised me a little.

Each morning during the week I escaped for about an hour on my way to the Health Care Center to stop by my "office" to use the time to study and reflect on the roots of the 12 Traditions and their possible application to a biblical understanding of the church.

Jorge emailed me and told me that on Sunday after worship he and Misha were getting together with her parents to fill them in on all that was happening with our group.

There wasn't any drama with any of our kids that first week back to school, and it seemed like last Sunday night's Liminal Plunge group had hardly ended before it was time to be back together at Stan and Karen's.

When Sunday night came it felt like a new season of our life had begun. I thought that it is interesting how the start of a school year seems to affect everyone's life. But this new season felt like much more than a new school year or the anticipation of fall events. It had the feeling of anticipating a move to a new city or the start of a new job or the beginning of married life or even something like anticipating the birth of your first child. Of course there was nothing as concrete as those expectations but it certainly felt like Tony sang in West Side Story "Something's coming, I don't know, what it is, but it is gonna be good."

Sunday evening, James met us at our house and the three of us went over to the Cruz's to pick up Jorge and Misha. On the way out to the Beckley's Misha filled us in on their time that afternoon with her parents. She said her parents listened with interest. They didn't offer much of an opinion about anything that was said but they did ask a lot of questions about what Mel was going to do. Misha said they didn't tell her parents anything about Stan and Karen's plans about their company but they asked her parents to keep everything they shared confidential anyway. Mel's life was too public and he was too famous for the media to get wind of what could happen before Mel actually acted on it. All-in-all they thought her parents were pretty open and interested in what might happen, depending upon what Mel did.

When we arrived at the Beckley's, Mel and Liz were already there and the table was set for dinner. It looked like we were going to have more than just soup and dessert like the last time. Karen asked us to come directly to the table.

I anticipated another Liminal Plunge group meeting with many surprises. I was not disappointed.

As soon as we had taken our seats Deb open a Bible and read the last supper passage from I Corinthian 11:23-26. Then she asked us to join her in prayer. It was a prayer of thanks for our forgiveness and for the food we were about to eat.

Karen then said, "Deb just read that whenever we eat and drink together we are to remember Jesus' love for us. As we eat could each of us share something that he or she remembers about a time when you experienced Jesus' love for you?"

She began with a story about a time that she felt so sad and lonely just after her father had died and as she prayed she sensed Jesus' presence and her emotions were flooded with an assurance that she would never be alone.

We began to eat and as we ate and drank we all shared memories that revealed God's quiet and deep desire for us to know that he loved us. It was one of the most encouraging times of worship that I had ever had.

We then gathered in the Great Room.

Stan got our attention and explained that since there was a lot for us to talk about that he had made an agenda. I think I heard an almost audible moan come from Jorge. Stan apologized for letting his business style invade the group but that he was anxious that we would not cover everything and get side tracked with small talk. He also asked our forgiveness for feel a need to be in control. He confessed he didn't know what to do with his fear of no control or structure and asked for us to please accept his lack of trust and he passed out the agenda.

I couldn't keep from laughing a little and I said, "Sounds just like me. I know what you mean and I don't think God is offended one bit. Let's see what is on your agenda. Maybe God help you put it together."

The agenda had six topics, none of which anyone objected to.

After we had a chance to look at the agenda Stan asked if anyone had anything else to add to it. I said I wanted to say something about our relationship with churches as a whole. Jorge said he wanted to say something about a concern he and Misha had been talking about. Liz said we should make sure we gave some time before we left for prayer. Stan wrote down the additional agenda items. He then said that it looked to him that the first two things on the agenda, 'Scripture Reflection' and 'Personal Sharing' had already been covered. Maybe God was in control. We all smiled and Stan continued, "So, the next agenda item. James, any word on Kara?"

"As a matter of fact, yes. I was able to track down Kara's husband, Father Witherspoon. He is an Episcopal priest serving a church in San Francisco. He told me Kara was killed in a car accident two years ago. He said they have three children, all boys, now ages, nine, seven, and five. He sounded very objective and professional, like he was reporting on someone other than his family. I also searched the internet and found several enlightening newspaper articles. One was about Father Whitherspoon coming out of the closest as a gay priest who had a male partner in addition to his wife. Another, about his Bishop applauding his honesty and integrity, and affirming his leadership of his congregation. And another reporting on Kara's accident. It reported that her car went off a cliff. She did not have on her seat belt and upon impact she was thrown from the car, hit her head on the rocks and died. There were no signs of skid marks, and an autopsy report showed that she had alcohol blood level of .35 in her system when she died. She was the only person in the car. It also mentioned that she was a recovering alcoholic with thirteen years of sobriety."

"That sounds like she committed suicide." Liz blurted.

"The article did not draw any conclusion." James continued. "Her husband called it an accident. As I read between the lines, I suspect she couldn't handle her husband having a gay partner. What I think happened is that she relapsed, went on a binge, and the alcohol killed her. I guess you could call it suicide. What ever happened, it is sad, for real."

After a long minute of silence, Misha said, "Can we pray for her kids, right now?"

We all bowed our heads and Misha prayed what I thought was an inspired pray for the kids protection from sex and drug addiction and for God's healing and redemption in the loss of their mother. She ended with a prayer for Father Witherspoon.

After the Amen, Stan thanked James, took a deep breath, and said. "Ok, let me now report on my Board and managers meeting."

He said that he had met with his Board and managers on Wednesday. It would take about a month to work out a settlement for him to sell his and Karen's shares of stock.

He then asked if anyone had had any further thoughts about how to use the money that would result from the sale.

Thinking James might have a suggestion about his work in Haiti, I glance over at him, but it looked like his mind was a mile away. He was now staring out the window in deep thought.

Jorge recalled that at the last meeting Liz suggested creating a Foundation.

Misha said, "It makes sense to me that that is the only way to insure it gets used for the children of poverty."

Stan asked if anyone had any other ideas.

Mel then said, "Creating a Foundation sounds right to me."

I echoed, "Me too."

Everyone looked around at each other and it appeared settled. We would create a Foundation. Stan verbalized what we all sensed. "A Foundation it is. And if my projections are correct we will be able to start the Foundation with about five hundred million dollars."

Jorge's jaw literally dropped open at the mention of so much money.

The room seemed to have had the air sucked out of it. It was as though someone had just locked us all inside an air tight vault. The enormity of what was happening hit us all at the same time. We all seemed to begin to take slow deliberate breaths. I think we were beginning to realize that Stan and Karen's surrender of their company was about to radically change all of our lives. Not that we were becoming wealthy but that we were about to share in distributing wealth. We were about to accept a lot, I mean a lot, of responsibility. Something about how I felt made me think maybe this is the way God want us to feel all the time about what it means to be his children. He has given all of his creation to share with each other, for the healing of others.

Stan recognized our state of shock and added, "That may seem like a lot of money and it is. I realize that it is a responsibility that we are now going to share with all of you, but I also believe God has given it to us so that we can participate in saving children's lives. The hardest part and maybe the risky part, is for us all to please keep this a secret until after it happens. Please do not breathe a word of this to your kids, parents, closest friends, not anyone. Ok! Please!"

Another slow breath with a long exhale.

Stan continued, "Of course there are a lot of detail for which we need God's direction. One thing at a time. Right now I think we should take this coming week to pray about what the mission of the Foundation should be and then use next week's meeting to come up with a Mission Statement. Does that sound right to everyone?"

"Can we take a minute right now to have some silence and each of us listen to what we think God wants?" Deb asked.

"Of course." replied Stan.

It was quiet and as we prayed silently it felt like fresh air filled the room again. After several minutes we all just lifted our heads about the same time and gave a relaxed smile to each other.

"I think God just said that it is all going to be OK." said Liz. "Am I right?"

We all made signs of affirmation and Stan said "Great!"

Stan then moved us on to the next thing on the agenda, which was Mel's report on his plans for relating to his church.

Mel told the group about our lunch conversation almost a month ago at Lew's place. He said he had prayed about it a lot and believed that God did want him to resign as pastor and also as a member. He said that what I had told him then was right too. God did not want him to leave the church. He said that he would simply be honest about what was happening, let go of any sense of control, and turn his concerns toward service and mission. After resigning as pastor he would only support that part of Apple Orchard that was reaching out. He would not support church programs that were discussions that did not lead to mission. And he would not support the buildings, staffing, or anything except making Jesus known through acts of mercy and justice and proclaiming the love of God in Jesus. He concluded by adding, "That is if you all confirm this and believe with me that this is from the Lord."

What he said had a ring of truth to me and it also made me feel rather uncomfortable. The thing that excited me the most was his request that we all confirm his sense of God's will. What made me uncomfortable was that if I confirmed what Mel was proposing for himself I was going to have to look more closely at my relationship to the church.

Stan wisely suggested that we again pause for a minute and pray.

He then, after almost exactly a minute of silence, said he supposed we should first hear what Liz thinks.

Liz said, "Oh, Mel and I have been talking and praying about this for a couple of weeks and he wouldn't have brought it to the group if I wasn't of one mind and heart with him. Yes, I think he should resign as pastor and we should both resign as members and that we should stay at the church and seek only the Kingdom of God; no more institutional wrappings."

We then went around the circle and everyone agreed. When it was my turn it took some courage but I couldn't deny it was the right thing for Mel and Liz to do. I also thought to myself, I bet their kids will really be happy about this too.

As we went around the circle I was interested to hear how Jorge and Misha would respond because I thought it could make them feel put on the spot a little since they were also on a church staff. But it didn't seem to faze them. When it came to Misha's turn she simply said, "Amen", without any comment, as did Jorge after her.

Mel expressed his gratitude and then shared the process for his resignation.

Stan then stated that the next thing on the agenda was the report of the women's lunch.

Karen said the women had designated her as the report person. She told us they continued discussing their confusion about the church. Basically, they agreed that what they had experienced all their lives fell far short of what they would expect the Body of Christ on earth to be.

Karen went on and said that they agreed it should be made up of believers who loved each other the way Jesus loved them, friends who supported and cared for each other, and didn't judge each other because of different political views or even moral differences. And that they agreed that the church should be a Christ-centered community of believers whose focus is on serving others through actions and words of forgiveness and grace. But she said they could not figure out how the church could be structured so that it didn't become self-serving.

As she spoke we could see Mel getting excited and wanting to interrupt. Finally, he could not retrain himself any longer and when Karen took her next breath he blurted out. "You are soooo right. Our thinking has been conditioned by the scientific method. But the church is not a logical deduction. It is about relationship. Western Christendom has replaced a relationship with the Father, Son, and Holy Spirit with an enlightened scientific formula. Don't you get it? That is why you, all of us, are having such a struggle with the whole idea of church. Our paradigm is all screwed up!"

"Yeah, right, we get it." Jorge said with some sarcasm. "Like we all really understood what you just said."

Deb chimed in and said, "I get it a little, I think. And that may be exciting to you Mel, but it doesn't answer our confusion about how to structure our group. How do we organize ourselves? What is the alternative to the structure of the church that we currently have? How do we live together in this world where the Kingdom of God has come, but is not yet fully here? We are confused. Is there an alternative to the organization that we currently have?"

Mel answer. "I don't have an answer but this thought came to me. You know, the word, ecclesia, which is translated in the Bible as church, does not mean what we think of as church, like the church building or an organization or institutional structure at all. It means a gathering of people, and assembly or a community. Maybe that helps, maybe not. Just a thought.

I finally said, "Maybe we need to pray and expect God to show us something new."

We prayed. This time with rather lame, not very articulate prayers. Each person struggling to find words, like when you sometime pray for someone who is facing an incurable disease and you don't want to offer pat optimism. But you also don't want to pray with gloom and doom. Stan ended the prayer time with, "God, grant us the serenity to accept the things we cannot change, the courage to change the things we can, and the wisdom to know the difference." And then added, "Lord, we are surrendered to you, we don't need to be in control, we just need to know what steps to take next. Amen."

I thought, *sometime the best prayers are groans and moans.*

Stan continued. "It is now after 9:00 p.m. and we agreed to leave some time before we leave to report on our kids and pray. Mel and Liz, if you don't mind, can you fill us all in on what is happening with your kids since last week when you and Odell left for the police station. I know, most of us, have been in touch but I think it would be helpful if you could bring us all up to date. How should we pray this week?"

Mel looked at Liz as if to say, 'you talk'.

Liz reported that she and Mel had attended Naranon with Deb and me on Thursday night and that it had really helped her to trust God to be in charge of Elijah. Mel agreed. They said the treatment program at Walcott had Elijah on a 'black out' and that he was not allowed to talk to anyone for the first two weeks. Mel then reported that he'd had his second dinner date with Andi on Thursday night and that it was really helpful for both of them to share their fears about Elijah. He also reported that Andi was going to go to Naranon with them next Thursday.

I asked Deb to report on our kids and she shared the first week of school seemed to go well for Billy. He liked soccer practice and had meet several guys on the soccer team that he seemed to hit it off with. She also said that our twins seemed to be back into the school routine and that all seemed normal with Jimmy. I added that Jim seemed to be relating to Jenn like he always had and that Jenn didn't seem to be worried about him. I asked everyone to continue to pray for Jim because I knew from my teen years how easy it was look one way at home while at the same time living a gang life on the street.

Karen asked us to pray for Brenda. She seemed to be more withdrawn than usual and not as excited about school starting as she had always been in the past. Stan said he thought that maybe she was worried about him quitting his business.

Misha said everything was fine with their twins. They were in their junior year and had their group of friends that were good kids; for which they were really grateful.

Stan then ask us to pray for the smooth sale of their interest in the company.

Mel asked us to pray for him as he prepared to talk to the church.

We then spent the next half hour taking turns praying. As we left for home we were again blown-away with what God was doing in all our lives.

Twenty Four

As we just turning out of the Beckley's driveway Jorge said. "I suppose I should have share a concern that Misha and I have at the meeting but I really didn't see a place to fit it in. Can we at least share it with you three anyway?"

"Of course!" I answered. "What is the problem?"

"Well, as you are aware, since before Misha and I got married we have been reaching out to kids on the streets of Homewood. In these twenty years or more we have gotten to be close friends with many others who have also been seeking to serve people on the streets. Just like you and Deb have, 'O'. Some people who work with streets people have been doing it as an expression of God's love in Jesus. Some have been doing it simply because they care about people in need. We have all seen a lot of trauma, pain, suffering, and heart ache. Two years ago, in one year, I conducted seventeen funerals for kids that had been shot by other kids. We have also watched kids die of an over dose of drugs and from AIDS. Many of our friends who are providers of services to the homeless have known and been close to mentally ill friends who have committed suicide."

"I know that is true." Interjected Deb.

Jorge continued. "As a result of experiencing close up, all the pain, suffering, and trauma of so many others, we ourselves suffer from a kind of, what is called secondary post-traumatic stress disorder. It creeps up on all of us who are so close to suffering and we don't realize it until we get sick or depressed. It is more than simple burn-out, it is a kind of compassion fatigue or empathy exhaustion. We haven't identified it yet in ourselves but we have seen the result in many of our friends. Misha and I sat down this week and listed about seven people who we know, who have been direct care providers of the poor and that have died or gotten a fatal disease in their thirties and forties. You guys know some of them too. And from what we have learned, we think their shortened life can be directly connected to the intense stress of being so close to so much pain, suffering, and tragedy.

"We think that part of the reason this happens is because front line care providers of the poor are some of the least paid servants in the caring professions and they cannot afford to take periodic breaks to recover and be restored. On top of vicariously experiencing the trauma of others they have the personal experience of their own stressful lives trying to make ends meet and raise a family."

Misha added. "Catholic religious orders must have recognized this stress toll many years ago because they almost all require and provide time for Nuns and Priests to take a spiritual retreat on a regular basis. But low paid providers for the poor can't afford such self-care and spiritual renewal."

Jorge went on. "Misha and I have this vision of creating a way for these providers to learn to take care of themselves and to get away for periodic times of rest and renewal, maybe even have available for them counselors who would be trained to help them process and recover from the secondary trauma that they are experiencing every day. Almost like the kind of help soldiers coming home from war need if they are going to ever be emotionally, relationally, and spiritual healthy."

"I know what you mean." I said. "I know a number of recovering addicts who had many years clean and where involved as outreach staff to those suffering from addiction. Over time, because of lack their resources to take a break and some rest the physical damage that was a consequence of their past life took its toll and they developed heart problems, not to mention, diseased livers, diabetes, and cancers. All health issues that may have caught up to them eventually but because they had so much stress without a break their health problems attacked them prematurely. If they had been able to have a less stressful daily experiences, they may have grown in health rather than become a victim of their disease.

"Well, we need help to figure out what to do. First, we need Misha and I need to learn how to take care of ourselves. Second we need help to discern what God is saying to us through what we are realizing."

Deb answered, "We can pray!"

"I can do that." I said. "And I would encourage you to mention this to the others when we get together at the picnic."

James then added. "I would like to pray about this right now."

James prayed a beautiful pray for God's leading and sustaining in Jorge, Misha, and all of our lives.

Monday was Labor Day, the kids didn't have school, and the Health Care Center was closed. Deb went grocery shopping, did some laundry, and cleaned the house. Jenn, Jim, and Billy just hung out; except for Billy taking an extra-long run. I ran some errands, cut the grass, and spent about two hours reading my Bible, looking for stuff that I was familiar with in the Twelve Steps and Twelve Traditions. Around 5:00 p.m. I grilled some chicken on the grill and we had a quiet family picnic.

One of the things Deb and I had done with Jenn and Jimmy since they were small was to spend time at the dinner table each night after dinner having each of us share a High, a Low, and a Hope from the day. We hadn't been doing it so regularly in the past couple of years as all of our schedules didn't allow for our family to have regular consistent evening meals together. So, to introduce Billy to our tradition and since none of us had anywhere to go, I suggested we do High, Low, and Hope; but instead of reviewing the day, reviewing the first week of school. Jenn and Jim reluctantly agreed.

Jenn went first. Her high was just getting back to school and seeing all her friends. Her low was realizing that the summer was really over. Her hope was that Billy found some friends.

Jim was next. His high was being glad that the summer was over and that school was starting so his life would have some structure. I thought that was interesting since I was assuming structure was the last thing he was looking for. Maybe my suspicions about starting to live two lives were wrong. His high also made me wonder if it was a con or if he was really hoping to distance himself from the gang bangers. His low was seeing a number of his friends including Billy going out for soccer and it being too late for him to try out. His hope was that the Steelers would win their opening game against Cleveland that coming Sunday.

Billy then shared that his high was meeting a lot of new people at school. His low was feeling a little on the outside at soccer practice. His hope was making the soccer team.

Deb said her high was the lunch she had with the LP wives. Her low, learning that a long time patient to whom she was close, had advanced metastatic ovarian cancer. Her hope was that Mel would meet with a good response from his congregation when he told them this week that he was resigning.

I said my high was our LP group meeting, my low was feeling some guilt about the waves of doubt and anxiety for real change, and my hope was for what God would do as a result of the trip to Haiti.

When we were done sharing it struck me that there was no mention of the discussion about the Beckley's wealth.

The Carr's Labor Day was much more emotional and intense than was ours. Liz was worried to death about Eli and couldn't stop being anxious for him. It would be another week before they could talk to him. She couldn't wait for the Naranon meeting on Thursday night.

Mel spent the day making phone calls and setting up a meeting with the Elders and Trustee of Apple Orchard Church.

Andi was the only one who seemed to be relaxed. She spend most of the day reading, texting, and watching TV.

Karen Beckley started the day off getting in a fight with Brenda. It started at about 11:00 AM when Brenda, just getting up and showing herself in the kitchen, asked her mom what was for dinner. Karen had answered that she was not sure, that maybe they would ask the Carrs over for a spontaneous picnic. That led to Brenda saying something, in a sarcastic loud voice about how maybe they should have the whole LP group move in with them. Stan was coming into the kitchen to get a third cup of coffee when she was waxing her sarcasm. He stopped her and asked what was going on. Karen said that Brenda was feeling threatened by all the changes that where happening. Brenda screamed that she didn't know what she was talking about, forget it, whatever happened with dinner was fine with her, and left the room crying. Stan told Karen to just leave her alone for a while and he went back to his office. Karen was left there not knowing what to do but she couldn't just let Brenda go to her room in tears. So after a few minutes she went to up to see how Brenda was doing. When she got upstairs and was walking down the hall towards Brenda's room she could hear her talking on the phone, so she waited outside her door and listened. Brenda was saying, "They're crazy, they want to give all our money away and move to Haiti, I think. They are both going through some kind of mid-live crisis. And these people that I have never seen in my life are as crazy as them. I think they are forming some kind of a cult. I am scared and I don't know what to do. My whole life is about to fall apart. It is all so insane."

There was a pause, like Brenda was listening to whomever was on the phone, and then she said, "Thank you, grandma, for listening. Can you please talk to them? I love you, bye."

Grandma, was Karen's mother. Her name was Ruth Bowlick. She grew up the only child of a Pittsburgh steel worker's family and was a 'speak your mind', blue collar, Pittsburgher. She had a great sense of humor, was very accepting and everyone loved her.

Karen decided not to go into Brenda's room and went back down stairs.

Brenda stayed in her room, talking on the phone with friends most of the day and then finally came down about 4:00 p.m. to see what was going to happen for dinner.

Karen simply said they were going to have cold cuts out by the pool.

Stan had spent the day in his office sorting out papers and getting ready for meetings with some accountants, lawyers, and his top management. He was in the pool when Brenda came out with her suit on and got in the water.

After about ten minutes Karen came out for a swim too. The three of them swam in silence for about ten minutes and then they all got out of the pool, first Karen, then Brenda, and finally Stan. As Stan was drying off, Karen's mother came out of the house.

Karen's dad had died of a heart attack about seven years earlier and her mom, at Stan and Karen's encouragement, had bought a house about two miles from Karen. They had always been very close and Brenda just adored her Grandma Ruth. Grandma Ruth was a "'what you see is what you get', no nonsense kind of a person. She told you like it is but you never ever felt judged or less loved by her. She could strongly disagree with you but you knew she respected you and respected what you thought. You could trust her and you knew that she cared about and loved you.

Grandma Ruth would just drop in unexpected almost any time; but this day Karen had called her after hearing Brenda on the phone and asked her to come over. As this attractive stout 70 year old came out toward the pool, the timing couldn't have been more right.

As she emerged Grandma Ruth loudly said, "OK, now what's going on, I heard you guys are getting too big for your britches. I've always thought Stan was on kind of wacky and from what Brenda tells me, I was right. You should have never married that religious nut, Karen. But I guess he did help make a beautiful granddaughter and he makes lots of money. Brenda, what were you trying to tell me this morning?"

Brenda felt safe now and was almost laughing. "Like you don't know Grandma. I'll bet mom has told you everything about what they are up to, about their meetings, and the picnic a couple of weeks ago. And I'm sure you know about how Dad's friends went to Africa when he was in high school. Can you please talk some sense into my parents?"

"Honey, your dad is one of the smartest, sanest, reliabilist men I know. He is a good man and your Mom is a wonderful woman. They are doing nothing crazy and they'll will leave you and me high and dry without any money. Maybe, they're just, finally, getting their priorities straight."

"What do you mean, Grandma?" Brenda asked.

"I mean, Honey, that there are a lot of things more important than money. A lot of things, like you, and me, and world peace, and ice cream, and birds, and the mountains, and the oceans, and just being together and eating cold cut sandwiches. You know what I mean? Maybe your Mom and Dad are going through a mid-live crisis. Sometimes we all need a crisis to brake our apathy. Yeah, your Mom has been telling me what is going on with them. I don't think you need to worry about it. And I like what it is doing to your Mom."

"But what about me. What is going to happen to me?" And Brenda started to cry again.

Ruth walked over to Brenda and wrapped her arms around her – getting her slacks and shirt all wet – and hugged her for several minutes. Then she said, "Like I said, don't worry about what will happen to you or me or them. We'll all do the next best right thing and we'll love each other."

Brenda had stopped crying but was still sniffing, and said, "How do I explain what is happening to my friends? I don't know what to expect. Until a couple of months ago my life was pretty predictable. Now, I don't know what is going to happen next."

Ruth let go of Brenda and held her at arm's length. They were both about the same height. She looked her in her eyes, wiped away some tears on her checks and said, "No one knows what will happen next, ever. Next is not what's important. Now is what's important."

Then her Mom said, "True friends, like Grandma, will always be true friends."

Her Dad then spoke and said, "Brenda, I love you. As we try to figure out what is next we want you know that what is best for you will always come first when making changes. I guess we haven't said that. Sorry, I assumed you would know that but I suppose the way we have been acting has been pretty alarming to you. Do not worry honey, we want what is best for you most of all. Some things may be hard to explain to your friends, just like it is going to be hard to explain for your mom to her friends and for me to my friends. We will just have to do the best we can. And it probably would help you if we all could be honest and share what we think about anything. Isn't it refreshing how Grandma just says it right out sometimes? And we can take it and she can take our disagreement because we know we love each other. Know, honey, that we love you!"

"But honey," Ruth interrupted. "I gets in trouble sometimes because I can say some things before I have showed people that I care, that can hurt them. Take it from me, always try to think before you speak. Like I just thought – what's there to eat? I could have put on my swimming suit and showed off my varicose veins and gorgeous figure, but I came over to eat.

Brenda smiled and strutted down the pool side showing off her trim young body.

The Cruz family went over to Misha's parents for a family picnic on Labor Day and invited James to join them.

James spent the following day with his secret roommate.

Rita had moved in the last week of August. James was in his glory both with her and with hope of big bucks from the group. At the same time he felt a growing ache in his spirit over his deceit. Also as James and Rita got to know one another they each shared with each another their hope and desire to one day they wanted to be very wealthy. Neither of them thought that the desire for wealth was any different from almost everyone they had ever met. Rita then began to fanaticize about how they might steal the money that James was raising for the orphanage. She shared her musings with James and a plan began to take root. He would get Rita a job at the orphanage as the business manager, they would disappear with the money, and live happily ever after on an island in the Caribbean. At first they both just fantasized and joked about such a scam and neither felt serious about it. But the more they shared their dreams of wealth out loud, the more they began to get seriously seduced by such a dream. Rita then began to a scheme to use their physical relationship to keep James focused on stealing the money. James thought he could keep Rita interested in him by keeping her focused on the money. Their scam plan grew and developed. All James had to do was to make sure Rita's existence stayed a secret from the LP group.

After Rita moved in with James she began to have her regular get together times with Marcie so they could maintain their friendship. Marcie shared with Rita her discovery of God's love in Jesus and her decision to daily seek Jesus' presence in her life. Not long afterwards they began to meet with Patty to study the Bible and talk about what it meant to follow Jesus. At first Rita felt good about this Bible Study because it would help prevent any suspicions about their scheme when she moved to Haiti.

Twenty Five

The 10th grade counselor, Ms. Rogers, had made an appointment with Billy to see how he was adjusting. Billy's appointment ended early, so he was early getting to the cafeteria for lunch. He arrived just as the ninth graders were leaving. He happened to pass Jenn and Jim in the hall and said hi. He felt good about his new family but it made him miss his African friends. And his heart was aching with the absence of his mom and dad and brother and sister.

Deb had packed him a lunch so he just got a Coke and went to sit down. It was only about 30 seconds when the bell rang for the 10th grade lunch and change of classes. As the kids came swarming into the lunch room, it seemed everyone knew his or her self-assigned seats. During the first week of school he had swarmed in with them and each time found an empty seat at a table with someone he had just met, but on this day he was seated first and sat alone at a table. No one came to sit with him. He was deep into his feelings of loss. At first he really didn't notice that he was still alone. When he did notice he thought it was just as well because he didn't really feel like talking to anyone anyway.

As he sat there slowly eating his peanut butter sandwich and sipping on his Coke he overheard some kids at the table behind him. One of the kids was saying, "Oh, that is that new kid who has been adopted by Jimmy Ogden's parents. It's weird, he is white and they are black. And he has an odd accent. I think he is from South Africa. He is strange too, acts like a nerd but doesn't look like one. I'm going to stay away from him. And I think he could be in trouble if Jimmy becomes part of the Henley posse."

Then he heard another kid respond by saying, "Have you noticed that he is really quiet. I don't think he has ever been to school. I heard that he is real religious and his parents were missionaries who sent him back to the States because they don't have school in the country were they were. They were living there in order to convert the illiterate pagans in the jungles."

"Yeah, maybe he hardly knows English." speculated another kid.

Billy just listened and wondered what other rumors were going around. It made him miss his African home more than ever.

When the bell ran for the twenty minute 10th grade lunch period to be over, Billy refrained himself from saying something sarcastic in Swahili to the kids at the table behind him. He went to the gym where the rooster was to be posted of those who made the boys soccer team. The posting wasn't up yet and he realized he would have to wait another forty minutes until the 11th and 12th grade lunches were over. So, he went on to his Study Hall.

When the bell rang to end his Study Hall Billy hurried back to the gym. When he got there, most of the kids trying out for soccer were crowded around the bulletin board. Not only was there a posing of those who made the team but also what were their positions for each of two squads. Everyone was quietly talking to each other, some excited, some upset, some just listening. When Billy got to the board he saw his name posted as center midfielder for the Blue Squad. Nobody said anything to him and he just walked through the crowd to go to his next class. He was really happy inside but didn't feel he could share his excitement with anyone. As he walked down the hall, all he could do was pump his fist down by his side.

At soccer practice after school he seemed to get a stone cold shoulder from everyone in the locker room. Wondering what this was all about, he spoke to Steve, the kid whose locker was next to his. He hoped he could develop a friendship with him. He asked him why no one was even saying "hi" to him and why the locker room got so quiet when he came in. Steve said many of the guys had been playing soccer together since they were little kids and that Billy had taken away the position that Carl had had since they had all started playing soccer together when they were little kids. He told him Carl was thinking about quitting the team and half the team was really upset because of the change. Billy thanked Steve and started to go toward the field.

One of the assistant coaches was standing at the locker room door to keep the kids from exiting. Everyone stood there in silence. When most had gathered, the head coach, Mr. Thomson, came out of his office and directed all the kids to go back to the meeting area in the locker room and have a seat. All twenty five kids who made the team were present. They sat there looking up at the coach. The three assistant coaches stood behind him and off to the side. Billy was sitting by himself behind the other kids.

Coach Thomson gave a warm welcome of congratulations to everyone and then laid out the ground rules and expectations for practice and his strategy for the season.

As they walked out to the field, Carl, one of the leaders on the team from past years, laid back until Billy caught up to him, Carl stuck out hand and they shook hands. That simple jester made Billy feel good, but no one else said a word to him. He thought it was hard to tell what anyone was thinking and even though as new kid he still felt a little shunned by the other guys, he felt good about being on the team.

The woman met for what was becoming their standing Tuesday lunch at Panera. Karen could not join them. She had a previously scheduled luncheon at the Club.

Karen was part of a women's charity group call the Flowers of Heaven. Their objective was to do charity events to raise money for the Make-a-Wish Foundation. The last event they held was a Woman's Golf Tournament. Tammie Harris co-host for Dancing with the Stars was their speaker at the dinner following the tournament. They had raised forty thousand dollars for Make-a-Wish. Karen was Chairwoman for this year's planning committee and this Tuesday was their fall planning meeting. They were hoping to plan a Christmas Fashion show.

When Karen got to the club she was the last one of the eight women on the committee to arrive. Everyone, including Karen, looked like they were auditioning to be in the fashion show. Karen had on a bright yellow business suit complete with a large brim hat. Several of the woman greeted her with ceremonial air kisses and they sat down. Their lunch orders had been called in with their reservations and their salads and drink were already at their table. There were even name cards for where they were to sit.

As they took their seat, Karen remain standing. She paused for a second to pray. Then she called the meeting to order and opened the meeting by passing out an agenda.

Then as she facilitate the reading of the minutes, financial report, and sub-committee reports, she felt more and more like she just did not belong there. She wasn't sure what her feelings were all about. Make-a-Wish was a wonderful organization.

It made a lot of deserving kids enjoy an experience that was not otherwise available to them, and for some an experience that could be their last. Why was she feeling like she wanted to get out of there? She looked around at these women and the surroundings and she almost started to feel sick. Maybe she was getting a flu bug. It was getting to be that time of year and she hadn't gotten her flu shot yet. Two other thought popped into her mind. Why did they have to put on these events? If the fifty women or so who came to them just gave the money they won't have to endure all the phony socializing. And she could be in Africa or Haiti putting her energy into feeding people who were starving instead of sitting in this opulent setting spending twenty five dollars for food that would do her body more harm than good. Then she began to feel guilty for having such judgmental thoughts. She was so perplexed about what was going on inside of her. These thoughts were all so new to her and in some ways surprising.

She finished running through the routine business of the agenda and was hoping to sit down and start on her salad. She felt herself wishing the meeting was over so she could leave. There was a realization stirring within her that she had a lot of latent guilt about not being true to her heart for many years. But this was not the time or the place to vent her feelings so she pushed past them. As she started to think about introducing a discussion about were to have the fashion show one of the woman anticipated what was coming next and asked the group what they thought about using Heinz Field as the venue for the fashion show.

Karen sat down to eat and felt relieved that someone else was showing some interest and that she did not have to keep the meeting on task.

Someone asked if anyone had any contacts with the Steeler's front office.

As the discussion continued Karen returned to her musing about the strange new feelings she was having. One of the things she also realized was that most of her feelings had been always been there underneath the surface and it sort of felt good to be getting in touch with them, maybe for the first time. Her guilt began to be lifted as she could see that she was entering a new life of freedom to follow Jesus.

She took a deep sigh of relief and moved forward with facilitating the meeting.

When the agenda was completed and all the sub-committee had their assignments for the meeting in December and as the as the chocolate cheese cake was being served, Karen said, "I am afraid I won't be able to attend our December meeting. I am going with some friends to Haiti. It would also probably be best if Mary took over as Chair for the Fashion Show because I am not sure what I will be doing next Spring. Stan and I are going through some changes."

"Oh, we are so sorry, Karen." responded one of the women. "I remember how hard it was for me when I got my first divorce. It will get better, honey. Just make sure you get at least have of what he's worth."

Karen quickly replied, "Oh, we are more in love than ever. We are not getting a divorce. We are just looking to realign our priorities and commitments. You might say we are undergoing a character adjustment. You see some close friends of ours who were missionaries in Sudan were killed. In our shook and sadness it has made us look at what is really important to us. The truth is, we, or maybe I should say, I am feeling like I am having a mask ripped off of me by our friends' tragedy and I am discovering a person under that mask that I really like. I want that person to come out and be free. Out of a fear of being rejected the person I have been is someone who has pretended to have it all together. Almost my whole life I have worn a mask of respectability and felt angry at being somebody who had to perform. I am now starting to feel release from that fear and anger and want to be someone who isn't so wrapped up with herself. This place and this suit are not really me."

Mary said, "Karen, I will be happy to fill in for you while you recover from your grief, but I expect you will be back to lead us again. It is understandable that you are angry at God. You know we are not all really as self-absorbed as you are describing yourself. I am sure God will get you back on track."

Karen thought, *I think I have hit a nerve,* but she said, "Thank you Mary, you are right. Only God knows what to do with me and I expect it will be all good. And thank you all for listening. I hope you can understand. I am just speaking about what I am experiencing. Like a friend of mine told me, when you share your story with other don't talk about theirs, just share your experience, strength, and hope.

The ladies all gave weak nods. Karen, noticed that one of the woman got a little twinkle in her eye which made her wonder if she was familiar with recovery jargon. Maybe she was in recovery and thought Karen was an alcoholic who was drying to stop drinking too. She wanted explain but let it go.

Everyone had finished her cheese cake and starting with Mary they all got up to leave.

Back at Panera while Karen was with the Flowers of Heaven, Misha, Liz, and Deb were having their Tuesday lunch time together without her. After sharing their uneventful Veterans

Day, Liz, almost through tears, thanked Misha and Deb for their acceptance of her.

"I have been so lonely for so long, always feeling like I am playing a role. It is such a relief to feel like I can be myself and you still accept me. Thank you, thank you so much. You don't know how good it makes me feel." she said.

"I think acceptance is what everyone is looking for," stated Misha. "Isn't it weird how when we strive for acceptance by putting on a mask we just isolate ourselves; but when we start to care about caring for each other and are honest about our own insecurities we discover we are accepted."

"Yeah, you know, like if we care about others more than ourselves then we are the ones who benefit the most." added Misha.

"Thank you!" said Liz. "I think that no matter what, if we want our friendship to grow we need to stay real. We have to be committed to staying honest and open with each other. Maybe the most important thing in being the church is establishing relationships that share sins and insecurities and fears and mistakes and stuff like that."

"I can hear that." responded Misha.

Deb added, "It is what makes us a spiritual body. And, I think it is what enables us to hear God's voice through His Body."

"And when we lose that intimacy we become prey to the deceitful values of our self-centered world." added Liz.

"Aren't we the fountains of wisdom?" Misha announced with a laugh.

"Yep, out of the mouths of babes," Liz added. And they all laughed.

"Speaking of being honest, I need your prayers." continued Liz after the laughter subsided. "Tomorrow night Mel is going to meet with his elders and staff and resigning as pastor and as a member of the church. I am anxious for him and for me. I am afraid a lot of people are not going to understand and be upset. And that some of our old friends will feel rejected and betrayed. I don't want to be rejected and I don't want anyone to be hurt. I'm also concerned about Mel relationship with Elijah. Eli has told his counselor at Walcott that he doesn't want to talk to him and Mel feels shut out, like he has lost his son. He is hurting. We both are. Maybe the Naranon meeting Thursday night will help."

Deb asked, "How is Andi doing?"

"Oh, she is the one bright spot right now. Thank God for her." answered Liz.

"Odell is anxious about Jimmy too. And so am I. And I worry about Billy adjusting to all the changes in his life," Deb said thoughtfully.

"Jorge and I need your prayers, too. We are so confused about our future and afraid if we stop doing youth ministry at the church that my parents will feel like we are abandoning the church and the kids. I just wish God would give us some direction for how we can follow him without getting rejected by my parents and the church. Maybe we can still do the kids thing and also figure out how to address our discovery of premature deaths due to compassion fatigue like we spoke about Sunday night. It's confusing. Maybe this whole direction about questioning the church and culture is all wrong. Or maybe I am just still afraid of my parent's rejection."

The three women were quiet for a minute. It was as though they all knew there weren't any answers for each other and yet at the same time there was a sense of it being okay not to have answers. No one felt like she wasn't being listened to by the others. Just getting their fears and confusion out on the table gave them hope.

While they were silent, the waitress brought their check.

Liz finally said a short prayer of thanks. They all expressed their commitment to pray for each other. They paid their bills, gave each other a hug and went home.

In the parking lot, Liz remembered they needed to plan for Sunday night meeting and yelled out to the others that she would call them about planning for the group.

As soon as I got to work on Tuesday I called Mel and asked him if we could have breakfast the next day. I wanted to get his input regarding the application of the Traditions of the 12 Step Program to the Church. He agreed. H then told me that he was going to submit his resignation letter to the Apple Orchard Elders and Trustee at a meeting he had called for tomorrow night and that he would also like to review it with me. We decided to meet at Ritter's. It felt really good that Mel would respect my input.

Around the same time that Billy was meeting with his counselor, Mel got a call from Eli's counselor at the Walcott Center. He told Mel that Eli was cooperating with all the rules and reluctantly attending all the meetings, and so his black out period was being been cut short to two weeks. He could have visitors for the first time on Saturday afternoon. However, when asked to make a list of who he wanted to see he did not list him Mel. He did put down his mother. The counselor told Mel that Eli said he was not ready to talk to his dad. He said

Eli had not told the counselor what he was feeling but even if he had, the counselor could not tell Mel without Eli permission. The counselor tried to console Mel but Mel's mind was being controlled by his heart and he did not hear another word the counselor said. Mel told him thanks and that Liz would be calling that afternoon to make an appointment for her to visit Eli on Saturday.

Mel hung up, turned back to what he was reading and found the page was all blurry through the tears that had formed on his eyes.

Twenty Six

Wednesday, September 5, 2007

It was in the low fifties as Billy and I went for our morning run. Our pattern had become running two miles at my pace and then he would pick it up and I would keep on prodding along. Usually when I got back to the house after my five miles he would have finished his run, taken his shower, had his breakfast and was ready for school. Today was no different. We often had some good conversation during our fifteen to twenty minutes together each morning but this morning he was quieter than normal, which means he hardly said a word. I asked him what was up with his silence and all he stated was that he was learning that American teenagers where more absorbed with themselves than he had suspected. He said that kids in Africa were more concerned about each other's needs than their own even though, or maybe because, they did not expect their own needs to ever be met.

I got to the diner about five minutes before my appointed time of 8:30 a.m. Mel was already at a table with a cup of coffee. Rose showed me to the table and brought me my tea. Rose had been a fixture at the diner for twenty years. Mel ordered. Rose just nodded to me. She and I had known each other for the last ten years, and my breakfast order had always been the same: Oatmeal with brown sugar, whole wheat toast, and a cup of tea.

Mel asked how Billy was doing with school and I said I really wasn't sure but that he had made the soccer team.

I asked if he had heard anything about Eli and he told me about his call from Walcott. He and Liz were going to attend the Naranon meeting on Thursday. I apologized and told him that Deb and I would not be coming because we needed a night to just stay home. Mel also asked about Jim, to which I really had nothing to report.

Then Mel pulled out a piece of paper and asked if I would read it and tell him what I thought. I read,

> Dear leaders and members of Apple Orchard Church,
>
> About two months ago on my plane ride back from Texas I had a conversation with the passenger next to me that caused me to question my discipleship to Jesus. He was the head of a secular international business organization and it shocked me to realize that he and I were living the same lives. In the process of being your pastor and becoming wealthy and famous, I have neglected my wife and children, and most of all Jesus. I believe God wants me to pause, reevaluate my call, renew my discipleship to Him, and discover anew what it means to be His disciple. I have shared this need for transformation with Liz and we are of the same mind and heart.
>
> Therefore, as of September 30, 2007, I am resigning as your Pastor and as a member of this congregation.
>
> In the past twelve years I have been on a phenomenal journey with all of you. I hope we can continue to journey together. I have gotten distracted on this journey and I ask your forgiveness. I began with a vision for us to become a body of believers who love one another and love their neighbors as themselves. My plane conversation on the ride back from Texas made recognize that it has become an institution that has filled me with pride because of its popularity as

a successful corporation. God has confronted me with my arrogance. Over the past two months I have experienced God's forgiveness and grace like I couldn't have imagined. He has already begun to retransform me. I believe my resignation is what He desires and I hope you will not feel abandoned or judged, but will know that God is truly with you, in spite of me.

Thank you for how you all have supported and loved me and my family over these years.

Many of you are not only my friends but my extended family and I trust that will not change but only be enhanced by this decision.

I also trust that God will more than replace me. You are His children, He loves you, He will provide for you, He will nurture and discipline you, He will guide you, He will comfort you, and He will never leave you. God is not finished with Apple Orchard or any of us yet.

Your brother, In Christ,
Mel Carr

"Mel, I am not a writer, that is your gift, but I like to read and this is a good read. I think you are being honest and humble but without a "poor me" attitude or self-righteousness. Some people could feel that between the lines you are saying that Apple Orchard is not Jesus' Body and that is alright. Eventually that is going to be asked. I don't think you should hardly change anything, except maybe add something about encouraging the church to use this as an opportunity for self-evaluation."

"Good idea." replied Mel. "Thank you, I am more than a little nervous about this. I want to say the truth but I don't want to sound like I am judging the church. What Apple Orchard Church has become is mostly my doing, yet I know every one of us is responsible for his or her own decisions. I have been in denial of having been seduced by the values of our culture and have taken others with me.

I could identify with Mel's feelings of being between a rock and a hard place. I too had been at in denial about my lack of being a member of the Body of Christ. I had been viewing myself as set apart from the Church and I hadn't taking responsibility for exercising my gifts for leadership.

"Mel," I responded, "We have been so much alike, just playing to different audiences. It is time for us to try and clear the cobwebs and learn how to follow Jesus and seek His Kingdom. We need to seek the Kingdom in a fresh new way without regard to our own importance or to how we appear to any audience except Jesus. God will be with you. Don't worry too much about what to say, He will give you the right words, and He will speak to each person who is open to hear Him and only let them hear what He knows they need to hear. As they say in the rooms, 'take the best and leave the rest'."

"In the rooms? Explain."

"That is how the recovery community refers to Twelve Step meetings."

"That reminds me of why you wanted to have breakfast." said Mel. "So, you could bounce off of me what you have been thinking about the Twelve Steps and the Church. And now it is already 9:30. But to tell you the truth, I was hoping before you shared, we could first go to the 10 o'clock recovery meeting. I want to learn more of what the Twelve Step program is all about before I respond to what you want to share. At the meeting we went to three weeks ago, I was blown away by how much of it sounded like the church of the first century. Besides I need to go to a Twelve Step meeting so I learn more about how to understand what Eli is going through and learning. I hope you don't have anything you need to do right now, so we can go to that meeting, and then you can share what you have been thinking."

"That would be great," I said. I was excited that Mel wanted to go to another meeting, just not for Eli's sake but for how I wanted him to understand what I was thinking about the future of the church.

Rose brought us our checks. We paid for our breakfast and left separately planning to meet at the recovery center.

I stopped by the Heath Care Center to check any emails I might need to respond to and then walked over to the meeting. Mel had already gone in and sat down. He was talking to the man sitting next to him. I recognized him and was glad they had met. I almost felt it was like God had put them together. I sat down about two rows behind them. The meeting place was nearly full.

As I sat down, the Chair went to the podium and opened the meeting with the Serenity Prayer and proceeded with asking various people to come forward for each to read one of the readings. This was followed by the Secretary report, the General Services Representative report, and Clean Time. Next the Chair introduced Lew Hammer to come give a "lead."

I smiled to myself. The man next to Mel raised his 6'5"s frame off his seat and went to the podium.

Lew stood there for a few seconds until the meeting got quiet and then said, "Good morning family, my name is Lew and I am a grateful recovering addict. I give all honor and glory to my higher power, He put you all in my life. I used to take, now it feels good to give. My clean date is December 25, 1992. Before that date I used heroin for almost twenty years.

I grew up on the lower Hill during the fifties and sixties. I was one of four children at home plus I had three other half-brothers in the neighborhood who were my dad's kids from other relationships. Mom was at home and Dad was on the street; drinking, dealing, pimping; into everything. To say the obvious, my Dad was not around much but he did bring some money home once in a while. It was a matter of survival. My mom had been one of 12 children. Her maiden name was Sholler. My dad was one of 16. You all know, there are Hammers and Shollers all over the Black neighborhoods of Pittsburgh. When I was a kid, I had to learn how to survive too. It was me against the world, and even though I had a huge family, I felt alone and scared. Everyone seemed to be on their own. My dad was in and out of jail all the time and never seemed to be there for me. He was killed in 1970. I learned early that you do what you need to do, no matter what. I grew up knowing, like my dad, I too would steal, sell drugs, and do anything I needed survive. Other early memories I have are of parties, especially around the holidays, with everyone drinking and feeling good. I used to think as a kid and teenager, 'This is great, everyone is have a good time'.

But when they weren't drinking they were yelling and arguing. And they could be mean. But the drinking made them feel good and they acted happy. So, I grew up thinking that the fast life, drinking, selling drugs, and being totally hip and super slick was what life was all about. But inside I felt confused, and like I didn't belong. I think all I really wanted was to be accepted. Acceptance was the most important thing to me; and for me that meant being accepted by my dad and the other role models I had on the street. I wanted to be part of the Hammers.

I never liked school because I had a hard time learning. But as I have thought about school, it really wasn't that hard, it was just that I felt so much pressure from everything in my crazy family and life that I couldn't concentrate. I was just lazy about school and didn't care about learning stuff. My sister got A's and that made me feel inadequate and stupid. What motivated me was basketball because I was good at it. So, I dropped out of school in the 10th grade and spent a lot of time playing hoops at Mellon Park.

As early as 8, I was drinking, and by thirteen I was selling and using marijuana. At fifteen I had graduated to selling smack. I was also crazy for girls and liked to fight. By the time I was seventeen I was living on the street and using everything I was selling. My mom talked me into going to trade school where I became a welder. So, about the same time I became addicted to heroin I also got a well-paying job as a welder in the ship yards, building barges. At twenty I got married. So, I now had a good wife, a well-paying job, and I started to have children, but I was still searching for acceptance. And no matter how I tried I couldn't get rid of the monkey on my back. I would have problems at home and at work because of using, and during the 70's and 80's would go into detox every six months or so. I'd get clean for two weeks or a month and then start using again. I would sell drugs and use. The drugs used up my pay plus I also owed everyone. To feed my habit I would also "swoop." I would hide in dark doorways or narrow alleyways and when someone walked by who looked like they might have some money, swoop down on them and take their money.

It wasn't until 1990 when I kicked out of the house, lost my job, my wife and kids, and started sleeping under bridges that I hit bottom. One night I swooped on an undercover cop, big mistake. I was high, he was an ex-navy seal. Best thing that ever happened to me. After I got out of the hospital, Drug Court sent me to Gateway Rehabilitation Center and I finally had to admit that I was an addict. In the past, I had gone into detox to rest, catch some meals and get a break from the streets. I was always in denial. I had been shooting heroin for almost twenty year but I didn't think I had a problem. For the first time in my life I surrendered. I went in to rehab this time because it was either there or jail again; but when another patient approached me about making a connection after we got out I snapped. It was like a spiritual bolt of lightning. I "went off" on the guy and I realized I didn't want to use anymore. I started to like the meetings in this treatment facility.

My wife also played a big part in my getting clean. She came to see me and when I got out welcomed me back. I don't know how she did it. She went to meetings with me and I started going to church with her.

She died of cancer in 1993. And out of respect for me and her, her funeral was the first family gathering ever where there was no alcohol or drugs. Always in the past everyone used a funeral or any occasion to get high, but not that time. I saw that the change that God had made in my life could also make a difference in other people lives.

My wife died about 9 o'clock at night. In my anguish over her suffering and death I wanted to use again in order to escape the pain. I knew that I needed a meeting, but there weren't any late night meetings that I knew about in Pittsburgh at that time. By God's grace, I called my sponsor and he listened to a lot of pain that night. That winter was when Odell asked me to help him start a 10 o'clock at night meeting in a store front that he and others were opening for recovery meetings. I said yes and we got the first Late Nite meeting started. That experience has taught me to believe you only keep what you have by giving it away.

And that is what still motivates me. I want to help others. I find fulfillment in seeing others find a new way of life. I remember one night not long after the Late Nite meeting got started I was a little late to open the doors and when I turned the corner to where the meeting place was about 60 recovering addicts were waiting for me. I couldn't believe that God had used me to make a difference on that corner. I also remember that not too long ago how bad it used to be on that corner and how dealers were always asking everyone who walked by if they were looking for drugs. Now dealers know that corner is about recovery and new life.

I have three kids. My dad never once gave me a hug like we do `in the rooms', but I hug my kids today. Two of them are grown and out of the house. The third is my angel, she is twenty five but has the intellectual development of a five or six-year-old and requires twenty four hours a day supervision. It is such a gift to be loved by her and love and care for her. We are friends and we care for each other, and respect each other, and accept each other. We pray together each day, at meals, at bed time, when we get up, when I come home. She is often with her hands in prayer waiting for him to join her.

I spend time in prayer alone with my God every day. I still call my sponsor at least once a week. I am working the Twelve Steps for the fourth time. I sponsor others. I go to meetings. I try to be available. I have a home group. I have found I have more acceptance of myself when I care for others. People see me and see that my life has changed from being self-centered to helping others. I feel accepted by both God and you all. I play new tapes in my mind now. They used to be of using drugs and beating myself up, they are now of helping others. In the rooms I share the joy, the pain, the happiness in my live with you and you celebrate with me and care for me. Thank you!"

I knew Lew well and as he spoke I looked at Mel. Mel was looking around at the audience as they all were listening. I sensed how this tall imposing man with a gravel voice was making each one feel safe and have hope. Lew had started NA meeting all over the city. He no longer held any position in them but as he told me once he liked to be by the door to tell people they too can be helped. "My job," he told me, "is by the door, accepting people and giving a hug. I want the new comer to feel like they are home. I don't need a title or a position, my place is by the door. God loves me. God accepts me. That is more than enough for me."

Lew finished his story with, "God is in this place, miracles happen here. My name is Lew and I am not only a grateful recovering addict but a happy and free lover of God."

My eyes moved from Mel and scanned the room. I saw Jeannie, Kenny, Tisha, Michael, Sarge, John, Bo, Sissie, Millie, Terry, P.J., and many others all with expressions of acceptance and hope on their faces. They were all men and woman who were living a new way of life because of the hope that Lew had given them.

After the meeting Mel and Lew must have talked for fifteen minutes while I got caught up with a couple of guys whom I hadn't seen for maybe five years. They were both doing really well, one living in Cleveland and the other whom I hadn't seen at a day time meeting because he had a great job that was keeping him from attending. He said today was the beginning of a two week vacation for him. He was just staying around town and chillin.

It was almost noon when Mel and I left the meeting, so we decided to go across the river to Jimmy Wan's. We left Mel's car in the Recovery Center parking lot and I drove. On the way over in the car Mel shared how much he felt that he could see the Bible reflected in the couple of meetings he had attended and how hopeful it was to see people being honest, open, and surrendered to new life. Again, I could not help but think about how judgmental I had been of him. And again I told him so and asked for his forgiveness. His reply was that I did not need to apologize, that my judgment was true. It was just that God was changing him before my eyes. It sent chills through my body.

As soon as we were seated at Jimmy Wan's Mel asked me to tell him what I had been thinking.

I started by asking him, "Mel, tell me your first impressions about the couple of NA meetings you have attended with me?'

"I have noticed three things. First, the meetings were perhaps the most authentic times of gratitude to God that I have ever witnessed. They were genuine, honest, times of praising God, not with pious religious words, that's for sure, but with real life expressions of gratitude. Second, I was struck by how much of the whole program of recovery is biblically based from the Steps and Traditions to Sponsorship and Service. Third, I was impressed by the depth of insight and the intelligence of those who shared." Mel replied.

"Maybe you can see why, for me, NA has almost been like my church. Anyway, that first Sunday night meeting when our small group experienced a time of confession I have been preoccupied with thinking and researching about how the Twelve Traditions might apply to the church. It seems to me that they are what have kept the Twelve Step movement from becoming institutionalized. Maybe I am mistaken, but from my point of view institutional structures are what tend to control the church and make it a rigid organization rather that a living organism whose life flows from the Spirit of God." I said.

"There is no question that for me, personally, I had become subtly seduced into running an institution that fed my ego. I became the head of an institution that is consumed with buildings, programs for its members, administration, budgets, maintaining rules, and appearance. I know you have seen our wonderful campus. We say our mission is to love God and love our neighbors but the truth is that Apple Orchard Church spends over ninety percent of its budget on itself. Stan told me his research showed that half of the people in the world are suffering, dying of malaria, AIDS, TB, starvation, war and religious oppression. They are widows, refugees, and orphans and about half of them have never heard the name of Jesus. And Apple Orchard does better than most churches. He told me that the church in America spends a little more than one hundredth of one percent on sharing the love of Jesus with the one and a half billion people of the world who have never heard about God's forgiveness and the resurrection of Jesus. And it spends ninety-nine point nine percent of what it calls 'mission giving' on programs for its church members. The church in America spends nearly all its resources on itself while half the world's population is literally suffering to death. That doesn't sound to me like loving our neighbors as ourselves. And Jesus said what you do or don't do to the least of these you do or don't do to him. That could mean we don't even love God, regardless of the wonderful worship experience we provide for our members.

"Sorry, I guess I am preaching. It is just that to think about how upside down I have made the Gospel upsets me. If there is some way to make it right then I would love to discover it." Mel responded.

So, I began to share with Mel some of my thoughts and we continued a lively discussion. It was so good to get his knowledge of the Bible and see how the scripture was applied in the Twelve Traditions. We could have keep sharing for the rest of the afternoon but I glanced at my watch and saw that it was 1:30 p.m. So I had to call us to a stop and said. "Mel, I hate to stop our discussion. I am really feeling encouraged by all we have shared but I have to be at a meeting at 2:00. Can we pick this up another time soon?"

"Sure." Mel answered. "I too have really appreciated and been challenged by our whole morning. We need to do more of this. And thanks again for your help with my letter."

Twenty Seven

Mel had his regularly scheduled monthly meeting that night with his twelve elders and the eight pastoral staff members plus his private secretary, three other clerical staff, and the executive administrator. There were twenty five not including Mel.

They gathered in the 'Upper Room' just off Mel's office. Because Mel had called everyone ahead of time, everyone was present. They were anxious to hear why he had given each of them a special reminder. The head elder, an elderly, bald, portly, man with kind eyes opened the meeting with prayer. He then asked the treasurer for the report on the offering and worship attendance for April. Then the balance sheet and investment earnings report was called for. Next came the building maintenance report, the children's and youth ministry report, young adults ministries, seniors ministry, small group ministry, homeless and indigent ministries, addiction ministries, local and worldwide missions, and finally the Senior Pastor's report. Each report was written and distributed by the appropriate staff. Each was given with an upbeat expression of praise and gratitude for God's grace and provision. As Senior Pastor, Mel's report summarized several follow-up responses from participants at his June speaking tour. He informed the group that he had received about a half-dozen requests for speaking engagements. He reported on four weddings he had been performed as well as three funerals. He also reported on his hospital and nursing home visits and the monthly clergy association meeting. He concluded by affirming all the staff for their fine jobs and welcomed back a couple who had had vacationed during the month of August. Then, as was their tradition, there came a time of group prayer that not only included thanks for what had been reported but also a prayer concern list that had been collected from that month's prayer cards during worship and distributed to those present by the pastoral care committee. After maybe half an hour, Mel offered the closing prayer. It was now Mel's time to share words of encouragement and motivation. This had been their pattern for the past twelve years as the church had grown from that first worship services following the founding picnic back on July 4, 1995.

He started by asking everyone to join him in another prayer. This in itself was a break from the pattern. He then began by announcing that he was canceling all his speaking engagements for the next two years and would not be accepting any new ones.

The room became still and the atmosphere changed from distraction to anticipation. Mel continued, "It is obvious that you are all wondering what this is about, why am I stopping my most effective ministry?"

He paused.

"I don't know how to say this, except to just say it. I am also resigning as your pastor and as a member of Apple Orchard Church, effective the end of this month."

It was as though a huge vacuum sucked all the air out of the room and you could hear everyone gasp.

Mel continued, "I will give my resignation letter to Fran at the end of our meeting."

He had to pause again as he could feel his emotions starting to cause him to choke up and tears started to form in his eyes. Stan, who was one of the elders, could also feel his emotions coming to the surface and began to pray silently for Mel to have peace.

Everyone in the room could feel Mel's emotions and waited respectfully.

Mel collected himself and began again, "On my plane ride back from Texas in July, the passenger next to me in first class was the President of Rotary International. We got acquainted and our conversation caused me to question my discipleship to Jesus. It dawned on me that my fellow passenger and I were living the similar lives. In the process of being your pastor over the past 12 years I have become wealthy and famous but I have also neglected my wife, my children, and Jesus. I believe God wants me to stop, reevaluate my call, renew my commitment to Him, and discover anew, or maybe for the first time, what it means to be Jesus' disciple. I need to get out of the way and let Jesus continue the transformation he began in me twenty years ago. This has been a phenomenal journey with all of you and with this congregation. I want it to continue but with no strings. But I have gotten distracted and I ask your forgiveness."

Mel's throat filled up and he could not speak for a minute. He stopped talking and everyone waited.

"I have led us into becoming an institution of which I have become proud because of its fame as a successful corporation. Maybe that doesn't sound so bad to you. I believe it is a distortion of what a local Body of Christ is meant to look like. I'm so sorry. You are all my friends before you are elders or staff and I trust that will never change. I even hope by not being your pastor our friendships will be enhanced. I believe this is an opportunity for Apple Orchard Church to also evaluate where it needs to go in the future without my overbearing influence. But that is up to you. I only ask that you don't just outright reject me and my family. I still love Jesus, in fact more than ever, and I love you and this church. I trust that God will more than replace me and I know that he will provide for you, nurture you, guide you, comfort you, discipline you, and never leave you. God is not finished with me or Apple Orchard or any of us yet. I want to end with this these words from Philippian 3:15. 'I've got my eye on the goal, where God is beckoning us onward—to Jesus. I'm off and running, and I'm not turning back. So let's keep focused on that goal.' And Ephesians 3:14-21, I 'get down on my knees before the Father, this magnificent Father who parcels out all heaven and earth. I ask him to strengthen you by his Spirit—not a brute strength but a glorious inner strength—that Christ will live in you as you open the door and invite him in. And I ask him that with both feet planted firmly on love, you'll be able to take in with all followers of Jesus the extravagant dimensions of Christ's love. Reach out and experience the breadth! Test its length! Plumb the depths! Rise to the heights! Live full lives, full in the fullness of God. God can do anything, you know—far more than you could ever imagine or guess or request in your wildest dreams! He does it not by pushing us around but by working within us, his Spirit deeply and gently within us. Glory to God in the church! Glory to God in the Messiah, in Jesus! Glory down all the generations! Glory through all millennia! Oh, yes!'

"I can't imagine what some of you might be thinking or feeling. You must have a lot of questions but I do not think it would be very helpful to try and answer all you are thinking and feeling at this time. And besides I am not sure I could handle it and I know I cannot satisfy everyone's question; mainly because I have a lot of them myself. For example, I just said a successful corporation is not what a local Body of Christ looks like. One question I have found myself asking is 'What then is a local Body of Christ supposed to look like?' I would just ask you to trust our Lord. He is always faithful and he will be with me and Apple Orchard. Thank you."

After about 30 seconds Chuck, the head elder stood up and said, "Brother and sister will you all please join hands and let's pray for Mel and this flock, for we are all the Lord's." And he prayed and closed the meeting with a benediction.

After the benediction, there wasn't a rush to ask Mel questions but after a while a group of three or four joined Mel at one end of the room and talked for about ten minutes. Mel tried his best not to say anything negative about the church or all the thoughts he had been having recently. Stan tried to talk to some of the other men about the Steeler's game coming up on the week-end. Most of the staff just quietly left. A number of them went to Eat & Park to get something to eat and also to digest what had just been sprung on them and what it might mean to the congregation and their futures. As everyone was leaving Bob Franks, who had been the founding elder of the church, pulled Mel aside and tried to talk him out of resigning. Stan went to his car to wait for Mel. Bob told Mel he just needed to give it time that we all burn out now and then and we just need to ride the waves and everything would be OK. Mel just listened; he knew Bob well enough to know he just didn't get it.

Mel met Stan at his car and they decided to take a deep breath over another cup of coffee at Starbucks. The first thing they both did when they sat down was to take a big sigh of relief.

The next morning on the bottom of the front page of the Pittsburgh Post-Gazette the by-line read, *APPLE ORCHARD PASTOR QUITS*. The article began.

> The Rev. Melvin Carr, the thirty nine year old founding pastor of the 20,000 member Apple Orchard Community Church announced to his elders and staff last night that he was no longer going to be their pastor. He did not give any specific reasons except to say he was reevaluating his call to be their pastor. One

> member, who wished to remain anonymous said she believes he may be going through a mid-life crisis. He has written three best-selling Christian books and is a popular speaker at Christian leadership conferences around the world. It is reported that he also intends to cancel all future speaking engagements.

Mel could have kicked himself. He did not expect someone to leak his resignation but he had also forgotten to ask everyone to not say anything until he could share his decision with the congregation the coming Sunday.

Liz and he speculated about who could have called the paper. Their guess was the one of the elders told his wife, she told someone else and everyone was soon on their cell phones texting and talking about it. And an alert reporter got the word.

It was 6:00 a.m., so immediately after reading the article, Mel unplugged the house phone and made a mental note to not turn on his cell phone. Everyone may be calling one another this morning but he and Liz were going to have some peace. Then he went to the computer, got on the church web page and copied his letter of resignation with a couple additional paragraphs of affirmation and appreciation. He also said that at next Sunday's worship he would preach at all four worship services and explain what he thought may be God's word for him. He then went on his personal website and blog and wrote a similar note. Next, he suggested to Liz that they go to Ohiopyle and hike and picnic for the day. It was going to be a beautiful early fall day and Liz was thrilled.

Andi was up and ready for school by then. Liz told her about the meeting last night and the newspaper article so that she could be prepared if kids at school quizzed her.

On Thursday morning Mel met with the church pastoral staff and shared some of his thoughts. He told them that he believed that the world is in a spiritual battle and that it is most important to identify the enemy and at all costs be faithful to Jesus. He also talked about being a disciple of Jesus and seeking the Kingdom of God. They had about a two hour discussion, much of it around how to handle all the questions that were already coming. He felt that most of the staff understood where he was coming from much better than he had. In fact, a few shared how refreshing it was to see him being vulnerable and challenged in his walk with the Lord. He asked Dick Smalley, the Executive Administrator to become Head of Staff. He told them that he would preach this coming Sunday and then the last Sunday of the month. The other two Sundays he wanted the two Associate Pastors to each preach one of the Sundays. They ended their meeting with an extended time of prayer.

Sunday, September 9, 2007

Mel took his text from Philippians 3 and began his sermon that Sunday by telling the following story.

"On my trip back from Texas God interrupted my life. I was sitting in first class reviewing the last twelve years of my life. I remembered what felt like miracles as the Frank's and Liz and I watch Apple Orchard Church materialize. We were caught up in the amazing success and growth of this congregation. It has resulted in many wonderful programs for thousands, not just in Pittsburgh but all over the world. But as I mused about this journey I felt a strange kind of confusion and depression. I started to pray and no sooner had I asked Jesus to open my eyes and ears to see and hear what he wanted to show me, the man in the seat next to me interrupted my prayer and asked me what time it was. I was focused on my prayer and unintentionally blurted out, "It's time to see."

The man said, "Excuse me."

I said, "I'm sorry, I meant it's time for me to listen, what did you ask?"

This then lead to us getting acquainted and for me what was a very revealing conversation.

The man's name is Bob Blick and he is the President of Rotary International. He told me all about Rotary, which I had never really known too much about. His told me that Rotary International was a dues paying membership service organization made up of community leaders from around the world. They meet in local chapter for lunch or dinner once a week. At their meetings they fellowship, sing together, do the business of the organization, take up a donation, and have a speaker. They have strict membership rules and expectations to volunteer and support their leadership education and development programs as well as do local community and world services. I struck me how similar it was to Apple Orchard Church without the religious language but with greater focus on outreach services. One of their projects is providing clean water filtration systems. That threw me; and has had me thinking about what church is ever since."

Mel didn't say anything more about what his thinking about church is or is not. He also didn't talk about the Liminal Plunge group. He did, however, go on to share his neglect of his family and wife, his infatuation with self-importance, his lag of genuine accountability, his loneliness, and his neglect of Jesus. He asked the congregation's forgiveness for leading them into what he was realizing is a business model corporate expression of Jesus' Body instead of being radical followers of Jesus.

He concluded his farewell sermon by saying, "I am resigning as your pastor and a member of this congregation but intend to continue with all of you to press on toward the goal to win the prize for which God has called us heavenward in Jesus Christ our Lord."

Twenty Eight

Sunday night's Liminal Plunge meeting for me had that rare feeling of being able to relax and feel safe to be yourself, like coming home is supposed to feel.

Our simple warm meal together and our time of reflection and praise made it feel like Christmas around a fire place. What Liz, Deb, and Misha had planned for our meal time and worship was perfect.

When we gathered after supper Stan distributed an agenda. We all looked it over and then looked at each other. Karen started by saying as gently as she could, "Thanks, honey for helping to keep us moving forward but honestly I am not looking forward to a business meeting. This has been a hard week for me and I really need some time to vent and sort out what is happening to my life."

Misha, in not as sensitive a tone, piggy backed with, "I can 'Amen' that. I feel like I have entered a dark tunnel without a light in any direction!"

Through a sheepish grin, Stan responded, "Hey, I'm cool with setting planning aside for a while, let's forget the agenda for tonight. I am not really sure what to do next anyway. To tell the truth, if it weren't for you all, I would be either on the verge of getting depressed out of fear of the future or wanting to run back to the security of what I know how to do, which is serving the god of making money. And today that really would feel like a dark tunnel without a light at the end."

So, I said, "Why don't we just share what is on our hearts. I get the feeling this has been a rough week for everyone."

"Good, I'll start." Karen moved up to edge of her chair. "I have belonged to a charity organization called 'Flowers from Heaven'. In fact, I was this year's Chairperson. This past Tuesday, I went to our monthly meeting at the Club instead of going to lunch with Misha, Deb, and Liz. I quit the Flowers. Liz listened to a lot of my stuff this week but I need to share my feelings with you all."

Karen then proceeded to vent her anger, shame, guilt, and a bunch of other stuff related to taking off her mask and now feeling so exposed but free with anxiety about what direction her life will take.

I was impressed how everyone listened without trying to fix her or give her some clichés of encouragement.

When she was finished, Liz shared a little about how she was now feeling free but also lost. She said she had not expected it but with Mel giving his resignation on Wednesday and then a farewell sermon that morning had her now wanting to run back to the known like Stan had just said. She said sometimes the security of knowing what to expect, even though you are miserable is easier than the fear of the unknown. She said she still hated her past life as a pastor's wife. But maybe it was better than the future darkness that she was facing. Maybe, she thought it would have been better to have a plan for the future before leaving the past. And she said she was afraid of what was going to happen to Elijah, and she also had to admit that she was worried about what Mel was going to do and if he would get depressed or have a nervous breakdown. She then began to cry.

Mel did not show any signs of being defensive, but listened with love, and reach over to take her hand.

I glanced over at James and it looked to me like he was feeling a little frustrated or perturbed at the two women emoting their fears. Or maybe there was something else bothering him.

Misha began to speak next. "I think I can identify with what you are feeling Liz. I am still scared to death about being rejected by my parents if Jorge and I quit our youth ministry. I thought I was over the insecurity but it is still worrying me. Maybe we should just be friends with you all and not change anything about our lives."

Still everyone just listened and didn't try to take away the tension and anxiety of the moment.

Then James spoke up and said, "Maybe Misha is right, maybe you are just going too fast. Maybe what you are doing is just a little irresponsible. Stan is giving up a billion dollar business, Mel is quitting the most successful Christian enterprise in the country, Karen is quitting her charity work, and you two are thinking of quitting your successful youth ministry. All for what? I am excited that you all what to help the orphanage in Haiti but maybe you shouldn't change your whole lives and give up everything, just because a friend was a martyr."

I thought, "Just because a friend was a martyr.' Where are you really coming from anyway, James? Those martyred were part of one of the best families you could have ever known. All we are doing is trying to stop being so self-absorbed and follow Jesus."

I could see the disbelief on Karen's and Liz's faces.

Mel came to their defense. "What we are doing is the right thing to do and I believe it is the Holy Spirit that is doing it. Transformation is not without suffering and pain. When Jesus called his disciples he did not tell them where he was going, he just said 'follow me'. This is about taking up our cross, not about being comfortable. But at the same time, for me, and I think from what we have all shared, we already have more peace and joy than anything the past has provided, except maybe when we were together in Africa 20 years ago ministering to those babies dying of AIDS. I say regardless of how dark it may seem right now that we move through this dark tunnel until it is shattered by the Light of the resurrection. That's all, I'm finished preaching."

Karen, Liz, and Misha postured a relaxed demeanor, almost like they were saying, "I know and I agree, thanks for letting me vent." James did not look either rebuked or reassured, he just sat without any body language that revealed his feelings and he did not respond.

I felt conflicted inside. Part of me felt relieved and thankful for Mel's courage. Part of me felt excited. I could also sense some old cynicism surfacing with the sarcastic thought of, *"You're right Mel, just like you felt when you started Apple Orchard."* But my dominant sense and feeling was that of trust and peace. I believed we were doing the best we could to be obedient to the Holy Spirit.

After a few seconds of waiting for someone else to say something, Stan said, "Is there anything else anyone feels a need to share? Thank you Liz, Misha, Karen and Mel for saying what a lot of us are feeling. We are walking into unknown and uncharted territory but the Lord is with us and we do not need to be afraid. And James thank you to for having the courage to say what you said."

Deb, in her own sweet way than said, "What was on your agenda, anyway?"

We each picked up our agenda and looked it over. We saw listed:

Personal Sharing

Up-date from Mel

Haiti trip report from James

Date on disposition of Cyper Market and creation of Bryce Foundation

Stan looked at the agenda and said, "Well, I guess we have done some personal sharing but I think it would also be good to hear how Billy is doing, --- and Elijah."

"And Brenda." I said.

"Billy seems to be doing well, we are still running in the morning together and he said school is going OK. Kids exclude him a little but he said he can deal. He likes soccer."

Mel then said. "We don't really know about Eli. He doesn't want to see me. I think you all knew that. Well anyway, he doesn't. Naranon is helping me deal with that. The topic this week was the First Step, 'We recognized that our lives were unmanageable and that we were powerless over our addiction'. People shared how they had tried to manage the lives of their loved ones but they had to recognize that the best thing they could do was let it go and do nothing. They had to stop trying to save their loved ones and admit they were powerless to change them. It hit home for me because I saw a biblical truth in what they shared. Jesus' absolute humility is what gives him absolute power. When we absolutely surrender, God's power can take over in our lives.

"Oh, and I know, like she shared, Liz is worried about my emotional resilience, but I honestly think I am fine. The reactions I have gotten from my resignation has been much better than I expected. People seem to be more accepting of me than I thought they would.

"And, oh, yes, Andi and I are having our second monthly dinner date next week."

Karen then said, "Brenda is doing fine. In fact she now wants to go on the Haiti trip and wants to ask a girl friend of hers to come with us."

"I guess that bring the agenda down to me." James said.

"Wait," interjected Stan. "Does anyone have anything else they want to share?"

"Not now", I responded. "But later in the meeting if we have time."

"You sure you want to wait?" Stan asked me.

"Sure, no problem." I said, which really meant, like so often when people say 'no problem', that it was a problem. But I would held back my enthusiasm and wait.

"Ok then, James you're up."

"Thanks, Stan." James began. "I have communicated with Fr. Jacque in Bois Joli and he is making arrangements for the fourteen of us to be at the orphanage from December 15th through December 21st. He will have lined up an excellent itinerary for us that will include some helpful physical work on building repairs, time with the children, and some visits to partnership ministries like the clinic and school, plus an opportunity to worship and share with the local Christians."

Mel interrupted. "I count fifteen not fourteen."

James answered. "I didn't count Eli because I didn't think with him being at Walcott that he would be allowed to go."

"I hope he will be back at home by then," Mel responded.

"I wouldn't count on it," I said. "But I think if we could show the judge that it would be a positive experience for him and that we would keep him in line that he may be allowed to go. I also am thinking that perhaps we could ask a good friend in the recovery fellowship by the name of Sunny and his wife to come with us. Sunny could serve as Eli's sponsor, and be responsible for his conduct. Sunny would be a wonderful, and I mean a wonderful influence on Eli.

"If something like that would work out, that would be great. I met Sunny at the NA meeting and he would be terrific. That would make seventeen." said Mel.

"I think my mother, might like to go too," added Karen.

"Eighteen would be fine, but where we are going to stay can't handle more than twenty." James said, and then continued.

"Everyone needs to get his or her Passport if you don't already have one that is up to date. You should do that now. It can sometimes take up to eight weeks to get them processed.

"Everyone going also needs to get the vaccination that I have listed on the information sheet I am passing around.

"As we get closer to when we leave for Haiti we can talk about what to wear and what to take and about the Haitian culture.

"Fr. Jacque is arranging transportation once we get there too; and our meals.

"The flight will cost about eight hundred dollars a person and our stay will be less than two hundred a person, plus each of us should take about a hundred spending money. So, a total of about eleven or twelve hundred dollars each. Oh, and Customs will require a fifty to hundred dollar exit fee, depending, as I have learned, upon which custom official we get and their mood at our time of departure."

"So, the total cost for all of us, if we end up with twenty people, will be around twenty five thousand dollars." inserted Stan.

I thought, 'How did he do that in his head so fast?'

"That is about it for now, to get us started." James concluded. "Any questions?"

As each of us looked down at his or her handout, it seemed like no one had any immediate question, so Stan said. "Thanks, James, well done. Now let me fill you all in on what has happened with Cyper Market this week.

"First, I have talked with a lawyer about creating a Foundation and all we need to do is write a Mission Statement, create a few By-Laws, which he will put into legal language, and name at least 3 Directors who would be the incorporating directors. I would like to get that all done this week so that next week we can file for incorporation. The lawyer will move the process through quickly, he has had lots of experience with the process. So, tonight I would like us to do two things. One, agree on who will be the 3 incorporating directors and write a Mission Statement. Next week we can talk about who else should be on the Board when we approve the By-Laws. I want to suggest too, that Odell and I meet this week to write the By-Laws. That all sound OK with everyone?"

Misha and Mel said "Amen" almost in unison and everyone else nodded.

"Ok, then who wants to be listed as the incorporation directors?"

There was a very brief and Stan continued. "I nominate Odell, Jorge, and Liz. I don't think Karen or I should be on this legal document for fear of the appearance of creating a conflict of interest."

Mel then said, "All in favor of Odell, Liz, and Jorge in that order for President, Treasurer and Secretary, say, 'You bet!'.

Everyone yelled, "You bet!"

Liz, Jorge, and I looked at each other.

Stan looked at us and asked, "You guys cool with that?"

We all nodded.

"Great." said Stan. "Now for the Mission Statement. I have been thinking about this and I'd like to make a suggestion to get us started. The conventional wisdom is that a Mission Statement should describe the purpose of the organization succinctly enough that you can write it on a T-shirt. So, here goes. The Mission of the Bryce Foundation is to "Share the love of Jesus by providing financial resources for meeting the needs of those who suffer in the world, especially children."

"I like it." I said. "It is direct and specific but open to almost any need, yet puts a focus on children, and it witnesses to Jesus. But ---" I said grinning. "--- it will need to go on and XXXXL T-shirt."

"Very funny," retorted Stan.

"I like it too." Jorge said. "But it sounds a little presumptions. By saying that money alone will meet the needs of those who suffer. How about if we just changed the word 'meeting" to 'helping to address' so that it would say, "Share the love of Jesus by providing financial resources for helping to address the needs of those who suffer in the world, especially children"?

It was silent for a minute.

"I take our silence to mean we all agree?" asked Stan.

"Since we are doing this in honor of his family, I think we should run it by Billy before we carve it in stone." said Deb.

"Me too," said Mel.

"Ok, then, this week Odell and Deb would you ask Billy for his input about the Foundation Mission Statement. The rest of us please think and pray about it for a week and see how it feels. Let's come next week with what we think God is saying." concluded Stan.

"Now let me tell you what I think is really exciting news. I haven't even told Karen this. This week one of Cyber Market's Board members got a call from one of our competitors offering to buy Cyber Market. They did not know anything about my planned departure or us selling our stock and the Board member did not tell them. Their offer is five points above the stock market price of the company's stock on the day of the sale. They believe together with their current company and eliminating our competition in the current economic climate that it is a win-win for both of our companies; if we are willing to sell. We had an emergency Board meeting again this week and given my departure, the Board agreed to sell. The closing date is October 9th, just two months from now. This is starting to get real, friends. And it is a little freaky how it fits in with what has happened to us personally."

"God is very good. He loves us so much. Why does it always surprise me when He blesses me? Thank you, Jesus!" Karen said as her eyes began to fill with tears.

Automatically, we all bowed our heads and you could hear everyone whispering thanks to God, and then James began to sing and we joined in, singing, "The steadfast love of the Lord's never ceases, his mercies never come to an end, they are new every morning, new every morning, great is thy faithfulness oh Lord, great is thy faithfulness." We sang it softly three or four time and then all was quiet for a while.

I looked at my watch and it was only 7:50 PM. So, I broke the silence and said, "Stan, when we started I said if we have time, I wanted to share something. It is now 7:50 PM, could I share a couple of thoughts with us?"

Stan replied, "I am not in charge here, we all are, what do you all think? Should we go home, stay here and watch Sunday Night Football on our huge screen, or listen to Odell?" Everyone smiled, looked at each other, paused for a few seconds and yelled, ----- "Watch Football! ---- just kidding, listen to Odell"

I was anxious for those few seconds, then smiled broadly and said with a sarcastic tone, "Deb, please write this down, Odell got higher ratings than the Cowboys and the Giants. Thanks family, I recognize the sacrifice you are making."

Then after a pause I continued, "You all recognize I'm sure, that since I turned my life over to God's will and the care of Jesus, the church has never lived up to what I saw in Jesus life and teaching in the Bible. I have been pretty arrogant and very judgmental of the church as I have experienced it over the past 20 years. I am ashamed of myself for that attitude. What I have been experiencing in the last couple of months I believe has broken through that self-righteousness."

I paused for a few seconds to get control of my emotions. They were unexpected emotions, mixed with my deep feelings of shameful arrogance and at the same time in awe of God's grace and mercy.

"Over the years, at the same time as I have as been spurning the church yet seeking to follow Jesus, I have also been nurtured and supported by the fellowship of Narcotics Anonymous. Recently that has gotten me to thinking about why AA for seventy years, and NA for maybe forty years, been able to stay true to its mission when the church hasn't. They both have the same temptations of being seduced by self-interest and the values of the culture.

"Mel has come to a couple of NA meetings and gone to a couple Naranon meetings and at lunch this week he and I had a great discussion about what causes the church to take on the values of the culture and what has kept Alcoholics Anonymous in its short seventy year history, true to its founding. We want to share what we think so far.

"First, ----"

"Wait, Odell, you just said something that we were talking about at lunch this week. I want Misha, Deb, and me to share before you go on." Interrupted Liz, as she pressed on. "You just said that it has been the *fellowship* of Narcotics Anonymous that has supported you as you have sought to follow Jesus. At lunch, fellowship is what we were talking about and in one fashion or another it is what we talk about almost every time we are together."

"Yea," added Misha. "We think what the church is really about is fellowship."

"Something special happens when people who have met Jesus and are seeking the Kingdom of God experience what we went through as kids in Africa and are now going through together. It is hard to define except maybe to say it is like being a family that absolutely loves one another." Continued Liz.

"I think it is not just our desire to follow Jesus; lots of people in our experiences with the church really do want to follow Jesus; but it is also being vulnerable and willing to live transparently with each other. I mean being honest and open, like we have been doing, sharing our sins and feelings, mistakes, plans and dreams, or lack of them, our struggles and needs." Deb said.

"I couldn't have said it better." I said. "What you just said is the first thing I want to say. Our fellowship, the friendship we have that is bonded by the Holy Spirit, is what defines us as a church, not signing up as a member.

Mel picked up what I was saying as though it had been scripted. "What I am about to share is so different from what I have known in the church. I means that there should not be membership requirements to be a member of the church. No joining, no expectations for contributing money, no catechism, no membership rules, pledges or promises. You are a member when you say you are. You become a member when you say you only desire is to follow Jesus and seek first the Kingdom of God. That is when you become part of the family. The desire to live a new life in Christ is what initiates you into the family, the fellowship. No formal membership rolls or promises to keep. The eternal connection we have is a result of our common, life-saving, interdependence in Jesus.

"There's another thing that Odell and I have talked about. Odell is it OK if I go ahead and talk about church authority? Ask Mel.

"Sure, of course." I responded.

"I want to introduce this part because it is such a transformation for me personally. We don't think the church should hire any professionals, including pastors, teachers, prophets, evangelists, administrators, priest or leaders."

'Wait a minute," Stan interjected. "You can't be serious. Without someone to give direction, how does the church know what to do? Somebody has to be given the responsibility of coordinating or at least facilitating the group. Who will make decisions when the fellowship gets bigger that a handful of us. Sure when there are only nine of us consensus is possible but not with nine hundred. And besides, some people are gifted to be on that list you just ran down. I don't want to sound too much like the manager that I am, but if someone doesn't manage the church how is it going to be managed? I know too, in fact I have been taught by you Mel; that the Bible says some people are given gifts for those functions. Peter's letter to Timothy has some specific qualification for deacons and elders. Personally, I like to think of them as administrators, but various traditions have called them Bishops. Mel, you are confusing me. Are you sure you are not being just reactionary because you feeling a little confused right now?"

I looked around the room and it seemed that everyone, except Mel and I, was nodding their heads in agreement. They all also had a look of anticipation as to how Mel was going to answer.

"Mel, let me try and answer some of this." I said. "The whole question of church governance has some other issues connected to it as Stan has alluded to.

"First of all, we are not saying that what some refer to as the five-fold ministries that list that I ran down, is to be abandoned. What we are saying is that what the Body of Christ <u>does</u> must grows out of what the Body of Christ <u>is</u>. We want to suggest that the Fellowship should be separated from the ministry. The ministries are where we the church needs administration and the other gifts. The Fellowship is an organism, the ministries are what require the institutional organization.

"I get it, Jesus is the Head of the Body, the Church. But how then is Jesus' leadership as the Head of the Church going to work? How is this non-institutional fellowship managed?" asked Stan.

"Just like our little fellowship has been doing these past few months." I chimed in.

"That seems to mean that each "fellowship" or church as you are describing it must stay relatively small and that's fine." Stan responded. "But, … I don't want to sound condescending but what about a fellowship that doesn't have trained or experienced managers like we do?"

"Then one fellowship relies on another fellowship until they get the experience and are trained." I responded.

"Amen" said Mel.

Misha added. "Yea, that makes sense."

Then Karen spoke up. "I hope you guys don't mind. I know that figuring out who we are and how we move forward is important but it is getting late. Don't some of you need to be getting home?"

"It is almost 8:30 PM and I suppose we should be heading back to make sure our kids are OK." responded Mel.

Stan then spoke up again and said, "For me this has all been very stimulating and helpful but I am not sure I fully understand or agree. I would like to suggest that we think and pray about what Odell and Mel have been saying and then continue our discussion at a future meeting. And right now I think we need to spend some time praying before you all go home."

"Good idea." Deb said.

We all then prayed with James ending the prayer time by singing "Be Not Afraid."

As we were getting up and starting to say good night. Stan got our attention and asked, "I was wondering, would it be alright with the group if I ask Karen's mom, Ruth to join us next week. Karen and I think she might really benefit from the fellowship and she has always wanted to follow Jesus, though she is not the most orthodox person I know?"

Liz responded immediately and said, "Of course, please ask her to come."

Several of us nodded our head in agreement.

I then used the opening to ask. "I would like to also invite a couple. Their names are Sunny and Sara McFarlyne. Sunny is the person I had in mind to be Elijah's sponsor, if he get permission to go with us to Haiti."

Mel answered, "Sunny would be great to have a part of this group. Anyways, I think we were just trying to suggest that anyone could be a part of this group as long as they desired to be a disciple of Jesus."

Heads nodded in agreement again.

We all got up and departed.

On the way home, I was driving and Deb was in the front seat. James and Jorge and Misha were in the back. We had not gone more than five miles when Jorge said. “I think I am having a heart attack.

Twenty Nine

"You're what!?" exclaimed Misha.

"I think I am having a heart attack."

"What makes you think so?" Asked Deb.

Misha remembered that Deb was a nurse and restrained herself from starting to ask a thousand questions.

Jorge replied. "During our prayer time I started to feel really tired, like I had just climbed up a hundred steps. Now I am starting to sweat, and my chest and arm hurt. Well more like my chest feels like it is being stepped on and my left arm is aching. And I feel a little short of breath."

Deb reached back to take Jorge's pulse and asked him, "Have you ever felt like this before?"

"No, not really." answered Jorge.

Deb told James to call 911 and silently counted Jorge pulse. When emergency answered, James gave the phone to Deb. Deb introduced herself as a nurse and then said, "I'll hold." In about fifteen seconds someone came on the line. Deb introduced herself again and described Jorge's symptoms to the person on the phone and answered questions that were being asked of her. All I could hear was, "About ten minutes ago." "Yes." "We are on I-369 about fifteen minutes from town." "Yes, his pulse is eighty two. He's thirty eight years old. Yes. I don't know. Let me ask."

Deb paused to ask Jorge if he was on any medication. He said no. Deb went back to the phone. "No" she said. "Ok", "Shadyside Hospital", "Henley Health Care Center." "Thank you, I will. Good bye."

Deb reached in her purse and pulled out some aspirin and told Jorge to take one. Then she told me to go to Shadyside Hospital Emergency Room. She told us all that the triage nurse on the phone said. Deb then paged the on-call doc at the Health Care Center. In a couple of minutes Dr. Billard returned her call. She told him what was going on and he said he would meet us at Emergency.

Seeing the fear in Misha's eyes, Deb reached over and squeezed Misha's hand. I then suggested that we pray for Jorge. We held hands and we prayed that Jorge and Misha would feel God's peace and the Jorge would be alright.

In about 15 minutes we were at Shadyside Hospital. As I was turning into Emergency, Jorge said he was feeling fine now and began to protest going in. He said that it was probably only indigestion and gas. Deb said he needed to get checked out. He protested more strongly. We all looked at each other and finally Misha said, "What's up? Why are you giving us a hard time? If you are having a heart attack I don't want to have you die in bed next to me tonight."

Jorge said, "Honey we don't have any insurance and we make too much money to qualify for charity care. If I walk through those doors we will have a five hundred dollar bill before they even run any tests; and by the time I leave our saving for the kids to go to college will have been spent. I am alright now. Let's just pray and go home. God will take care of me."

I cut in and said, "Yeah, God will take care of you and Misha and your kids. That is why you are going into that hospital."

He looked at me as if he wanted to get into a real argument, and then he looked at Misha and Deb and James. We were all staring at him with conviction in our eyes. He sighed and exhaled, "OK, let's go in."

We went to the reception area and as Jorge was checking in, Dr. Fred Billard from the Health Care Center came in the Emergency Department. Deb greeted him and gave him a detailed account of the last half hour. She then introduced him to Misha and James as the Medical Director of Henley Health Care Center.

Jorge came to join us when he was then finished registering. Deb introduced Dr. Billard to Jorge and we sat down to talk. Dr. Billard asked Jorge a number of questions. Jorge described his sensations at the meeting and in the car, plus he answered some questions about his family's health history. Dr. Billard then went into the emergency examining area and returned in about five minutes to tell us that the Emergency Room doctor would examine him and most likely she would run some tests to help determine how to proceed.

Jorge was then escorted into an exam room. The emergency room nurse took his vitals, hooked him up to a cardiac monitor, drew some blood, asked him questions about his medical and family history, and what if any medications he was taking. The emergency room doctor then came into see him.

While Jorge's condition was being assessed Misha went to the registration desk to express her concern about them not having health insurance. The receptionist had her fill out the paper work to apply for welfare medical assistance. When she was finished Misha told me that she was worried because she knew from her own experience with trying to help a lot of people get medical assistance that they would not qualify.

Dr. Billard went to the exam room and returned. He reported that Jorge's cardiogram did show some irregularities and they were going to admit him to the hospital. He told us that when Jorge got to his room they would hook him up to heart monitor and put in an IV to give him a medication called a thrombolytic to prevent any further heart episodes. Then in the morning he would be given an echocardiogram. The results would help identify whether any area of his heart has been damaged and isn't pumping normally or at peak capacity. Dr. Billard then said that God is the Great Physician and is in the healing business.

A nurse then came out of the exam room area and said we could all go in and see Jorge for a few minutes. When we went into his room he had a sheepish smile on his face. Misha hurried to his side and gave him a kiss. No one seemed to know what to say. Dr. Billard then asked if it would be alright if he prayed for Jorge. Jorge responded with a real smile and said, "You bet!" We all joined hands and Dr. Billard put his hand on Jorge's head. He prayed for God's wisdom, Jorge's heart, and all of our peace. He then assured Jorge that he was in palm of God's hand and we would all continue to pray for him. Misha then said to Jorge. "Don't worry honey, you are going to be alright, and we are going to be just fine. God has always taken care of us and he is not going to stop now.

Dr. Billard then gave us all a hug and left to go back home. I went out with him and shared with him that Jorge didn't't have insurance. Fred reminded me that it would not make any difference as far as the Health Care Center was concerned, but the hospital bill would be another matter. He said if Jorge and Misha did not qualify for medical assistance the hospital usually worked out a payment plan based upon the income of the patient.

When I went back in, James asked if I could take him to his apartment which was only about two miles away and Misha and Deb said they would wait with Jorge.

It was about 10:00 p.m. when James and I left. Deb called Karen to let her know what was going on and to ask her to pass the word for prayer. Misha first called their kids and then called her parents. Deb also called home to tell our kids what had happened and that we would be home later than expected.

When I returned from taking James to his apartment in Oakland an escort had already taken Jorge up to his room and Deb and Misha were waiting there for me. We didn't't say much on the way home. Deb led us in a short pray for Jorge and Misha. We dropped Misha off at her house. The twins were still up and we waited until she was in the house before we drove away.

On the way home Deb called Karen back. She quietly and tactful explained the Cruz's financial stress. Deb told me later that before she could finish Karen said, "Tell them not to worry about any of it; that is what being in the Body of Christ is about. Doesn't't it say in Acts that they shared everything in common and now one was in need? Stan will talk to the hospital and it will be taken care of no matter what the cost."

I hadn't heard what Karen had said, but I saw tears running down Deb's face. She thanked Karen repeatedly and said good-night.

The next morning I got to the Center early and Fred and I decided to go to the hospital together after he had seen some patients in the office. He said from 10:00 to noon he had some free time designated as administrative time and that the hospital would have gotten the remaining test results back on Jorge by then.

On the way to the hospital I quickly filled Fred in on the past several months. I had shared with him about the Bryce family and Billy, but not much about the group and the radical changes that the Carr's and Beckley's were making. I made a point not to talk about the sale of Cyber Market or the start of the foundation, just telling him about our fellowship and how Mel and Stan had come to some NA meetings with me.

I focused mostly on James and Jorge and Misha. I talked the whole way to the hospital. He only had a chance to squeeze in the comment, "Sounds like a God thing to me."

When we got to Jorge's floor, Fred went to the nurse's station and I went to Jorge's room. He was sitting up in bed looking fine. He was still hooked up to a heart monitor. Misha was already there.

Jorge told me they drew more blood last night and had him on an IV drip all night. He also said that they disconnected the IV about an hour ago and that they he'd had an echocardiogram. I told him about the Health Care Center not charging him and what Karen had told Deb. As he comprehended what I was saying, I watched his blood pressure on the monitor drop and the tension in his face relax. I thought to myself, *"It is amazing what stress relief can do for your heart."*

Dr. Billard came into the room, smiled at Jorge, went over to Misha, gave her a hug, and then stepped over to the side of Jorge's bed, sat down, and said, "Things look pretty good. You do have the beginning of atherosclerosis but you are young and your heart is not significantly damaged. Atherosclerosis is the result of cholesterol building up in your arteries creating plaques. What happened last night was that a small plaque ruptured, a small blood clot formed from the site of the rupture. When it got to your heart it caused a strain on your heart but did not block it. The aspirin you took dissolved it before it could cause you real distress. God loves you Jorge and He is looking out for you."

"That means no operations, right doc?"

"Right, but it also means that if you want to live long enough to see your grandchildren that there are a few things you need to do. This experience is a 'heads up" for you. This is not about a serious heart disease – yet. It is about learning how to live in a way that is treating your body like the temple that God has designed it to be."

"I can hear that doc. What do I need to do?"

"Let me start with a few observation. First, you told me and the doctor in emergency that you did not know anything about your father, only that he was from Cuba. It that right?"

I interrupted, "Jorge would you like me to leave while you two talk about personal stuff? I know we know each other really well but I also want to respect your privacy."

"No, no, please stay. I think I am going to need someone to help hold me accountable. I think I have an idea of what is coming." Jorge said.

"Ok, I am happy to stay."

Fred went on. "You don't know your father's medical history, right?"

"Right, and really not my mother's either. I've never talked to her about that and she died about two years ago."

"OK, well a person's family history gives us a clue to one of the risk factors for heart disease, but we will have to stay in the dark about that. It also can help us understand one of the reasons why your cholesterol is so high. A healthy cholesterol should be under 200 and better if it is under say 140. Yours is 240. That is way too high for someone who is 38 years old. One of the pills you got this morning was to lower your cholesterol. You will need to take it every day.

Your blood sugar level also shows that you are at risk for developing diabetes and diabetes is another risk factor for a heart attack.

A third risk we know about is that your blood pressure was 160 over 100 when you came in and it pretty much remained that overnight. The second pill you got this morning was to lower you blood pressure. We want your blood pressure to be about 120 over 65.

Now, you answered that you did not smoke or use drugs. It that true?"

"Yes, I used drugs about twenty some years ago but not since I went to Africa – but that is another story."

"Good."

"I understand from what 'O' has told me that you have been working with teens in Henley for the past 15 years or so. In my experience, someone on the front lines of the suffering of people, especially kids, lives with a lot of other people's pain and though they often look like they are doing well, their bodies are taking a beating as a result of the stress they live with every day. And then there's the stress of always having to be ready for whatever might happen. They never really getting a break, often because they can't afford to get a really restful vacation. Do you think these stressors are true for you?"

"Doc, you don't know the half of it. I don't think now is the time but I can tell you about a number of good people who have gotten sick and even died as a result to what I have learned is called compassion fatigue. But I think from what you have just said that you already understand. Yes, my life is full of stress, if that is what you are asking."

"That is what I was asking and suspected. Stress can be a significant risk factor for heart disease.

"And last, how about physical activity?"

"Do I look like I get much physical activity?"

"Well, that gets me to a pivotal factor in what I suspect is the underlying cause of your heart problem. Your BMI is 33, it should be less than 24. That means for your height you should weigh less than about 175 and you weight 240. Bottom line is that you need to lose a little more than 60 lbs."

Fred paused to see how Jorge would react.

Jorge did not say anything. I was quiet as well. Misha just sat looking at Jorge.

Fred continued, "I still want to have you take an exercise stress test to get a better idea of whether your heart has been compromised. But here is what I think we have got. You are a relatively healthy early middle age man who loves Jesus and serves him. You are happily married to a lovely woman and have two healthy gifted teenagers, and I think from what Odell has told me, you are feeling like you are just about to embark on a major change in your life. Odell shared a little about what you all have been confronted with in the past couple of months. God is touching you and maybe launching you on a new direction in your life. But, you are at risk of dying prematurely from heart disease.

However, that danger is preventable, and if treated, will most likely not be the cause of your death, even if you live to be 100. Your risks come from; one, your excessive weight, two, the stress in your life, and three, your diet. Also is sounds like you don't get enough regular exercise. All of which are manageable, but demand some changes in your life-style. You are here not because of an illness but because of how you care for yourself. I say all this in this way because I know God love's you and you love him and I do not think God or you would want me to pander you. I can treat you with drugs and perhaps that will put off surgery for a number of years: or you can decide to change some things about your life."

Jorge didn't't hesitate. "I hear you doc. Thank you. What do I do?" Jorge asked with a quiet but sincere humility.

Fred smiled and said, "You're a good man, Mr. Cruz. Well, first, I want you to learn what to eat and what not to eat. Joining Weight Watchers is a good place to start. It has built into it several things that are good habits to replace bad habits. The Mediterranean Diet is a good guide for what to eat. I will have Deb get you a copy.

Second, I want you to exercise, preferably every day but at least four out of seven days in a week. Start by taking a brisk walk for 15 minutes a day and work up to being able to run two to three miles four days a week.

Third, I want you to take a vacation. You need a rest. Say for a month. You need to let go of some stress and rest in the Lord.

Fourth, I am going to put you on the cholesterol and high blood pressure meds that you are taking here in the hospital. I want you to stay on them until you have lost 65 lb. and have a regular exercise routine for at least three months. And then we will reevaluate.

And last, I believe you and Misha have in your little group one of the best prescriptions for a healthy life that God has designed. You are part of a community of believers who are learning to surrender to the Lord and love one another. We all need that to be healthy and God has designed us to live like that. If I could I would write a script for all my patients for that exact thing. God did not create us to be individual lone rangers, he made us for him and for each other. We are a corporate creation and we find our identity with the whole.

Do you have any questions?"

"Thank you doc. Yeah, I do have a lot of questions, but right now I just need to digest all that you have said. It all sounds very simple and hopeful but it is all a really big challenge for me. I love to eat, I am in terrible shape, I am always on the go and would love a vacation for a couple of days but a whole month sounds like running away from being responsible. I am too dependent on doing something meaningful to not be involved with people's pain.

I really appreciate everything you and everyone have been doing for me. God is so so good to me. I will definitely call you when I have a question that other than, 'How in the world do I do this?'"

"You do it with the grace of God and with gratitude." Fred answered. "And I will look forward to your calls. I will also ask Odell to keep me up on how you are doing. If that is alright with you."

"Yes, of course, it is alright with me. The more accountability I have the better."

"I believe nothing really happens without prayer, so would you like me to pray with you before I discharge you?"

Dr. Billard prayed with his characteristic humility, which made us all feel so grateful and confident in God's sovereignty. Then he told him that he would go write up the discharge papers and the nurse would come in and discharge you, and also arrange an appointment for you to come in and have a stress test. He told Jorge that the discharge papers would have written on them what he had discussed with him and that the nurse would also give him scripts for the meds he would need to be taking. He then gave us all hugs and left. As he went out the door, he called back to me that he would be ready to go back to the Health Care Center with me as soon as he completed Jorge's discharge papers.

One of the folks I was supporting in his recovery was also in the hospital for a liver transplant so I told Jorge and Misha that I wanted to stop in on him and see how he was doing and that I would be back in about 15 minutes.

I returned and shared with Jorge and Misha that I thought it might be a good idea to cancel the group meeting the coming Sunday and give them and everyone a break. They agreed. Fred appeared at the door. I gave Jorge and Misha a hug, said good bye, and Fred and I left to go back to the Health Care Center.

Thirty

On the way back to the Center I shared with Fred the vision that Jorge and Misha had about supporting those on the front lines of ministry with the homeless, drug addicts, and mentally ill. I told him about their observations related to Secondary Post Stress Disorder and compassion fatigue. We both agreed that what had just happened to Jorge was a clear confirmation that God was calling them to a ministry that addressed this need. He thought it had the potential to save lives with exponential results for many who were served by these unrecognized sacrificial heroes. Fred asked me to please keep him up to date on how things might develop. I was tempted to tell him about the pending formation of the Bryce Foundation and it was hard to not share my wonder but I managed to keep my mouth shut and wait until the sale of the Beckley's company.

When we got back to the Health Care Center I filled Deb in on our time with Jorge and Misha and we agreed that it sounded like a good idea to cancel this week's LP meeting. So I called Stan, Mel, and James to let them know. Deb emailed the women. The women also decided to cancel their lunch.

After some wait the nurse came with Jorge's discharge papers. Misha and Jorge finally got home around 5:00 p.m. The boys, as well as Misha parents, were anxiously waiting for them with lots of questions. After an extensive debriefing there were many sighs of relief and expressions of gratitude. After a light dinner at Jorge's request, Misha's parents went home and the relieved family of four settled down to have a peaceful night watching soccer on TV.

That Thursday, September 13, 2007 was Billy's first soccer scrimmage. It was against Foxwood High School at the East Shore Tigers Field. Billy was feeling like this was going to be test for whether or not the team was beginning to accept him or not. The coaching staff to set up the positions. The team was organized into two platoons consistent with how they had been practicing. Carl had been elected Captain by his teammates. The coach had assigned him to the Blue Platoon and moved him to Center Forward with Steve at Right Forward and Cowboy at Left. Billy had taken Carl's life long position at Center Midfield. Although they had been practicing together and seem to communicate well on the field, Billy still wasn't sure if he was really part of the core.

The Blue Platoon started the game. For the first five minutes both teams were clearly just feeling the other out.

About seven minutes into the first half, Foxwood began to become more aggressive and went on the attack. The Red Platoon, which was designed to be the stronger defensive Platoon went in and responded well. They held Foxwood to only two shots on goal, both of which were deflected before they reach the goalie.

The coach made only two substitution during the first 12 minutes. The Blue Platoon was starting to get extremely anxious to get in, especially as most of the guys on Blue had been watching and had picked up some of the weakness of the players who would be marking them. Things like which kids over-committed on defense and how far the goalie came out of the box to cut off the angle on the goal. Billy noticed too that the left defender wasn't nearly as fast as the right defender. It was like watch scouting taps. Billy mentioned this to Cowboy, Carl, and Citters and all three said they had noticed it too. They agreed that when they got in they would look for a way to take advantage of it.

Then with about two minutes before the end of the half the coach switched Platoons and the Blue team when in fired up. There still has no score and Foxwood and the Red Platoon were both showing some fatigue.

As the Tigers entire Red Platoon came off the field and a new on came in you could see the Foxwood players stop in their tracks for a minute and just look at each other.

The ball had been kicked out of bounds by Foxwood. Sammy, the Blue Platoon Sweeper threw the ball down the line to Cowboy. Cowboy passed it to Carl who dribbled it past mid-field and toward the center. Cowboy, who was much faster than Foxwood's left defender, took off down the side line and Carl passed it back to him. The sweeper came over to head off Cowboy and Cowboy passed it back to Carl. As the Foxwood defenders moved to cover Carl he passed it back to Billy who was moving fast down the center of the field. The goalie came out to cut Billy's angle off since the defense was pulled over defending against Carl and Cowboy, Billy stop, touched the ball, Carl's defender came after Billy, the goalie was out of goal, Carl broke from right behind Billy. Billy, with lighting foot work, tapped the ball to Carl and bang - GOAL.

Cowboy, Carl, and Billy, with Steve and the rest of the Platoon all came running towards each other with hugs and high-fives. Billy guessed rightly; now he had been accepted as part of the core.

That same day, Mel got a call from Eli's counselor at Walcott saying that he would like to meet with him and Eli the following Wednesday at 10:00 AM. He didn't say any more than that and for the next week Mel was more than preoccupied, ruminating about the meeting. All kinds of wild speculations were running through his mind, from there being some kind of probation agreement to catastrophic thinking that Eli had brain damage from drug use and would be hospitalized the rest of his life or that he had slit his wrists in an attempted suicide and was being placed in a mental hospital for the criminally insane. He felt like he was praying more for his son and himself than he had forever for anything. He was also riddled with guilt about neglecting Eli all his life.

Mel must have called me five or six times that week expressing his anxieties. I listened to what he was going through and understood. Although I didn't say this to him, it was rather refreshing and hopeful to me for see this man who had always projected such an aura of having it all together to be so vulnerable.

On Wednesday, September 19th Mel arrived at Walcott at 10:00 a.m. on the dot. The receptionist directed him to a small private waiting room with two doors that had signs on them that indicating that they were the offices of counselors. One said, Dr. Barry J. Harding, PhD. This was person who had called him. Within three minutes, his door opened and out came a tall thin man in his mid-forties with a long pony tail, bushy mustache, and wire rimmed glasses dressed in blue jeans and a short sleeved gray dress shirt that revealed a tattoo of a cross surrounded by fire on his forearm. He no more looked like a shrink than Mel looked like a coal miner. He introduced himself as Barry and Mel responded with his first name as well. Dr. Harding had an engaging smile, warm eyes, and greeted Mel with a hand shake that communicated assurance and support. As he ushered Mel into his office Mel saw Eli sitting in one of two chairs opposite Dr. Harding's desk chair. Eli sat with his head bowed down and did not look at his father as he came through the door but as Barry came in Eli stood up, looked at his dad and said, "Hi Dad." Mel responded with "Hi son."

Everyone then sat down, Mel in a chair facing Eli and Barry with his back to his desk facing both of them. Then Barry explained that for the past month he and Eli had been meeting together several times a week and that he felt Eli was making excellent progress, that he recognized many of his issues and was dealing with them. Then he asked Eli if he had anything to add. He said no. Then Barry said that he understood that the last time that Eli had seen Mel he said he did not want to talk to him but that now Eli did want to talk and that he had some things he wanted to say to his dad. Dr. Harding then looked at Eli, indicating it was now his turn.

Eli was silent for a minute, just sitting looking at his feet. He then looked up at his dad and said, "First, dad, I want to tell you that the best thing you ever did for me in my whole life was to not bail me out when you came to get me at the police station. I have hope now and I know you love me for the first time."

Mel started to cry.

Eli waited.

Mel collected himself but could not respond and Eli continued.

"Second, I need to say that I have been angry with you."

Barry caught Eli's eye.

Eli continued, "I mean really really angry. I have been angry because I have never felt like you were a father for me. I have felt like I was in your way, like I was a bother, like you never said no to me and you never cared what I did or didn't do. And I have hated the way you have neglected mom and taken her for granted. And I have wanted to just take Andi and run away because I felt like you thought she was in your way too. And right now I don't feel bad about telling you all that because I think I have been right. I love you dad but you have been a terrible father."

The whole time Eli said this he looked confidently right into Mel's eyes. He then looked and Dr. Harding and Dr. Harding looked at Mel.

Mel had stopped crying and wasn't sure what to say at first. He had just been listening and taking in what Eli was saying rather than thinking and planning how to respond. He felt no need to justify himself.

After about 10 long seconds Mel said, "You're right, Eli. I have been a terrible father and husband. I have neglected your mother and you and your sister. I have been more concerned about myself, with an inflated idea of who I am, than with raising you and your sister or loving your mother. I am sorry more than I can tell you. But I want to tell you. You have a right to be angry. The truth is I haven't tried to be a father so I haven't learned how to love you. I do love you so very much but I haven't acted like it. I hope someday you can forgive me. Please forgive me."

Eli did not respond.

Dr. Harding was quiet, not looking either one of his two clients.

Then Eli said, "Barry can I say something?"

With eyes of kindness, Barry nodded his affirmation towards Eli.

"Dad, I am forgiving you, I need to so I can be free of my anger and resentment. But dad what are you going to do to change? I cannot return to the past. I am a drug addict and if I live like I lived I'll do what I did. I need a new life and if you stay the same way, then I can't have you in my new life."

Mel thought, *"My son is growing up and he is insightful."*

With a deep breath, Mel replied, "I can't promise you anything Eli. But let me bring you up to date on what has been happening to me too. First, I have been going to Naranon and I realize that the disease of addiction is a family disease and I, too, need a new way of life. And the first part of that new way of life is to not to now start to over compensate and make up for all my mistakes by trying to tell you how to live. Second, the night I came to the police station with an old new found friend, I was coming from a meeting with a group of people who were my closest friends when we were in high school. We are now all reevaluating our life and our future. And part of that is that I have quit my job at the church and I have stopped my writing and well as my speaking and teaching engagements. I have no idea what the future holds, except it will be in an accountable relationship with these new long lost friends. And third, your mom and I are in this 100% together and we have not been happier in the last 20 years. I don't know if that helps or hurts your recovery but it is a beginning of some change, and I guess rather major change."

"Wow!" exclaimed Eli.

Barry nodded in agreement.

And then he followed up with, "I think we have some new beginnings here. This has been more than a good first step. Eli, has more work to do and has to complete his rehab and sentence and graduate from high school, but it sounds like we are well on our way to a new way of life, free from a number of addictions.

Also during the two week break between Liminal Plunge group meetings; Stan and the Cyber Market board continued arrangements for the sale of the company. Stan and I and his attorney worked on the Bryce Foundation by-laws, board selection nominations, incorporation papers, and bank accounts. Mel and I met to talk some more about how to protect the LP group from institutionalism. James worked on arrangements for the Haiti trip. And everyone who was committed to going on the trip, worked on getting all of their medical and passport needs. The woman also met to plan for the next LP meeting.

Thirty One

Sunday, September 23, 2007

The LP Group resumed meeting that Sunday. During the two week break, Sunny and Sara McFarlane, Karen's mother, Ruth, and Fred Billard and his wife Susie, had all been invited and all attended. I admitted to Deb as we were on our way to pick up James, Jorge, and Misha that I had a little apprehension about how the group dynamics might play out with five new people who had not experienced the common transformative experience that had bonded the rest of us over the last couple of months.

Deb's response lowered my anxiety a lot. She said that the Body of Christ was not dependent upon shared common experiences but upon surrendered hearts. She reminded me that we are bonded in Christ by the indwelling of the Holy Spirit. Her words helped me a lot, mostly to remember that God is in control. By the time we got to James' apartment I was feeling peaceful about the meeting.

When we arrived at Stan and Karen everyone else was already there. The first thing I noticed was that Mel and Sunny were in a conversation and Stan and Fred seemed to be engaged as well. Deb and Misha joined the women who were preparing dinner. I joined Sunny and Mel and James and Jorge joined Stan and Fred.

After about ten minutes Karen called everyone to the table. I was impressed with how well the dining room table expanded to accommodate the fourteen of us.

Before we were seated Ruth asked us all to stand and join hands. She then led us in a beautiful prayer, thanking God for providing not only the food we were about to eat but also for the new life in Christ that we continue to experience. I was struck by her positive straight talk and enthusiasm for the future. She then led us in singing the doxology. We sat down and Karen passed around the soup that Liz had made, the lettuce salad with strawberries that Misha had brought, and the homemade bread that she had made. We all enjoyed the meal without any discussion about an agenda for our meeting that would follow or business talk about Cyber Market or Apple Orchard Church or medical stuff or even the war in Iraq. It was really a nice time together with a very diverse group of people. Nobody even tried to draw out any of the new comers' theology. I thought to myself, *'Maybe we are getting past the religious stuff and learning to be spiritual. There seems to be an unusual amount of acceptance and gratitude around this table.'*

After dinner, the "experienced" group members as well as our new members Ruth, Sunny, Sara, Fred, and Susie, automatically gravitated to the Great room. Karen and Misha, stayed back in the kitchen to finish clearing up the dishes No sooner had everyone been seated than Karen and Misha emerged with trays full of plates of apple pie and ice cream for everyone. Jorge declined as did Sunny.

Stan started the meeting. He began, "It is a joy to have Ruth, Sunny, Sara, Fred, and Susie with us tonight. What a delight! Welcome! May the grace of our Lord Jesus bless your hearts.

"For me the past two weeks have seemed like an eternity. I have missed being together. We have a lot of stuff to talk about tonight. But as we have learned, first things first. What seems like business and details can wait. I think what we need to do first is to get to know one another. Does anyone have anything they think should trump that?"

A couple of people shock their heads and Stan continued, "This may sound odd to those who are with us for the first time, but, what has brought us together was the martyr of a couple old friends and two of their children. I think that we have all come to the realization that our lives in Christ are broken. It appears that God needs to break us over and over again in order for His Kingdom on earth to come live in us. Since these old friends of some of us were murdered by a children's army in the Sudan, our lives have begun to be dramatically transformed. We will perhaps get to that later. But for now, I think it would be appropriate for each of us who have had this happening to us share a short version of what that transformation has been about for each of us. And then, so that we could get to know you who are new, would you, if you feel comfortable enough, share something about yourself.

"One more thing before we get started. I recently heard what I think is a very important ground rule for any group that shares personal stories. That is that confidentiality is a spiritual foundation for trusting relationships, it reminds us to respect others and put others before ourselves. So please, what you hear here let it stay here.

"Does all that sound right and good to everyone?"

"Yep." "Sounds good." "Makes sense to me." "Sure."

"Mel, would you be willing to start?"

"Sure Stan, but I am not sure where to start. I'll try and keep it simple. "For the last 15 years or so I think of my life as being pretty messed up to say the least. But I don't think it would be helpful to share all my poor decisions. Let me just say that what may have appeared to the world as the top of success has been the bottom of the pit for me. I have had everything that

America says are the goals of being a Christian but they have been the furthest thing from being a disciple of Jesus as anyone could be. By God's grace he has intervened in my life and he is beginning to change me. I am no longer what I used to be and I believe and hope that I am ready for whomever God wants me to be. I have a beautiful daughter that I am beginning to get to know, my son and I are just beginning a new way of life free from our addictions. His addiction had been drugs, mine has been ego. And for the first time in many years my wife and I are of one heart and mind. That is the sum of it. I know that is not many details but I hope you get the picture. I have recently resigned my job as a pastor and am open to whatever God has for me from here on. I more than willing to share the details later with anyone, but for now, let's just say I am right at the beginning of getting to know myself again."

"I would like to go next," said Liz. "My name is Liz, Mel's wife and I have been a major contributor to our disastrous life. For years, really most of our life together since Mel went to seminary, I have sat back and been the submissive wife. I have not been honest and have not spoken up about what I really believed or felt or thought. Silence in the face of danger can lead to the destruction of not only the one who is facing the danger but everyone that person touches. God's intervention in Mel's life along with the shock of the death of our missionary friends in the Sudan have shaken me loose from my cowardliness and given me the courage to face myself and stand up for what I believe. I had been resenting and blaming God rather than doing or even saying something myself. This courage has made me realized too that when it came to our children, Eli and Andi, my fear and lacking of faith was hurting them as well. I had been such a wimp, running away for faithfulness to Jesus. In fact, until Mel's realization and the Bryce family tragedy, I was seriously contemplating actually running away, just disappearing. But no more. I may not know what to say or do now, but when my gut tells me something just isn't right I am not going to keep my mouth shut anymore. And I want you all to hold me accountable. So, that is what has happened to me. I am free, I am a liberated woman, a liberal conservative evangelical. But most of all I am just so grateful for what is happening to our family, especially Mel's relationship with our kids. It is simply miraculous. Thanks for letting me share."

I spoke up next because I was just bursting with excitement. "Fifteen year old Billy is the only surviving family member of our close friends who were killed in the Sudan. We were named in their will as his guardians and he is living with us now. He has shared with me that in the East African Christian Revival when someone is first introduced to someone else it can often take an hour. Their introduction involves each person giving his or her conversion testimony. I feel like we are doing something similar here.

"I have been a part of Narcotic Anonymous for twenty years. A cornerstone of recovery is what the Twelve Step program calls a Lead. A Lead is when someone share their experience, strength, and hope. It is their testimony and it helps others to have hope. It keeps their new life of recovery alive just like introductions keep the revival in East Africa alive and spreading. Maybe the sharing of transformational experiences is what ushers in the Kingdom of God. I think we need to do this regularly to practice surrendering and gratitude.

"Twenty years ago I was a drug addict and dope pusher and God had to break me. I had to admit that my life was unmanageable, that I was powerless over my addiction and that a power greater than myself could restore me to sanity.

God broke me and I surrendered my will and the care of my life over to Jesus.

"What has happened to me recently has been another breaking of my will. Those who know me, know that I have had some pretty strong judgments about the church. They know that in my arrogance I have always thought that I have known better than everyone else, about almost everything, but especially when it comes to what it means to be a disciple of Jesus and what is wrong with the church. I used to think nobody has had the same experiences as me, so nobody understands as well as I do. Well, Mel's confession at our first meeting confronted my arrogance. It hit me like a bolt of lightning. I was confronted with how I had always been such a judgmental and self-righteous idiot. I had always made God's battle my battle. That night I was face to face with the reality, as evident as this may have been to everyone else who knows me, that the truth is, the battle is not mine. It is God's and he is most capable of fighting it and winning it, even with me in the way. I met the enemy and I am he. And now I am so in awe and excited that God loves me anyway. Now, his grace is more than enough. I feel like I am free of an addiction all over again. I can stand up for what rings true to me and what I believe, but I can let it go. I don't need to be right. I can now trust that not can God speak through my experience, but He also speaks through the Body of Christ. For me that surrender is huge. God has broken my self-centeredness again.

I'm done."

Deb then shared that what had happened to her was that she confessed her anger at me for never being content with a church, her anger about the Bryce's murders, her sense of inadequacy in being prepared to raise Billy, her anger about what had happened to her satisfying life as a nurse and mother, and her self-righteous judgment of her complacent apathetic parents. But she said she was now finding new enthusiasm for life among these new friends and a renewed sense of adventure rather than a need to accept the status-quo. Her last words were, "It is strange, but where there was anger, there is now a mysterious joy."

Jorge then shared with a quiet humility, "I have been such a weak excuse for a disciple of Jesus and yet he has been so gracious, forgiving, and good to me." Jorge then went on to share that at our revival meeting he was convicted of his fear of confronting gang leaders or, for that matter, any injustice. He said was learning that it was his lack of faith in God's love for him was at the root of his fear and lack of courage. He said that what Dr. Billard said to him in the hospital about God giving him a wake-up call was like God telling him again, showing him again, that he was really accepted and God's beloved. He told us in the past week he had been able to stop eating so much and start exercising and just being himself. He had actually let go of needing to perform for Misha's parents or the church.

He concluded with, "I cannot tell any lies here; my new doctor is present. The truth, for real, is that this past two weeks have been perhaps the best two weeks of my life, next to Misha and my wedding and honeymoon. Not only am I motivated to love myself as my neighbor and start taking care of myself, but Misha and I have had some great conversations about our future. Whatever it takes we are going to pursue our vision of addressing the self-care needs of the front line servants of the Kingdom. And I have a fresh new freedom to be bold about doing what is right and good. So, you all can expect us to looking to this fellowship for support and guidance. I am doing well, thanks to God's mercy and Dr. Billard's doctoring. Thank you, doc."

Misha went next explaining that all her life she has had confusion about who she was. She said she was not sure why but she has gotten in touch with her fears, especially in the past couple of months. She has felt accepted, not only by Jorge but by the fellowship of the old friends in the group. She said she has been feeling God love for her more than she has ever felt it in her life. She talked about no longer being afraid of disappointing her parents, and that she was falling in love with Jorge and her kids all over again. She was talking fast and it seemed it was hard for her not to go talking on and on about everything that was being released within her. But she got control of herself and simply concluded by saying she was so excited about creating a new ministry with Jorge.

As Misha ended Karen spoke up. I was sure she would talk about Stan and her decision to sell their company, but that is not what she shared with the group.

"Since the Bryces were martyred I am no longer concerned about pretending to be someone that I think other people want me to be. I am quitting my charity performance charade and trying to take off my mask of respectability. At the luncheon after the funeral I think I blurted out something about picking up where Brandon and Emily left off. At the time I really didn't know where that was coming from. Since then what I do know is that my life has been turned up-side-down. I am free of needing to pretend to be the wealthy socialite and model Christian lady. I just want to be someone who has a heart like Jesus and not care whether the so called right people accept me or not. And to tell the truth, I don't think I care about money anymore either. Jesus was homeless and destitute. Why should I think I need to be better off? He was a servant not a capitalist. He never profited from his healing, teaching, or preaching. Six months ago I would have never have said this but I am really looking forward to going to Haiti.

"Maybe what I just shared doesn't really say much about my life and my past but I hope it says a lot about who I am tonight.

Stan was the next one to share but he didn't say much, which seemed rather uncharacteristic for him. He simply said he was excited to be seeing the changes in Karen and that he thought God was in the process of showing him a whole new way to live. He said it scared him to death but he also felt more secure than in any other time in his life. "I am just taking one day at a time and waiting on the Lord. I am relieved to be leaving the competitive corporate world and excited about discovering the Kingdom of God. But honestly, I am not sure what that means. I only know it means not going back to where I have been."

"Well, I guess it is my turn," said James. "I haven't had the "about face" that everyone else has been talking about. But I am excited that the changes in your lives provides an opportunity to make a difference in my life. After Sally, my wife, died in 1994, I floundered around at a church in Atlanta and then as a YWAM volunteer. I was searching for what to do with my life. I finally found a niche in Haiti helping Dr. Pete Palmer and Father Jacque Lamont. And now I am trying to raise money for an orphanage that I am starting in Haiti and I am exciting that in December you all are going to see first-hand the need and the potential for improving ' quality of life. Do you know that there are approximately 200,000 orphans in Haiti in need of care and that half the children in Haiti die by the age of five? I have learned it takes a lot of commitment and money to even begin to make a difference. Thank you for wanting to help."

Ruth was sitting next to James and I could see her getting a little impatient with his speech so as he paused, she began, "I'm Ruth, Karen's mom. First, I want to say, Karen, it is about time you started to get off your high horse. If God is responsible for it then, 'Praise the Lord!' And Rev. Carr it does my heart good to see a big shot celebrity like yourself taking a good look at himself, trying to get his priorities right, and paying attention to what's important in this life rather than trying to do God's job. So, there, that's off my chest.

"Now let me tell you all a little about myself. A number of years ago, when Karen was in college, I was at the beauty parlor. No response is necessary. I was sitting under the hair dryer reading *Decision Magazine* when the lady next to me noticed what I was reading and said to me, 'I see you are reading *Decision*, do you read it often?' I replied, 'Why yes.' She said, 'Do you enjoy reading it?' I said, 'Yes, very much!" She then asked, "Do you like Billy Graham?' I said, 'Yes, I watch him every time he comes on TV.' 'Oh,' she came back at me. 'Are you born again?' 'No, I said, I haven't died the first time yet.' She looked sort of surprised and just went back to reading her *Ladies Home Journal.*

"I decided to follow Jesus when I was in my teens but I have never really understood what the Church had to do with it. For me what it's meant to follow Jesus has been to try and be honest, be a faithful wife, and be the best mother and grandmother I can be. That usually means trying to keep my mouth shut, be kind and generous, and care for other people more than I do for myself. I know that Jesus forgives me for not being very good at most of that, most of the time, because he gave his life for me. If there is a hell after we die, worse than the hell that so many people live in this life, then I trust that Jesus' love for me will keep me safe with him when I die. Regardless, he sure has given me a full and fulfilling life now. That's about all I have to say about that.

"I'm 76 years old and was married to a strong man who was my angel for forty-five years. He died ten years ago. I have two awesome children. Pete, my oldest, who lives in Seattle, is single, maybe gay but celibate, I hope. He's got a good job in management with Seattle's Best. And I have one budding granddaughter who is the joy of my life right now. Stan and Karen have been very kind and generous to me and I am very grateful that this group has welcomed me. I am a little scared about going to Haiti with all of you, but I am also up for a new adventure.

"I think that's enough for now, you may get to know me better than you want. Basically, what you see is what you get."

Susie was sitting beside Ruth so she went next.

"I'm Susie, Fred's wife. We have 6 kids between 19 to 6 years old, three boys and three girls. I love being a mom, singing in our church choir, jogging, swimming, helping out at our neighborhood toy exchange program, and nursing part-time every other Saturday at the Health Care Center. I grew up a Catholic and became a born again Christian at a Baptist Church in Boston while in college at Amherst. Fred and I now worship at St. Stephen's Episcopal Church in Henley.

"I think this is a great group and I feel at home with your vulnerable honesty. Thanks for including us tonight."

There was a pause, some silence, and then Susie looked at Fred which was followed by everyone else looking at him.

So Fred said, "Hi, I guess you all want me to tell you something about me. My name is Fred Billard." He smiled and added. "I am Susie's seventh child. She also forgot to mention that we have 2 dogs and a cat. I am a family practice physician." He paused, thought for a minute and after several false starts he finally said, "Maybe it would be best to start my saying I enjoy being a doctor. I love my wife and family. I love Jesus. I believe God has called me to serve the poor. I am grateful for every one of the 70 staff at the Henley Health Care Center. I am in awe of how God has blessed me. I enjoy going on missions to Guatemala and Honduras. And I think from what I have just heard, and from what "O" and Deb have shared with me, that God is revealing his Kingdom through you. I am humbled to be among you."

He then paused again and then said, "I am anxious to see what God does. Thanks so much for inviting Susie and me to join you tonight. I hope we don't get in the way of your hearing God for what is next."

Only Sunny and Sara were left, so Sunny went next. "My name is Carl McFarlyne, almost everyone knows me by "Sunny." He flashed his huge bright smile. "And I am a grateful recovering sinner and drug addict in the process of being transformed. I am originally from Michigan and the second of eight children. My substance abuse started when I was eight years old and I was addicted by the age of thirteen. I chased mind altering drugs for nineteen years. I have been clean and sober for fourteen years. For the years when I was using I was a very scary and wild person. I was a gangster and a thug and in and out of prison. But today Jesus is my God, not the drugs, and I chose to seek to have him run my life instead of letting the drugs run my life. Odell saved my life. He got me into treatment and introduced me to the Twelve Step fellowship. Jesus is now my, what we in that fellowship call, 'higher power.' He is my strength and hope. I should have died at least four times and as I look back I realize that God's grace brought me back to life. I am free of anger and no longer confused or lonely. I have peace today and my smile is for real. I know that God loves me. I am just learning how to live for the first time and I have learned that you stay clean by staying honest, humble, and grateful. I have a job today and I tell the truth today. My mother even likes me today. My kids respect me. And I have a wife that has loved me through everything. And believe me she has been through a lot with me and really knows me and yet she still keeps loving me. She is the strongest evidence of God's love for me.

I understand that this support group is trying to figure out what the church is. I have never really understood what the church is either; though I really didn't pay attention until the last few years. What it seems like to me is that it is a social club where everyone wears a mask, thinks alike, and pretends they are better than anyone else.

Well, for me, and this is only for me, as I have looked at the Bible and what Jesus seems to identify as church is that the church is a new way of live, a family living out God's will. And, like, the closest thing I have found to Jesus' church is the Twelve Step Fellowship. We are a fellowship of recovering sinners discovering a new way of life, free from our addiction. You know, everyone in the world is addicted to something, and God wants us to all be free to follow Him. Sara it is your turn."

"Thanks, Sunny. I won't be long. This has been great. I feel so honored to be privileged to have you all be so open with me. I have just loved listening to you.

"I met Sunny while he was a Black Muslim. He had been clean for maybe a couple of years. When we met he was gorgeous, had his great smile, and such a gentleman. He swept me off my feet. But when he started using again my life became a nightmare. I never knew if he were dead or alive and I rarely saw him. All I could do was pray.

"I had grown up in a Christian home and had been in love with Jesus, but those years really tested my faith. I joined Islam to please Sunny. You would have thought that I should have known that another religion based on rules, like Islam is, and not based in grace and love: would not provide a higher power strong enough to defeat a mind altering addiction. I am five years younger than Sunny and I was so smitten by the man. I prayed to Jesus and cried and cried and prayed. And after eight years God heard my pleas.

"While he was using drugs I went to Pitt, got a degree in Elementary Education, and for the past 16 years I have been teaching the second grade.

"The first couple of years of Sunny's recovery were for me filled with fear and anxiety, but God has healed my post-traumatic stress and the past 10 years have been a dream come true. I am so blessed."

Sara, stopped and was quiet.

"Aren't we all so blessed?" Stan summarized. "It is so good and encouraging to hear how uniquely God so faithful share his extravagant loves for each of us. I am learning that as we share each of our experiences of God's love we see it more clearly. The sum of the whole is greater than each individual part. Our individual experience of God's love is wonderful but our combined shared experience of his love is amazing. For me, this time of sharing has been really good. Regardless of what else we do tonight this time together has already really blessed my heart. We now do have a lot more to get caught up on though.

"First, Mel, I understand you had a break through time with Eli this week and I hear that Billy had a little breakthrough of his own. Perhaps there are some other 'kisses from God' that some of you would like to share. Then I need to bring you up to date on the Bryce Foundation By-laws and Board development, we need to clarify some things about the Haiti trip, and I think we need to pick up where we left off the last time when Odell and Mel were sharing about preventing the Body of Christ from becoming an institution of man. Mel will you please tell us all about your time with your son?"

Thirty Two

"My son, Elijah. I am on cloud nine. Some of you know that he is at Walcott and he was refusing to talk to me. Well this week his counselor asked me to come in and meet with them." Mel then, almost verbatim, told us about his healing time with Eli.

I then shared a little from what Billy had told be about the soccer game and how he was starting to feel accepted by the team.

James then reminded us of details related to our preparation for our trip to Haiti. He let us know that he had been in touch with his partners in Haiti and they said they could accommodate as many people as we brought, as long as we weren't too picky about where we slept.

Deb leaned over to me and whispered, "I wonder what not being picky about where we sleep means."

When James finished, Stan passed out the Foundation's By-Laws that he, his lawyer, and I had put together, and filled everyone in on what they said. He also suggested a couple other people as possible Board members, one a lawyer and one an accountant. He said he thought they would both get excited about the mission of the Foundation and he was sure they would welcome being involved. We all agreed. Then he asked us all to not breathe a word to anyone about what he was about to share with us and to also not make any stock transactions related to Cyber Market. He told us that the sale of Cyber Market was set for Tuesday, October 9, and that it would be sold to Internet Marketing, Inc. for one dollar a share above what the market price was when the market opened that day. He said the money that he and Karen would realize from the sale would go directly into a Trust account established to hold the funds for the new Bryce Foundation. We had a little discussion around some of the details about the requirement for Board members.

When Stan was finished he ask Mel and I to pick up where we had left off about our ideas for how to be the Church without becoming an institutional corporation.

Mel with his practiced skills as a group facilitator began with a very clear summary of our last discussion and handed out printed outlines of what he called the five 'boundaries' we had suggested.

This was all new to Sunny, Sara, Ruth, Fred and Susie. I could tell from the look on their faces that they were wondering what they had gotten themselves into. I saw Fred glance at his watch. I imagined that he must be wondering what this was all about and how long it was going to take since we had already been meeting for two hours, and what was coming sounded like it could last for several days.

So, assessing their nervousness, before Mel introduced the next thing we were planning to present, I interrupted him and said, "It might be helpful to let the first timers here in on what we are talking about. You see, not only did the assassinations of the members of the Bryce family cause us to get in touch with our separation from Jesus, it also surfaced our need for a community of disciples. That has led to considerable confusion about just what is the Church and how we be a Church. So, we have been searching for that community and life style. Mel and I have been working on some suggestion for this group. Hopefully, you all can help us think this stuff through. We desperately need some direction for how we are going to move forward in support of one another as we abandon our past lives and seek to follow Jesus. But it has been our experience that to be in the world but not of the world seems almost impossible. We seem to get subtly seduced by our fallen nature and our need to control our lives and therefore the Church."

"Can I say something?" asked Sunny.

"It is my experience that there are a lot of people who are looking for a church fellowship. There are probably many thousands of people in recovery from addictions of every kind who live with a stigma that prevents them from being their honest self in the church. Personally, I think that the way our culture stigmatizes exposed sin is one reason it is so hard to be honest in the church and maybe even with ourselves. Our masks seem to keep church member's sins hidden from each other. I think people, especially those who have exposed their character defects in their recovery from addictions, need to feel they belong with a fellowship that accepts them in their sin. I am very much interested in what you guys have been thinking."

"Thanks, Sunny." I said.

Fred then spoke up. "I can identify and understand where you are coming from and I really appreciate and respect what you are struggling with. But the Church has been around for a long long time. Over the centuries many people have tried hundreds of various life-styles, forms, organizations, and more. I don't know anything about what you have suggest so far but from what you have handed out it looks like you are applying some of the suggestion of the Twelve Steps programs. I would just caution that besides being a young movement of only a seventy year history. The Twelve Steps fellowship is also a rather small and obscure movement. Are you sure Odell, that you are not simply so involved with recovery that it becomes a window through which you see hope for everything?"

"Let me respond, Odell." said Mel. "Fred, your points are well taken. But most revolutions throughout history started with a very few surrendered risk takers. Plus, though the Twelve Step movement is not publicized it is still a movement that is significantly influencing hundreds of thousands of people. There are over forty-one different types of Twelve Step Fellowships of one kind or another in the world. In additions to AA and NA. AA and NA are the ones that address healing from addiction to drugs and alcohol. But just with them alone there are over one hundred and fourteen thousand AA fellowship groups in the world and fifty-eight thousand NA fellowship groups. In the greater Pittsburgh area there are maybe over nine hundred AA and NA fellowship groups meetings a week. Compared to institutional churches in the greater Pittsburgh area, the Yellow Pages list eight hundred and ninety-six Churches from all denominations.

"Plus, the start of the Twelve Step movement took the founders of AA eleven years of trial and error to settle on the Twelve Traditions. We haven't even shared ours, let along started to experience if they make sense."

"Good answers, Mel. I'm open and I think, if Susie is in agreement, we would like to explore with you all for a while. If, like your handout says, the only requirement for membership is a desire to follow Jesus, then we are members. But, now that I said we would like to pursue this with you, I am going to have to apologize, we need leave. I just got a page from the hospital that one of my patients was admitted to emergency. So sorry we have to go. This has been a great time, thank you all so much for including us. Odell and Deb, will you guys please keep us in the loop? Please don't let our leaving interrupt this discussion. This time has built my faith and hope."

"Fred, I think I would like to stay, if Odell has room in his car and can take me home." Susie asserted.

I responded, "We do, and I would be glad to."

"Thanks 'O'." Fred nodded.

Fred got up and Stan accompanied him to the door. They hugged and parted. The rest of us were silent as we waited for Stan to return to his seat.

"Folks," I began, "It is almost 8:30, we want to all be on our way by 9:00 so I want to try and pick up where we left off a couple of weeks ago. The institutional church has most often organized itself around programs for the purpose of worship, instruction, and mission. The last point in the summary that Mel sent out is that in addition to being a church fellowship, the members are to create organizations, as an outgrowth of the church, to provide ministries of mercy, healing, compassion, justice, teaching, and preaching. These organizations are not the church; they are the ministries of the church.

"It seems that so far in our experience as a little group we are discovering the church is for the purpose of being a community that loves one another. We are learning to accept each other and feel free to confess to one another and hold each other accountable. We are becoming interdependent with each other and sharing our lives with each other. We are fellowship, a family of God. We are being a church.

"But we don't yet have the programs and ministries that institutional churches have. By the nature of being an institution, the institutional church finds definition for itself by its programs and ministries, not by being a community that loves one another. And yet, if being a church is defined by loving one another and not by its programs, what about Jesus call for the church to have ministries of healing, teaching, and preaching?

We want to suggest that the Church, Jesus Body, the fellowship of the followers of Jesus who we are. The ministries of the Church are what the followers of Jesus do; like the person of Jesus is God in the flesh and the ministry of Jesus were what he did; healing, teaching, and preaching."

As I looked around, Mel nodded his head and so did a couple others but most everyone else looked a little lost. I thought maybe if we just keep going it will become clear to everyone what we are trying to say.

Mel than spoke up. "We have one primary purpose, to love one another. We have already suggested that the church, with the purpose of being a fellowship, should have no professionals. We want to also suggest that the church as a fellowship not have any, what we usually think of as programs. Our suggestion about what to do about a mission or ministries is to create mission entities. There is a church in Washington, DC that is made up of about twelve people. They try to love one another. Their fellowship is their church. They also have a housing mission or ministry, called Jubilee Housing, where they manage about two hundred and fifty housing units. A couple of the church fellowship members are on the staff of the Jubilee Housing and they hire about 6 other people, who are not part of their church fellowship. They have a mission vision to house the poor, but that is not their church, that is their mission."

"I get it!" Stan exclaimed. "How have I missed it all my life?"

"How have we all missed it." answered Mel. "We have missed it because we have swallowed the value of our culture that says are worth is tied to our productivity. God, however, says our worth is tied to his unconditional love for us. We are loved just because of who we are regardless of what we do."

"This is getting interesting." Stan interjects again. "So, now we don't create a church program, but we create an independent mission organization. How do we decide what our mission or missions are to be? We also do not have any church hierarchy to give us directions, right? How do we make a decision about a mission?

"Group conscious!" Blurted out, Sunny.

"Thanks, Sunny." I said. "I thought you would catch the drift.

"Group conscious is Twelve Step jargon for consensus. This group has been functioning by making decision as a group. We have been agreeing together about what we are to do next by consensus."

"I hate to be a pain. Maybe I am being a little defensive, since I have spent my career being a decision maker, but unless we stay a small group, it is not possible to have a consensus with more than about twelve or so people. We already have 14 at tonight's fellowship." responded Stan.

Mel answered. "Our culture's value that bigger or more is better has taught us to assume that we should grow. Yes, a goal of the Kingdom of God is for all of creation to be reconciled to a love relationship with God, but that does not mean that the family of God is to be organized into mega churches. If you look at how the church functioned in the New Testament, you see 3,000 or more believers immediately after Pentecost, yet in Acts and the Epistles and even for the first 300 years of the church, the fellowship met in members' homes. In that culture, especially among the common people, I doubt very much if they had homes that could accommodate more than about, say twenty people. They met in small fellowship groups. Also, you see in the Gospels, the model that Jesus set was a group of twelve or maybe as many as twenty, if you include a few woman. Yet, many many people followed Jesus from time to time, but he never organized them further than the twelve.

"I think what we are suggesting is that when a local church adds member so that the group becomes more than about fifteen or eighteen consistent members then that group, spins off another local small group church fellowship."

"Then how do we stay connected?" asked Misha.

I answered, "That is where there is a need to have a mission ministry that has a calling to provide communications between fellowships. And maybe that ministry also plans and coordinate stuff like educational literature, and common gatherings for worship, encouragement, and information sharing."

At this Liz interrupted. "I'm sorry guys but it is getting late and my brain is again on overload. Can we call it a night?

"Good call." added, Ruth.

"Mel and I don't have much more to add. That is it. That is what we wanted to suggest for tonight," I said.

"Can you guys write up what you have been suggesting over the past two meetings about how to structure ourselves and email it to us so we can digest and pray about it." asked Karen.

I said. "Sounds right." And added with a smile. "Do we have a consensus?"

Everyone around the circle nodded. It was again curious to me that James seemed to be off somewhere daydreaming during most of this church organization discussion and I don't even think he heard the question because he didn't respond at all while everyone else was engaged.

Then Karen spoke up again and suggested that we have a Columbus Day picnic with all our families. She offered for it to be at their house. Again everyone, including James, nodded. Karen said she would email everyone and organize it. Then she asked for the new members to please give her the contact information before they left.

James then seemed to perk up and offered to lead us in a song. We sang, "Seek ye First the Kingdom of God", and Stan closed us with a prayer. We all expressed our gratitude to each other for sharing and our appreciation for the evening and finally we started for home.

It was past 10:30 p.m. as we drove away. On the way home I reflected on how it seemed like the vulnerability, honesty, and humility we had shared is leading us to trust each other, even when people have extreme differences in life experiences, like Sunny and Stan or Karen and Misha.

Thirty Three

As we drove home I wondered who else might be sucked into this whirlpool in the Kingdom. It was obvious that the next three months were going to radically change all of our lives.

When James got back to his apartment he filled Rita in on the development of the Foundation. Then, as they slipped into bed, they agreed that it would be best if Rita found her own apartment in case anyone from the group wanted to stop in to see James.

On Monday Mel and I got together for lunch to work on summarizing the group's discussions about the church. I agreed to email the summary to everyone in the group. That afternoon Mel also contacted Eli's counselor and asked if Eli could come to the Columbus Day Picnic. The counselor said if Eli wanted to go to the picnic he would give him permission. He would talk to Eli and would let Mel know.

On Tuesday morning Stan had another meeting with his Board finalizing the details of the sale of Cyber Market. Stan estimated that if the market stayed strong and Cyber Market held its value by the day of the sale on Tuesday, October 9th the new Bryce Foundation would be established with assets of about $590,000,000. In the afternoon he met with his Accountant and Lawyer to finalize the incorporation papers for the Foundation.

Also on Tuesday, Deb, Karen, Misha, and Liz resumed their Panera lunch get together. They talked mostly about the summary regarding the church that I had emailed to everyone. And they did some planning for the Columbus Day picnic.

On Wednesday morning Sunny and Sara went to the Post Office to apply for Passports and then to the Health Department to find out what shots they needed for a trip to Haiti.

Also on Wednesday, Jorge and Misha got together with Stan and Mel to talk about Jorge and Misha vision of preventing direct care providers of the poor from suffering the consequences of compassion fatigue. Jorge left the meeting feeling like with the administrative experience and connections of Stan and Mel their vision might have a chance of becoming a reality.

Wednesday night, Jorge and Misha and their twins had dinner with Misha's parents. They shared everything God had been doing in their lives with the exception of the sale of Cyber Market and the Foundation's formation. Misha's mom was very understanding and most supportive. Her dad had a lot of questions and reservation, especially about how, if they were going to start a new ministry, they were going to finance it and support their family. All they could say was that if God were in it, it would all work out. Jorge did mention his meeting with Stan and Mel but he had nothing specific to tell them. In the end Jorge and Misha presented her dad with their letter of resignation effective June 1, 2008. They would leave their jobs after school was out and the church program year was over.

The rest of the week was uneventful and went by quickly. Billy had two more very well played soccer games, Mel and Liz went to an Naranon meeting in Henley with Deb and me on Thursday night, and Mel and Andi had their September dinner date on Friday night. Before we all knew it the Sunday night LP group meeting was here again.

Prior to our Liminal Plunge group on Sunday night, September 30, the first official Bryce Foundation Board meeting was held. Billy was invited as an honored guest. Also invited to become members of the Board were Sunny and Ruth, Dan, a friend of Stan and Mel's from Apple Orchard Church, Barb, an attorney, and Kent, an accountant. Barb and Kent were both business friends of Stan. Stan's personal attorney facilitated the formation and organization of the Board. As agreed by our group, I was elected President of the Board. When the meeting was turned over to me I passed out papers with the new Bryce Foundation Mission Statement, the Incorporation Papers, and the By-Laws. The Mission Statement read,

> "To share the love of Jesus by providing financial resources for helping to address the needs of those who suffer in the World, especially children"

After the close of the meeting, Stan's attorney firmly admonished everyone not to breathe a word about the sale of Cyber Marker and the creation of the Foundation until Wednesday, October 10, 2007. It struck me that on that very day it would be four months since Billy's family had been assassinated.

After the Board meeting, Stan and I invited Barb, Dan, and Kent, to stay for the group but they all said they needed to get home. They mingled a little and expressed their enthusiasm about the new Foundation. They also shared their sympathies with Billy, assuring him of God's love.

Thirty Four

Fifteen people found a seat at the table, on which was set with large bowls filled with an assortment of salad makings plus dressings and homemade bread.

To everyone's surprise, before we could all sit down, Ruth spoke up and said, "Will everyone please join me in thanking the God of abundance for all his blessings?" And then this little senior among us began to sing an original psalm of praise that she had written. She then passed out the words to each of us. And then began to sing it again. We all joined in. Those who could began to harmonize.

We sang it another time and when we finished all was silent and still. Karen broke the stillness by taking some salad greens and began to pass them around along with various vegetables, raisins, nuts, fruits, chicken, ham, hard boiled eggs, and dressings. Everyone began eating and conversing with one another.

I kept to myself. It felt good to be relaxing with this group of friends. As I looked around I began to feel amazed. Sunny was talking with Stan and both were listening intently to each other's words. I couldn't hear what they were talking about because there were several conversation going on at the same time. Sara and Liz were in animated conversation. At the end of the table Billy was sharing with Ruth. At the other end Karen and Misha were engaged about something. Next to them were Susie and Deb, probably talking shop about the Health Care Center. I could pick up a word or two that sounded like Mel and James were talking about our teen mission trip to Africa 20 years ago and our planned trip to Haiti.

Jorge who was sitting directly across from me, caught my eye and smiled, like he could tell what I was thinking and feeling. We were touching and tasting the Kingdom of God with this extremely diverse group of friends. Fred, who was next to me, poked me and said, "A penny for your thoughts." I responded by saying, "Just thinking about how God does things that we can't even imagine and I am so grateful. And wondering what he will surprise me with next.

"Fred, would you consider going to Haiti with us? I was thinking about it this morning and thinking not only would it be a good chance for you and Susie to get to bond with the others who are going, but it also would be a chance to see what Dr. Pete Palmer is doing. That is if you could get away. I know you have been on a number of third-world mission trips but I remember a couple of years ago you giving me a book about Dr. Palmer's work in Haiti. Personally I am not only excited about what James is trying to do but I am also looking forward to see what Palmer is developing."

"You are make it very tempting." replied Fred. "Let me talk to Susie about it."

Karen spoke up and got everyone attention. "Deb, Liz, Misha and I were talking and wondering what our times together as a group will be like after we get beyond all the changes that we are trying to work through. We like eating, singing, and praying together and we were saying we probably should do a Bible Study together, or something like that. But we honestly do not want look at the Bible just to get better and better at understanding it. We want to apply it. We want to look at it for what it tells us about how to live. We don't want to bisect it, we want to life by it. We have started on this discipleship journey and we want to keep going."

"Yea." Said Misha. "I, for one, am sick of picking the Bible apart and never changing anything in my life. I know my life has not been living up to a lot of what the Bible says."

"So, what does everyone else think? Would we like to try having Bible Living session? In fact, before leaving our meal time, Liz is prepared to get us started." Karen said.

Everyone sort of looked at each other and gingerly nodded our heads, like, 'OK, do we have a choice'. I thought to myself. *So much for consensus. But I guess we asked them to prepare a devotional time for us.*

Then Liz read aloud Matthew 5:3, "Blessed are the poor in spirit for theirs is the kingdom of heaven.", and asked the question, "If you are poor in spirit how do you act? What do you do?"

And after a few minutes a lively discussion was in progress. Sunny eventually spoke over the group and said "I think basically, we are saying that to be poor in spirit is to be open and honest about our insecurities, struggles, mistakes; our live."

Mel agreed, "We are to humbly confess to one another."

I responded. "Well then I think every time we get together we need to ask the question, 'Does anyone have anything they feel a need to share?'"

I paused. Everyone waited for what I would say next.

I continued, "Just saying we are to be free to be open and honest sounds scary to me. But I think we have discovered in the last few months that sharing our feelings of guilt and fear are the first steps in learning to walk as a disciple of Jesus. And for me I know every day has its' guilt and fear and struggles and mistakes and sometimes just a bunch of stuff that I have to let go of."

"I agree." said Susie.

I was happily surprised that someone new to the group responded with such affirmation when she had not been part of any of the times that we had already been vulnerable with each other.

"After all this heavy discussion, I feel a temptation right now." blurted out Jorge. "Where is the dessert, I could eat a tub of ice cream. Just kidding. I'll have whatever or nothing, but whatever, if it is pie, would be nice."

"You got it, why don't you all go into the Great Room and Deb, Liz, and I will finish cleaning up. Mom and Misha would you guys please slice up the pies?" said Karen. "And, Jorge, you can take orders, we have apple, pumpkin, or rhubarb pie, but sorry no ice cream. Just kidding. But only vanilla."

"Wait!" Deb said. "Does everyone agree that as a result of this 'Bible Living' study that whenever we get together as a group we should always make an available time for anyone to openly and honestly share anything that is troubling them?"

"All in favor?" asked Stan.

"Everyone resounded "Amen!" But, I noticed, everyone accept James, who just stayed silent.

Then everyone got up and went into the Great Room where James sat down at the piano and began to play some gospel songs with jazz improvisation. We all took a seat, Jorge had gotten a pad of paper from the kitchen and went around taking dessert and drink orders, and Stan went into his office to get the agenda for the discussion following dessert.

Coffee and pie were served by Ruth and Misha while James entertained us with a jazz-gospel concert.

In less than ten minutes, when we were just about finished with our pies, Stan got our attention by asking James to stop playing and passed out an agenda with the summary of church life organization suggestions that I had emailed to everyone earlier in the week. Then after praying a short prayer of thanks and surrender of the meeting, he said, "Ladies, that Bible Living was a great idea, thank you. We have a number of things to accomplish tonight and it is already 7:30 PM, so let's get started.

"First, let me report on the founding Board meeting of the Bryce Foundation, which we had before our fellowship meeting."

He then shared what had happened at the meeting.

"Next, as you can see on the agenda, I think we need to make sure we are prepared for our Columbus Day picnic next week."

"Excuse me." interrupted Jorge. "I appreciate your organizational skills and help to keep us on track and moving forward, but didn't we just finish our Bible discussion by saying that every time we get together we need to ask the question, "Does anyone want to share anything that is troubling them?"

"Oh, brother, I am sorry." answered Stan. "You are right and not only I am now feeling guilty, I hadn't even realized I was falling into my old need to be in control. I almost feel like the evil one is trying to find a way of diverting me from following Jesus and letting him be in control. Please forgive me."

"Oh, Stan, it didn't even cross my mind that you were trying to be in control." Jorge replied. "I meant that I needed to confess my guilt over the past couple of week. I need to tell on myself. It is not about food, I have been doing well with that, and with exercise too."

Everyone was surprised at Jorge's honesty as he began to openly share.

"It is that it seems a lot this week I have had these crazy angry thoughts come into my mind, thoughts about wanting to kill drug dealers and brutal police and men who oppress woman, and other just plain mean thoughts. I don't try to think them up, they just appear. I don't dwell on them and can dismiss them by thinking about something else, but they come and I wonder what is wrong with me. Where are these thoughts coming from? I needed to share that because I need your prayers and I need forgiveness, I think. I am not really a bad person, why do I have bad thoughts?"

Fred replied, "Thanks for being so open and honest, Jorge. I think we also need to proclaim Jesus' forgiveness to one another. So, I want to say to you Stan that Jesus forgives you for wanting, even out of habit, to take control again. New ways of life are about progress not perfection.

"And Jorge, I feel a need to say to you that you are not alone with your evil thoughts. My experience is that everyone struggles with unhealthy thinking now and then. I believe Jesus understands and he forgives you and everyone else who has garbage passing though their minds. We may not fully understand where those thoughts come from; maybe personal hurts buried in our past. We just need to be careful not to let those thoughts divert us from seeking the Kingdom of God, sort of like Stan's control issues can divert him from his life in the Kingdom.

." I don't want this to sound like an excuse, but the reality is that we live in a world that is full of darkness, and evil is all around us and even within us. We are fallen creatures, but Jesus redeems and restores us."

"Thank you doc for reminding me." Replied Jorge.

"Does anyone else need to share?" Asked Stan.

"Can I add something?" Billy asked.

"Of course." Replied Stan.

"I agree with Dr. Billard and in my experience if we get diverted from Jesus we can also become a pawn of evil. I think I have shared with this group that the kid who shot me when I was in Africa was once my friend and playmate. Well, he was also a really good kid. Perhaps the nicest, kindest, caring, and most friendly kid I have ever known. However, before he was kidnapped he hadn't yet surrendered his life to Jesus. The people who took him made him see and do terrible things, and he became someone who was able to kill without hesitation. I think that the prince of darkness in this world not only works within our spirits, minds, and hearts but also through our destructive experiences brought upon us by the presence of evil in others. I think that without Jesus we are all capable of the worst kind evil. It is only Jesus who has the power to deliver us from evil and keep us from temptation. There really is a spiritual war going on and it can show up in relationships and in places of worldly power as well as in our spirits, minds, and hearts. Anyways, I felt like I needed to say that because I have seen it. Thanks for listening."

"You got that right, my man." inserted Sunny.

"Thanks Billy. Always feel free to share. Does anyone else need to share?" asked Stan.

There was a silent pause. No one else spoke up until Mel said, "Let's pray." Mel then led us in a prayer of thanks and protection from evil, followed by a time of silent prayer.

After a few minutes, Stan said, "Are we all set for the Picnic next week? I am assuming that since we are having the picnic on Monday that we will not be meeting on Sunday night. It that right? And I also am assuming that all of our families are invited. And that it is going to be here. And that the Tuesday lunch group has it all organized. And …."

"Stan!" Karen broke in. "You know what they say about the word 'assume'"?

"Oh man, am I embarrassed. And so soon after asking for everyone's forgiveness."

"It's okay, honey. All your assumptions are right. And I'm sorry for embarrassing you. We did talk about the picnic and organizing the food. Either Deb or I will be calling you all to ask you to contribute to the food. And we would hope that everyone's kids can come. We thought they all had a pretty good time last time. We thought we would get started around 2:00 PM. If anyone wants to come earlier to ride our horses, everyone are welcome. We can always ride in the afternoon too."

"You have horses?" asked Susie.

"Yes, four of them." answered Karen. "So, I think you are right Stan. We have got it together. But we do need to ask. Do we want to skip the Sunday night fellowship next week because we are having the picnic the next day?"

"I think that is a good idea." Mel said.

"Everyone seemed to nod in agreement."

"Good, then I hope everyone can make it next Monday," said Karen.

"The next thing I think we need to check in about is the Haiti trip." said Stan. "James, are there any up-dates?"

"Just one," answered James. "So far the number that is planning to go is about nineteen. That is if Sunny is going and if Eli can get permission. The school has guest accommodations for only eighteen, so I have been talking with Fr. Jacque and he has gotten Dr. Palmer's permission to use their conference facilities. It sleeps twenty five and has a kitchen and dining area as well as a meeting room. So, that leaves room for six more.

"Also, everyone needs to make sure they have up-to-date Passports and check with the Health Department to see if you need any shots. That's about it."

Stan then added. "One other thing. We need to get our plane reservations made soon. I will call everyone this week to get your information and then have my travel agent make our reservation. I'll put it on my card and anyone who is able, without hardship, can reimburse me what amount they can. But please don't contribute if you can't. Remember we are one family. Is there anything else that we need an up-dated on before we get back to our church discussion?"

Thirty Five

No one said anything, so Stan said, "Mel and 'O' the evening is yours."

"Thanks, Stan." replied Mel. "I think we should all watch the Sunday night football game."

Everyone looked around at each other in dismay, except for James, who reached over for the remote.

Then Mel said, "Just kidding. You can put the remote back down, James.

"To refresh our memories I have brought copies of the summary of what we have discussed so far. But before we talk about them, Odell and I have four more suggestions.

"There are many passages in the New Testament that call for Jesus' followers to be self-effacing, unassuming, and unpretentious, such as; when you pray do so without drawing attention to yourself, when you give do so in secret, build one another up, give the other guy the credit, lose your life for Jesus' sake, the first shall be last, be a servant, do good to those that persecute you. We could each contribute additional verses from the Bible. Jesus' life example demonstrates how those created in his image are to practice values of humility, surrender, and service. He said he never did anything unless his Father doing it. He taught his disciples with words like, 'I did not come to be served but to be a servant.' And 'Anyone who would follow me must deny himself.'"

"So this is what we would like to suggest as values for the church. They are also based on what has worked for the Twelve Step fellowship.

"Our first two suggestions require us as a group, that is, the church, to surrender self-interest. The hope is that these two suggestions will protect the church from problems of money, property, prestige, public controversy, and diverting us from being the church."

Then I began to share. "Our first suggestion is that our common welfare should come before personal interests. Our love for one another is how the world will know that we are a fellowship of Jesus' Body, the Church. Our life as followers of Jesus is dependent upon our common unity. Without accountability we too easily follow other gods.

"Our second suggestion is that as a church we should not have any opinions or give support, financially or otherwise, about or to, anything beyond sharing the love of God known in Jesus Christ.

"We also think that to protect us from getting diverted from seeking the Kingdom of God we should never accept contributions from anyone or any group outside our local fellowship of followers.

"Any questions?"

"Yes, I have some questions," pronounced James. "First, about accepting money from those not part of the group. What if I am a part of this non-traditional local church like you have been suggesting and no one in my fellowship has enough money to eat. I am not talking hypothetically, that is a common situation in Haiti and in the majority of the world."

Mel answered, "That suggestion about not accepting outside money is to protect the integrity of the group. It does not mean that we cannot accept money if we are starving. That would be absurd."

I added, "Of course anyone who would want to help someone else is encouraged to help that person. We are just suggesting that someone can't come along and give a church a pile of money to then later try to tell the church how to function. That is a danger for individuals too, but perhaps that is where the support of the fellowship can help. In fact, if the common welfare of the Church comes before personal interest, then it would be expected that if anyone in the fellowship has something for them to eat, he or she would share what they have with the person who is starving. And I would think that would go for those in another group or anyone at all."

"That is exactly what I witnessed when I went with a group to Honduras some years ago." Mel added. "I had a pair of shoes that I gave to a young man who did not have any. He did not keep them but immediately gave them to an aging man who had never worn shoes in his life. He did it simply out of compassion for him. I don't know, but I don't think he was a believer in God. He just knew that the old man had suffered more than he had."

"Okay, I have another question." James continued. "You have suggested that the church not have any opinions nor take a stand on anything in order to influence others. At least that is what I think I heard was your second suggestion. Do you mean to suggest that the church should not take a stand on justice and moral issues like abortion, free speech, global warming, human trafficking, woman's right, racism, politics, homosexuality, or anything? You're saying that the only purpose of a church is to just be a fellowship that loves one another. Is that right? Isn't the church to take a stand on what is right or wrong?"

Karen answered, "What I hear Mel and Odell saying is that the Church needs to stay focused on God's love and grace and not become legalistic and judgmental. I sort of agree with them. It seems to me that when the Church starts to take a position, regardless of the biblical arguments or the unanimous convictions of a local church, those convictions invariably alienate those who have different convictions and stymies them from seeking to follow Jesus. It causes them to feel like following Jesus mean that they must agree with the convictions of that local church. That is when a controversy can arise, which eventually alienates someone, and diverts the church from loving one another. It makes being right take priority over love. Take the history of women's rights or the history of racism and slavery for example."

"I know many recovering drug addicts who don't want anything to do with the church because they have felt judged." inserted Sunny.

"Okay, I get the point, but doesn't the Bible tell us that following Jesus is to do what is right? Doesn't Micah 6:8 say that the Lord requires you to do justices?" asked James.

"Of course." answered Mel. "But if the focus is on being right then we put rules before relationships. Justice too is about right relationships not about being right or wrong. God's justice is a love relationship with us based on grace. And our love of one another is also about grace. If we make moralistic judgments then we stymie God's grace and our love of one another."

"I disagree." responded James. "God is just and he judges between right and wrong. And the Church throughout the centuries has been what gives moral values to societies throughout the world. How else do we know what is right or wrong, good or evil."

"Excuse me." said Sara. "But why do you or I need to know what is right or wrong? Or maybe I should ask, what makes you think anyone can know what is really right or wrong. Yes, God is just, but he is the only one who is just. God is the only one who knows right from wrong because he defines right and wrong.

"I had a daughter who used to always complain that her brother got to do stuff that she didn't get to do. She would always be telling me that it just wasn't fair. Finally one day I said, 'Who decides what is fair?' She wisely replied, 'God.' "I agree with just doing our best to love one another. I think that next to loving money, loving to be right, is what causes all the problems in the world. Anyway, that is what I think. I am sick of people telling me they are better than me."

"Me too, but that sounds like a cop-out." said James.

"Whatever." responded Sara.

Sonny gave one of his signature smiles, and the tension relaxed.

"I think we all need to have an idea of what's right and wrong, Otherwise how do we decide what to do. And I think the Bible is the best guide for knowing what's right or wrong. But it is wrong to try and impose on others what you think is right. That is what can cause fights. So there, we're all right." Ruth inserted. "And you had all better agree with me."

Sunny flashed another big smile.

To try to put an end to the argument, Mel said, "I think this disagreement is a great example of the changing paradigm that we are suggesting. When the church is understood as what is does, it get its definition from a set of rules or doctrines. When the church is understood for what it is, it get its definition from the love relationship we have for one another. Our suggestion about not having an opinion to influence what is right or wrong beyond demonstrating our love for one another is, in part, an attempt to protect the church from becoming a set of rules, doctrines, or laws and to keep it centered on being a loving fellowship. But it does not stop anyone from making decision based on what they believe is right or wrong. It protects the church from becoming the opinion of men and women and keeps it surrendered to God's judgement."

It was clear by the expression on James' face that he was not sold.

Sunny then spoke. "I want to make another suggestion. I think it is extremely important that when we communicate about our church fellowship to the general public, such as the media, that we leave out of the communications our personal names or the name of the church fellowship. We should refer only to Jesus or God."

"What do you mean Sunny?" asked Stan. "What is wrong with letting others know who we are or about the church where we fellowship?"

"No big 'mes'; no little 'yous!'" pronounced Sunny. "That's the bottom line. What I have learned in my recovery is that anonymity is a spiritual value that keeps personalities from destroying the unity of the fellowship."

Stan replied. "You know, I think I started to answer my own question as I was asking it. I don't mean to be hurtful Mel, but I think, the big 'me', that Sunny just identified, is what had drawn you and me away from following Jesus. I take back my question. Forget I asked it. I think anonymity is a good idea. At least for me."

Then Fred spoke up. "I have been listening to what you have all been sharing, and also looking at the other suggestions that you passed out. I am trying to process what has been happening to you all because of the tragedy that happened to Billy's family and I continue to really like what I am hearing. This all has a ring of truth to it. And though it may not be a finished product I think it makes a lot of sense. However, I see a danger. That danger is that this new paradigm of church could lead people to focus too much on each other and separate that church from the pain of this world. And I believe that, like Jesus, we are to enter into the world's pain. I know we all have our issues. To love one another we have to deal with those issues and live with each other's stuff, but that is not what I mean. I mean entering into the consequences of sin in all the issues that James was listing and, frankly what Billy has experienced."

"That self-centeredness is one of the primary reasons Mel and I left KFC." said Liz.

"I don't understand. Isn't KFC a fast food chicken place?" inquired Ruth with a very perplexed look on her face.

Mel then shared a quick explanation about their time with Kerygma Fellowship Church. Then he said, "I want to get back to what Fred has raised because I think if it is missed then we do become a self-absorbed, insulated, and isolated narcissistic group. And frankly I believe that describes a lot of our churches. Fred, in the suggestions that I passed out, one of the things we talked about at the last meeting, as you perhaps remember, was that a church may create ministries of healing, mercy, compassion, justice, teaching, preaching, and celebrating. In a way, I would rather say that a church 'should' or even 'must', as they are able, create those ministries rather than 'may' create them. The church is who we are; ministries are what the Church does. So, what we have suggested is that, out of a calling or whatever you want to name it, we are to put into actions towards others the love we have received from God and one another. That way others too may experience the love of God. If we don't, how can we love our neighbors as ourselves? And I believe that if we are not loving our neighbor we are not loving Jesus."

Then I said, "It is the ministries that need organized and administered and funded, but the Church, Jesus' Body, needs to be protected from being a corporate institution."

Suzie then expressed some impatient. "This is all very interesting and it sounds to me like this whole package of suggestions is at least worth trying. It can't hurt, because let's face it, what many people experience as the Church just doesn't cut it and it is for sure not what Jesus is looking for in a bride. I would like to make my own suggestion. Odell or Sunny or somebody said that it took ten years for the founders of AA to come up with their Twelve Traditions. It was a trial and error process. So, what I want to suggest is that we all try being a church with these suggestions for a while and just see what we learn. Maybe Mel could put them into a format that would help define and guide what we are doing. If we need to we could change as we learn. What do you think?"

"Amen!" exclaimed Deb.

"You go girl," added Ruth.

"If Ruth and Deb and Suzie agree then I think we have a consensus," joked Stan. "So, let's all go home and get a good night's sleep. Everyone agree? See everyone next Monday for a fun afternoon."

"Sound right to me," I said. "But, before everyone else agrees and we break up I need to say something that has been personally bothering me. Also I hope we can have a time of prayer together before we leave."

"I hope you know I was trying to be a little funny when I called such a quick end to our time together. Sorry. Please share what is on your heart Odell. Don't let my poor sense of humor make you feel cut off," said Stan.

"What has been bothering me is that I am really excited about how this group is emerging and developing but I have also been convicted about my lack of commitment to the traditional institutional church. I know in the past at these group meetings I have said some very strong negative things about that institution but regardless of how broken or enculturated we just can't abandon what we have inherited. I know it is hard for you to believe that I am saying this, and it may sound contradictory, but I've been thinking I should get involved in a traditional institutional church, in addition to being a part of this group. We seems to be moving towards identifying a new structure for a local church and maybe for the church as a whole. I am feeling a pull and call to both. I need your prayers. I am so excited about the possibilities of what we have been suggesting, but for the first time I don't feel I can just ignore the traditional institutional church."

Mel responded. "Odell, I remember you sharing some advice for me when you were helping me sort out my relationship with Apple Orchard. It was helpful advice for me and I think you too need to listen to yourself. As we discover God's love for his church we have a responsibility to care for what is our heritage. What we have touched on the last few meetings about the difference between being the church and doing the ministry of the church is, to me, exactly the point. I need to continue to be a part of Apple Orchard and help direct it into identifying and becoming a *ministry.* I want to help move it from what it thinks a church is in the institutional sense, to doing the ministry of the church. And I want you to join me."

"Thanks Mel. Why is it we can sometimes see what is so evident for someone else and not see how that is exactly what applies to ourselves as well?" I said.

"I think I should join you two in that calling." said Stan.

"And I think that your wives should too." said Deb. "At least I think I should."

"And if it is alright with Sara, we would like to be a part of that too." said Sunny.

"And Dad, would it be alright if I was part of that ministry too?" asked Billy.

I was blown away that Billy referred to me as Dad.

"This is not what I expected," I said. "But I think, the way you are all jumping in, that it is another God thing! Can we talk more about it informally at the picnic?"

"Can we pray now?" Ruth said with a little tone of exasperation. "These old bones are getting tired."

"Let's do that." Stan said.

And at that, Billy got on his knees. Several of us joined him and Mel began a time of prayer.

When we ended our prayer time we left for home with hugs and with everyone expressing how much we were looking forward to the picnic the on Columbus Day.

Thirty Six

Monday, October 8, 2007

Columbus Day was here before we knew it. In fact Sunday slipped by as though it were an extended Saturday. I didn't realize that I missed it. Maybe that was because our family hadn't been in the habit of going to worship, the group didn't meet on Sunday, and I was looking forward to the picnic. So, in my anticipation Monday turned into Sunday. Everyone in our house was up and dressed by nine o'clock, ready and excited to get going. The plan was for everyone to get to the Beckley's around noon if we wanted to get a ride on the horses. The ride out to Apple Orchard took about forty minutes. Even Jim was excited to get to ride a horse, bragging about how he knew exactly how because he had visited a horse farm once at Day Camp when he was ten years old.

At ten thirty Jim got a phone call from a new girlfriend. Jen shared with Deb and I that her name was Tammie and that he was spending a lot of time with her at school. Tammie invited him over to her house for a picnic at one o'clock. He asked us if we could drive him back after he rode a horse but we had to tell him we weren't sure he would have ridden by then. He understood that it would be rude for us to just get there, ride, and then leave. So, he decided he wanted to go over to Tammie's house instead of coming with us. He said her dad would come pick him up and that she only lived about a mile away. He sounded very disappointed about not getting to ride a horse but also excited that this girl had asked her over and that he would meet her parents. At ten after eleven Tammie's dad had not yet come to pick him up. So that we wouldn't be late the rest of left anyway, trusting that Jim would be okay. We said we would be home around eight. He said he was sure he would be home way before that.

On the way out to the picnic Deb expressed that she had a funny feeling about Jim wanting to go to the new girl's house for a picnic and that her dad was picking him up maybe two hours early. She said she could put her finger on it but it just didn't feel right. I told her not to worry.

Deb, Jenn, Billy and I were the first ones to arrive at the Beckley's, except for Grandma Ruth who has slept there overnight. Jorge and Misha, with their twins, were picking up James. Sunny and Sara were coming with Fred and Suzie and three of their kids.

Not long after we got there, Mel, Liz, Andi, and to our surprise, Eli, arrived.

Billy and Eli seemed to hit if off right off right away. Stan showed them where the game room was and Eli offered to show Billy how to play pool.

Karen and Brenda took Andi and Jenn out to the barn not long after the Carr's got there.

Not long after that everyone else began to show up. Stan and I went out and got the grill started. The ladies gathered in the kitchen. The rest of the men were watching football and talking in the Great room. Some of the kids joined Eli and Billy in the Game room. When the girls got back from riding the horses Karen took Eli, Michael, and Juan riding. Billy said he wanted to go watch the football game.

After about 15 minutes of TV Billy went back to the Game room where the girls had gone after getting cleaned up from their horseback ride. He then took the opportunity to offer Andi some chips and sat down to talk to her. She was more than happy to get to know him better. They sat sharing with each other until I came around announcing that lunch was served.

The equestrians returned as Liz was just bringing out some pumpkin pie for dessert. After we had all eaten, to everyone's surprise Andi announced that we should just enjoy ourselves because Jenn, Brenda, and Patty, Fred and Suzie's oldest daughter, would do all the clean-up.

As soon as the girls finished the clean-up James got our attention and said that he would like us all to gather in the Great Room because he wanted to give us all an orientation session in preparation for the Haiti trip. James wrapped up our discussion about 5:00. We spent about half an hour in prayer and then we all headed home.

It was one of the most enjoyable days I had had in a long time, no drama or hassles, good friends, and a relaxed time together, filled with anticipation of a new experience traveling to Haiti.

When we got home Jim was in the living room watching TV. He said he had a wonderful time at Tammie's house. And we told him of the great time we all had at the picnic. Jenn grinned as she told was him how Billy opted out of horseback riding to spend time with Andi.

At ten a.m. the following day, Tuesday, October 9, 2007, it was announced at the New York Stock Exchange that Internet Marketing, Inc. (INI) had just bought Cyber Market for $1.5 Billion.

Stan and Karen Beckley, the principle stock holders, realized $600 million. The Dow Jones closed that day at 14,164.53, the highest it had ever been. The business news in the Wall Street Journal on Wednesday, October 10 head lined the purchase with a side article announcing the deposit of the entire revenue from the sale that the Beckley's realized was going to establish a Foundation for children in honor of Brandon and Emily Bryce and two of their children who were murdered in the Sudan where they had been serving as Christian missionaries.

That afternoon as soon as Jenn got home from school Deb began to give her the third degree about Jim and Tammie. What was her last name? How long had he known her? Where does she live? What does her dad do? Does her mom work? Does she have any brothers or sisters?

Jenn told her mom that she really didn't know Tammie. She said Tammie was a year ahead of them in school and that she was new to their school. She was African American, slender, and beautiful. She also told her mom that Tammie looked like she could pass for 20 years of age. Tammie's mom was a single parent and Tammie was an only child.

Deb wasn't satisfied. What Jim had said about her dad picking him up for the picnic and what Jenn told her about her mom being a single parent made her wonder what Jim and this Tammie were really all about. When she shared her this information with me I felt some relief but Deb's intuition was usually pretty on target so I too began to feel some concern. My suspicion, however, was not so much about Jim and Tammie's hormones, but that this may be another excuse to be a part of the drug gang that had been pursuing him. Maybe there wasn't even a picnic at Tammie's house at all and whoever had picked up Jim was a gang banger. But at the same time recently it felt like Jim was making some good decisions, especially since he was already home when we got home the night before and he freely told us about his day.

As I thought about Jim I also had a new realization that he was turning into a young man. I realized that in the last year Jim had grown several inches, his muscles were starting to develop and his voice was getting deeper. He reminded me of myself at his age. No wonder a beautiful girl, as Tammie was reported to be, would be attracted to him. I guessed this was all good. But now maybe Jim's hormones did give Deb and me more than the drug pressure to worry about.

Not until Jim shared the real story while we were in Haiti, did we learn what Deb and I could have never guessed. The truth was that Tammie's mother was a prostitute and drug addict and Tammie was part of the drug gang that Jim had secretly joined. And that he was beginning to be accepted as part of the leadership because of his relationship with Tammie. He wasn't using yet but he was selling outside of school. Both he and Tammie, since she was new and I was his dad, were putting on a positive show to their school friends. But after school they had another life with growing connections in the drug abuse teen sub-culture. Jim had gone over to Tammie's house that evening but her mom wasn't home. He and Tammie had planned their drug distribution for the rest of the week. Tammie's dad didn't live with Tammie and her mom. He was more like her mom's pimp and he was a major drug dealer with higher up connections. Tammie and Jim were his primary distribution source to younger teens. Jim's relationship with Tammie was giving him a prominent place among the other drug dealers with the teens. It was also giving him high standing in the drug gang that he had joined.

Jenn and Billy had not picked up on all this yet because her circle of friends at school stayed away from the drug scene altogether and Jim made sure at school to stay away from the known drugees as well. In fact Jim had developed some lunch time and class change friends who were part of Jenn's click. And Billy hung out with the Soccer players, who, all but two, also stayed away from drugs. So, Jim's dual life was starting out to work real well, in every way.

If I would have known all this at the time, I probably couldn't have done anything about it without driving Jim further into the drug culture. It again would have reminded me of me at his age. But I was, at this point, clueless.

During the next several weeks Stan and Karen visited Jorge and Misha a couple of times and talked a lot about the development of a respite service to provide some relief for low paid frontline social service workers who are involved with urban ministry. It would be a ministry designed to provide renewal, especially those who serve the homeless, recovering people with the disease of addiction, HIV support workers, youth workers, and others working with the poor. Part of their discussion included using the Beckley's home as a "Country Club for the Poor" type retreat center.

The first step was to make plans for Jorge and Misha to get certified as Compassion Fatigue counselors. They had heard about a psychologist in Canada that offered a certified training for people wanted to become Compassion Fatigue counselors specializing in Secondary Post Traumatic Stress Disorder.

Also, during the next couple of months, Mel and I had a weekly meeting together to talk about how we might incorporate what we had been discussing at the Sunday night group about how to keep our group from becoming another traditional institutional church. The group decided to refer to our suggestions as Church Life Traditions and we began experimenting with using them as a guide to keep our Sunday night group focused on being a loving fellowship of Jesus' disciples. We also agreed that we needed to be careful not to make these "traditions" into laws but to remember they were just suggestions to help keep us from putting our reliance on them instead of on Jesus. Everyone in the group had begun to refer to the group as The Liminal Plunge Church (LPC).

Sunny, Sara, Deb and I, with our kids joined Dan, Stan, Karen and Brenda, and Mel, Liz and Andi in attending Apple Orchard Church on Sunday morning. As part of our Apple Orchard involvement strategy the ten of us would meet twenty minutes before worship began at Mel and Liz's home for prayer. One of our intentions was for Mel, Liz, Andi, Stan, Karen, and Brenda to introduce Sunny and Sara and our family to as many people as they could each Sunday. We also decided that we would not express any criticism of the institutional church but try and listen honestly to the needs of the people we got to know.

The beginning of November, Mel began to contribute all royalties from his books to the newly formed Bryce Foundation.

By the end of the November their hidden relationship from the LP group and their plan to steal the money had develop way beyond what they first intended. Rita said she had set up an account with a Swiss Bank. James had made arrangement with Fr. Fritz for Rita to become the orphanage's financial manager. All that needed to be done was to make the plane reservations to Nassau and deposit the money when the Foundation made the grant. James imagined that they could realize about one and a half million dollars as a result of the Foundations grant and other money he had raised. It was almost past the point of no return. At the same time Rita was increasingly conflicted about all what was going on inside of her. She was pondering all that Marcie and Patty had been sharing with her and what she was learning from the Bible. James too was almost a basket case feeling so guilty about his intimate relationship with Rita and his plan to take the Beckley's money. Both were so confused in their minds and hearts that it was driving each of them crazy. But neither one had yet shared this struggle with the other.

During these months leading up to the Haiti trip Billy was not only achieving acceptance at school with the other students but also impressing his teachers with outstanding grades and study habits. His time was usually divided between studying, running, soccer practice and games, and an evening walk and quiet prayer time. Most morning I ran with him for about a half an hour and then he would pick-up his pace and by the time I got home another half an hour later he would have not only run three more miles but have taken his shower, gotten dressed, eaten breakfast and be going out the door with Jenn and Jim to go to school.

Our new little family life appeared to be falling into place and so was our new found Christian body life. About every other week-end our family would get together with the Billy's grandparents, Bill and Ann Bryce, at their home. Or they would come to ours for a visit and sometimes a meal.

Our small Liminal Plunge Church (LPC) got together every Sunday night. We always had a small simple meal and a meaningful time of sharing. We then started a more structured time by reading what we were calling the Church Life Traditions. This was followed by an opportunity to confess our realizations where we fell short in our discipleship. Sometimes this included honest admission of painful distractions from our desire to be faithful to seeking Jesus and loving others. We then had by a practical discussion around a scripture passage and a report on what we each had tried to practice as a result of what we believed the scripture had spoken to us the week before. Our fellowship usually ended with a time of singing, and reports on plans and events in which each of us were involved, plus a time of prayer. We were beginning to notice that our meetings were taking on a regular order or format.

Thanksgiving Day was split for the Ogden family. We had a special morning breakfast with just the five of us, got together with the LPC fellowship for a large noon time meal, and went over to the Billy's grandparents' house for dinner. By the end of the day we were all totally drained. We were so stuffed from eating so much. We vowed as a family that next year we would not try and do everything in one day. Jim, Billy, and I especially didn't like how all the football games were interrupted by our need to get from one place or another.

The LPC fellowship agreed to have a grab bag for Christmas and we also agreed that our family gift exchange would be replaced by taking small gifts like soccer balls and shoes to the children in Haiti. All our children were a part of the decision and they learned later that it was perhaps the best decision they had ever made.

The beginning of December Sunny, Mel, and I met with the Judge who ruled on Eli's sentencing and he gave permission for Eli to go on the mission trip to Haiti with Sunny as his escort.

James finished his class the week before our departure date. He planned to fly ahead of us to make sure all the arrangements were in place and everything was prepared for our arrival and stay.

He and Rita had planned one last special night before they left. She told him she would be in bed reading and waiting for him when he got home that night.

Jorge and Misha had had a good-bye dinner for him and then him off at his apartment in Oakland. James felt anxious when he noticed that the light on in his apartment bedroom window. He remembered Rita had promised to be reading in bed, ready and waiting for him when he got home. Paranoid thinking filled his mind. He was so worried about the chance that Jorge or Misha may have noticed the light and would suspect her presence. On the way up the steps his fears subsided and his thoughts shifted with anticipation for the night ahead. Yet deep inside he was struggling and more confused and conflicted than ever. He was going back to Haiti, a fornicator, a liar, a deceit and a con-man. What had happed to him?

When he got up to the apartment and went into the bedroom, sure enough Rita was waiting for him. But not like he expected. She was fully dressed, sitting in the corner chair reading.

"Hi Honey," he began. She set her book down. "Rita, I have been thinking. I was so paranoid when I saw the light on in here. I was afraid Jorge or Misha would see it and suspect you were here and then our whole scheme would be blown. I know that is not rational. I just got scared and then coming up the steps my emotions change and I couldn't wait to be with you tonight. I ----."

Rita interrupted, "James, I have a confession to make. I am having a lot of second thoughts about our whole plan. Something has happened to me that I need to tell you about. I have been meeting every week to study the Bible with my old roommate, Marcie, and with Patty, another CMU student. I know that may not sound like me and how it happened is a longer story, but as a result I have asked Jesus into my life. I have asked him for his forgiveness. He has forgiven me and I feel clean inside for the first time in a very long time. I want to follow him and there are changes to make in my life." Rita paused for a second. "I don't think we should have sex anymore, and I can't go through with our plan to steal all the money you are raising for the orphanage."

James was silent for a minute. Tears began to form in his eyes and slowly roll down his cheeks. He responded with deep emotion and said, "I am so relieved! I have been feeling so guilty and mixed up. I just can't go through with our selfish plan to feed our greed either and I have got to reign-in my desire for your body. Please don't think I am a terrible person. Please forgive me."

"I do! But really it is you who needs to forgive me. The honest truth is that I have been using our sexual relationship to keep you on board so we could steal the money. I am the one who has been the terrible person, please forgive me. I think I have found real love in Jesus' love for me." Emoted Rita.

"Maybe we should try to just be friends and see if anything more develops while we are in Haiti. Maybe we really do care about each other and maybe we don't." replied James. "Are you still going to Haiti? What should I tell Fr. Fritz?

"Yes, I want to go to Haiti more than ever. I think it is what Jesus wants me to do, to share his love with the kids. And yes I would like to just be your friend and see what develops. Being friends sounds right to me." Answered Rita. "For tonight, I am moving back in with Marcie until I leave for Haiti. Tomorrow, after our emotions have settled down and we have had a chance to think about what has just happened, would you like to get together for breakfast before I take you to the airport? We can begin to talk about where God may directing each of us?"

James was beginning to feel like he could breathe again and Rita couldn't believe how free she felt.

"That sounds right to me, how about we meet at Ritter Diner at 9:00 a.m..?" James suggested. "I don't have to be at the Airport until 2:00 p.m."

"It's a date." Rita replied with a sheepish smile as she stood up and went to the closet to get her packed bag.

As Rita went to the door, James approached her to give her a hug but thought better of it, so he just opened the door for her and they said good night.

Thirty Seven

December 14, 2007 arrived much sooner than we anticipated. Everyone had all their credentials and shots. Packing was fun and a challenge, especially for the teens as they tried to figure out how what and how to pack so that they could both leave the clothes they took for the people in Haiti and to also fit everything into the one suit case allotted to each person. Twenty three people ended up going. Besides Fred and Susie being added to those who were going, Stan and Mel's friend from Apple Orchard Church, Dan Kawalski, had been recruited to go. Barb Jenkins had asked if she could go too. Dan and Barb were both on the Bryce Foundation Board. Dan had been a missionary in India for ten years and was currently working as the Director of a community services agency in Aliquippa. He and his wife, Nancy had two kids in college. Barb was an attorney for a large firm that focused on human rights. Her husband was also an attorney. They had one child whose name was Marcie and they belonged to St. James Roman Catholic church in Wilkinsburg.

At 4:00 in the morning on Saturday, December 14, 2007 we all met at the Pittsburgh International Airport. Mel passed out yellow Pirates hats for everyone. He said in his experience in traveling with groups it was easy to lose track of each other in airports. When we got to Miami we should all put on our hats so we could all stay together, that the hats were like tethers holding us together. To my amazement, no one had more than one bag to check. We also had ten boxes of gifts of sport equipment, clothes, and medical supplies that Fred had collected. Our American Airlines flight was scheduled to leave at 5:35 AM. We would fly to Miami and there change planes for Port-au-Prince.

The flight arrived in Miami on time at 8:25 AM. Our connecting flight was scheduled for 10:15 AM, so we had a little less than a two hour lay-over between flights. We planned to get some breakfast at the airport while we waited.

Right before we landed in Miami Mel yelled out so everyone on the Boeing 747 could hear him, "Put on your hats, you Pirate fans." His booming voice woke up everyone on the plane, including Eli, Jim, and Karen. The Miami Airport was mobbed and as we disembarked I think we were all glad we had our hats. In fact, Brenda and Andi had refused to put on their hats, but about ten yards past the Gate they looked around and at each other and pulled out their hats out and put them on. We found a Bob Evans at the airport and we all had a big full breakfast. We made it to our flight to Haiti with about ten minutes to spare.

After about an hour and a half the plane began to descend. I looked out the window and could make out an island in the expanse of ocean. The sea looked like it was made of blue and green stained glass. After about ten minutes the pilot came on and said we were approaching Port-au-Prince and we should fasten our seat belts, put up our trays and seat backs, and turn off all electrical devises to prepare to land. As we got closer, I saw off to my right beautiful beaches with shiny flickers of light along their edge. I learned later that what I was looking at was the city of Cape Haita on the northern coast of Haiti and the shiny flickers were the suns reflection off the tin roofs of shanties lined up along the edge of the sea. We were then over land and from our altitude, in places, it looked like the left half the mountains were shades of green and lush foliage and the right half was painted with shades of dull brown and looked like barren desert mountains. This was unexpected and seemed odd to me. Almost like the island was painted on the water and had a line drawn down its middle. I mentioned it to Billy he said the right was Haiti and left was the Dominican Republic. I asked how could we see the boundary and why the two different colors. He told me that because of the greed of the Haitian rulers for a hundred years, deforestation made way for cash crops and no care was taken for replenishing the soil or replacing the forests that had been removed. The arable land had been slowly eroding, taking the top soil to the sea and raping the land of its ability to reproduce. In the Dominican Republic this had not been the case and that half of the island had remained healthy. It made me think that perhaps greed was one of the reasons that even with the removal of the evil dictatorship of Papa Doc poverty in Haiti continued to be so tragically prevalent. As we continued to descend I could see the urban center of Port-au-Prince.

Our landing, which seemed to come quickly, was unexpectedly smooth. But what I didn't expect was how I was hit by the heat and the shock of a putrid odor as I walked down the steps from the plane. It was like opening an oven door that had a mixture of spoiled garbage and feces inside. As I walked towards the small terminal I looked around to see were the odor was coming from but I could only see some trash here and there. Slowly I began to realize that the smell was not coming from any particular source but was just part of the general odor in the air. As we move towards customs and the luggage pick-up bay I was overwhelmed with the heat and stench as it mingled with the body odors and sweat of the crowd.

James was waiting for us there and to my amazement we all went through customs with no hassles, questions or hold ups. I heard James whisper to Stan that he would explain later. We all boarded a crowded old school bus and left the terminal.

I was overwhelmed a second time by the scenes that confronted my eyes as we rode into the city. Port-au-Prince was a sprawling urban city. The streets were mobbed with thousands of people of all ages, some with bundles on their backs; children seemed to be everywhere, people, and cars, and old trucks, and lots of bicycle. People were dressed in every imaginable and unimaginable kind of clothing. Most were barefoot. Some of the main street were rudely paved but most were like dirt alleys and full of huge ruts and garbage. There was no particular direction to the traffic, no left or right for movement, everyone was on their own. James told us there was a nice part of the city and a business/government district that we may see before we went home, but most of the city's over 800,000 residence lived in conditions like we were riding through. On the edges of the roads, there were tin roof shanties with no walking area to define the road. Instead there were drench gutters with puddles of liquid which did not smell like water. I saw a young man peeing in the gutter and no one was even taking notice – except for me and the rest of our group. The trash and garbage boggled my mind, it was everywhere. Children were playing tag, laughing and yelling. I saw a group of young boys sitting on top of a twenty foot wall. There was what looked like three or four year old children going through a pile of garbage eating whatever they could find. Flies were swarming all around them. The sights, sounds, and smells assaulted my scenes.

We took Route #3 north out of the city. The first half of the trip was on a paved highway but the second half was on deep rutted, bone jarring, dusty roads. This part of the trip was more like navigating a trail littered with gravel, boulders, and huge deep pot holes the width of the road. The trip with its sights and smells was emotionally draining as well as physically exhausting. It took about three hours to go the forty eight miles to Cange. When we got to the Central Plateau we drove alone a large lake for about two miles. Mel who had researched Haiti more than most of us said it was Lake Pe'ligre and that it was created when the Artibonite River was dammed with US money and engineering in 1957. Then as we began to drive up the hills to the village we began to see some farms and then shanty houses and eventually more houses and more developed homes. The village of Cange was rather large and much cleaner and full of foliage than I expected. In fact the mountain side had a full lush growth with mature trees and flowers in abundance. The views of the mountains and valleys were full of beautiful trees and vegetation, in stark contrast to most of the country side that we had just gone through.

When the bus stopped, the driver said, 'Bas Cange.' Bas I would learn meant 'lower' in English, sort of like saying, 'The Lower Hill District' in Pittsburgh. There were destitute people everywhere. We were in front of a beautiful large white stucco building with a cross on top. The bus had left off and picked up many people along the route, but everyone still on the bus got off at Bas Cange. Our group, though mixed in skin tone, stood out as well dress foreigners and as we stepped off the bus children seemed to appear from everywhere running up to us; older ones were asking to carry our bags and the little ones were asking for candy. James had told us not to give anyone anything because if we did it would attract a swarm of kids like bees to flowers. I looked around at the hungry children and thought of the kids I saw eating garbage. I was caught off guard as I began to feel overwhelmed. Despite James' wisdom, I reached in my pocket and gave an adorable little girl the bag of peanuts that I had saved from the snack handed out on the plane from Pittsburgh.

The kids began to swarm at the motion of my hand to my pocket but then I had my third shock wave since landing in Haiti. The little girl, whom I would guess was about 10, though I found out later was probably in her teens, open the package of peanuts, gave a wave to the kids that were coming over and they formed a line. There was no pushing or bullying. They came to the little bag of peanuts and this angel gave each child one peanut as the line moved past her, no one asked for more or grabbed for the bag. When there was one left she ate it, turned, gave the little snack bag back and said "Thank you", in perfect English. My eyes were damp and I don't think they got dry for the rest of our trip.

I then saw James approach a tall older balding gray hair man with an obvious natural charisma. He was standing at the top of the wide steps leading up to the front of the church. There was a large well in the courtyard at the foot of the steps. The elderly man had a blue bandana around his neck and wore a blue dress shirt, blue jeans, and sandals. He and James exchanged a few words and then they both began to walk down to our group that was now standing at the bottom of the steps. I could feel a sense of excitement among us as we anticipated meeting this interesting looking man. The only ones among us that seemed to be talking to each other were Billy and Andi.

When James and his companion got to within a couple of steps from the group, James got our attention and said, "Everyone, I would like to introduce you to Father Jacque Lamont. He is our pastor here in Cange, he has been the pastor in this village for the past 40 years." James told us the school campus that Father Jacque and his wife started was behind the Church and the large and renowned medical facilities that he and Dr. Palmer had started were about a half mile down the hill. You could see people waiting on the side of the road as you looked down the hill. The site of the orphanage that James said he was raising money for was about a quarter of a mile up the hill from where we were standing.

When I was searching the history of Cange on the web, I saw pictures of Father Lamont. In the pictures he was always wearing a clergy uniform with a collar and black shirt and looked bigger and younger than in person.

The community's spiritual leader welcomed us with the demeanor of a humble and warm gentleman who made you feel safe and strangely at home. As he was talking I caught a glimpse of Billy, who was intently looking at this humble, and I saw tears running down his cheeks.

Father Lamont then led us about a quarter of a mile down the road to a walled in large newly build house. We went through the locked gate and walked onto a beautiful porch. Father Lamont went up to the front door and walked in. In a couple of seconds he came out and with him was a tall thin man dressed in a khaki shirt and pants. I also noticed he was wearing Asics running shoes. Father Lamont then said, "This is Pete Palmer, he will be showing you where you will be staying."

I glanced at Fred and I could tell at the sight of Dr. Palmer his day was made.

Dr. Palmer welcomed us, told us we were at the guest quarters of the Zanmi Lasante Clinique Bon Sauveur, and invited us to come in. When we were all inside, he shared that Zanmi Lasante meant "Community Partners in Healing" (CPIH) in Haitian Creole and that ZL was started 23 years ago by Father Jacque and himself. He told us that Clinique Ban Sauveur was started by ZL in 1985 with the financial help of Thom Blackwell, a Boston business man. He explained that the international organization of Community Partners in Healing had ten other medical facilities in Haiti now and that this year they would complete the building of a 54 bed Hospital in Locolline. They expected to provide about 1.3 million patient care visits in 2007. He told us CPIH was in eight other countries beside Haiti and that they were committed to providing state of the art medical care to the poorest of the poor at no cost for care. He also shared what he thought might be of interest to us, because he had heard that we had a special interest in children, that in Haiti they were just beginning to manufacture their own locally-produced peanut-butter medicine called "medika mamba" to treat severely malnourished children.

He informed us that our meals would be prepared and served for us in the dining area to our right and that our rooms were upstairs. He said he felt most privileged to have us as their guests and hoped that our short time at Cange would encourage us in our desire to follow Jesus.

Unfortunately, he informed us, he was only going to be around for one more day because he had to be at Harvard to teach a class on Tuesday, and that the rest of today he would be busy seeing patients. So he wasn't going to be able to spend much time with us. He hoped to be able to have dinner with us in a couple of hours. Then he introduced us to Pierre, the host for the Guest House.

I looked at my watch and it struck me that is was already 4:45 PM and Dr. Palmer said he would be spending the rest of the day seeing patients. Apparently his day did not end until sometime later.

Pierre welcomed us again. He was a charming man, maybe in his 30's, who spoke English with a strong Haitian accent. He said dinner would be served at 6:30 PM and showed us up to our rooms. As we were on our way up-stairs, I saw Fred introduce himself to Dr. Palmer. Then he ascended the stairs right behind Stan who had stopped to talk to James for a minute.

Upstairs there were twelve rooms with two or three beds in a room. We somehow managed to organize ourselves so that everyone was happy with their roommates. It work out so that each of the couple had their own room, Brenda, Andi, and Jenn shared a room, Billy and Eli had a room together, Jim, Juan and Michael shared a room, and Ruth, Barb, and Dan each had their own room. Once we were in our rooms James came around to each room and explained that we were all to gather in the meeting room down stairs in a half an hour to talk about our schedule for the week ahead.

When we gathered in the meeting room James laid out a schedule that he, Father Jacque, and Dr. Palmer had worked out for us.

We read:

Monday through Friday

6:30 AM -	Breakfast
7:30 -	Morning worship with Father Jacque and the school, orphanage, and ZL staff in the Church sanctuary.
8:30 -	Stan, Mel, Sunny, Billy, Eli, Jim, and I would help with the construction of the orphanage. Dan, Juan, Michael were to work on helping to repair and improve someone's home. Fred, Deb, Misha, Brenda, Suzie would help as directed at the hospital. And Karen, Sara, Jenn, Andi, Jorge, Barb, Liz, and Ruth were to be teacher-helpers at the school.

12:00 -	Lunch and break back at Guest House
3:30 PM -	Everyone play soccer, do crafts, or just play with kids at the school
6:00 -	Dinner
8:00 -	Group Meeting - discussion of the day

James said that Fr. Jacque and Dr. Palmer had learned over the years that the relationships that were developed with the Haitian by visitors were what had the more long lasting effects for change, healing and progress than any anything else. He said that it was best to stay with one activity all during your stay rather than move around from one area to another. They strongly suggested for everyone to spend the whole five days with their assignment and if anyone wanted to change that now would be the time to do so.

Billy said he understood; and though he enjoyed hard work, he would like to be with the group that was going to be helping the teachers at the school. Ruth said she would be happy to switch with him and work with the men. Of course, Billy didn't mention that Andi was also in the school group, but I noticed a little twinkle in her eyes as Ruth said she would switch. I also noticed that Andi had a little smile on her face when Billy asked for the switch.

James said that switch was fine. Then he asked if anyone had any questions.

Stan asked, "What is the plan for tomorrow and next Saturday before we leave on Sunday?"

James answered. "Tomorrow is a day of rest and everything is closed except the hospital. We will go to worship in the morning and then the rest of the day you are free to roam around and explore, but please stay in groups of three or four."

He said this was a very hopeful and caring community but it still, like every place in the world, has those who would do you harm and seek personal gain, especially because you stand out like Americans. He strongly urged all females to have a male present with them. Something that is not publicized much is the human traffickers in Haiti. With the Haitians they offer young female orphans a nice home and lots of food and sexually seduce them. They sometimes outright kidnap children and young adults, especially girls. Then they are enslaved and sold as servants and prostitutes across the border in the Dominican Republic. "Even though you are not from Haiti, please stay together." James said.

I looked at Billy and could see him getting emotional. During our runs, which had continued during soccer season and on, he had shared now and then, thoughts and feelings he was having about the loss of his parents and brother and sister and his past life. I knew what James had just said would touch a tender painful place inside of him. The pain of orphans' lives being destroyed and used by the greed and thirst for power was always with him.

James was continuing. "Also remember at one of our preparation times together about what I told you to wear. Ladies and girls, no shorts or exposed shoulders or bellies."

He told us that next Saturday we will stay at a nice Hotel in the tourist section of Port-au-Prince, relax and process all that we would be experiencing."

I think most of us were very impressed with how well planned and organized the week was going to be. At first my cynical side told me that they were making us special and giving us the VIP treatment because James had told them that we had big bucks to hand out. My second thought was that Father Jacque and Dr. Palmer had been hosting visitors for over 20 years and they had learned how to do it right after many lessons learned. And I also realized that Pete Palmer had done so much all over the world through Community Partners in Healing and with his connections with the World Health Organization and the World Bank, that no matter how much of a contribution we could provide it would be peanuts compared with what they had already raised over the years. So, I concluded that they must treat everyone this way. It really helped me see that James had hooked up with some real world changing disciples. I had the feeling that I was about to learn that what I had experienced so far of the Kingdom of God was only a taste of how awesome and amazing is the love of God.

At 6:30 PM we had our first Haitian meal. Somewhat to my surprise everyone appeared to enjoy it. Pierre told me later that was the first time in his ten years of introducing people to local food that no one refused any of the food. Part of that might have been that we hadn't eaten since the breakfast we had between flights and also that in our preparation orientation James had told us how offensive it could be to refuse food that you were offered.

After dinner we simply sat and talked for an hour or so about all that we had experienced that day. Dr. Pete, as we learned was what everyone called him, Father Jacque, James, and the Head Master of the school, Claire Lavelle joined us for dinner. The conversations were lively and full of discussions about life that none of us, even Billy, had ever encountered.

Around, 9:00 PM, you could tell by the lulls in our conversation that we were all getting exhausted, so we thanked our hosts and bid each other good night. Deb and I commented, as we laid in our beds, that they were not like our bed at home but they were beds, we had arrived safe, we had eaten well, had a roof over our heads, one much better than we had anticipated, and that we had meet some unbelievable servants of the Lord. Our hearts were full of gratitude as we prayed and thanked Jesus. I don't know when Deb fell asleep, but when I woke up I couldn't remember when our prayers had ended.

Thirty Eight

We heard Church bells ringing and roosters crowing as the sun came up in the morning. When I went down the hall to the men's bathroom and shower Billy was coming the other direction. He had just finished showering after a run.

"Dad, you should have seen the awesome sunrise this morning. Eli and I went for a short run, the hills were a challenge but the sky was unbelievable."

I was a little taken back to think that Eli got up and went for a run, but sure enough when I went into the bathroom, Eli was just finishing getting dressed.

Breakfast was a fix your own. Pierre had put out a variety of Haitian breakfast foods and everyone was to eat what they wanted.

The Church bell rang again at 8:00 AM calling everyone to worship. In the silent morning air the bell could be heard for miles in all directions. Worship was scheduled to start at 8:30 AM. We discovered it really started when the church was full. We also learned that very few people, among the population of about eight thousand five hundred, had watches or a means of telling time. Everyone who was going to worship began to move towards the Church when they heard the bell ring. The large two story sanctuary, which held about 1,000 people was full 20 minutes after the bell tolled. Our little group went up together and arrived about a half hour after the bells rang, at 8:30 AM, the time we were told that worship would begin. With the church packed we wondered where we would fit, but James met us in the court yard and escort us into the church down the aisle to chairs in the first row that Father Jacque had saved for our group.

I commented to James that I was impressed by the large crowd. James said that at 11:00 the bell would ring again and there would be at least the same number coming to the second service and the same thing would happen at 1:30. Each service would be about two hours long. It was obvious that Father Jacque had made a difference in this village and that he was most revered. He began years ago by learning from the people and becoming a part of the life of the village. He had spent over forty years suffering with the people, building their trust, and becoming part of their families. He had gained the reputation as someone who cared and who could be counted on to be there when you needed someone, no matter what. He was a big reason why Pete Palmer came to Cange,

The service began with a fifty member youth choir all dressed in bright robes, some in red, others in blue, and yellow, and orange. They began by singing the most beautiful a cappella praise song in Haitian Creole. It seemed to transition into another song and then another. The crowed began to join in and it wasn't long before everyone both inside and outside the building was clapping and singing along. Some were dancing. This music celebration lasted about a half an hour. Father Jacque then opened with prayer. Following his amen the youth choir began to sing again; this time a soft hymn accompanied by ten liturgical dancers. They emerged from beyond the crowd outside and as people made a path they gracefully danced into the church. It was like out of a movie.

As they ended, Father Jacque offered another prayer, read a passage of scripture and began to share from what he had read. He spoke in Haitian Creole but every couple of minutes he would summarize with a sentence or two in English for us and some other visitors who were standing with medical staff. He preached for about thirty minutes. When he was finished an elderly woman came forward and led us in prayer. The choir director led the congregation a closing hymn. Father Jacque ended the service with a Benediction.

People began to disperse but many stayed around talking with one another. Soon the square began to fill up again with new people coming to the 11:00 worship. The church bell rang. I looked at my watch. It was 10:30 AM.

Deb and I decided to look at the Well in front of the church. There was a Cross hanging from the rope where normally a bucket would be. The Well was obviously not functional and served as an icon or monument. We learned later that in the early 80's a water distribution project was instituted. It was really what totally changed this poverty stricken displaced community. Previously there was just one well in the community and now there were four water stations around the village for people to get clean water. The hospital, school, guest house had piped in running water.

We began to talk about what we wanted to do with the day when Jim and Jenn came up to us and asked if they could go look at the school with Juan and Michael. We said that would be ok but be sure to stay together. I thought the school was probably one of the safest places in the community. Next, before Deb and I could resume making plans for what to do next, Billy, Andi, and Brenda approached us.

Andi said, "What are you guys going to do with the day?"

"Yea," Brenda added. "Can we hang out with you?"

Deb answered. "Sure, we were just starting to talk about what we would like to do."

Billy said, "I would like to spend some time just getting to know some older people in the village and learn what their life is like."

"Sounds good to me. And I think I would like to just sort of do a "walk about" in Crocodile Dundee style," I replied.

"But we don't understand Haitian Creole and we don't have a translator." said Brenda.

"Or know where to go or what we were looking at from the locals' perspective." added Deb.

I felt like we were just standing there looking lost, so not knowing where to go, I started to walk back towards the Guest House and the rest followed.

We had slowly walked about a hundred feet when we saw Pierre coming out of one of streets alone the side of the church. He greeted us and asked what we were going to do till dinner.

Brenda, asked, "What about lunch."

Pierre said there wasn't any lunch provided for guests on Sundays.

Billy asked if he knew of anyone who might show us around. He said we were interested in meeting some elders in the community who could share some local stories with us.

"As a matter of face one of the jobs I had before becoming the Guest Host was that of a translator who gave tours of the community, I would find it a privilege to show you around." offered Pierre. "But I have to be back to prepare dinner by late afternoon."

"That works for me, I want to get a nap before dinner too." I said.

"Then let's get going." said Andi.

"This is probably a good place to begin." Pierre began. "Right over there." He pointed to an empty lot next to the church that had been made into a flower garden. "That is where in 1962 Father Jacque build the first church in Cange. That primitive building was torn down and replaced by the current church building, and the Well was built to serve as a symbol of Jesus, the living water. I'll tell you later about the water; clean water has been what is giving us new life, just like Jesus gives us new life. Asking us to follow him, he then began to walk back down the hill to the walled-in medical compound. As we walked he talked about the damming of Haiti's largest river, the Artbontie, in 1957. The Dam flooded the valley and destroyed the original village as well as surrounding homes, farmland, and country side. The purpose of the Dam, which was funded by the United States, was to provide hydroelectric power for the development of Port-au-Prince about fifty miles away. The area around the dam within four or so miles now had a population of about thirty thousand of which Cange the center. Most of the people now were subsistence farmer, with a few cash crop farmers, shop and market workers, and a number of people who worked in the hospital and school.

About halfway back to the compound we ran into Stan and Karen and Mel and Liz coming the other way. They had just left the Guest House. We told them that Pierre was showing us around and they asked if they could join us.

Pierre took us down to the medical area which was a huge walled-in compound. There were people waiting to get in. They were crowding the sides of the road, sitting on walls, almost up to the Guest House. When we entered the Courtyard of the Hospital's Clinic it was filled with patients waiting to be seen. Many were lying on the ground along the paths throughout the complex. We didn't spend much time there because we knew if we were to get a full tour of the several medical facilities that that alone would take all day.

After a quick fifteen minutes, Pierre took us back to the Guest House. He got the Guest House van and we started on a driving tour. As we traveled through the beautiful mountains, he told us all about the history of the school and the medical facilities. He showed us the Dam and farm country, the market and back streets, and even the landfill for the village. There were not only small farms with chickens, goats, and gardens but also fields planted with corn and other marketable crops. He talked about Haiti winning it independence in 1804 and the deforestation that began and escalated in the early 50's. It was apparent from all that had happened as a result of the development of this community that the land was being reclaimed and Pierre was excited as he talked about it.

We returned and dropped off the van and then started a walk about. We must have covered ten miles and by 1:00 PM we were all ready to collapse. I hadn't looked my watch but know it must be 1:00 because I heard the church bell ring again. We ended up back at the Well in front of the Church. The Church was full again with people even spilling over outside. Pierre said he had to get back to the Guest House but before he did he wanted to introduce us to someone who could answer any questions we might have about anything related to Haiti. He took us down the road to the back of the Flower Garden where there was a modest well-kept house with a vegetable garden and chicken coop in the back. There was an old woman sitting on the porch in a rocker.

"Friends,' he said, "May I introduce you to Yolanda Lamont. She is Father Jacque's wife. She told me this morning if the opportunity arose that she would be happy to share about Cange and answer any question you might have. She was born in Port-au-Prince and she and Father Jacque have lived here in Cange for the last forty five years."

Yolanda was a beautiful 83 year old with the demeanor of royalty. She smiled and stood up and it almost felt like I should bow. She told us all to have a seat, welcomed us, and she would be right back with some water. Liz asked if she could help and was welcomed.

In a couple of minutes they brought out a pitcher of water and some glasses. Pierre said good-bye and that he would see us at dinner. We all thanked him and he started to walk back towards ZL.

Yolanda started the conversation by asking, "Well what do you think about the Kingdom of God in Cange?"

I blurted out, "I am overwhelmed, from all that I have read and heard about Haiti and the little I have seen so far your village seems like another country. As we drove out here from Port-au-Prince I was overwhelmed by the devastation, the bareness, the deplorable living conditions, the garbage and lack of sanitation, the odors and immense poverty, but here there are large trees, foliage, flowers, birds of paradise, clean streets, well-kept homes with back yard gardens, and thousands singing the praised of God. There is a state of the art hospital and a huge school. How did this happen?"

Yolanda smiled and said, "When the Haitian Episcopal Church sent Jacque and I here from Mirabelair to start a church in 1962 the Central Plateau was one of the poorest areas of Haiti. The infant mortality rate was well over 50% plus over 25% of the young children were dying of TB, Malaria, dysentery, AIDS, and starvation. Probably 80% of all the children in Haiti were infected with parasites. Most of Haiti is still like that. Mothers in Haiti for years have had many children with the hope of a few surviving. And in 1957, all the people along the Artibonite River, had their homes and land destroyed by the flooding caused by the dam.

We struggle to help the people survive and eventually focused on providing an education for the children and their mothers, beginning with nutritional education. Then after a long twenty years, with the assistance our Bishop, beginning of the 80's we helped develop a water system project and very soon after that Pete Palmer came and we helped him start a clinic."

We spent the next hour or so discussing the history and needs of Haiti and in particular the area of Cange and the Central Plateau.

About the time we were getting ready to leave Father Jacque arrived home from the last worship service. He looked as tired as we felt; but in spite of the exhausting day he greeted us enthusiastically with a warm smile. I looked at this robust old man and wise healthy old woman and thought, "*God is faithful and when two or three gather together in Jesus name there he is in their midst; and where ever Jesus is the Kingdom of God has come.*" We all shared with him what an amazing wife he had. He almost blushed.

When we got back to the Guest House it was 4:00 PM. We were all exhausted, so everyone went to their rooms to take a nap. Stan said he would set the alarm on his watch and wake us by 5:30 PM in time for dinner.

As everyone gathered for dinner I noticed that Fred was not there but Suzie was. I asked Suzie if Fred was alright and she said Dr. Pete had asked him if he wanted to on hospital rounds with him after worship and he jumped at the chance. But she said that meant they would not be finished with rounds until about 12 midnight.

At dinner I sat next to Sunny and asked how his day went. He said he and Eli spent the afternoon together, just the two of them walking and talking and playing with some kids. He told me they had some great discussions about addiction and recovery. They agreed to get together for an hour every day at 4:00 PM and talk about different aspect of recovery.

At 8:00 PM we had our first group discussion about the day and then James asked Mel to fill everyone in on what we had learned from Pierre and Jacque and Yolanda.

Everyone, except Fred, was in bed by 10:00 PM.

Thirty Nine

The Church Tower Bell rang and roosters crowed at sun rise the next morning as it would every day of our stay. It was about 5:15 AM. Billy, Eli, Brenda, and I had agreed to go for a short run each morning and sure enough we all were ready to get going about 5:30. We ran for about 3 miles as my pace and were back in time to wash off, change, and be at breakfast by 6:10 AM.

After worship James delivered the four groups to their assignments. The rest of the day and the rest of the week went as planned. James did not attend our discussion in the evenings. For me the discussions were very much like being at a small NA discussion meeting. Each person shared emotions and insights with which everyone else could identify. One of the most unexpected things that happened at that first evening meeting and then at the next three meeting, though after the first time it was not such a surprise, was that Billy shared, often through tears, how much of what he was experiencing brought memories of his life and the grief of his losses. Deb and I talked about how this was the best thing that could have happened to him and so necessary for healing.

Dan, Juan, and Michael's drop-off was at the home of Jules Basque. Jules was a single dad with two kids. His wife, Marta, had died about three years earlier of Tuberculosis as a result of contact with a visitor whom they had taken into their home while she was waiting to be admitted to the TB hospital. Marta was unable to fight off the TB. Treatment for her TB was unsuccessful because she had neglected to take her HIV medicine, and as a result her AIDS had become active. Jules was also HIV positive, and their six children were all born HIV positive. All were now doing well on their medications and four of them were grown and out on their own with jobs in Port-au-Prince. Dan and the Cruz boys were unaware that in 1987 Jules was one of the first people in Cange to be treated for HIV. Over the years he had been the leading advocate in the community for breaking the stigma of the disease and encouraging everyone to get tested and treated. Hundreds of lives were saved because they were educated about how to prevent HIV, tested, and treated when found to be positive. Jules was unemployed due to an unfortunate accident a couple of years ago in which he lost his leg when a truck overturned on the road while he was walking home from helping a friend on his farm.

The Basque house was a small concrete block structure with a tin roof. It had a low wall around it that was falling down. The roof had rusted through in a couple of places, one side of the house was covered with a canvas tarp where a few of the concrete block and a window had fallen out. The front door was missing and much of the inside of the house was a damaged from the rain coming in. The original hard mud floor that once was smooth as glass was now rutted unevenly caked mud. Michael was totally shocked. He couldn't believe that people were living in this place.

Jules greeted them with a hug smile. He was a joyful man of about forty. The children, girls, ages six and eight, had just left for school. Jules offered the small work crew something to drink. They accepted and he brought them three cokes, which was a surprise and a treat, even though they were warm. Juan wondered where in the world did he get the cokes and how did he pay for them. After discussing the needs of the house, Dan asked if he could talk to the boys alone for a minute.

He said he had an idea. "Guys, you know that TV show, Extreme Make Over in which Ty gets a bunch of volunteers to tear down an inadequate house and builds a new one in one week. Well we may not be able to build a new one and this project is way too big for the three of us to even make a dent in it, but maybe we can do something similar. If we could get the material and enough volunteers, I think we could make this house livable at least. What do you think?"

Michael looked at Juan and said with his usual halting speech, "He even sounds like Ty. Sure why not, we three sure aren't going to make much of a dent."

"Good, here is what I want you two to do this morning. Go door to door and ask anyone who can to volunteer and come to Jules house after mid-day. I will go over to the orphanage construction site and see what materials and tools I can get, but first I need to take stock of what we need," Dan offered.

Juan asked, "How are we going to communicate, we don't know Haitian Creole?"

"We have to trust God for something." replied Dan. "Now let's get going, I'll explain to Jules."

When the orphanage construction crew of Stan, Mel, Sunny, Ruth, Eli, Jim, and I arrived at the construction site there were already nine men at work laying concrete blocks and rebar reinforced walls. There were footers and two stories of steel girders frames in place for three buildings whose foundation has been poured. Three men were at each building. One was mixing mortar and two were laying blocks. There was also a fourth building laid out with stakes. As our group arrived, one of the men came over to us and introduced himself as Andre' Heroix. He spoke English and said he was the foreman and had been looking forward to our arrival and the help we could give. Stan had to tell him that only Sunny had had experience laying block. It didn't seem to bother him. Stan then introduced everyone and Andre' took us to each of the work building sites, leaving Eli at the first site, Jim at the second, Mel and Sunny at the third, where Andre' had been working, and then took Stan, Ruth, and me to the staked out building. At the first two sites, Eli and Jim were quickly taught how to mix mortar and the man mixing mortar then went to lay block with the other two. At the third site, Mel was taught to mix mortar and Sunny was directed to help Andre's partner laying block. At our sight Andre' explained that the staked out outline of the building with cord strung between each stack was where the footer was going to go. He gave Stan and me a pick and shovel and told us to dig a trench alone the cord. He said it should be three feet wide and two feet deep. Then he took Ruth over to a trailer that looked like it was being used as an office. Her job was to provide us all with water and to run errors for Andre'.

After about an hour, Dan showed up at the orphanage construction site and asked if he could talk to the foreman.

The sign at the entrance to Clinique Bon Sauveur in Cange read: Zanmi Lasante: Complexe Sociamedical de Cange. Inside the walls and beyond the court yard there was a two story hospital with four operating rooms, a critical care area for post-operative care, a dental clinic, a woman's health clinic, a family planning clinic, a pediatric clinic, a TB treatment facility, and an eye clinic. There were several other buildings that provided support for these services, including an educational building for Harvard medical students.

Because Fred had become familiar with the medical facilities and had met a number of the staff he took Deb, Misha, Sara, and Suzie with him to the clinic while Pierre took the remainder of our group back behind the Bon Sauveur to the school.

After Fred shared a lot of what Dr. Pete had shown him, he then introduced Misha to the Receptionist at the TB facility, Brenda to the Receptionist at the Dental clinic, and Suzie to the Nurse Supervisor at the Woman Clinic. Then he took Deb with him to the post-op area where they would begin by caring for the patients returning from surgery. He told her that after she rounded with him in post-op that he would introduce her to the medical surgical Nurse Supervisor. Deb was for the first day to shadow one of the nurses to be oriented. Then the remainder to the week she would become part of the nursing staff. Fred said then he was going to the pediatric clinic. Dr. Pete had asked him to help out there because that was where providers were always needed the most.

When the rest of the group got to the school they were surprised by its size. Those who were on the tour the day before had just driven past what looked like a playground and small school. But now once beyond the walls, they could see this was a campus with several buildings. Pierre showed them around before they went into the administrative building. There was a primary school, a middle school, a high school, an athletic field, a huge playground, a building for a nutritional education program, and an agricultural teaching field and garden. The group was overwhelmed by all that they observed.

When the group ended their tour at the Administration building, Pierre left them with Claire Lavelle. They had gotten to know her a little at dinner on our first night. She was a delightful attractive woman in her mid-thirties who had been educated in the US and had a PhD in Education from New York University. She had been born in Haiti but had grown up in New York and was fulfilling her dream of what she referred to as her "assignment" from God to serve the children of Haiti. When you were in her presence she made you feel like you were the most important person in the world, even when the room may be filled with people. After welcoming the group, she explained that the school started at 8:30 a.m. and since it was now 10:00 a.m. and time for the primary students to have morning recess, she would take a minute to share a very brief history of the school and it development. She told the group that the enrollment was currently at about one thousand students and was growing every year. The next expansion plan was to develop a scholarship partnership with several colleges in the U. S. She then asked each of the group what grade they would like to assist in. Karen, Brenda, and Jenn said any grade in the primary school. Jorge and Liz said they would like to help in the 8th grade. And Barb, Andi, and Billy said in the High School. Claire ask each of them to tell her a little about themselves to give her idea of where each may be the most helpful. Then she took the group out to the playground where maybe two hundred children were playing at recess. She introduced Karen, Sara, and Jenn to Zoe' More, the primary school principal. She then promptly moved the rest of the group to the middle school building. There she left Jorge and Liz off and, based on what Jorge and Liz had shared about themselves, suggested teacher assisting assignments to E'mile LaBlac, the middle school principal. From there she took Barb, Andi, and Billy to the high school. There they met Ines Baudoin, the High School Principal. Again she gave the principal the suggested teacher assisting assignments for Barb, Andi, and Billy, wished them well, and told them to please feel free to just stop in her office or track her down if there was anything they would like to discuss or need. From the time they had met Dr. Lavelle until the time they parted it had only taken thirty minutes. Barb was most impressed with this woman's efficiency as well as her grace, warmth, and captivating charisma. After meeting the teachers, to whom they were assigned, they helped with the students for a little over an hour before it was lunch time.

Everyone's first day on their assignments ended about 3:00 p.m. They all returned to the Guest house except Fred and Deb who stayed at the hospital until dinner time. As the group gather together everyone was animated, talking all at once about what they had seen and experiences. Everyone was wet from sweat but the home repair and orphanage construction crews were totally drenched and covered with dirt. After a few minutes most of the adults went to their rooms to take a nap before dinner. Karen, Brenda, Jenn, Andi, Billy, Eli, Jim, Michael, Barb, and I went over to the athletic field together because we had told the older kids we would come play soccer with them. We took two of the boxes of soccer balls with us to give to the kids. Michael took his camera, which he had been taking everywhere we went.

Fred and Deb were back in time for a dinner that was inhaled by everyone. After grace was said we all started to talk at once and the sharing didn't stop for a couple of hours. Juan seemed to be the most excited. He shared that when they were sent out by Dan to look for volunteer to help with the repairs they were apprehensive because they did not know how to speak the native language. They walked passed a couple of houses before they got up the courage to try to talk to someone. At a thatched roof mud hut they there was a man kneeling in his garden weeding. They introduced themselves in English and waited as the man did not respond right away and kept on weeding. He then looked up and said, "How can I help you." Juan was shocked by his perfect English. The man's name was Luc. They explained who they were and what they wanted to do. Luc told them that the whole village felt like they owed their lives to Jules. Twenty years ago Jules had the courage to tell them about being HIV positive and urge them to get tested and treated if needed. He said people didn't listen to him at first, but after several people died of AIDS and he stayed healthy, they listened. Father Jacque and Mother Yolanda helped educate the community about safe sex and now that the clinic provided medication and condoms only a few people a year were being found to be HIV positive. Luc said he would be happy to go with them to round up volunteers. Around noon people began to gather at Jules' house with rakes, shovels, hammers, and other tools. Dan drove up with a pick-up truck filled of concrete blocks, sand, and cement, tin and lumber. There were about 50 neighbors who said they wanted to help and that they would come every day as needed.

Dan reported to the group that the demolition of part of Jules' house was done, the floor was almost refinished and that the roof would be replace the next day. Jules and his family were doubling up with a neighbor while the work was being done. He also said he wanted to stay at Jules' house until dinner each day but he thought that Michael and Juan could leave for the afternoon soccer time with the kids.

Ruth said she felt useful but that maybe she could be more helpful on another crew. Fred said the Pediatric clinic was extremely busy and that they could use another receptionist, so Ruth decided to move to help out there. The rest of the crew agreed.

The medical crew shared that they thought it would be good for all of them to stay with Fred and Deb until dinner each day. Since none of them were planning on playing soccer we all agreed.

The next four days most everything went according their adjusted schedule.

Jules house was not only totally renewed but Jules and Luc decided to start a ministry of repairing neighbors' homes with volunteers. Dan said he would serve as a contact in the States to raise money and recruit groups from the U. S. to come help.

By the end of the week the footer for the fourth building at the orphanage construction was dug and the concrete poured and the first floor of block walls for the other three buildings were finished.

Those who worked in the hospital got to know their co-workers well as everyone welcomed them and free shared their life's journeys. They also became attached to many of the patients and when they were free found time from their duties to listen to their circumstances and pray with them.

At the school the crew grew emotionally attached to many of the kids and the staff made everyone feel like they were part of the teaching and nurturing team.

Everyone, on the trip develop what felt like new life-long relationships.

It was extremely difficult for everyone to leave.

To help with the transition from Cange to back home we had made plans to stay at a resort in Port-au-Prince on Saturday. In our planning we thought that we would need the time to recover from the hardships of stressful and sparse living conditions. But we had discovered that our simple living, hard work, predictable days, and time for relationships were much less stressful than our lives back in Pittsburgh. We also thought we would need some time to process all that we had been experiencing. So, Saturday morning, the two LZ vans drove us back to Port-au-Prince to the Resort Hotel La Villa Creole. It was a five Star Caribbean Resort with all the amenities. We arrived about noon and stayed there for the rest of the day. We were to catch the plane at 10:25 AM the next morning.

During the afternoon at the hotel, some of us sleep and some of us swam and laid around by the pool.

As I laid by the pool so many thoughts and feeling ran through my mind. And as I looked around at others in our group I imagined they were having the same kind of thoughts. To me the contrast between the poor in Haiti and the opulence of this resort was shocking. It made me realize that even the poor in America lived in affluence compared to the poor in Haiti. And yet the joy of the majority of poor I had gotten to know in Haiti was in contrast to the gloom and depression I saw so many in America. I thought that it seemed to me that the common struggles that those in Cange experience created a community for them, while the insecure competitive world of America kept us separated from one another. The faith of those I meet in Cange had an honest trust and acceptance of God's grace and love. There was a peace about most of them, even though many were in the midst of suffering. I felt thankful that God had given me a glimpse into the lives of brothers and sisters who were also His beloved.

That evening we had a very nice American food dinner in the hotel conference meeting room.

As we finished our meal Mel got our attention and started our evening's discussion. "I, for one, am overwhelmed by what I have experienced this past week. I am so excited to get back to work. And I don't mean being a pastor or going around speaking. I don't want to just talk about furthering the Kingdom of God; I want to do it. On one of my speaking trips a couple of years ago one of the other speakers was a lawyer by the name of Ben Gregory. We had lunch together one day and one of the things he said to me was that as a lawyer his job is to collect information and memorize facts and he said that he thought that is exactly what the church has been doing with it members; collecting information, memorizing stuff about God and Jesus, and learning how to talk about knowing Jesus. He challenged my perspective on pastoral leadership. First, he expressed that he thought as believers we hardly know each other and, second he told me he thought we followed Jesus at a distance. The church, he believed needed to get to know Jesus by doing what Jesus did, not by just studying Him. That is what this trip has done for me. It has raised my awareness of the needs of children around the world and it has motivated me to start to put into practice what I know so well about what Jesus did and taught.

I think we all need to process what the week has meant to each of us. At least that was our plan. So who wants to go next?"

"I'll go next." Answered Liz. "Like Mel, I too am overwhelmed by all that I saw, heard, and experienced this past week. And I am so grateful for the relationships I made with so many people in Cange. It was such a blessing. I think the dominant sense I am going home with, like Mel, is new motivation to stop sitting around talking about Jesus and start putting flesh on what I say and to whom I am surrendered and committed. And for me that translated into doing something about providing opportunities for those kids that I met at the school to help them go to college when they graduate. That may feel impossible to them but I believe it can become possible. Why can't they go to college? So, what I am going home with is a drive to find a way to help Claire develop partnership with colleges in the States so that her students can get a college education."

"May I talk next?" asked Fred. "Because what the week said to me goes along the lines of what Mel and Liz have been saying. Not so much about new motivation but about new vision. I have been on a number of medical mission trips, mostly in Latin American countries. They have all been primarily rural to communities where the only medical care that the people got was when medical teams came and set up clinics a few time a year. This trip was the first one where there was an established comprehensive medical facility that was providing care for the poorest of the poor. It is something that not only could expose doctors to the needs in the world first hand but could be used to train doctors like Pete has been doing. I am going back home with the thought of trying to establish a family practice residency program that would use Community Partners in Healing as training sites all over the world. Right now it is just an idea but I think the resources are available. The idea and resources need to be connected and developed. The other thing that excites me is that training sites like Clinique Bon Sauveur would not only educate docs to the health care needs of developing countries but they would also expose them to the Gospel through the lives of believers in those training sites."

"That sounds exciting," Deb said. "What impressed me was just the people and the place. I think I fell in love with them. It was so amazing to see how the land was being redeemed, and so many people made me feel like family. The people I encountered were so accepting and welcoming. I definitely want to go back."

"I am going back. And to stay." Exclaimed Ruth. "Don't you two get upset or hurt, honey," she said as she looked at Karen and then Brenda. "But I feel like I have found myself again. Cange is a place where I can contribute and have a sense of call. In the back of my heart I have always thought about wanting to follow Jesus among the poor. I'm not sure how much time I have left on this earth but I want to make the most of it. Like Deb shared, I too have fallen in love with the people in Cange. If you all will pitch in and give me the money, I think God wants me in Haiti."

"Don't feel bad, Grandma, I, and I think and all of us have a little bit of the same feeling. You go for it Grams and we will all be coming down to visit. I think." said Brenda. At first she spoke with great assurance but as she talked her words slowed down with a hint of apprehension. But then her mother also spoke up.

"Mom, Brenda is right. I too feel it is right and good that you give the remainder of your life away. We love you and love having you around to keep us real but I saw how alive you were in Cange and I agree, God is calling you. And I for one will give you all the support you need. If Stan and I can give the company to God surely we can give a little bit of our personal stash to my mother. I feel like I bonded too with the life and people of Cange. What I have come away with is feeling like I am part of something much greater than myself, not only because I got outside myself while we were here but also through our time of prayer in the morning at the school. They made me feel a part of what Claire and the other administrative staff are trying to do. They included me. They made me feel like I belonged. Mom, you go, and Brenda and I will be with you all the way." Said Karen.

A couple of Amens could be heard from the group.

Ruth responded, "Thanks, but that is enough about me."

"But not enough about me." Brenda said with a smile. "I just want to say that the main thing that I got out of this trip is that I too felt like I belonged. I mean, you know, without feeling like I had to act a certain way or fit in like I have always felt with my friends at home. I was most impressed, even though I could not believe how poor everyone was, by how the children loved me and how easily they accepted my love. Even the older kids, my age, didn't have a hidden agenda, no game playing, they were just themselves and loved me for just being myself. I was like they didn't even care about making a mistake in how they related to me and they didn't care if I made a mistake. It was ok to be real about my feelings. It has been so good to just be myself and in the process to learn a little about just who that self is. I know I can't stay here now and I don't know what my future will be but I am sure glad and grateful that I came on this trip."

"That makes me want to say something." said Andi. What got me was the pure joy of the kids.

They were really happy kids. I mean it was real. The kids have diseases, many are malnourished or orphaned. All are poor, living without anything. And they had a smile on their faces and enjoyed almost everything. Boy, what a gift. The joy of the kids is what impressed me the most."

"Yeah, me too." contributed Jenn. "And how they looked out for one another. They not only shared everything with each other, like the candy bar I gave one of the girls when I first met her, I also noticed when we were playing soccer if someone wasn't getting the ball very often, someone else would be sure to pass the ball to them. And it wasn't just one person who was sensitive, it was almost all of them. Like it was just how they assumed you were to treat one another. They were so unselfish. They put me to shame. If I acted that way back home I would get so taken advantage of and laughed at. I wouldn't ever get included in any activity. Back home we are so competitive in everything. Here, I am learning that it is like they are all one person. If that is what poverty does to you, trying to be number one is so overrated."

"Me too." Juan chimed in. "Everyone, just not the kids was always willing to help each other. They came out of the woodwork; well, I guess not the woodwork, there wasn't any. They came out of the woods from everywhere to help with Jules' house. Like Jenn said the kids cared about each other more than they cared about themselves. This trip has changed my whole impression of what the poor in this world are like. I always thought they were poor like a lot of my friends at home. We are not poor but we are really poor, if you know what I mean, like poor in awareness and caring. The poor of the poor are rich in relationships and community. We have more than we need but we are all alone.

"You got that right." said Eli. "What impressed me the most was the unselfishness of everyone, especially the kids. Jenn, I couldn't have said it better. Life is not a "me" thing for these people it is a "we" thing. And that is something I have been learning in my recovery. Another thing that impressed me was the genuine community of the Haitians that we met. Also after we were done playing soccer with the kids each afternoon Sunny and I spent time together talking about addiction recovery and life. My friendship with Sunny as well as this trip have put a lot of stuff in perspective for me. Thank you, Sunny. And thank you, Dad. And thank you, Stan. And thank you, 'O'. And thank God for Mesi, my friend, in Cange. And thank you everyone. God has been so good to me. I feel like the past couple of years I have been so screwed up. The cloud is being lifted and my life is about to start. I was dying but now I am alive, maybe for the first time."

"I want to say something else." added Juan. "I have watched my brother come alive this week as well. The kids made him feel a part of them and he loved them back."

"I can share for myself." said Michael. "Yes, I hide behind my camera some of the time. That is because I don't know how to talk with people in a way that they don't think I'm weird. But it is also because I love to take pictures. Is it ok for me to talk like this? Doesn't matter. The kids taught me to just be myself and that I am OK! I hope I am OK with everyone here too. Like some of you, I have a dream now too. I want to take pictures of the needs of children in the world so others can know about them and want to help."

"Thanks for sharing Michael. You will make a difference to a lot of kids someday," Mel affirmed.

"I can't stand it anymore. I have something to say. Dad and Mom, Jenn and Billy, I hope you won't think the worse of me, but I just have to get this out or it will kill me," interrupted Jim. "I think this trip has saved my life. I can really identify with what Micheal, Jenn, Eli, Juan, Andi, and Brenda have shared. The kids I have gotten to know here have shamed me and taught me that life not about me. Back home I have been pursuing only what I want. You guys may not know this, though I think Dad suspected a little, but back home, in the last six months I have gotten involved with the LA gang and have been selling crack cocaine and other stuff. In fact I am now one of the key dealers in Henley. That is because I have hooked up with this girl Tammie whose dad is one of the major connections for Pittsburgh with the cocaine traffic from New York."

Jim paused, and had a hard time trying to speak again as he started to fill up with emotion. Everyone sat quietly and waited. I wanted to just go over and hug him, but I let him hurt because I knew he needed to get his pain out and externalize his guilt.

And we all needed to listen to him. I could also see Sunny and Sara's intensity and knew they were praying as I was. Tears started running down Jim's face. Finally he began to speak but this time it was a prayer.

"Jesus, please forgive me for being a part of killing your precious children with drugs. I am so sorry and so selfish. Lord, please forgive me for being so deceitful and turning my back on my family and you. I am a real scum bag. I am so sorry," Jim began to weep softly and couldn't control his tears. Then he continued as his words made their way through his tears. "I am especially sorry for how I have kept secrets and turned my back on Jenn. Lord restore our relationship, and please give me the courage to walk away from Tammie and the LA gang." His weeping words had settled to a quiver as he continued. "Thank you Jesus for the orphans at Cange, for showing me what is important, what gives life joy. Lord, make me a person of gratefulness and take away my self-centered life that only destroys what is important to you."

Now I did get up. I walked over to him, knelt down and gave him a hug. And Sunny and Eli and Mel and Billy and Jenn and Deb, and several other others came over and reached out to touch him. And then everyone else joined the group. Billy unexpectedly said, "In the Name of Jesus, you are forgiven. Jim, you too are one of his precious children." And several in the circle said, "Amen."

Everyone went back to their seats slowly. Jim lifted up his head and his eyes met mine and then he looked around the room at the gentle smiles from each of us.

Misha was the first one to speak. "I can't follow that, but Jim I think in one way or another, we all can identify with how you feel to some degree. In fact, maybe we have been humbled like that repeatedly. God's love never stops. Like Billy prayed, God loves you Jimmy. Sorry, I mean Jim."

"Jimmy is fine, I'm Ok with Jimmy today."

There was a short pause of quiet.

Misha continued, "I guess it's my turn now. What impressed me this week was the consistent positive and gracious attitude of everyone, I mean everyone on the hospital staff. That is not easy when the stress is so constant."

"I was impressed the most by the faith of the people." added Sunny.

"For me it was the quality of the teachers at the school and the potential I saw in the kids. Karen, I would like to help you with your dream of helping to provide an opportunity for the kids to have a chance go to college" said Sara.

"I too was surprised, though I am not sure why, with the quality of all the staff I met and their commitment, in addition to their faith in Jesus. One of the reasons I wanted to come on this trip was to evaluate the risk of giving a grant to the orphanage. I am now ashamed of my condescending attitude. I would trust Father Jacque and anyone he trusts with my life." said Barb.

"This week has been very healing for me." Billy shared. "Not only was I able to get in touch with my grief over my losses but I also felt at peace, and at home with the kids. I bonded with one of the older kids and that has really been redeeming for me. I could explain later, if anyone is interested. But I think you all understand since I have shared so much this week about my family's sacrifice. God has been so good to me, thanks to you all. Thank you!"

Jorge was next in the circle

"It looks like I am next in line." began Jorge. "What has struck me, besides identifying with so much that everyone has said so far, is that I believe that mission trips like this one could really help recovery from Secondary Post Stress

Disorder. This has been spiritually rejuvenating. The physically exhaustion has even been refreshing. As Misha and I move towards developing a Care Givers Ministry I now want to add a mission trip component."

Dan was next. "I am leaving with a new vision for developing a ministry that addresses the housing needs in Cange. When we get back I want to contact Habitat for Humanity and see what they have going in Haiti and if I can help start a project in Cange."

Suzie then said, "I was overwhelmed by how much is going on and had been done in Cange, but also by how much needs to be done, not only in Cange but in all of Haiti. I have always heard how Haiti is the poorest country in the Western hemisphere but experiencing it up close has given that a whole new meaning. Living in Henley, which is a poor urban American community with violence, poor health, and broken families, does not come close to what we have experienced this week. I am leaving with such a heavy heart."

Stan was next and as it so happened I would be last.

"Next to my wedding day and the birth of Brenda, these have been the best days of my life. I feel alive again like I felt twenty years ago when we were in Kenya. I feel like what I did this week was why I was born. Not necessarily the tasks that I did but the reason I was doing it. It made me feel like I was born to share with and care for the least in this world. I also feel like my relationship with all of you has grown and we have become a family. What impressed me the most is what was going on inside of me, the awakening I was feeling and the contentment that I experienced. I am going back, feeling freed from my success driven past, and excited about finding a way that we who are wealthy can personally experience the poorest of the poor in this world. We need, and by that I mean, the rich like me, need to catch a vision for how we can eliminate poverty in the world. Only the Holy Spirit can change peoples' hearts; but I believe the poor can soften our hearts and open the door for the Spirit to work. The rich need the poor for the sake of their souls and the poor need the rich for the sake of their bodies. I want to create a ministry that opens the hearts of the wealthy to the needs of the poor. That sums up what I got out of the week."

Finally it was my turn. So much had gone through my mind as everyone else was sharing. As I listened to Jim my thought had wondered to my childhood. I also thought about how I had been so humbled by Mel and Stan and Billy and everyone in the group. I wondered about the future. I really didn't have my thoughts together and I wasn't' prepared to share all that was swirling around in my head. Hardly anything was clear to me. So, I said, "What has the week meant to me? I am not sure. I have been having a hard time separating it from everything that has happened in the last six months. I am a little in a fog and feel like I can only see what is directly in front of me. I feel broken and surrendered, yet peaceful and excited. I am looking forward to whatever God has for me and for us as a group. I am excited about learning with you all how to be disciples of Jesus seeking the Kingdom of God together. And I am excited about what I can see right in front of me. For real, what has most impressed me is what has been shared just now by all of you. I hear and see our hearts, and our visions and dreams, and how God has been changing us and I am awestruck. This trip has been part of it but it has been so much more. I feel like my life is just beginning. I feel like I did when I first turned my life over to Jesus."

As they all boarded the flight home on December 21, 2007, Rita Cruz was getting off the same plane they were boarding.

Forty

The trip home was uneventful. Most of us slept on the plane from Miami to Pittsburgh.

About half way home, Jim asked his mom if she would switch seat with him so he could sit next to me. He woke me up and said he wanted to talk to me.

"Dad, from what you have shared with Jenn and me about you when you were a teen, I am sure you have a good idea what has been going on with me. I want to let you know that this trip has been a wakeup call for me and it is you and mom who are my stability zone. You two have given me the safe place to wake up to. I imagine it has been very hard for you guys to not try and find out what has been going on with me and try to prevent me from making bad decisions. Without your unconditional love I would be confused out of my mind and right now be wanting to run away. Back home it was like my life was starting to go dim but because of this trip and your love the light has been turned on again. I was falling into darkness and now I am leaning into the light."

I responded, "Jim, I am so relieved and thankful. As you know, I've been there, done that. But for me it was more like a new birth than waking up. I didn't have a family like you do. It blesses my heart to know that our family makes a difference. Now, however, it is what you do after you wake up and see the light that matters. Your mom and I will always be here for you but it will take God's grace and a lot of continual surrender to walk in the light. I especially like what you just said about leaning into the light. You know you cannot walk unless you risk leaning forward and take the first step."

"Well, first of all Dad, I want to tell you that I have not been using drugs. I have not even tried any drugs even though I have had easy free access to them. But as I shared in Haiti before we left for home, I have been selling them. And I feel terrible about that. Second, I want you to know that I turned off my cell phone last Wednesday and have not communicated with anyone back home since. And now, the first thing I am going to do when we get home is go over to Tammie's and tell her face to face that I am done with dealing and with her and she cannot expect to see or hear from me again."

"Are you sure that is wise? I don't know the extent of how hooked in you are with the whole gang drug dealing thing, but it can be dangerous to leave with what you know about contacts and sources. Don't you think her dad will have something to say about you quitting? Maybe I should go with you."

"Thanks Dad, but the truth is he doesn't really like me. He didn't want me messing around with his daughter and he can find a dozen kids like me. And for real, I don't know who is who in the chain of command, except for the kids I was selling to. My competition will be happy to hear that I have been cut loose. I think I have been in more danger from competitive gangs than I will be from Tammie and her dad and mom."

"I hope you're right." I said. "Can we pray about that right now?"

"Sure."

Jim and I prayed. It felt so good to hear my son tell God about his gratitude and dependence on him and ask for forgiveness, courage, protection, and direction. When we said "Amen" I gave him a hug and told him I needed to get some sleep.

We landed in Pittsburgh about 8:30 PM. It was Saturday with just two days left before Christmas morning. I can't explain it, but Christmas felt different to me that year.

On the way home in the car I told the kids they could all sleep in Christmas morning.

As soon as we got home Jim announced that he was going to go to break-up with Tammie and tell her that his days of drug dealing were over. Deb was adamant that it was too dangerous and that he needed to wait until morning. I supported Jim and told her I would explain later. The car was uncomfortably quiet the rest of the way home.

When we got home and unpacked, Jim left and said he would be back by 11:00 and not to worry, God was going with him. He said it with great sincerity. Deb objected and told him he had to stay home. Jim was determined and said he could not wait until morning, it was something he had to do right then. Billy and I quietly let it play out. Jenn supported Deb. After about ten minutes Jim just walked away. Tammie lived just about a half mile away and as he walked away, Deb began to cry and simply said to me. "I don't feel good about this."

As Jim turned the corner to walk down the street where Tammie lived, he heard about ten rapid fire gun shots, looked up and saw a car speeding away from Tammie's house. He stopped, shocked and scared, he searched for what to do. He wanted to run see what happened and if anyone was shot but that didn't feel sensible to him as he reasoned the cops would surely be coming in the next few minutes. So, shaking, he decided to find a place to hide and wait to see what happened next. He found a dark space between a couple of garages, sat down behind a garbage can, praying and waiting. As he prayed, he sensed a quiet peace that he could not explain. He relaxed and felt safe in the presence of his Lord. He stood to see what was happening at the house but all he could see was a body lying on the steps up to the porch and the door to the house, so he sat back down behind the garbage cans.

In about five minutes the police and an ambulance with flashers turned the corner and went flying past him. He stood up again to watch. Two more cop cars arrived from the other direction. Then another ambulance arrived from that direction. About the same time an unmarked car arrived. He could see two men who looked like they could be undercover cops, get out of the car. One started taking pictures of the man on the steps and the other went into the house. After a few minutes two uniformed cops covered the person on the steps up. Soon someone who looked like he or she had been wounded came out of the house on a stretcher, that victim was put in one of the ambulances, and it left. Next they put the person on the steps in a body bag and put him in the other ambulance. This was followed by two cops carrying another body bag out of the house and putting it in the ambulance with the first body bag. That ambulance left. Soon two of the cop cars also left. To Jim it seemed surreal, like he was watching a movie. But he knew it was real and could feel his heart starting to beat hard and his stomach feeling tight.

He sat where he could see a little and waited, afraid if he exposed himself they might see him and he would become a suspect. The remaining police and the two detective stayed in and around the house for about thirty minutes. Neighbors began to come out of their houses and a few gathered to discuss what was going on. Then someone in handcuffs was escorted out of the house to one of the cop cars and it left. Then almost at the same time Channel 4 and Channel 11 arrived.

Jim wondered what to do. After a few more minutes as the TV reporters began to interview people, he decided to slip out of his hiding place and walk slowly back home. It was about 10:45 p.m. As he walked home he thought; *What if I had left fifteen minutes earlier, I could have been killed. Maybe mom was right that I shouldn't have gone. Who was taken to the hospital and who was killed? It looked to me like it was Tammie's dad who was arrested but I really couldn't tell. What if Tammie was one of the ones who was killed? She had a really sweet side to her. She was too young to die.*

He caught his breath as tears streamed down his face. God was surely looking after me, he thought. Thank you, Jesus. Thank you for protecting me and saving me from a life that only leads to prison and death. I want my live for you. Please show me how?

Forty One

Back home we had been praying. During that time of prayer, Deb said she felt her anxiety had been replaced by God's presence and peace.

When Jim got home Deb, Jenn, Billy and I were waiting for him. Jim was trembling as he filled us in on what had happened. We were in shock at such a terrible drama but we at once also in awe at God's protection of Jim. My heart was torn between grieve and gratitude.

As Jim was sharing, Jenn turned on the 11 o'clock news. And there it was, live, just as Jim had witnessed as he hid in the darkness. Two persons, a male and a female had been killed. Another male had been wounded and a third man, who hadn't been shot, had been arrested on drug charges. No names were given and no suspects responsible for the shootings had been identified. An investigation was underway.

We all joined hands and thanked God for protecting Jim and asked God to bring his will and Kingdom out of this tragedy.

In the morning the Sunday paper said that Tammie and her dad had been killed and that Curt Wheeler had been wounded and arrested, and that someone Jim didn't know by the name Lenny Doyle was arrested for possession of cocaine. It was suspected that the Cribs, a rival gang of the LA gang were behind the shooting.

Billy was silent as I read the paper out loud to us all at we sat around the breakfast table. Deb cried a little. Jenn said that she was in awe with how God had protected Jim and what a difference the Haiti trip had made in him. Jim said it just wasn't the Haiti trip, it was how we had all loved him even though we thought he could have been going down the wrong road. Billy then spoke up and shared that he believed that we are all faced with choices every day and if we choose to receive God's love known in Jesus that he will direct us to make choices for good and not evil, even sometimes when we can't see the outcomes.

"Jim," he said, "You are choosing to accept Jesus love for you, that blesses his heart, and he will guide you to make choices that are for good not evil."

The rest of the day we all stayed home. We didn't go to worship but it was a day of grateful hearts, silent praise of God, and rest. We took turns on the computer, made phone calls, did laundry, watched football, took naps, snacked, and generally adjusted to the culture shock of being back in our home. Most of the day consisted of short discussions about not only how awesome and surprising the evidences of the love of God had been in our individual lives, but also in our growing church fellowship. We continued to share about what we had experienced in Haiti. And we all went to bed that night filled with hopeful anticipation for what God was up to next.

We didn't have our Liminal Plunge Church fellowship meeting that night but we went to the Christmas Eve service at Apple Orchard.

Christmas Day was unlike any our family had ever experienced. Before leaving for the trip we had all bought our presents for each other and had decorated the house. When Christmas morning came it was almost like we had forgotten about the presents or any Christmas morning ritual of opening our stockings and gifts before breakfast. Instead, we all slept in. I was up first and put together a pancake breakfast for everyone. Billy shared what Christmas was like as he grew up in the Sudan. Jim read a poem he had written that expressed the birth of Jesus in the small stable of his heart. The baby Jesus was a refugee fleeing from violence. Jenn, to our surprise, sang a Christmas song in Haitian Creole that the kids at Change had taught her. I read Luke's account of the birth of Jesus, and Deb lead us in prayer. We didn't open our gifts to one another until after lunch.

When 2008 rang in a week later it felt like the beginning of a new era not just a new year. Our family had expanded not just by adding a new son but by recognizing our nuclear family had been incorporated into a new extended family. I personally was full of new energy and hope.

We had our LPC fellowship meeting on New Year's Day evening. We all expressed feeling of having a renewed purpose in life. We were excited with anticipation for a life together full of challenges to serve, continued transformation in our individual lives, and more surprises.

My first surprise came on Thursday, January 10, 2008. After my morning run, I showered and sat down to read the paper while I ate my breakfast. The Post-Gazette headline read, "Analysts lining up to predict recession in 2008." The article began. "Fears are mounting that the nation is about to be thrashed by a recession. In recent days, several heavy hitters on Wall Street have said the economy is teetering on the edge." It went on to describe what could be an economic disaster for the whole world.

As I read I was filled with emotion and a deep concern for those in our neighborhood, the patients at the Health Care Center, and the poor around the world who would be the ones who would suffer the most if such a global economic collapse became a reality. And as I began to pray about it, I was struck by how my feelings were so different from times in the past when I had felt such concern. In the past I would have immediately become worried and dismayed. Then I would become cynical and judgmental about the self-centered decisions of banks and big business. This would have let into my usual anger towards the wealthy. This morning, my passion for the poor had not diminished; but instead of dismay, judgment and anger, I felt an overriding sense of God being in control. There was even an underlying feeling of hope.

As I continued to pray, I wondered why I was feeling this way. My mind went to thinking that it was exactly seven months since I picked up the paper and read about the Bryce family's assassinations. I realized my perception about myself, others, and the church had all changed since then. And the lives of those who had been on the original trip to Kenya twenty two years ago had transformed.as well.

I thought about how my attitude towards the future of the church had totally changed from despair to hope. I thought about how Stan's values had changed from accumulating wealth for himself to divesting himself for others. And how Mel had escaped the clutches of the institutional trappings of the church and found freedom to love and to discover new visions for life in the Body of Christ. I thought about how Misha, Liz, and Karen are discovering the courage to be true to themselves and the Spirit of God within them. I was filled with gratitude as I reviewed the miraculous changes in all our children. God had not only protected some of them falling into paths that would have led them to lives of destruction, but He was giving them a heart for the least in this world. I was in awe at how God had brought us all together and in the process attracted others to join our new adventure. I could have never dreamed or imagined all that had happened.

I realized that our new developing community life was the result of our courage to surrender and our willingness to risk being open to experiment with a new structure for the church.

I felt humbled and grateful. I was in awe of God's love and grace and how He had turned tragedy into new life.

Epilogue

Rita Cruz became the Business Manager for the orphanage on January 2, of 2008.

In February, 2008, Barb Jenkins and her husband started attending the Liminal Plunge Church fellowship meetings on Sunday nights. From then on almost every couple of months someone new joined the fellowship. The meetings continued to have a character of honesty and vulnerability. Deb, Karen, Liz, Misha, and Ruth planned the meal and devotional times which were always new and often unique. They even had everyone dancing a time or two. Without James our times of music changed, first to Mel's guitar leadership and then once a month when the kids also came, Juan led us with the piano.

The group slowly was slowly beginning to have a character acceptance and an atmosphere that produced hope. We become more confident as the months passed that we truly were discovering the birthing of a church for the future. Our energy remained focused outreach and service to those who were suffering and without hope.

One of the interesting things that happened was that our meeting times began to have a regular pattern of order to them, almost like a liturgy. Each meeting began with a meal, a time of confession, prayer time, affirmation of God's grace and forgiveness in Jesus. Often some of the ancient liturgical prayers with a Eucharistic format were part of their meal time. We would then sing some praise songs followed by the reading of the Church Life Traditions, a Bible study which we continued to call Bible Doing with reports of what our last study had called us to apply to our life, and other personal sharing. Sometimes a birthday celebration would be included and if time allowed more praise songs and more prayer time at the end. It began to feel like it really wasn't "church" without the meal, confession, forgiveness, "Traditions" reading, "Doings", singing, and prayer. About once a month they discussed how each of their visions and callings for mission ministry was going.

With permission from Walcott Detention, Eli was allowed to join Jenn, Jim, Billy, Andi, Juan, Michael, and Brenda, to have a fellowship meeting of their own. On Sunday night they meet in the basement playroom at Beckley's. The exception was the last Sunday of the month when they went upstairs to the adult LPC fellowship meeting.

On February 29, 2008 the Bryce Foundation gave $1,000,000 to the orphanage in Change.

In June, Billy had his 16th birthday. In July he got his driver's license. In August he and Andi began to date.

James did not say anything to the group about Rita until the beginning of 2009 when he wrote them a lengthy letter announcing their engagement and inviting everyone to their wedding which they were planning for February of 2010. He introduced Rita as the Business Manager for the orphanage. In the letter James also confessed his temptation to steal the money, his contrition, and Rita's conversion process. He also shared how their new relationship in Haiti had found a foundation in Jesus and grown into as a close friendship and then blossomed into a love that felt God's call to become one.

By the middle of 2009 Jorge had lost 100 lbs., was running three miles a day with Billy and me, and he had been taken off his high blood pressure medicines. That year Misha, Stan, and Mel started a ministry to provide urban and overseas missionaries with an opportunity to be refreshed and renewed from the emotion and physical fatigue resulting from the intense personal relationship of serving those who suffer. They used the Beckley's estate as the Retreat Center.

Also in 2009, the Bryce Foundation gave $1,000,000 to start a scholarship fund for Haitian kids to go to college. Dan made two trips to Cange with some supporters of Habitat for Humanity. These trips lead to plans to create a partnership between Habitat and a group that Jules and Luc had organized.

In February of 2010 James and Rita were married at Cange. There wedding was attended by everyone in the LPC, which had grown to about thirty adults and their fifteen children.

That year the Bryce Foundation gave $100,000 to The One Acre Fund in Kenya to teach Maasai children farming productivity, planning and techniques.

Also in 2010, Juan, Michael and Brenda went to college, Jorge and Misha moved to the Beckley's house and Stan and Karen moved into Jorge and Misha house in the city. The LPC fellowship continued to meet in what was now being called the "Restoration Retreat Center."

Also in the fall of 2010, Sunny and Sara, Mel and Liz, Fred and Susie, and Dan spun off from the LPC fellowship and with three couple from the Henley neighborhood started a second church fellowship in Henley. Just before Christmas, 2010 Stan and Karen started to attend this new group. To distinguish it from the Liminal Plunge Group it was being called the Henley Church Fellowship.

They each meet every Sunday night and both also worshipped weekly at the Apple Orchard Community Church on Sunday mornings. They did not become members of Apple Orchard but attended worship, participated in church social functions, and developed relationship with many of the members.

Then in 2011, Stan, Dan, Fred and Odell started a ministry of take people on mission trips to orphanages in Haiti, Honduras, Sudan, and Kenya. Many of the people from Apple Orchard as well as people from Henley signed up for these trips. Fred and Stan, also recruited people from their professional relationship in the medical and corporate communities.

In 2012, Billy was one of the Keynote speakers at the One Young World gathering in Pittsburgh. His topic was "Converging Worlds." He spoke about the coming confrontation between the hope of an impinging movement of Jesus' resurrected love and the Kingdom of God spreading all over the world; and the despair felt from escalating weather catastrophes, weapons of mass destruction, terrorism, cyber warfare, disease, and starvation. He described how the two clashing world views; one of surrendering to love and the other surrendered to greed and lust for power were creating a point of decision for individuals and even nations throughout the world.

In 2013, the Apple Orchard Community Church faced a conflict within its leadership because many wanted the congregation to become solely a mission agency and other did not want to give up their institutional church identity. About two thousand people left Apple Orchard and started the Children's Rescue Services with the mission of restoring oppressed, abandoned, and orphaned children to a new life and family. They become partners with both Bob Goff's Restore International and with World Vision International. Most of this new ministry were organized into small group churches like the Liminal Church Fellowship and the Henley Church Fellowship. There connected expression was called the Resurrection Fellowship Churches. The new Children's Rescue Services was organized and incorporated in the spring of 2014 and no longer meet as a large Sunday morning Church worship service but began meeting weekly for worship and fellowship in there small groups.

That same year, Fred and Suzie began serving six months a year with Zanmi Lasante Clinique Bon Sauveur in Haiti.

By 2016, just nine years from the Bryce family murders, there were over one hundred and twenty Resurrected Fellowship Groups (RFG) in the greater Pittsburgh area, all pattern after the original Liminal Plunge Church fellowship meeting, most were involved with the Children's Rescue Services ministry. Each small church fellowship was independent but used the Church Life Traditions as a guide from their fellowship structure. The Resurrected Fellowship Groups began meeting quarterly for a Resurrected Fellowship Conference and worship time together. At the first Conference on July 10-12, 2015 there were about 3,000 attendees including about 500 who came seeking to learn what this movement was all about.

By 2018 the RFG movement had spread to six other cities and had established over 25 ministries, ten of them were spin-offs from the Children's Rescue Services. Each city had its own quarterly RFG Conferences.

Appendix A

Church Life Traditions

For the purpose of assuring the freedom for the Church, the following traditions are suggested. When followed they seem to keep Jesus as Savior, Lord, and Head of the Church.

Definition and purpose: Each local church is a fellowship of followers of Jesus. It has but one primary purpose: to love one another as Jesus loves each of them.

Membership: Anyone can be a part a local church and therefore a part of the Body of Christ, as long as they desire to be a follower Jesus.

Values of Surrender: The following directives are to protect the local church from problems of money, property, prestige, and public controversy, and from being diverted from the Church's primary purpose.

- The common welfare of the local church comes before personal interests.
- Whenever a local church gathers together in fellowship as disciples of Jesus they shall make opportunity to honestly express their needs, short coming, and struggles to one another. Acceptance, grace and forgiveness shall take priority over fear, shame, blame, and pride.

- The local church is never to be used for personal interests or for influence beyond its primary purpose of loving one another.
- The local church is never to be used for personal gain.
- Anonymity is to be practiced when serving anyone or when representing a local church.
- All local churches shall never accept contributions from anyone or any group outside their local fellowship of followers.

Governance: For the purpose of a local church's life and fellowship there is but one ultimate authority; God: Father, Son, and Holy Spirit, as they may express themselves in the church's group conscious. Leaders of local churches are trusted servants they do not govern. No one is a paid professional; but ministries may employ workers. A local church should not grow beyond the capacity of its members to each fully participate in a group conscious. A suggested maximum number of members is 17 to 20.

Ministry: A local church is not to be organized as a structured institution; but as disciples of Jesus, in exercising their gifts for ministry, its members may form organizations for the purpose of creating ministries of healing, mercy, compassion, justice, teaching, preaching, and celebrating. Each ministry shall be accountable to that organization's Board or Committee.

Connected Church Relationship: Each local church should be autonomous except in matters affecting other local churches or the world-wide Body of Christ.

Acknowledgements

I am most grateful to Jesus for the journey he has had me on over the last seventy three years of my life and for how his consistent unconditional love has persistently been transforming me into his will for me and drawn me closer to him through so many unforeseen joyful and sometimes painful experiences.

My gratitude is beyond description for my patient wife, Nancy, who has been my editor, encourager, and partner in producing this book. She is also the most incarnate expression of Jesus love for me that I have experienced in our 50 years of married life together.

I am also extremely thankful for the many friends whose composites have provided the stimulation for the characters, the extended Body of Christ that has have been my family, the opportunities for ministry, and the models of Christian servant. They have together provided the content of this book. I cannot list all the mentors and circumstances that have contributed to this expression of my love for Jesus and my hope for the Church. I am especially thankful to Jesus for the Fellowship of the 12 Step movement, the East Liberty Family Health Care Center, Metanoia Fellowship Church, and Young Life Campaign for each of their unique demonstration of the Kingdom of God coming to earth in my life.

And to Barb Carter, my Inspiring Voices coach, I am indebted and grateful for her constant patience, freedom, understanding, support and encouragement.

Made in United States
North Haven, CT
02 May 2025

68518950R00226